UNLOCKED

JAMES CHRISTIE

Other works by James Christie:

Blink Once to Spread Snow (2007-2020)
Gracehill Press

From I-80 to Galway Bay:
Searching for an Exit (2015)
Gracehill Press

Cover design by James Chrsitie
Deep Brain Stimulation image photographed by Andrew Janson.

For my sons Scott and Michael

PART I

MOSES, his CHILDREN, et al

Kendricks

April 2017

Assistant District Attorney Louise Kendricks pushed the partially-opened door just far enough into her boss's office so her words would have a visible source. "Gotta minute, Barb?"

"Sure." Barb Breckenridge closed her laptop screen. "Come on in and have a seat."

Louise did as she was told. "Enjoy your time off?" she asked as she straightened her back and crossed her legs. Her boss had been out of the office for the last three days and Louise was hoping to put a little excitement into the DA's Thursday morning.

"Yes. But it's always good to get things back to normal. I love my mother to pieces, but…" The DA smiled and let her sentence be interpreted however Louise wanted. "Now, what's up?"

"We have a guest coming in this afternoon."

"Oh? Who might that be?"

"A gentleman by the name of Wally Foster."

"Should I know the name?"

"I don't know. I know I didn't, but I've only been in the area for a couple of years. He said his mother's remains were found in 2010 and that an investigation resulted in next to nothing. He evidently had been and still is very disappointed in that outcome."

Without hesitation Breckenridge blurted out "Christine Foster. I wasn't involved but I remember the story. I actually had your job then.

The PSP investigated but couldn't come up with enough information to do anything with the case. I'm guessing you are more familiar with the details now than I am."

"I don't know about that, but I spent yesterday afternoon learning as much as I could. Bones with an over-the-shoulder vinyl bag and purse were all that was left."

"Found in a cave or something, if I remember correctly."

"Where an underground stream empties into the Susquehanna down in York County. The river water backs up into the opening and is fed by the stream below the surface. She was found on a ledge inside the opening. From the photos, you would never know there was anything there but a hole in the rock wall. And the only time you would even notice the hole is when the river is low. The guys who found her had been following the stream underground after it was exposed by a sinkhole. They evidently were looking for a cave with enough water to dive in."

Louise paused and opened her laptop. After a few swipes on the touchpad she started to read the notes she had compiled from yesterday's research.

"She disappeared May 12, 1972. Just vanished. Her husband Lucas, after surviving five tours in Vietnam, died the previous month, an unsolved murder in San Diego while off duty at Camp Pendleton. He and his wife had two children. Christine was described by her brother-in-law Moses Foster as being devastated by her husband's death. Her mother had died several years before her husband's death. Her father deserted her and her mother when Christine was in junior high.

"For the next three years after Christine's disappearance, Moses and his mother raised the two children. Then in January of seventy-six, a few months after the grandmother died, Moses officially adopted Wally and his younger sister Lisbeth. Moses taught math at Pine City High School until he retired in 2012. He never married.

"The coroner ruled Christine's cause of death as undetermined, theorizing that she somehow drowned in the flooding caused by Hurricane Agnes. The theory is that the force of the floodwaters drove her body into the underwater cave where the corpse was somehow trapped in the rocks and remained there until her bones were discovered by the divers. There was nothing to suggest foul play, but by 2010 there was not much left that forensics could work with. The flesh was long gone, probably eaten by critters that could swim in and out of the cave. There was a crack in her skull and a few broken bones, but they could have been the result of the turbulent water and river debris.

"She was officially identified by DNA samples from her son although her driver's license and an expired credit card issued by Mobil were found in her purse beside the bones."

"So what's the reason for the son's visit?"

"He didn't' say. Only that he had some new information about the case, and that he felt the state police hadn't been too enthusiastic in 2010."

"Do you care whether I'm there or not? I've got a pile of stuff to get through."

Louise tried to keep her surprise and excitement contained. She had assumed that her boss would want to be involved. Doing the interview herself after her research yesterday would be a bonus. The son must think he has something of value.

"No, not at all. I'll be more than happy to do it."

"If his new information has any relevancy, you can fill me in afterwards."

"Will do." Louise closed her laptop and got to her feet.

"When is he scheduled?" the DA asked.

"I told him two o'clock."

"If I can help in any way, buzz me."

"Thanks. I will." As she closed the door behind her, she was already thinking of more questions for Wally Foster and wondering if this might be the case that would springboard her out of Mercer County and into a DA's job somewhere with more political possibilities.

* * * *

The clock on the wall in front of her had seemed to be operating at twice its normal speed prior to two o'clock as she prepared her questions, then every minute after two o'clock seemed like five. Finally, at 2:13 her secretary rang to announce Wally Foster's arrival.

He could have looked like Brad Pitt, but Louise would likely not have noticed. She was too focused on his walk. And then his extended hand. Her guest obviously was suffering from some misfortune, most likely Parkinson's. His steps were at best unsteady and his hand, although extended confidently, shook slightly from the shoulder. Once in her grasp though, his hand felt like anybody else's. In fact, there was more man in his hand than the hands of some healthy lawyers she greeted from time to time. She sensed a slight reluctance from her guest to let go, as if he enjoyed the security that her hand provided to his. She let him be the one to release.

"Thank you for seeing me," said Wally, looking directly at the eyes of his host.

"Please, have a seat, Mr. Foster." Louise fought the urge to physically guide her guest to his chair. Instead she gave him the momentary privacy of her back as she made her way to the other side of her desk.

When they were both seated, she said, "I spent yesterday afternoon getting familiar with the details of your mother's disappearance and discovery. Now, what would you like to tell me that I don't already know?"

Wally looked at his hands clenched into fists and pressed firmly against the edge of the desk, almost as if he were bracing himself for the impact of his own words.

"I'm sure you have noticed that I have some physical issues."

He hesitated as if he expected Louise to confirm his assertion, but she refused. His physical condition likely had nothing to do with why he was in the office. *Why was he even mentioning it?*

Sensing her unease, he quickly took back the lead. "I only mention it because my Parkinson's is complicit in why I am here."

"I don't understand. You were only a child when your mother disappeared?"

"My symptoms started shortly after her body was found. I don't know if there is any connection but…"

Feeling that she had been misled by Wally's phone call, Louise started to interrupt, but Wally raised his left hand from the desk, the fist still there. Someone unaware of his disease might have thought he was making an aggressive gesture.

"Please, Attorney Kendricks. I will try to make this as brief as I can. Last month I was fortunate enough to begin a new treatment. Until then my condition had been steadily declining to the point that I was barely able to get out of a chair by myself. The procedure is called DBS, short for Deep Brain Stimulation. Electrodes are connected by wires to a gizmo, something like a pacemaker, that is implanted under the skin of my chest. The device sends electrical pulses through wires that were inserted into my brain, blocking the renegade impulses that are causing the tremors. The results have been more than I thought possible. So good that I decided to have another operation on the other side of my brain. That had been the plan all along, but I wanted to wait to see how the first one went.

"This time, day before yesterday, for whatever reason, something unexpected happened. When the electrode was implanted, and the electricity was turned on for a fine tuning of the placement and current intensity, I experienced an image of a room with a little girl who was asleep. When the charge was increased, the image became more vivid and I could see the room was mine as a child. From old photographs I knew the girl had to be my sister. When the position of the probe was adjusted, I could hear what sounded like my mother screaming in the next room. Not loudly. More like she had a pillow on her face. I told the doctor what was happening, so he adjusted the electrode once more, but I was still in the room with my sister Lisbeth. This time I could hear a man's voice. It sounded like my Uncle Moze."

After her visitor went silent for a few moments, Louise asked, "I don't suppose your memory included what he said."

"Yes."

Again, Wally hesitated.

Louise was getting irritated with the drama. "Well then, what did he say?"

"'I'm not taking them. If you're coming with me, the kids stay here.'"

"I went home after the procedure and got out the family photo albums and tried to figure out how old Lisbeth would have been. In my DBS memory she had a pink ribbon in her hair that matched several photos, and near as I can tell, it would have been around the time my mother disappeared. I had just turned five and Lisbeth with her pink bow was in a photo of me with my birthday cake. The clarity of her image Tuesday was even better than the photo, and I know I haven't looked at that album in ages."

Louise remained quietly stunned. The questions that she had prepared were pretty much useless in the face of what she had just heard. What she needed to do, what she *would* do as soon as he left would be to call his doctor to confirm what Wally Foster had just said had happened on Tuesday.

"Ms. Kendricks, please understand that I did not want to tell you this. I am not accusing my uncle of anything. I am just as dumbfounded by all this as surely you are. Of course, I questioned the reality of what took place, but everything was so vivid. And then when I saw that photo with Lisbeth and me... Oh, and something else that helps set the time... the room in my memory... we only lived in that house for a few months before my mother disappeared.

"The neurosurgeon said this was a first for him, but he had read of other occurrences usually in different parts of the brain. Research is actually being carried out using DBS to enable dementia patients to unlock memories that have become lost."

"Fascinating," said Louise. Then after catching herself staring at Wally, she dropped her astonishment and returned to inquisitor mode, a flurry of questions at the ready.

But her visitor was talking again. "My Uncle Moze became my dad. And he has been a great one. He is the last person in this world that would've hurt my mother. I only tell you about the memory because I– Maybe somehow this will get the case reopened. I've never believed that she would have just walked out on us without a good reason.

"Maybe Moze has always known something and just didn't want to tell us. I *don't* want to get him into trouble. I could have been wrong about the voice – I mean I was all of *five*, for Christ's sake. And I was hearing him through the wall."

Kendricks thought it peculiar that Foster felt the need to suddenly shift into a defensive mode for his uncle. She had not questioned anything he had said or made any accusations.

"Have you told him about Tuesday's experience yet?"

"No. I can't. I am afraid it will sound like I'm accusing him. I haven't told Lisbeth either. She will be very angry with me for telling you. He raised her also. She adores him as much as I do." His unfocused gaze at the wall on the far side of the room fell and his eyes closed.

Louise could see by the movements of his hands that her guest was becoming agitated, so she gave him a few moments to regroup, to maybe recover from his imaginary confrontation with his sister. All the while the blower in the heater beneath the double window rattled behind her. Such a pathetic individual, she couldn't help thinking. His history, his disease, his dilemma.

"I know the case files say you didn't, but do you ever remember any contact from your mother after the night she disappeared?"

"No. I don't." His eyes opened and his head came up. "But I know she wouldn't have left us voluntarily."

He stared at Kendricks in expectation, but she remained silent. Finally his patience lost the battle with his curiosity. "So then, will you think about re-opening the case?"

"I will want to talk to your doctor to corroborate what you say happened, and I will want to talk to your uncle and sister before I decide to go any further with this. Right now, I'm not sure this information will be enough. I was looking at the PSP report from 2010-2011 yesterday. Your uncle was questioned extensively and apparently had a pretty solid alibi, so I don't think there's much for you to worry about there."

"But if my DBS memory is right, *somebody* was in that room. Somebody wanted her to leave with him, and the next morning she was gone."

"*If* your memory is accurate." Louise quickly added something she had been thinking about for several minutes now. "The screaming you say you heard – did it sound like your mother was in pain?"

Wally hesitated for just a moment then said, "Do you mean do I think it could have been the sounds of sexual excitement? I don't know. Possibly. My DBS memory was created when I was five. It's probably a little like reading a translation of a book written in another language except I'm the one doing the translating with a different part of my brain influenced by all my life's experiences after that day. All I know is the words asking her to leave were not hostile or angry."

"And your memory did not include her answer?"

"No."

"And you said that your sister was there with you?"

"Yes, but she was asleep."

"So, you don't have any knowledge of what happened later that night?"

"It's all probably stored in my brain somewhere." After a moment he added, "I have always remembered getting up the next morning and not being able to find my mother and then calling Moze and Granny Ann a few minutes later and them coming right over. We moved in with Granny Ann and Moze that same day. We were all together until Granny died."

"Do you remember the police asking you questions? Wouldn't you have told them then that you heard your mother yelling and that somebody asked her to leave you and go with her?"

"No. I don't remember any police. Maybe Moze would know. Or Lisbeth. But if I don't remember, I doubt she will."

"Can I get their phone numbers from you?"

Wally started grabbing at his jeans pocket. "Just a minute, I'll get them from my phone. I never dial the numbers from memory." His movements were awkward and Louise could see that he was getting frustrated. When he stood up, he momentarily lost his balance. Finally, he had the phone in his hand and read both numbers to her.

"And the name of your doctor?"

"Martin Chang-Lee. He's with UPMC in Pittsburgh."

"Okay, Mr. Foster, let me hear what these folks have to say, then I'll get back to you. But I have to be honest. There's not much here to warrant any more investigation than what I will be doing with your family and your doctor. I know that's not what you want to hear, but it always comes back to money and time. And, as always, we're short of both." She stood up and extended her hand. "Thanks for coming in. You will hear from me one way or the other, hopefully within the next couple of weeks."

Wally Foster was still fumbling with getting his phone back into his pocket when she stood. He shifted it to his left hand and took her hand with his right. "Maybe I'll have another memory for you the next time I see you. I have another fine-tuning session next week."

2

Wally

April 2017

Apart from the obvious loss of co-ordination and mobility, what bothered Wally the most about his disease was the various states of fear he now experienced on a regular basis. Fear of falling, fear of dependence, fear of being mocked... fear of the future. He didn't think he used to be a fearful person at all. In fact, it had been just the opposite. Other than photos and the one short video of Granny Ann after his parents' wedding, he barely remembered her, but he would never forget an image he had of her shortly before her heart attack. She had only been fifty-nine when she had gathered him into her arms one afternoon after he had chased an aggressive dog away from Lisbeth. She'd told him that he was going to grow up to be just like his Grampa Ned, her husband, one of the bravest men there had ever been, and Wally's father Luke, who had fought in Vietnam. She said that Wally was already the bravest eight-year-old in all of Pennsylvania.

Moze had filled him in on the details of Grampa Ned's bravery a few years later and then again when Wally had been old enough to really appreciate what his grandfather had done. With the 101st Airborne he had fought courageously in many of the worst battles in Europe during World War Two, bringing home with him a Bronze Star for his heroism at the Battle of the Bulge. After his discharge he'd met and married Granny Ann and within two years they'd produced Moze and Wally's dad. Although Grampa's job at the big foundry in Pine City had paid good money, he'd thought the smart thing to do was sign up for the Army reserves and pick up some easy money to help get a little ahead. Next thing he knew he was in Korea, fighting another war. For two years he fought off the Chinese and North Koreans only to die in an incident involving friendly fire.

Moze had also told Wally about his father Luke receiving two Bronze Stars and three Purple Hearts during his five years in Vietnam. Wally later suspected that the special bond he shared with Moze likely had its roots in their common losses of soldier fathers although Wally had never felt like he had lost a father. There were no memories. None. Just photographs and Granny Ann and Moze giving Wally *their* memories of his father.

If left to Wally, there would never have been an *Uncle* Moses. Wally had started dropping the word Uncle early on, had even started calling him Dad a year or so before Granny Ann died. But she had quickly put an end to it, firmly reminding him that Moze was his uncle, not his father. Although Moses hadn't encouraged the kids to call him Dad, by that time he had developed all the instincts and feelings that fatherhood required. He had savored those moments when the kids would defy their grandmother if she was thought to be out of earshot. After a few slipups, however, and having to witness Granny Ann's tears of disappointment with them, the kids and Moze had realigned their verbal relationship according to Granny Ann's wishes. By the time she died, *Uncle* Moses had become just Moze. After her death Wally and Lisbeth would be inconsistent in what they called him. When he was their friend, he was Moze. When there was emotion, he was Dad, or, as was often the case with Lisbeth, he was Daddy.

Wally had been so relieved to hear the DA's assistant say that Moze was very unlikely to be considered a suspect. Until his DBS memory, he had never considered the possibility of anyone thinking Moze might be involved. Still didn't for that matter. All that he had wanted anybody to know was that somebody had been with his mother that night, and that the person who had been there had wanted her, likely forced her, to leave with him, and that person was someone who had *sounded* like Moze.

Moze had always been there for him, good times and bad... his doctors' appointments, his best man, his rock to hold onto when Junie had left him a year after his disease attacked him. And, Wally was certain that whatever happened in the future, Moze would continue to be there.

But Moze was seventy-one now, and although he was in great shape physically and mentally, Wally did not want to be the cause of anything negative in his father's life. No matter how well he was aging, there would come a time when his father would be the one to need somebody. In fact, what drove Wally more than anything else to beat his disease, or at least manage it on his own, was to make sure that he would be there for Moze when that time came.

It was hard for Wally to think of Moze as seventy-one. Maybe if they only saw each other a few times a year, Wally would take more notice of the changes. But he saw him several times a week, making change difficult to discern. For Wally, Moze aged primarily in Lisbeth's comments after her visits, forcing Wally into a reality that he did not want. He also suspected that his failure to perceive changes in Moze was partly due to the Parkinson's. Being dependent on someone made it even more difficult to perceive the roles reversed, especially when Moze had defined and executed his role so well over the years.

Maybe the special relationship between the two of them had been fostered by the de facto grace period they'd shared with one another following his mother Chrissy's disappearance, a void that allowed each of them to find the other's value. Moze's first role had been as Granny Ann's back up, someone to give her a break, help with oversight and logistics. Lisbeth had been only four and her curiosity and energy sometimes challenged Granny's capabilities. Moze had made sure his mother had what she needed and had the extra set of eyes to keep track of the two children when her focus was required elsewhere.

But what Granny Ann had needed most from Moze had been money, especially after Chrissy disappeared. Although Granny's house had been inherited by her late husband from his parents, her income was limited to survivor's benefits and the money she made by selling pies and cakes to a local lunch counter near Pine City Castings. She had set aside her husband's death benefit for the boys' college fund. Eventually she'd had to take out a loan to get Moze through his last two years, but he had repaid her after a few years of teaching.

He had graduated with a degree in math education from Indiana University of Pennsylvania in August of 1969, almost three years before the kids showed up permanently. His college deferment had expired upon graduation, but the local draft board had granted him, at Granny Ann's pleading, a temporary deferment until such time as Luke would be discharged. She had argued that the drafting of Moze would cause her great financial and emotional hardship. Her husband had served four years of combat in one war and given his life in another, and her other son was currently fighting for his country in Vietnam. She hadn't wanted to risk the possibility of both of her boys joining their father in flag-draped coffins. When Luke had surprised everyone by re-enlisting for a second three years, the local board allowed the deferment to continue. And then Luke's death, followed by Chrissy's disappearance, removed any chance for Moze being drafted, especially after he adopted the kids.

During the years that Wally and Lisbeth lived with Granny Ann and Moze, Wally had never been in doubt as to who was in charge. Granny Ann had always been the long arm of the law, had her own ideas as to what was acceptable behavior. Moze was her oldest child but he was only twenty-five when Chrissy disappeared. In Granny Ann's eyes, not old enough and much too inclined to be their friend instead of a parent.

When she died, her years of discipline made the transition to parenthood easier for Moze. The children had feared and respected her, but they'd loved Moze and did what he'd asked them to do because they simply needed to please him.

Wally plopped down on the couch with his usual somewhat out-of-control landing and reached for the remote control. But, before he touched it, he changed his mind. He didn't really want to watch television. He didn't really want to do anything. He let his head fall backwards against the couch and closed his eyes. Half expecting the phone to ring with Lisbeth's vitriolic voice on the other end, he remained motionless. Would the DA's office have called her yet? She would be so pissed at him for getting Moze involved. He dreaded the call.

As close as Wally was to Moze, Lisbeth had always been closer. And that had never been a problem for Wally. He loved his sister. The two of them, having been orphaned by death and abandonment, had often taken comfort in each other's presence as the years had passed and the awareness of their situation became part of their identity… the Foster Children. Father dead, mother gone, grandmother dead. Raised by that wonderful man their uncle Moses. The man whose life Wally had likely just made a lot more complicated.

Wally opened his eyes and looked at the window a couple of feet to his right. It had started to rain. The nearby streetlight illuminated the drops sliding down the glass and the trails they left behind. His thoughts returned to his sister and the conversation looming in front of him like a root canal. His right hand started to shake, a somewhat common event when his mind became agitated.. Quickly he grabbed it with the left. Almost immediately he had the offending member under control.

"Just call her and get it over with," he relented aloud.

And then the phone rang.

As he put it to his ear, his hand was shaking again. Awkwardly he switched hands, sticking his right hand under his left thigh.

"Hey, Dad."

3

Lisbeth

April 2017

Lisbeth Dawkins put the phone back on the dining room table and stared at it for several moments as if it were a foreign object that she wanted removed. The day had been complicated enough already. Her favorite bar had called half an hour ago and asked if she could fill in for the act that had been scheduled. Ordinarily that wouldn't be a problem but she was playing violin with the orchestra tonight. She would have an hour to get from the last note of "An American in Paris" in Center City to the first note of her first song at the bar. She had done it before but she hadn't slept much last night. And now this… this call from the Mercer County DA's office.

She loved Wally, loved him to pieces. How could she not. But how could he do this to Moze? To all of them for that matter. What possible good could come from it? Their mother was ancient history. She'd been dead forty-five years – *forty-five!* For whatever reason, she'd abandoned them. How she died was irrelevant. Didn't matter whether Chrissy slipped on a banana peel and ended up in the river, or was pushed into the river, or jumped into the river. What Lisbeth knew for sure was that she and Wally could never have had any better childhood than the one they'd had with Moze. Mothers were so overrated. She had survived quite nicely without having one or being one.

Being pregnant for ten weeks… not exactly enough to qualify.

When the fetus had exploded from her in a torrent of blood and pain… well, she hadn't even wanted it in the first place. There had been a few motherly moments early on, mostly induced by attempts to convince Moze and Wally that getting pregnant would not ruin her life. But all thoughts of motherhood had ended with the miscarriage. So had her relationship with the man who would have been the father. His ultimatum to abort the pregnancy had provided Lisbeth with the last bit of insight needed to remove him from her future.

Two months later at the end of her first semester at Penn State, Lisbeth applied to the School of Music and was given permission to switch her major from Music Education to Music Arts with a minor in Performance as the end game. One summer session would be all that was needed to get her courses aligned, and eventually she would have to audition for the department head to demonstrate her competence, but Lisbeth had made up her mind that performing with a violin tucked under her chin was what she really wanted to do. Teaching had only been a suggestion by Moze. No doubt, Lisbeth's exposure to a teacher's life had been an influence in her original decision. Especially the summer vacations. But she did not have the patience that Moze had, and, although teaching would put her center stage every day, she decided it could never be a substitute for creating her own music in front of an audience that would recognize her for her talent.

. She had started violin lessons in sixth grade. In tenth grade she had started performing with a group of adults in churches and community events. Hoping to get her to commit to the music department, Pine City College had invited her to play with their orchestra her senior year, but she loved her softball and basketball careers too much to make the necessary time available. Not to mention she had already committed to play softball on scholarship for Penn State.

Two weeks before her sophomore year began Lisbeth auditioned for the chairman of the School of Music, and two professors of violin performance. Their evaluation was an enthusiastic thumbs-up with one caveat... Lisbeth would have to quit playing softball. The many demands on her time for practice and performances would have to be given priority. Mention was also made of the risk of injury, but the committee made it clear there would be no compromise concerning time. When Lisbeth reminded them her education was being paid for by her softball scholarship and that losing it would force her to leave school, the professors looked at one another with conspiratorial smiles. The chairman then looked at Lisbeth and said, "Our scholarship is better than theirs. We won't make you do early-morning wind sprints."

So her college softball career had ended. When graduation came three years later, she took a position with the Harrisburg symphony orchestra and gave private violin lessons to help pay the bills.

Lisbeth picked up her cell phone and checked the time. She had two hours to eat, get ready, and get into the city. That should not be a problem for her. She had never used anything but a taxi since moving to Philadelphia after her divorce. It just made life simpler. And after fifteen years of living with Conrad Dawkins, a former executive at Hershey, she had been more than ready for simple.

She put the phone back on the table, thinking about what she could have to eat. It would be a long evening – ninety minutes of playing the violin, then another ninety minutes of singing and playing the piano plus the between time. The leftover pizza in the fridge would have to do.

She would like to call Wally and read the riot act to him, but did not want to have that discussion added to the stress of keeping an eye on the clock. It would be better to give Moze a quick call instead... if the DA's office hadn't already called him.

No, she decided. Tomorrow would be soon enough. She would likely get too emotional and that was not the state of mind to have on a night that would be as demanding as tonight would likely be.

4

Moze

April 2017

Moze had thought about getting into his pickup truck and making the four-mile drive to Wally's house the moment he ended his conversation with the DA's assistant. Louise Kendricks sounded like trouble. Although his adopted son had long since become an adult, Moses Foster, like most parents, still felt the need to protect his children. He was certain Wally was in a bad way at the moment. The kid had enough on his plate these days with the Parkinson's.

A wave of guilt rolled over him for not insisting on taking Wally to Pittsburgh yesterday. This unlocked memory business surely had the kid in turmoil. And now he had the DA's office involved which meant Moze's life was likely to get a whole lot more complicated. But none of that mattered to Moze. As far as he was concerned, Wally had a free pass regarding anything. The phone, still in his hand, rang again. Moze looked at the caller ID and answered immediately.

"Yes, Ms. Kendricks. Must be you thought of something else you wanted to know."

"Sorry to bother you again."

"No bother here."

"I just got off the phone with my boss and she has given me permission to clear my schedule tomorrow. I know I had talked about maybe meeting with you next Tuesday, but I'm sure that everybody, including yourself, would like to get this all sorted out as soon as possible.

Any chance we could get together tomorrow?"

Moze didn't like the idea one little bit. He knew from their earlier conversation that the Assistant DA would like nothing better than to resolve everything as soon as possible all right... by putting him into prison for Chrissy's murder. What prosecutor wouldn't want a splash play like that? A cannonball into the still, dark water of an unsolved case from forty-five years ago.

"Jeez, I kind of already had something on my plate for tomorrow."

"Sure. We'll leave it at Tuesday then. Ten o'clock still good?"

Moze suddenly decided that he was really in no hurry to see this woman. She was a little too eager. He would need to be careful with his memories.

"Let me get back to you on that. I'd forgotten earlier that Wally might need me to take him for his next treatment and I think it might be Tuesday. I was just getting ready to call him when you called."

"Okay. How about we just leave it at ten unless I hear from you?"

"Sure."

* * * *

When Wally answered his phone, it didn't take long for Moze to regret calling instead of making the trip.

"You've had a tough day, I'm guessing," said Moze.

"She called you already?"

"Yeah... twice, as a matter of fact. Me thinks she thinks I sound sexy."

"Twice? Oh, shit, Moze, I'm sorry about this."

"No big deal, Son. She's just doing her job and that's what you really want, right?"

"Yeah, but —"

"Now, tell me about the treatment."

Wally paused for a few moments. "The Assistant DA told you about the memory?"

"I believe she might have mentioned something, yes," he said finishing with a quick laugh. "You're sure about it? Nineteen seventy-two was—"

"Oh, Moze. It was sooo real. A home movie in 3-D. The pink bow in Lisbeth's hair was just like the one in a photo we have from my birthday the year Mom disappeared."

"She wore that thing everywhere. I bought it at Easter and put it on her basket. Chrissy put a barrette through it and we all made a fuss about how cute she was with it in her hair. Maybe your mother put it on her before she left that night."

"Maybe."

From the silence that followed, Moze knew that his son's focus was not on Lisbeth's pink bow.

"So how do think the DA's office is going to react to your visit?"

"You know how we've always said that Mom wouldn't have willingly left Lisbeth and me on our own. That's why I had to tell them. Please understand."

"So, you think I was really there?"

"No, no, no. I only said that the voice *sounded* like yours. I don't know what the rules of this game are, Moze. I'm hearing your voice, but I'm hearing it as you sound in the brain I'm using today. The voice was recorded in the brain I had then. They can't be the same, can they?"

Moze waited a few moments then said, "You know I wouldn't lie to you about this… right, Son?" Moze didn't wait for Wally's answer. "I'm not saying you didn't hear somebody, only that it wasn't me. I was with somebody that night. Somebody I shouldn't have been with. I have no doubt that her corroboration was what kept me from becoming the focus of the 2010 investigation. Your mom might have been with somebody that night in her room, but it wasn't me."

Moze chose every word carefully. He would not tell Wally lies. But he could not tell him everything that he knew about that night. Or the one before. He had his reasons.

"So, you're sure there's no way that the DA's office can use my words against you?"

"Not unless Vicky Voorhees would decide that she wasn't with me that night."

"Wait. You mean the Vicky Voorhees who was my high school principal?"

"Well, she wasn't the principal then, but yes. That one, and also the one who was married at the time to Joe Voorhees, the minister of the First Baptist Church."

"Holy Jesus, Moze! She must have been a bunch of years older than you." Wally paused while he tried to reconcile what he had just heard with his concept of the man who had raised him. "Did he ever find out?"

"No. At least I don't think so. Doesn't really matter now, does it. Remember, he died a few years ago. After Chrissy's disappearance Vicky and I saw each other a few more times, but we both never really were comfortable together again. In '72 there had been no serious investigation. Donnie Beemer was the one asking all the questions. He and I had hung out together in high school so he had next to no interest in questioning me. Besides, there hadn't been a body then. A lot of people figured it had all been too much for Chrissy and she had just lit out.

"In 2010 Vicky was seventy years old. She said that she and Joe had been married so long that the marriage could likely survive anything, but if it didn't, it was better for her to lose her marriage than taking the chance I might go to prison."

"So... Mrs. Voorhees... do you ever talk to her? I mean, is there any worry there that anything could change?"

"I went to Joe's funeral like several hundred others in Pine City. Vicky smiled at me and I returned it, but her daughter Deenie was with her and a bunch of others, probably in-laws. I haven't talked to her since those early days after Chrissy's body was found."

Several moments passed in silence before Wally spoke again. "Are you going to get in touch with her? If Kendricks reopens the case, she will want to talk to her eventually."

"I thought I would stop and see her after my meeting on Tuesday. That's when Kendricks wants to talk. I'd rather not deliver the news to Vicki over the phone. I'm sure she thought she had seen the end of this in 2010. And even though her husband's gone, she might be a little concerned about how Deenie would react to news of our little fling."

Wally had to reach for his bad arm. It had escaped the confines of his thigh and was twisting in response to the emotional agitation swirling in his head. He grabbed it and returned it to its holding cell for the moment, applying more pressure with his leg, his thoughts swarming with Mrs. Voorhees, Deenie, Deenie's husband. How could he have known they might be affected by his talking to the DA's office.

He wondered if Lisbeth knew anything of the affair. Moze would have been much more likely to have confided in her at some point.

Now his better arm started to twitch. Wally could not imagine telling her. If she didn't already know, Moze would have to be the one to tell her.

Audibly he exhaled. When did he become so fearful of his sister? He wished he had called her before finding out about Mrs. Voorhees.

"You okay, Son?"

"Not really. I'm thinking I should have kept my mouth shut."

"I raised you to never fear the truth and that's what I want you to do now. Whatever happens in the process, so be it. Don't worry about me, don't worry about Vicky, and most certainly..." Moze stopped speaking, not because he wasn't sure what to say next, but to give some emphasis to his next words, the ones that would fit with the grin that had spread across his face. "Don't worry about how your sister will react."

"How did Lisbeth get into this?"

"Lisbeth always gets into anything involving us. She's always here with us. The three musketeers, remember? Us against the world? Besides, I know you, Son. You have always been the peacemaker. And I'd bet every dime I have that you're wondering right this moment how all of this will play out with her. Our little prima donna already knows about Vicky and me."

When a few seconds passed without Wally responding, Moze again became the math teacher that Wally once had so many years ago when explaining a geometry theorem, laying out the steps for a proof. "Here's what I want you to do. First, when you next speak to Lisbeth, you tell her that you are going to tell the DA's office whatever comes out of that brain of yours because I asked you to. Lisbeth does not remember Chrissy, but I do. I loved your mom. She was like a sister to me. Like anybody who ever knew her, I want to know how she got into that cave. If these memories of yours can help bring some closure for all of us, then that's what must be done."

"And secondly, and this is going to confuse the bejesus out of you... no matter what comes out of that head of yours, there will be nothing that will hurt me. Even if you think it will. You just have to trust me on this."

Moze paused. "When's your next treatment?"

"Tuesday morning."

"Are you going to let me take you to Pittsburgh this time?"

"No. It's really not that much—"

"A taxi to the bus station here, then a taxi from the bus station in Pittsburgh to UPMC, then afterwards, a taxi back to the bus station, then a taxi from the bus station home. Yeah, I'm seventy-one, but I can still make it to Pittsburgh and back a lot faster than you did yesterday."

"Dad, you've made that trip so often. I think you're probably ready for some time off. It's really not that big a deal."

"What time?"

Wally hesitated then said "Eleven."

"Perfect. I was supposed to see Kendricks at ten. This will make her have to wait another day. I'll be at your place by nine."

"No, really, Moze, I–"

"Nonsense. See you then if not before. Bye, Son."

"Okay, you win. Bye, Dad."

* * * *

Moze stared at the ceiling. Sleep was not likely coming anytime soon. How complicated life could suddenly get because of a few phone calls. Once again the past had become the present. It had only been seven years since the two had last gotten tangled.

Chrissy's bones. There had at least been the relief back then of finally knowing for sure. Unfortunately, there had also been all of the hoopla with the press and the PA State Police and his adult kids getting the adult version of their mom's disappearance... not to mention that he briefly became the focus point of rumors and innuendo because someone in the investigation had leaked to the press that a family member was being questioned and would need an alibi for the night of Chrissy's disappearance. But Vicky had quickly and quietly made that nonsense go away again.

Still, he had not been nearly as much on edge in 2010 as he had been back in '72. Only twenty-five years old. No tenure yet. Wasn't even sure that he'd wanted tenure. He had often thought that he likely would have quit teaching if it hadn't been for Wally and Lisbeth. His mother needed money and time to take care of them, so he wasn't about to quit a job that could help with both, especially in the summer.

The summer of '72 had been complicated, to say the least.

And then almost four years later his mother had died, leaving him to become everything to Wally and Lisbeth. So, the teaching had continued.

LeeAnn Enders. What was she doing in his head tonight?

Whatever happened to her, he wondered. If not for the kids, she would have been his wife... at least for a while anyway. To think that his years with Wally and Lisbeth would have been lost in a trade for life with her. Damn, he had been lucky.

Not that he hadn't liked her a lot. Okay, he had probably been in love with her and had been miserable after losing her. But he had never regretted his decision. They had been dating the better part of a year and he had finally decided that the time had come to make it official. He had even purchased the ring, putting it in the same drawer where it was right now, forty-two years later.

LeeAnn had been fine with the kids, with the time they'd demanded of him... until Granny Ann died. After the initial turmoil and emotional stress, LeeAnn had given him an ultimatum, although she denied that it was meant to be one. An ultimatum in his mind had an expiration date that would invoke consequences. So many days, weeks, years before the alternative took effect. But that was something she refused to impose. She'd told him he had as long as he needed to unload the kids, but there would be no wedding until then. She wanted kids, just not someone else's.

But with every hug and kiss that he experienced with Wally and Lisbeth, each tear that he dried, each cut that he cleaned and dressed, each little giggle floated his way, Moze found LeeAnn's terms more disagreeable, until finally the thought of losing the kids became unacceptable. One month almost to the day after his mother died, he told LeeAnn what she surely already had figured out.

He dated a few times afterwards, but the pool of eligible partners shrank as he got older, and nobody was ever special enough for him to get serious. Besides, there had been plenty enough love in his life.

And now... he was seventy-one.

* * * *

When he woke, he was overcome with the need to talk to Lisbeth. He much doubted Wally's ability to defend himself should she go on the attack. Lisbeth had always been the tougher of the two. According to the norms of society, Wally should have been the musician. Not that he was the least bit effeminate. Wally had been athletic, had survived at least one fist fight, and had never given Moze reason to doubt his courage, especially in the wake of his Parkinson's and abandonment by his wife. Yet Lisbeth had always been the more dominant of the two. She had been the warrior, a fearless force that seemed to know which battles were worth fighting. And God help anyone who was on the other side because Lisbeth always made her side the right one and the winning one.

Lisbeth's mother Chrissy had had many of Lisbeth's talents... athletic, a singing voice maybe better than Lisbeth's, and the ability to sit down at the piano and play without sheet music.

"Moze?" Lisbeth squeezed her eyelids together trying to bring the caller ID into focus.

"Uh oh. I'm guessing you were sleeping." It wasn't the first time he had roused her from sleep. Since her move to Philadelphia, he would sometimes forget that her singing slash piano slash violin gigs often pushed her bedtimes into the early hours of the next day.

"Yeah, I was. Didn't get to bed until two. But you know I'm always happy to hear your voice."

"Sorry, Darlin'. I should know by now not to call you before noon."

"Don't you ever apologize for calling me." Her energy was catching up to the day.

"You probably, if you put your mind to it, can guess why I'm calling... that is, if you had a call from the Mercer County DA's office yesterday. Which I'm guessing you did."

"Yeah, I was going to call you today anyway before I let Big Brother have a piece of my mind."

"Lisbeth..." When he would say her name and leave it hanging in the air, Lisbeth knew what was wanted of her, that the path on which her words were taking her was most likely the wrong one. She had heard her name used like that so seldom in adulthood, so its employment now gave her even more reason to rethink what she was about to say, almost as if an internal GPS NAV system were saying *recalculating*.

"Okay. Then what's your take on all of this? After hearing what the woman said on the phone, you're the one I'm worried about, Dad."

"I'm safe. Wally only said the voice *sounded* like mine. And don't forget Vicky Voorhees."

"Is she still in the area?"

"Yes. I'm planning on a visit with her next week after talking to Kendricks in person. You knew that her husband died a few years ago?"

"Yes, you told me. I liked him."

"Well, I guess I kind of shit on him, didn't I."

She forced a laugh. "That was when you were young and reckless." After a quick pause she added, "You know... somewhat human like the rest of us?"

"Yeah, it was reckless all right. Anyway, Wally has another treatment next week. Maybe he'll have some more surprises for us. Did Kendricks tell you what made the time of his memory so certain for Wally?"

"No."

"The pink bow you had in your hair, the one you had on in a photo from his birthday party that year. Do you remember it?"

"Yes, but only because of photos. Otherwise I doubt I would have any recollection of it."

"Isn't that whole memory thing just... bizarre," said Moze. "To think that every moment we've ever experienced might be recorded in our brains somewhere?"

Lisbeth, seeming to give Moze's words some thought, did not speak for a few moments then said, "So, do you think it's really possible that he's remembering this stuff?"

"Yes. I do. His doctor told him that it's happened to others getting that treatment although not to any of his patients. I went online and checked it out. It's not a common thing, but some of the details that people recall are just incredible. So, give your brother some slack on this. He's only doing what he thinks he should do. Maybe this time around the powers that be will take the case a little more seriously."

"Well, I don't see how they can. What can they find in a pile of bones from 1972?" Lisbeth took a deep breath. "I worry that this Kendricks woman might be on a career-making witch hunt, and she'll end up turning you into the witch. All Wally's memory does is put your name prominently into the mix."

"No. What it does is put someone else into the mix. I have an alibi. Somebody was there that night who wanted her to leave her children. And Wally heard him. That's all."

"But where can that go unless he does remember something else? I just hate to see him get all worked up again." She stopped and thought for a moment. "Still, it must have been pretty cool to see the house the way it was for us back then and to see me so little. We were only in that place for a couple of months, right?"

"Yeah, wasn't long. It was just down the street a ways from Granny Ann and me."

"Well, with all that in Wally's mind right now, he'll be even more obsessed with finding a bad guy."

"I know you look at it differently, but we have to let him try. Maybe, if it all gets sorted out, you'll find that your feelings might change. Just don't worry about me."

5

Luke

February 1966

Freshman Luke Foster nodded at the large black senior who nodded back then disappeared into his private room directly across the hall from Luke's room. Two-hundred-fifty-pound Alex Seffers was a senior and the unquestioned authority figure for Langham Hall's first floor. If you were a freshman and were intending to participate in one of the athletic programs at Indiana University of Pennsylvania you were likely living in Langham.

Football season had been over for several months and Luke was officially on academic probation now that the second semester was underway. He had chosen IUP, not as a means to an education, but as a way to continue playing football. During the fifth week of the season, however, that part of his IUP experience had turned to shit. Life in general for him had occasionally done just that, primarily because of his temper. Most of the time, he would be on the lookout for those moments and do his best to control the craziness, extinguish the spark before ignition. But sometimes, well... the sparks were just too numerous or too hot.

And so it had been during practice on a Wednesday. The senior, third-string quarterback directing the scout team had fired a pass into the back of Luke's helmet as he was walking away. The two of them had tangled before. In an instant Luke turned and covered the five yards separating him from the offender with three steps and a leap that put his helmet into his teammate's knees, ending the season for both players. Luke might have escaped with only a suspension if he hadn't followed the hit with a punch that accidentally broke the nose of the offensive coordinator as he tried to yank Luke from the quarterback.

On this cold, February day he was a little surprised that his roommate was not in the room. He, too, was in Langham because of football, a transfer from West Point. Eddie Bruckman had left Army because the courses were out of reach for him academically, the science and math ones especially. His focus now was on becoming a phys-ed teacher. The one positive he had taken with him from West Point was a strongly-developed self-discipline which placed him at his desk studying most evenings, making him a much better student than his roommate.

Room 110 was on Langham's first floor, and like all the rooms on that side of the building, its windows faced the windows of the girls' dorm on the other side of a shared parking lot. Luke walked to his window and pulled open the curtains to take his customary survey of the rooms that were lit and available for inspection though he had only once ever seen something worth viewing… two girls with bras visible on the second floor. Because of the upward viewing angle, what else had been exposed he could only imagine.

After a few futile moments of searching, he turned and started for his desk. Again, there was a ritual that had to be performed. On his wall to the right of his desk, he had hung a magazine cutout that served as a poster tame enough to survive any surprise inspections by the dorm mother he had yet to meet. The subject… a photograph of Joey Heatherton performing for Bob Hope's USO Christmas TV special from bases in the Pacific and Vietnam.

"You studying that again? Too bad you never get quizzed."

Luke had not heard his roommate enter the room.

"Hey Eddie. You know a good roommate should cough or clear his throat when he walks in on his roomie having fantasy sex."

Luke turned and looked at the photo again. "She's almost enough to make me want to enlist. Did you see her on that show? Man, did she look good."

"No, I missed it." Eddie gave a cursory glance at the photo then dropped his book on his desk and lay down on his bed. "Did you eat yet?"

"Yeah."

"Anything good?"

"Spaghetti and salad."

Luke sat down at his desk and turned toward Joey Heatherton again, at the sea of soldiers in front of her. Hell, what were the odds of her going back to Vietnam when he'd be there if he did enlist? Slim to none. Still...

Eddie sat up on his bed and said, "I think I'll run over to the pizza shop for supper. You want to go along? My treat."

Luke turned away from his thoughts on the wall. "Naw, I'm not hungry at all. But thanks. I think I'll see what my brother's up to."

"I just saw him out in the lobby on my way in."

"No kidding?"

"Yeah, he and Jack Baird."

"Probably talking wrestling shit. Baird keeps trying to talk him into joining the team. Been after him since some guy got hurt and there's nobody now at that weight. Moze used to wrestle in high school. He was pretty decent but he doesn't want to put in all the time. He takes this place a little more serious than I do."

* * * *

In the lobby Luke walked over to where his brother and the wrestler were standing. Both were turned away from Luke and did not see him until he spoke. "Seems to me at least one of you guys should be studying."

"Hey, Luke," said the wrestler. "How's it hangin', man?"

"Never better."

Moze reached out and gave Luke a shove. "I was just comin' over to talk to you about a few things when the Bear here cornered me. Tell him will you, what a lousy wrassler I was so he'll let up."

"All I know is a couple of the girls he used to date told me how good he was with backseat pins. Spread eagle moves or somethin' like that."

"Doesn't matter how good he was, he'd be better than what we have now. One forfeit after another."

"I'm thinkin' maybe if you ask him next year, you might have more luck. All of this studying will get old by then."

Luke didn't see the surprised look on Baird's face, but he certainly saw the change that came over his brother who quickly turned to Baird and gave a brief shake of his head.

Silence. In the background, laughter from those watching "I Spy" with Bill Cosby and Robert Culp. Luke had forgotten it was on or he would have been on a couch watching it with a bunch of the other academic probationers, or playing pinochle on the second floor where there was a television *and* three card tables.

Luke finally broke the silence, "So we're playing 'I've Got a Secret' now?'"

"Let's go over to my place and we'll talk about it," said Moze.

* * * *

The walk from Langham took almost ten minutes. Luke had asked what was going on as soon as they got out of the building, but Moze told him to wait. Luke knew from experience that any further requests would only be wasted breath.

Because Moze was a sophomore, he had the option of living off campus. His apartment on Church Street was part of a house divided into five bedrooms with two occupants in each. All ten students shared the same kitchen, living room and two bathrooms. Moze's room was on the second floor.

Luke had been a regular visitor to the house and knew everyone. Terry Albrecht, Moze's roommate, was his favorite. But tonight Terry was nowhere to be seen which was unusual because both Terry and Moze were excellent students who seldom did anything but study on weeknights. Luke had to wonder if Terry's absence had been arranged.

"Sit down, Little Brother," Moze directed.

"Wow, this whole scene is freakin' me out," said Luke as he sat on Moze's bed. "You're not getting' me ready for some kind of bad news-type shit, are you?"

Moze pulled his chair away from his desk and positioned it in front of Luke. "No. Not *bad* news, just news. But I don't want you repeating it to anybody, especially to Mom."

"Scout's honor."

Moze paused a few seconds before announcing, "I'm enlisting in the Marines as soon as the semester's over."

"Holy shit, Moze! Are you serious?"

"As serious as I can get."

"Why?"

"I guess it's Dad probably as much as anything. You know, I just feel like I should do it. He went without having to. Honored himself, the family, our country. You know how proud Mom gets when she talks about him and how brave he was. He lost four years of his life because he enlisted in World War II then lost the rest of his life when he got called back for Korea.

"Every time I see stories about kids our age signing up and heading off to Vietnam, I feel ashamed that I'm back here in PA living the good life. I'll come back when my three years are up and finish my degree. I can use what I can save and the GI Bill to pay for it. That way Mom won't have to do any loans."

"So, when are you going to tell her?"

"Soon. I just decided for sure over the weekend. I wanted you to know first."

When Luke said nothing at the honor Moze had just given him and let several more moments pass in silence, Moze began to wonder if confiding in Luke had maybe been a mistake. Then suddenly he knew for sure it was. Luke jumped from the bed and stood directly in front of Moze, their knees nearly touching.

"I'm going with you!"

"The hell you *are*!"

"You know as well as I do, I'm not going to leave here with a degree. I came here to play football and to get you and Mom off my back. Unless I transfer or the coaching staff dies somehow, I ain't playin' any more football, here. You're not goin' to believe this, but I was thinkin' seriously about enlisting myself. You going just seals the deal. And nothin' you say is goin' to stop me now that I know you're goin'." Luke waited for Moze to argue with him, but he didn't. Emboldened by the silence, he added, "Let's do it tomorrow. Maybe we can get some kind of partial refund. We're not even close to half way through the semester, right?"

"No, three weeks yet. But you can forget about quitting now. We're going to finish the semester. Both of us. And you're going to quit skipping classes and assignments. Otherwise, you're going it alone when you face Mom." Moze knew how important it was for Luke to have his brother's support. Luke idolized his big brother and most of the time agreed to Moze's directions. Just telling their mother of the decision was something Luke would find so intimidating that he likely would just take off without saying good-bye unless he had his brother's support. "Understood?"

"But I'm already flunkin' everything except ROTC and geography.' Besides, I'm on probation, so if my QPA isn't above 1.6 at midterm, I'm gone anyhow."

"Jesus, Luke. You're flunking English, Math, and General Psych?"

"Exactly. And that means my deferment will be kaput. So, I'm goin' one way or the other... drafted for two years or enlisted for three. I'm thinkin' three. Maybe make a career of it. I don't see much else out there for me anyway." He glanced at his brother for a sign as to how he was going to react, but Moze just stared at the floor. Luke returned to his place on the bed.

Without looking at him Moze said, "Luke..." But then he stopped and stood up. Struggling with his composure, he said, "You've done a lot of stupid shit in your life, and that's entirely up to you." In a flash Moze grabbed the upper corners of Luke's coat with his right hand and closed them hard against the throat. "But dammit, don't you start lying to me. I called the Dean's office to find out what academic probation actually means."

Luke grabbed at his brother's hand to get free, causing Moze to squeeze even harder. A moment later he let go in disgust.

"You won't get kicked out until the end of the semester."

Moze grabbed his chair and slid it towards the desk then followed it and sat down with his back towards Luke.

"Do whatever the hell you want after May. But if you don't finish the semester with at least a 2.0, have a nice life." He waited for a response but didn't get one. Finally, behind him he heard Luke get off the bed and leave.

* * * *

When the Tuesday before Good Friday passed without hearing from Luke, Moze decided he had better check in with him to see what his plans were for the five-day break. To avoid any unnecessary contact with him, he decided to check in with his mother first. She answered on the third ring as she always did.

"Hey, Mom."

"Moze, is that you?" She sometimes had trouble telling them apart on the phone.

"Yes. Mom, I just wanted to remind you that we're off Thursday through Monday. Probably see you about six tomorrow night. I've got us a ride with LuAnn Thomas."

"Oh. Did Luke change his mind then?"

"What do you mean?"

"Well, he told me last night that he wouldn't be coming home this weekend. He said he had too much studying to do."

As much as Moze wanted to believe what Luke had told their mother, he was sure he had lied. In fact, he doubted Luke was even on campus. The little shit had enlisted and was in boot camp somewhere.

"I better check in with him just to make sure before I call LuAnn and tell her she'll have an extra seat."

"Well, you'll let me know then if he's changed his mind?"

"Sure will, Mom. I better get to class. See you tomorrow about six."

*   *   *   *

Had Moze expected to find Luke in his room, he would not have bothered to knock. He was glad he did. Eddie's voice called out, "Just a minute." A few moments later the door opened.

"Hey, Eddie."

"Hey, stranger. It's been awhile."

"Yeah, it has. Don't suppose Luke's around."

Moze knew the instant he looked at his brother's desk that Luke had not enlisted. His Joey Heatherton picture was still on the wall.

"You just missed him. He's got an eleven o'clock. Said he had to go to the library for something first."

"Library? Does he even know where it is?" asked Moze.

Eddie gave a quick laugh. "Yeah. Something's definitely going on with him. Says he's kicking academic ass. Showed me an essay on Hemingway that he got a B on. He's at his desk almost as much as I am."

"Yeah, but you're studying and he's drooling over that poster of his."

"No, really, man. He studies. It's the damnedest thing. I think he's going to make it this semester."

"God, I hope you're right, Eddie. Hey, tell him I was here." Moze turned to go then said, "You going home tomorrow?"

"Leaving as soon as my one o'clock is finished. You?"

"My ride leaves at four. Hey, thanks for the update on Little Brother."

"Good to see you again."

"Same here,"

* * * *

Luke had been relieved when he read Eddie's note saying that Moze had been there before Easter break, but he'd been glad that he had missed him. Luke had wanted to be able to tell his brother with absolute certainty that he was going to be able to enlist without being expelled from IUP.

Moze had been right. Maybe life in the Marines would not be what he wanted. Maybe he would want to go back to school with Moze when their time was up. At Easter Luke had not been ready to make any kind of pronouncement. Now, two weeks later he was sure that he was in control. In fact, he was hopeful that he was going to make Dean's List.

But instead of telling Moze in person, he opted instead to make a phone call. Eddie had already stolen some of his thunder by telling Moze how much things had changed. Now, with his grades a non-issue, Luke had become more focused on his military future and Moze's enlistment plans. Had his brother decided on a timetable yet? Was he still planning to include Luke? If the answer to each question was yes, then Luke needed to know what the date was going to be. And yes, if he was really honest about it, the memory of Moze's hand against his throat and the utter disgust he had thrown at him as he let go was fresh enough in his mind that Luke was still intimidated by the thought of being in Moze's presence without his final grades in hand. A phone call would be enough for now.

* * * *

After two attempts without an answer, Luke's third call was answered by Moze's roommate.

"He's in the shower, Luke. I'll have him call you when he gets back to the room."

"Great. Thanks, Terry."

"No problem— wait. He just came in."

Luke could hear Terry say "It's Luke."

The sounds of the phone being roughly passed ended with Moze's voice. "I am so proud of you, Luke."

"Why? How do you know I didn't screw up again?"

"Because you wouldn't have called me if you had. You'd be in some boot camp somewhere, and as of the day before yesterday you were in the library. The *library!* You are absolutely amazing."

"So, I've been under surveillance?"

"Yeah, a bit. Just in case I would need to get in your face again." After a quick pause he said, "So what's up, Brother?"

"Unless I break a leg or somethin', I don't see any way I won't get at least a 2.8. So I'm wonderin' what the plan is for the Marines?"

"I've got our tests and physicals scheduled for May 21st. That's a Saturday. All finals will be over the day before. Does that work for you?"

"I'm done on the 19th," said Luke.

"My last one is Friday at 2:00. First Aid. Shouldn't even need to study for that one."

Luke offered a quick laugh then said, "If we get sent to Vietnam that course might come in handy."

"You've got less than three weeks to stay on the academic bandwagon. Think you can do it?"

"You ain't gonna believe this, but if today was the last day of classes and I didn't have to take none of them there final exam thingies, I'd be on that fellow named Dean's list."

"Super. But it sounds to me like you need to get back to your studying ASAP, soldier. And stay away from me until finals are over. I don't want to catch whatever it is that you've got going on with your grammar."

"Yes, sir. Good night, sir."

* * * *

Luke walked out of Leonard Hall as sure as he could be that he had scored at least a B on his last exam in Freshman Comp. If it weren't for his shaky spelling and writing skills, he would have bet on an A. The multiple-choice part had been ridiculously easy. And the topics of his three short essays had not presented any problems. His writing had seemed to express what he wanted to say, but he knew from experience that Professor Vinzanni often took exception to Luke's language skills as evidenced by his many red-penciled suggestions. But whatever the outcome Luke was certain he would not be flunking out.

He and Moze were going to the Marines. Time to celebrate. Regardless that Moze had declared that he did not want to see his brother again until after finals were over, Luke decided to go over to Church Street and give Moze the good news. Besides, hadn't Moze said he wouldn't even need to study for his last final?

The house was absent the usual noise when Luke let himself in the front door. In the kitchen a radio was on, but Luke saw no one as he passed by on his way to the staircase. The upstairs was deserted also except for someone named Wiener Boy walking into his room at the end of the hall. Before Luke could say anything, Wiener Boy closed the door and disappeared.

Moze's door was closed also. Considering the possibility that his brother might not be there and Terry was there with his girl doing some celebrating of their own, Luke knocked.

"Come in," called Moze.

Luke burst through the door ready to explode with his exam news when he was stopped dead in his tracks by an image of his brother he had not seen before. Standing six feet away from him was Moze leaning forward on a pair of crutches.

"What the hell?" Luke blurted.

"Yeah, what the hell," deadpanned Moze. "I was going to call you later tonight."

"Okay… what happened?"

"Actually, it happened in Langham. Last night. "I only had the one exam left and Baird was completely done, just hanging around for his ride home today. One thing led to another and pretty soon we were showing each other some moves, both of us on the floor. Escapes, reverses, you know, just goofing around. Next thing I know I'm being rolled across the top of his back by a hooked arm, and I come down with all of my weight on the inside of my left knee flush against the floor. I spent the next two hours between the infirmary and the hospital. X-rays say I have some torn cartilage and need an operation to remove it."

"Aw shit, Moze. How you gonna get in the Marines with that?"

Moze pivoted and maneuvered his crutches so he could sit down in his chair. Luke watched his brother's face for signs of pain and found lots of them.

"I have to see a specialist next week after we get home. No enlistment for me for a while. ER doc said it would likely be two or three weeks before I could even get operated on, but that part was just a guess. He did say I would likely be on crutches for six weeks after that. How soon before I could do the stuff I would have to do in basic training, he couldn't say. All things considered, he figured my summer was pretty much shot."

"I can't wait that long."

"Sure you can. What else do you have to do?"

"I want you with me but I'm not waitin', Moze. That's just too long." Luke slumped to the bed, completely deflated.

"I'm sorry, brother. I really am. Baird was all busted up about it, too. Said he had no idea that he had rolled me so hard." Moze shifted his weight, trying to get comfortable with his bad leg stretched in front of him. "You can wait. You probably could get some work at the Castings."

"I'm really bummed that you can't go with me, but my mind's made up. I've been lookin' forward to this all semester. It's just time."

Nothing was said for a half minute or so. Finally, Luke said, "Can you go with me on Saturday anyway? Just to make sure I don't screw up somethin'."

"Sure. It'll be Monday before I'll be able to talk to anybody about a recommendation on which doctor to see, but I sure wish you'd at least think things over a little."

"Sorry."

"No, Little Brother. I'm the one who's sorry."

Luke waved the apology away. "Let's go downstairs and watch something on the tube."

Moze pushed himself up from the chair and grabbed his crutches. "Our last night ever on campus together, why not."

6

Moze

June 1966

The operation took place on June 14th, two days after Luke left for Parris Island and boot camp. After Moze was wheeled back to his ward, all he wanted to do was sleep. Shortly after midnight the anesthetic and meds finally wore off and the pain woke him. But even after he received more medication, he slept very little the rest of the night. The night nurse Mary was nice to him and did her best to manage his pain, even as Moze did his macho best to keep from showing it.

He found out from her that his surgeon had spent twenty years in the Army including three years in the Korean War and only recently decided to return to the service. A tour in Vietnam was scheduled for August.

Moze had just started to drift asleep when he heard some commotion at the foot of his bed followed by a curt "Good morning." It was his doctor.

"Good morning." Moze tried to be friendly but it all happened too quickly.

"Hurts like hell, right?"

"Not bad but thank God for—"

"Move your toes for me." His manner suggested there would be no time for chit chat.

Moze did as he was told.

"Now, I want you to lift your leg."

Although Moze doubted the likelihood of that happening, he made the nominal attempt only to experience the worst pain in his nineteen years of being on God's earth.

"Jesus," he said in a low voice, trying to hide his pain, but not so much that he would be asked to try it again.

"Look, I know it hurts some, but you need to work those muscles as soon as possible. Now try it again."

This time Moze, knowing the level of pain he was going to be hit with, gave a half-hearted try then grimaced and said, "I can't."

The doctor immediately grabbed Moze's leg and lifted it about a foot and a half above the bed. "I'm going to count to three and then I'm going to let go. I think you're going to want to keep it from falling. One. Two. Three."

Moze had no time to process what was happening, no time to argue, to plead, to formulate any response except the spontaneous flexing of the muscles needed to prevent the unimaginable slamming of his newly mutilated leg onto the bed. When he stopped the fall just before his leg hit the bed, the pain this time could not be concealed. "God!"

"There. I knew you could do it. Now, squeeze those muscles every half hour. I'll be back tomorrow." He turned to go then stopped.

"Your mother was telling me yesterday while you were in recovery that you're thinking about dropping out of school to enlist?"

Moze was still processing the doctor's promise to return tomorrow morning and torture him again, so it took a moment to sort through the question. "Yes, sir."

The doctor aggressively moved alongside the bed towards Moze, giving him the feeling that he was under attack.

"What in bloody hell would you want to do that for?"

Moze was dumbfounded. Why would somebody who likely had a successful surgical practice leave it to return to the army and question Moze's own choice to enlist? For a moment he thought he should let it go. He kept seeing his leg suspended in the air again. But his curiosity got the better of him.

"I feel like it's the right thing to do, I guess. You must feel a little that way if you're going back into the army."

The doctor, eyebrows knit, eyes squinting in irritation, stared at Moze as if he were trying to get meaning from a Rorsach image. "Listen– what's your name…" He looked down at Moze's chart again. "Foster. The only reason I'm going is to get kids like you back home alive." Moze noticed how the doctor's emotions were getting tangled with his words, but when he started to speak again the emotion was gone. "It's Korea all over again, just in a jungle this time."

He turned away, flipped the clipboard on the bed, and unintelligibly muttered something else before entering the hallway.

* * * *

Five days later when Moze returned home he was still thinking about the doctor's words the morning after the operation and the words he had for Moze on the morning of his discharge. Moze had just reluctantly given the doctor a demonstration of how far he could flex the knee, afraid that there would be some unwanted assistance in increasing the range as there had been two days earlier. Instead, the doctor had congratulated him on being so conscientious about doing his exercises and told him that he wanted to see Moze in two weeks. He then had shaken Moze's hand, holding on to it to give emphasis to his parting words, "Don't go, Moses. There is absolutely nothing you can do for your country over there." Still clutching the hand, he added, "War has already taken your father and likely has the scent of your brother." The doctor's grip tightened. "Get your education and be here for your family."

Two days later Moze told his mother he was thinking about attending summer school. There would be nothing else he could do for the next six weeks on crutches. He might as well get six credits.

She was elated.

7

Lisbeth

June 2010

The phone had been ringing all morning. Thank God for caller ID. Her husband just couldn't get it through his head that there was nothing he could do. The divorce was going to happen. She should have left him two years ago, but she had been weaker then, afraid to be on her own, to be separated from all that money and security... that lifestyle.

It hadn't always been that way, back when Hershey had just been a chocolate bar to both of them. But Conrad had promised her from the day they had met at a fundraiser for the Harrisburg Symphony, that he would someday make her life very simple... nothing but her music for as long as she would want it that way. She was going to write concertos by day and perform in the evening.

And Conrad had, for the most part, kept his promise. Hired by Tyco International near Harrisburg after getting his MBA, his fortunes soared as did the company's. Seven years later, at the height of Tyco's meteoric expansion, Hershey came calling and he answered without hesitation.

Conrad had always liked his beer, but the last two years at Tyco his preferred choice for a buzz had switched to whiskey. The company, making one acquisition after another, had Conrad worried that it was all happening too fast. The whiskey seemed to help with his anxiety.

Lisbeth had expected that the move to Hershey would fix him. And it did. At least the whiskey problem. Then two years ago, unknown to

Conrad, Lisbeth discovered the affair he had been having for nearly three months. When that ended, she'd discovered another. When the third one had started last week, she exploded then expelled him from her life. The phone hadn't stopped ringing since.

She had considered blocking his calls, but there was a bit of pleasure in listening to him grovel in his voice mails. Lately, however, he hadn't been leaving messages, so, if she wasn't going to get any satisfaction from the calls, maybe it was time to start blocking them. If he had anything to tell her, he could send her an email.

Again, the phone rang and she started for it with the intention of doing just that, but after the second ring when the verbal ID took place, she heard "Call from Wally."

"Wally!" Lisbeth injected some extra energy into her greeting. She had called both him and Moze two days ago to tell them of her decision to file for divorce and there had been tears. She would not be a downer again today.

"Hey, Little Sister. Sounds like you're feeling better today."

"Yes, most definitely. That son of a bitch is going to make all of my days brighter by the time I'm finished with him."

"Yeah, I'm guessing he's going to find out why I always let you win at everything."

"I think your memory's beginning to fail you. You never won because I wouldn't let you."

Wally laughed briefly then said in a much more serious tone, "You sitting down?"

"Should I be?"

"Yes, I think it's probably a good idea."

"What's up?"

"Somebody found Mom."

"Mom as in Chrissy?"

"Yes. At least what is left of her."

"Wow. Where?"

"In some cave next to the Susquehanna River down in York County. Some cave divers found her skeleton and her handbag. The state police called me about half an hour ago. Her driver's license and a credit card were inside. They're thinking maybe the strap of her bag had been around her neck until her bones eventually collapsed."

"Thirty-eight years. Christ. Well, now we know for sure that she's dead. I know that must make things better for you. You were always so sure that she wouldn't be living somewhere without us." She paused for a moment then said, "I wonder how she got there."

"That big flood in 1972. The cop said the cave opening is hidden by water when the river's high. She must have been forced into it by the fast water. I guess there's an underground stream that empties from it into the river. Photos were taken and the cop said we could see them if we wanted to. I am to go in tomorrow to give them a DNA sample just to be sure."

"So, is there going to be another investigation?"

"Damn well better be. I would like to know how she got there, wouldn't you?"

"But wasn't that all done when she disappeared?"

"Yeah, but now there's a body."

"I repeat... *thirty-eight years!* What can they possibly find?"

"I don't know, but they have to try."

"Well, don't expect too much." After a short pause she asked, "Have you told Moze yet?"

"I just got off the phone with him before I called you. He reacted pretty much the way you did."

The line went quiet for several seconds before Lisbeth said, "Now, I'm going to ask you if you are sitting down."

"I am, as a matter of fact."

"Did Moze ever tell you that Chrissy used to do drugs?"

Again the line went quiet. Lisbeth heard her brother sigh before he said, "No."

"She and our dad smoked a lot of dope."

"Marijuana?"

"Yes."

"Nothing else?"

"He never said anything about anything else."

"You're saying that her smoking marijuana might have had something to do with her death? I find that hard to believe. If she was having a joint now and then, more power to her. Husband dead. Raising two little kids on her own. What I can't believe is her leaving us alone."

Not wanting to start any kind of argument with her brother, Lisbeth dropped the drug topic. "All I remember is what we have photos of. I've always hated that I had no real memories of her."

"I remember her reading to us in my bed," said Wally. "One of us on each side of her, sitting up against the headboard."

Lisbeth heard the beep from her phone indicating that Conrad was trying to call.

"Give me just a quick few seconds. Conrad's trying to call and it's time to block him."

"I've got to—"

Lisbeth heard Wally's phone dropping and then a few moments of physical commotion as he picked it up.

"Sorry about that. Just so you don't think you're special, I did the same thing with Moze. Too much going on today, I guess. Is Conrad still waiting?"

"No. He hung up. I can block him any time. But the sooner I get rid of him the better."

"I'll call you when I find out anything more. Let me know if I can help with your break up or with anything around the house. You are getting the house, right?"

"I don't want it. But I'm not letting him know that. The day the divorce is final, I'm putting it up for sale."

"Then what?"

"Probably head for Philly. More chance of getting work there."

"Well, keep me in mind for anything that needs done."

"I always keep you in mind. Love you, Brother."

"You too. Bye."

You too. Wally had always had trouble verbalizing his emotions. You too or ditto was as close as he would come to saying *I love you*. When his failure to respond in kind to her words of love would begin to irritate her, she would remember an incident from high school that had been an early defining moment in their relationship. With Wally, love had always been more about what he did… not what he said.

Whenever either one of them had a basketball game, the other would always be there along with Moze to support the one playing. Moze would take the one playing to the gym early for the pre-game meeting and warm ups then go home and later return with the one not playing. After the game Moze would hang out until everybody was ready to go home.

Except Fridays. The boys always played Tuesdays and Fridays, the girls on Mondays and Thursdays. Both kids usually went to the youth center after Friday's game then found their own rides home. Most of their friends had cars. On rare occasions Moze would be the one to find himself a ride and give the keys to one of the kids on an alternating basis. That night had been Lisbeth's turn to have the car. And she had screwed up royally.

Kathy Barnett had liberated a bottle of gin from her parents' liquor cabinet and shared it with several of her friends including Lisbeth outside the youth center in Moze's car. After taking everybody home, Lisbeth, feeling not the least bit impaired, had headed home herself. A quarter of a mile down the road from her last drop off, a deer jumped in front of her. Lisbeth, after missing the deer, momentarily lost control and ended up in a shallow, muddy drainage ditch just off the berm. The car was still in drive but she had her foot planted firmly on the brake.

Quickly she shifted into park and turned off the engine. With her heart pounding and her breathing keeping pace, she threw her hands to her face and covered her eyes, searching for cover from the consequences. It was then that she understood the extent to which her life might change. The smell of the gin had been ignored by the laughter and good times with her friends, but as her hands on her face trapped it and forced the evidence of her sin into her nose, the odor seemed overpowering.

Moze would be waiting up for his children as he always did. His vigilance was not for the possibility of discipline. He only wanted to be sure all was well before going to bed. Tonight, with less than half an hour until her midnight curfew Lisbeth knew there would never be enough time to get rid of that much odor and get home on time.

She had never thought of herself as anything but honest with Moze, but she knew she had to come up with something that would cross that line now. The first thing she had to do was get back on the road before some well-meaning person came along and tried to help her. Especially if that person would know her or recognize her. Her athletic reputation had greatly expanded the latter. If word would somehow get back to the coach or school authorities that she had been drinking, her season would be over.

The back tires of the old rear-wheel-drive Buick station wagon spun for a few moments then grabbed solid ground under the mud. A few moments later Lisbeth had the car turned around and headed back for Sarah Washburn's house where she called Billy Quinton's house. Wally had told Lisbeth at the youth center that he and Billy were going there to play video games. Billy would then give him a ride home. Her plan depended on Wally still being at Billy's.

To Lisbeth's relief Billy answered the phone, eliminating the need for yet another lie. When Wally took the phone, Lisbeth could hear the fear in his voice.

"Everything's okay, Wally. I just need you to do me a huge favor."

"Well, everything is not okay if you need a huge favor at this time of the night. Are you at home?"

"No. I'm at Sarah's house. For the second time. Just after I left the first time, a deer jumped in front of the car but I missed him. I ended up in a ditch but I was able to get out and now I'm back at Sarah's. Can I come and get you so that you can take the car home? I'm going to stay at Sarah's tonight."

The line was quiet for a moment while Wally tried to understand why he was needed. "Sure, but you'll need to get here pretty soon or I won't make curfew. We were going to leave in about ten minutes."

"That's all I need."

* * * *

"What the hell, Lisbeth?" The smell of the gin hit Wally before he had his rear end on the seat.

Lisbeth looked at her brother in momentary confusion then understood. "Kathy had some gin earlier and shared it. I'm afraid that even if Moze doesn't smell it on me, which he probably will, I will blurt everything out."

"That smell is more than four girls sipping gin. Someone must have spilled it." Wally started the car, looked over his shoulder and backed the car onto the road.

Not another word was exchanged until Lisbeth looked at him before opening her door in Sarah's driveway. "Thanks, Wally. I won't forget this."

While she walked around the car, Wally rolled down his window then said as she walked by him. "Your secret's safe. This time." He wasn't sure she heard the light-hearted tone in his sarcasm, so he added, "My sister Lisbeth, the lush."

Lisbeth turned towards him without breaking stride and said, "You're the best."

Wally had kept his word, even after Moze had asked him out of the blue the next morning where the booze had come from. Wally explained that he couldn't tell him without getting somebody into a whole lot of trouble. Wally promised him that he had not personally had any and that it would not happen again. For Moze, that had been enough.

Eventually Moze heard the truth, but not until the night before Wally's wedding. It had come from Lisbeth who had wanted to finally set the record straight and be able to laugh about it when she and Moze would take turns toasting Wally later at the rehearsal dinner.

8

Moze

April 2017

Moze had been making the trip to Pittsburgh since he was a kid. In the old days it took nearly two hours. Today, using I-79 and I-279 he would have Wally at UPMC in an hour and fifteen minutes. That was the difference between getting on old Route 8 south of Slippery Rock then slow-dancing through all the lights in Butler and the rest of the Route 8's interruptions from there to Pittsburgh. Of course, back then he hadn't known it could be any other way. Besides, his friend's father who was always the driver with the tickets to Pirates games, would invariably stop outside Etna and treat everybody to the best and biggest ham barbecue sandwich in his world then and in his memory since.

He, Luke, and Peanut Morgan were the beneficiaries of the fact that Peanut's father handled the scrap iron from bad pours at the Castings. Mr. Morgan always got the best prices for the scrap from a yard in Beaver Falls and the owner of that yard had four, box-seat, season tickets at old Forbes Field that he liked to give to Peanut's dad two or three times a year to show his appreciation for the scrap iron. Third base line, second deck, front row... no matter how many different seats Moze had been in at Three Rivers and PNC Park in the years since, Mr. Morgan's seats had been the best. Moze knew his memory didn't have it completely right, but it seemed that those seats were so close to the field that if he would have dropped his Coke over the railing, it would've landed on the third base bag.

Wally had been unusually quiet for most of the trip down. Small talk mostly. No talk about *the memory* or the DA's office, and that was fine with Moze. He had decided not to tell Wally what he had discovered yesterday when he went to see Vicky Voorhees. Wally's day was likely going to be tough enough, especially if there would be any more memories unlocked.

Moze had changed his mind about seeing Vicky after tomorrow's meeting with Kendricks, choosing instead to find out her thoughts beforehand. As it turned out, it wasn't going to matter, but he wished he would have called her first. He had been going to, but the thought of having to tell her about the DA's office again, about Wally's memory – it just seemed to deserve a face-to-face delivery.

When the door finally opened after three presses of the doorbell, it had not been Vicky standing in front of him.

"Hi, Deenie," Moze said to the middle-aged woman still holding the door.

"Hey, Mr. Foster. It's been a while since anybody called me Deenie. Makes me feel young again."

"I wish somebody could call me something to make me feel young again."

They both laughed and Moze immediately felt her comfort level rise. He hadn't seen her since her father's viewing and funeral. Before that, not since her last day in his trig class her senior year.

"Is your mother at home?" he asked, knowing now that the only way he would be able to talk to Vicky would be to get her outside the house. No way he was going to whisper his way through his news.

Before answering, Deenie stepped around the door then closed it behind her. Moze backed up a couple of steps on the stoop to give her some space.

"I'm afraid she's not…"

Moze could see that Vicky's daughter was struggling.

"She always spoke well of you. You were one of her best teachers back when she was principal. Mine too."

"Thanks, Deenie. You were one of my best students."

"Truth is, Mr. Foster, Mom's not herself any more. Her mind… we're pretty sure it's Alzheimer's."

"Oh Christ," was all Moze could say. A few moments later he repeated the expression. Vibrant, intelligent Vicky not being able to read another book, dress herself, recognize family… the reality twisted him inside.

And that was before he understood the impact her words could have on him, on his future. His alibi was now most likely lost in the tangled webs of plaque spreading throughout her brain.

He immediately reached for some kind of a lifeline. "Does she ever have any good days now when she understands or recognizes her real life? Do you think she might recognize me?"

"Not likely. She thought I was her sister this morning."

"Oh no. Really?"

"That just started a couple of weeks ago. This morning was the third time in the last four or five days."

Moze's concerns for himself were gone. "I'm so sorry, Deenie. Are you in charge of her care now? Do you have any help?"

"I'm told there's a good possibility there will be a room for her soon at the Cottages. Somebody is expected to pass in the next day or two."

"Well, you certainly have my sympathy. I have always thought a lot of your mom." He paused, searching for the right words. "It's an evil disease."

"The absolute worst. But at least she has reached the point that I don't think she knows what's going on. And she doesn't seem to be in any pain."

"No, I guess the pain from her disease at this point is mostly suffered by the people that love her."

Deenie looked away as she fought for control. When she spoke, her voice dropped. "We'll lose her twice."

If Deenie were younger, more familiar, Moze would have tried to comfort her physically, but he wasn't sure he was entitled. In frustration, he exhaled. "I guess that's true."

A moment of unease stepped between them until Moze resorted to verbal comfort, "If there is any way I can help you, Deenie, find me in the phonebook and call. I can sit with her any time you need a break."

"Thanks, Mr. Foster. I've got lots of support. A whole church full really."

"Good. Just make sure you let them give that support to you, okay? For your sake and for theirs." He hesitated then said, "And I think it's probably time you stopped calling me Mr. Foster. I'd rather you just call me Moze."

"It'll be hard, but I'll try."

"Take care, Deenie."

"You, too, Mr.– Moze."

Before Moze turned to step off the porch, Deenie spoke again, "Oh, I thought to ask then forgot. Was there something in particular you wanted from Mom? Maybe I–"

"I just wanted to ask her about something from the old days. Maybe catch up some. Nothing of any importance." He turned to leave again, but again she stopped him with his name.

"Moze?"

As he did another about face, the thought occurred that maybe she was stalling, anything to keep from going back inside. "Yes, Deenie?"

"Something else I wanted to ask you. How's Wally?"

Deenie had been a year ahead of Wally in school, but both had been in the same trig class. When Deenie had been younger, she hadn't been all that interested in math, taking a consumer math class instead of getting into the more advanced algebra. The next year she changed her mind and went back into the sequence, putting trig into her senior year.

Wally would have gladly dated Deenie. But to do that, he would have had to ask her out. When Moze had questioned him about it once,

Wally had said that she was out of his league. Case closed. After graduation Deenie went to Pitt for her undergraduate work, married a dentist, then moved to Altoona where he had his practice. Vicky had provided Moze with the details in 2010. He had reciprocated about his own children, but Wally hadn't had his Parkinson's diagnosed yet back then, so when the question was asked on the porch, Moze was pretty sure she wasn't asking about Wally's health.

"Wally's good. He and his wife divorced a few years ago. Good riddance as far as I was concerned, but it was hard on him. So... it was hard on me. But at least for his sake there were no children involved."

"I heard about the divorce. Not that it is any of my business, but did she really leave him because of the Parkinson's?"

Well then, that takes care of the health question, thought Moze. He hadn't wanted to talk about it because he never wanted to talk about anything negative concerning his kids.

"Yeah, pretty much, I guess. I think she's always had a me-first approach to everything. She was afraid of childbirth, so there were no children. Wally offered to adopt, but that didn't fly either. She's just one of these people who doesn't like to have any responsibility. When the Parkinson's arrived, it was no surprise to me that she left. She denied that was the reason but..."

"Poor Wally."

She hesitated for a moment then asked, "How is he handling everything?"

"Wally's tough. Probably tougher than I would be. He's doing some experimental stuff with a specialist at UPMC. In fact, I'm taking him to Pittsburgh tomorrow for another treatment."

"Tell him I was asking about him, that I can identify with him a little regarding the divorce stuff. After twenty-eight years my husband the dentist decided that his hygienist was now the love of his life."

Moze could hear the bitterness. Deenie was probably fifty-one, divorced, and caring for her seventy-seven-year-old mother with

Alzheimer's. She was allowed to be bitter.

* * * *

Despite a bad headache, Wally was almost joyful when he got into the car after his procedure. There had been no new memories to report. As relieved as Wally was, Moze was even more so. Not because of any additional evidence he would have to battle to prove his innocence. No, Moze was more concerned about the effect any more surprises would have on his kids. He was still hopeful that some specific parts of the past could stay there.

By the time they were out of the city and headed north, Wally had become quiet. Moze looked over at his passenger and saw that his eyes were closed, so he decided to stop any attempts at conversation.

A short time later he noticed Wally's left arm starting to twitch. The right one was the one that usually caused the most trouble. The few split seconds that Moze had let his eyes linger on the moving arm was enough for the car to drift in that direction. The sudden vibration of the rumble strips under the tires startled both Moze and Wally. Immediately Moze brought the car back onto the highway.

"What happened?" Wally wanted to know.

"Just some old guy not paying attention to the road. Go on back to sleep."

"I wasn't sleeping. My head hurts too much."

"Is it supposed to?"

"It didn't the last time, but the doctor said that I shouldn't be surprised if it did."

Wally closed his eyes again. Several moments passed before he asked in a quiet, emotionless voice, "Is there anything you want to tell me?"

Moze had just looked at Wally's arm again to see if it was still moving when the question came. He looked up at Wally and saw that his eyes were still closed. The arm was motionless.

"What do you mean?"

"I had a phone call last night from Deenie Voorhees."

"Oh, shit. Look, Wally, I really don't need Vicky. I'm sure there's a record someplace of the questions she answered in 2010. And even if there isn't, I'll be fine. Nobody has accused me of anything."

Moze put his turn signal on and passed a slow pickup truck in front of them. "Why did Deenie call?"

Wally's eyes were open now. "Just to talk, I guess. She's having a really rough time. Said her husband left her. And her mother has tried to hit her several times lately. I feel so bad for her. If it weren't for the shakes, I'd probably consider asking her out."

"She's the one who asked about you first. And she's aged well. Go for it, Son."

"She's still out of my class, Moze. Especially now."

"I really doubt that she would care about your illness."

Wally's eyes closed again. "Maybe."

Fifteen minutes passed before Wally spoke again. "I'll bet Deenie would be willing to say that her mother told her about being with you that night."

Moze flipped the turn signal to the right and pulled off the road.

The car stopped abruptly and Moze's words flew hard into the windshield. "Did you tell her about Vicky and me?"

The force and incredulity in Moze's words startled Wally. "No. I would never do that, Moze. She really likes you. Said she really enjoyed talking to you. I just think if you told her all of the facts, she'd probably volunteer to do it."

Moze regretted the aggressive nature of his question, but the absurdity of Wally's suggestion of asking Deenie to lie had him even more irritated. "Dammit, Wally. I don't want you even thinking—"

"Sorry, Moze. I wasn't thinking straight. Let me blame it on the headache, okay? Sorry."

Moze looked at Wally for a few moments then reached out and

grabbed his son's head and rubbed the top. "Call her, Son. Ask her out. That's an order. But no discussing Vicky and me."

"I'll call her, but only as a friend. No date. I can't do that, not with this stupid disease."

"We'll see." Moze put the turn signal on and headed home, his focus no longer concerned with tomorrow's meeting with Kendricks.

Wally and Deenie? Wouldn't that be something.

9

Wally

April 2017

The phone rang just as Wally took the first bite of his left-over chicken. He hurriedly finished chewing and picked up just after the third ring. The voice belonged to Deenie.

"Hi, Wally. It's me again. Just wanted to hear how your treatment went and pass on some news in case you hadn't heard."

"Hi, Deenie. I had a doozy of a headache the whole way home, but everything's good now. So, what's your news?"

"Did you happen to see KDKA's five o'clock news?"

"No. Why?"

"I'm guessing they'll rerun the story at six. It's about your mother."

"No kidding?" He knew Deenie had to be serious so he did not wait for her reply. "What did it say."

"The DA announced that her office is looking at the possibility of opening its own investigation of her death."

"She went on TV?"

"Yes. She's asking for any information the public might be able to bring to light."

"I met her assistant last week, but she gave me no indication that they were about to go public."

"What's going on? Why now?"

Wally wanted to tell Deenie everything. He hadn't had anyone outside of Moze and Lisbeth to talk to about personal stuff in a long while, but this was not the time, especially now that Moze had lost his alibi. Deenie might focus on why he would've ever put Moze in such a predicament by going to the DA in the first place. Wally wouldn't be able to tell her that there had been an alibi. An alibi that would turn her mother into a jezebel.

"I... I don't want to say anything until the DA's office finishes what they're doing. It's too weird right now."

"Oh, jeez, Wally, now you have my interest piqued!"

Wally heard then saw the call waiting message on his phone. "Deenie, Moze is trying to call right now. I want to let him know your news anyway. Do you mind if I call you back?"

"No, no. You go ahead. I was ready to hang up anyway. As I said, I just wanted to see how you are and let you know the news."

"Thanks, Deenie. I really appreciate your concern. We'll talk again soon if that suits."

"Of course. I'll look forward to it. Bye."

"Bye."

"Moze?"

"Hey, Son. Only wanted to let you know about a phone call I just had from Kendricks."

"I'll bet I can guess what she said. I just had a call from Deenie."

"Another one? I told you she was interested."

"Kendricks told you then that the DA went on TV?"

"No, she neglected to mention that. She only called to cancel our date for tomorrow. That by itself had me a little concerned, as hot as she had been to make the appointment in the first place. Now, what's this about TV?"

"Deenie called to tell me she had seen the DA on the five o'clock news announcing that her office was considering reopening the case. She wants to see if anybody has any info. Deenie thinks they'll run it again at six."

"Well, I guess that's a good thing... that Kendricks is not just giving you lip service."

"I'm not sure how I feel about all of it anymore." Wally felt his right hand start to tremble with the phone against his ear. Quickly he switched hands and continued, "Did Kendricks reschedule?"

"No. She just said she would be in touch. Now I'm thinking she's going to wait and see if their public appeal will bring anything out from under the rocks."

"Do you think there's a rock somewhere with anything under it?" Wally noticed his right hand was now perfectly still. He couldn't help wonder if the short duration had been influenced by his electronic zapper.

"I hope so, but, no. I don't. Too many years have passed."

Neither of them spoke for a several moments before Wally added, "I think I'm going to ask Deenie out. Any objections?"

"No! I think that's a great idea. You absolutely ask her out. What are you—"

Interrupting himself, Moze said, "Wait a minute. Your interest in Deenie better not have anything to do with me losing my alibi."

"Of course not. You told me to forget about it and I have."

"Okay then, you have my blessing. Hey, you want to get a sandwich somewhere?"

"I just started to eat some leftovers when Deenie called. Besides, I'm really tired tonight. It's been a long day."

"Sure. We'll talk tomorrow. Good night, Son."

"'Night Moze."

10

Moses Hendershot

May 12, 1972

The small standing calendar that Uncle Bob's Insurance issued for advertising purposes sat perched on the countertop. From October until the end of March, motel traffic was mostly business driven. Salesmen. God bless them. But April was when the first signs of life appeared in the tourist end of things. Mostly older people, the retired segment, the great majority who spend their winters north of the Mason-Dixon line ready to get on the road and travel. Also, a small uptick because of the beginning of baseball season when the Pirates were home, but the motel's location was too far north of the city to benefit much from the sports teams. Besides, I-279 had siphoned a lot of the Route 19 traffic onto its red-light free, high-speed lanes bypassing Mom's Motel.

The mom in Mom's Motel was Moses Hendershot's mother. She was sixty, divorced, and increasingly happy to designate the day-to-day management of the business to her only child while she continued to manage the finances.

Moses was twenty-five and an honorably discharged veteran of the Vietnam War. He'd returned home in March of 1968, bringing with him his Purple Heart from the Tet offensive and a great affection for marijuana from his time spent *in country*. As far as he knew, Mom was aware only of the Purple Heart.

Mom was also unaware of the other source of income for her son… a small but thriving marijuana trade, mostly dependent on locals, but occasionally found its way into the lungs and suitcases of a few guests. It was for this reason that Moses worked the night shift. His sometime girlfriend worked days, and his cousin Toby worked evenings. Moses and Toby had an arrangement whereby Toby received thirty percent of any sales during his shift as long as he abided by the protocol which dictated no proactive selling.

The only permitted method of drawing the public's attention to the product was the display of an ashtray with a small rolled reefer butt sitting on the engraved name *Mary Jane*. The ashtray would be placed on the countertop only after each of the two employees would make a quick but careful evaluation of anyone coming through the door. A narrow counter three feet high defined the office area and provided a place for the ashtray, giving each of the staff time to get it in place or remove it if it had been forgotten after a previous display. Each customer received a paper asking for any special needs he or she might have. The word *any* was marked with a pink highlighter.

The system worked well, especially in the summer when the crowd was younger. Although Moses didn't figure on getting rich, in the June-July-August season he would clear an extra four to five hundred a month and have as much product as he could smoke gratis.

Just the night before last, a husband and wife who had been teachers in his high school before they retired bought fifty-dollars-worth when they checked in at eight and another hundred-dollars-worth before they left at midnight.

Tonight, business had been unusually slow. Mom's Motel had twenty-three rooms. By 12:30 a.m. twenty of them were still empty and none of the occupants had made any special requests. As was his routine, Moses had himself anchored comfortably in his padded swivel chair so that he could easily see both Johnny Carson and the motel's entrance from the door of his office. On the many occasions that Moses would end up asleep before he went off shift at 7:30, a bell positioned over the path of the door would wake him.

He had just started to drift off during the 12:40 commercials when that same bell pulled him back. A couple in their early twenties came through the door looking like they weren't sure they wanted to. Moses hurried from the office and set the ashtray on the counter.

"Evening, folks."

"Any rooms left?" asked the man.

"Yes, sir. How many would you like?"

The man offered a quick forced laugh. The woman remained expressionless. "Just one will do. How much?"

Moses tore a sheet from his registration pad and slid it across the desk. "Twenty bucks." Moses took the woman's mysterious indifference as a challenge. "For another fifteen you can have a bed, too."

This time nobody responded until the man said, "Do you take credit cards?"

"I'll need to see a driver's license."

"Sure." The man retrieved his wallet from his back pocket and pulled out a Master Charge and then a driver's license.

Moses saw the nervousness in the man's movements, as if he had never been asked for ID before. The woman also seemed uncomfortable as her companion placed the cards on the counter. Moses picked up the credit card with one hand and the license with the other. What he said next surprised himself as much as the other two people in the room.

"Holy Mother of God!"

Not waiting for an explanation, the male customer replied immediately, "What? What's wrong?"

"Nothing's *wrong*. A customer with the same first name as mine. *Moses*. It's about time."

"What a coincidence," the customer said without any of the enthusiasm coming from behind the counter.

And then, for the first time, Moses saw the woman looking at the ashtray. No, *studying* the ashtray. *Transfixed* by the ashtray. Moses couldn't help but be transfixed himself, not with the ashtray, but with the young woman. The sadness in her eyes that dominated her aura had become an emptiness as if she were already puffing on the joint he was sure she would soon be smoking in her room.

"I'll bet you've heard all the same jokes I have," Moses said to his namesake. Moses looked at the license again. "Jesus, we're even the same age! Maybe you were in the same river basket as I was. Maybe you too were accused of parting the waters to keep your feet dry. Did you know that we got those ten commandments from bubble gum wrappers? Or was it fortune cookies? And that there were originally twelve of them but we forgot two of them."

When the other Moses said nothing the clerk said, "Okay, must be you missed all of that." *This guy's got no sense of humor.* Looks like the two of them were born to be together.

Moses pointed to the registration sheet and said, "You'll need to fill this out and don't forget your license plate number."

"Chrissy, run outside and get me the number."

While the husband filled out the paperwork, Moses focused on the wife's backside as the bell rang over the door. When she returned, his eyes remained fixed on her. She really was a looker in a hard sort of way.

"64E00," Chrissy said as she approached her husband hunched over the counter.

"PA?" asked Moses Hendershot.

"Yes."

Chrissy's husband stood up and slid his paperwork toward Moses.

Moses studied it for a moment then said aloud, "Mr. and Mrs. Moses Foster. Heading anywhere in particular?"

"We're still trying to decide," said the husband.

"Well, you just give me a moment while I call in this card. I'll be right back." Inside the office Moses called Master Charge for approval, all the while sneaking furtive glances at Chrissy and Moses Foster. As he suspected, Chrissy was showing her husband the ashtray.

Moses quickly returned to the counter and handed Mr. Personality the Master Charge receipt to sign and the paper reserved for those having seen the ashtray. He then handed them the key to Room 213.

"Thanks for your business folks. Hope everything is to your liking." He paused for a few moments, then added as he always did whether the ashtray was in view or not, "And if there's anything I can do to make your stay with us better, just pick up the phone and call me here in the office."

Ten minutes later the phone rang. The woman named Chrissy Foster wanted his product. Five minutes later and one-hundred dollars in his pocket Moses Hendershot closed the door to Room 213, glad he could be of service to the woman with the sad face. To her husband Moses, not so much.

11

Lisbeth

May 2017

"How's my best girl?"

"Better now that I'm talking to you. How's my favorite father?"

"We'll get to that in a minute. First, you have to tell me what you mean by *better*. Has something been wrong?"

"Nothing serious. Minor stuff. Life's good for the most part. What's new with you?"

"Have you talked with your brother lately?"

"It's probably been three weeks. I was going to call and chew him out for putting you back in the crosshairs, remember, but you talked me out of it. Must be something's going on now though. You want to tell me about it?"

For the next ten minutes Moze updated his daughter on the developments regarding Vicky Voorhees and the DA's television appearance.

"In other words, Wally's little memory game is not such an insignificant matter after all."

"Please let it go, Lisbeth. I'm not worried. There is, however, some other news."

Lisbeth could tell by the tone of Moze's voice that whatever was coming was not good. "So, tell me what I don't want to hear."

"Let me back up to the Vicky Voorhees situation first. You remember Deenie, right. She'd been taking care of her mother until last week when Vicky went into the Cottages. Remarkably, she and your brother have had two dates since then."

"I thought she was married to some dentist in Altoona?"

"Divorced, and I believe happy to be so."

"After two dates I guess she knows about the Parkinson's."

"Yes, but from what I'm hearing, her knowing is probably bothering Wally more than Deenie. Although… there's been something of a setback."

"What happened?" Lisbeth's voice suggested she had been expecting as much."

"Wally fell last night in his living room. From the way Deenie described it, the fall had nothing to do with the disease. He just tripped over a leg of the coffee table and smacked his head hard on the floor. In the process of trying to break his fall, he twisted his right elbow to the point where he now has trouble doing almost everything."

"If you can pick me up at the airport, I'll get a plane this afternoon."

Moze's response was slow to come, then guarded, "I don't think that would be a very good idea, Lisbeth."

"Oh? And why's that?" She was irritated.

"The impact of his head on the floor evidently jarred the placement of the DBS probe and triggered another memory involving your mother and me."

"Oh, God." Their connection went silent. After several seconds, she asked, "What did he see this time?"

"He wouldn't tell me. He said he wouldn't tell anybody, especially not the DA. Whatever he saw, it clearly had him upset by the time I got there. And, of course, Deenie, was full of questions, all of which I answered as best I could."

"Moze…" She let his name hang like one of his reprimands to her. "You're scaring me."

"Don't be afraid for me. Have you ever seen me afraid for myself? It's Wally we should be worried about. Whatever Wally experienced last night, whether it ever happened or not, it was real for him. The fact that I've lost Vicky as my alibi already has him in knots. I would certainly like to know what he saw so I could try to explain it to him, but he made it clear that I would not get that opportunity, and I am not going to fight with him over it."

"Because you are not worried."

"Because I have no idea how Chrissy died. So, I can never help him find out what he wants to know."

Lisbeth had never had any thoughts concerning Moze's involvement in her mother's disappearance, but she was more than a little curious now as to what had upset Wally. Besides, her brother needed her help whether he wanted it or not. "Will you pick me up at the airport this evening?"

"I can handle things for now, really. Deenie has made it pretty clear that she wants to help."

"Yes or no, please. Or do I need to rent a car and drive from the airport to Pine City?"

"Of course I'll pick you up. But what about your career?"

"I have three days until the orchestra's next show. I'll take a personal day for that one, so I'll have a whole week free."

"That sounds great, Sweetheart. Call me from the airport before you leave Philly so I know what time to expect you."

"Sure. Can't wait to see both of you. Love you, Daddy."

Lisbeth put the phone down and flipped up the screen of her laptop. In a matter of minutes she had purchased her ticket for Pittsburgh. She'd be there by five. To give Moze an early heads-up she immediately sent him a text.

* * * *

Lisbeth stared at the clouds outside the window of Flight 709. Deenie and Wally. Who'd have thought. She remembered overhearing a conversation once between Moze and Wally in high school about her.

Wally had evidently had a crush on her and Moze was trying to convince him to ask her out. As far as Lisbeth knew, he'd never done it. And now two divorces later they were finally together.

Lisbeth had been two years behind Deenie, and had never travelled in the same circles. Deenie had been a cheerleader and on homecoming court while Lisbeth's life had focused on athletics and music. But Lisbeth remembered liking her. Deenie had never been the type to set boundaries, at least from what Lisbeth had observed, though it was difficult to tell sometimes when your father was one of the most popular teachers.

The fact that Deenie could see past Wally's affliction was reason enough to like her now. The sympathy factor involving her mother's dementia and the empathy factor because of her divorce only added to Lisbeth's willingness to do what she could to keep Deenie and Wally together.

Whatever shortcomings Deenie might end up revealing, Lisbeth was sure that she would find her much more likable than Wally's ex, June. What a bitch. From the day she had met her, Lisbeth had disliked her. For nearly a year Lisbeth had struggled to find some way to bridge their differences, to make herself like June. But there had been one too many references to Lisbeth's athleticism, one too many references to her *butch* haircuts, one too many *tomboy* stories June had heard from Wally and how *cute* they were. Still, Lisbeth had remained civil until her own divorce and June's comment that maybe Conrad had needed more femininity. Lisbeth responded by striking June with an open hand then saying, "You probably shouldn't piss off somebody as masculine as I am." Wally had spent the next few days convincing June not to press charges. But for Lisbeth, June's defining moment was her walking out on Wally six months after his Parkinson's diagnosis.

Because of something Wally had said to Lisbeth a year or so before June's exit, Lisbeth had been suspicious that June was seeing someone behind Wally's back. Without her brother's knowledge, she hired a private investigator to track June's movements and dig up any information that Wally should know, certain that June was the kind of woman who would cheat on her brother, divorce him, and somehow make it look like he was the one to blame.

It had taken less than a week for the PI to verify Lisbeth's suspicions, but she had said nothing to Wally. When June announced that she wanted a divorce, Wally refused to give it to her, sure that he could fix whatever was wrong. To think that she could be leaving him because he was sick was not the remotest of possibilities. June's response was an ultimatum— a divorce or she would sue him for divorce because he could no longer fulfill his duties as a husband. Wally was crushed.

That was when Lisbeth had stepped in with the PI's report, complete with dates and photos. After much persuasion Wally hired a lawyer himself and sued June for divorce. He would have been content to be rid of her, but again Lisbeth intervened. Her PI, during his investigation, had discovered that June had been hiding nearly five-hundred thousand dollars she had received from a trust when she had turned thirty. Lisbeth pointed out to Wally that he should consider the possibility that he might get to the point with his Parkinson's when he would need more money than he had. Through his lawyer he told June he was keeping the house and half of her money. She could have the car. Most of his work creating websites was done from home and he feared his driving days would soon end anyhow. In the meantime he'd find something cheaper than the BMW that he never wanted in the first place.

If June would not agree, he would be willing to let a judge decide, knowing that her infidelity and her original plan to divorce him because he was not going to be able to please her in bed would not be looked upon favorably, possibly even cause her to lose everything. No support payments from him would be necessary because of June's real estate business.

Lisbeth knew that Moze had been irritated with her meddling, especially when she had told him about hiring the PI. But when June accepted Wally's terms for the divorce and disappeared from their lives, Moze had thanked Lisbeth apologetically.

That was one of the many traits she loved about her father, his ability to forget his pride when he would be wrong on an issue, sometimes before the other person was even aware that a mistake had been made. But such mistakes for Moze were rare. He had a gift for clarity, able to eliminate the noise, then process the facts with common sense and logic.

Lisbeth had the same abilities but sometimes her fearlessness would make her life more difficult than it needed to be. When Moze would point out that she took after her birth father in that way, Lisbeth would take offense, always choosing to identify with Moze in any way she could.

She abhorred dishonesty. If she didn't speak her mind, she saw herself as hiding what she felt or what she was thinking and therefore being dishonest. Although it was her skill set with her violin that allowed her to create music, it was this constant need for honesty that elevated her playing to an art form. She channeled the emotional truth that the music stirred within her into the music. The same held true with singing. It was always more than the notes themselves. Moze had taught her not to fear her honesty, that it was like the naiveté of a child. It was who she was, part of the structure of her soul.

She wished there was something she could do to help him now. Regardless of what he had said, she knew he had to be worried about the DA. Lisbeth had been more irritated with Wally than worried for Moze. But now that Vicky's alibi was most likely gone, she found herself obsessing over his vulnerability and her brother's foolishness in taking his memory to the DA's office.

And what was this new memory of Wally's? What if this business with Chrissy ended up in court? Could Wally be forced to tell what he remembered? Not if the DA didn't know about the new memory.

Nobody else knew it existed. Did Wally, she wondered, even say for sure that it involved Moze and Chrissy or did Moze just assume it did? And did Deenie know? Lisbeth wasn't convinced yet that she could be trusted.

12

Moze v. Kendricks Part I

May 2017

The woman looked up from her desk, repositioned her glasses and asked, "Can I get you something to drink, Mr. Foster? A cup of coffee, can of Pepsi, bottle of water?"

"No, thanks," said Moze.

He had been waiting for ten minutes for Louise Kendricks to see him. She had called him late yesterday afternoon just before he left to get Lisbeth at the airport. His first inclination had been to tell Kendricks no, giving her Wally's accident as an excuse, but then decided he just wanted to be done with it. He had put her off once, which was likely why she had done the same with him. Now, hopefully, they were even. The sooner the interview was over, the more likely it would be that everything would get cleared up and get the waters calmed between Wally and Lisbeth.

"Ms. Kendricks shouldn't be much longer, now."

Almost on cue, the assistant DA's door opened and another woman, still not fully turned towards the room said, "Thanks, Louise. I'll talk to you again before you leave." She completed her turn and flashed a political smile at Moze. "You must be Mr. Foster." She quickly covered the few feet that separated them and extended her hand. "I'm Barb Breckenridge, Mercer County's District Attorney."

Moze got to his feet and caught the DA's hand as it rushed at him. "Nice to meet you."

Kendricks had followed her boss into the room and smoothly took the handoff from Breckenridge when she'd finished with Moze. "Louise Kendricks, Mr. Foster. Nice to finally meet you in person." Moze made a point of letting go first.

Kendricks motioned with the released hand toward her open door. "Please."

Inside the office Moze waited while she said something to her secretary. A few seconds later Kendricks entered and closed the door behind her.

"Thanks for coming in. Have a seat."

Moze unknowingly seated himself in the same chair Wally had occupied nearly two weeks earlier.

"Well, now, where should we begin?" Kendricks said in a genial tone of voice.

"I doubt that you invited me here for my opinions on the Pirates' chances this year," said Moze facetiously.

"No, it's probably going to be no different than any other year since 1990," said Kendricks.

Moze tried to laugh but nothing came out. Didn't matter. Kendricks laughed enough for both of them.

After a few moments of silence, she asked, "How are Wally's treatments going?" The tone that she used irritated Moze. It implied sincerity. Moze was sure there was none.

"If you're asking if he's had any more memories... no, not that I know of."

"Do you have any idea why he would remember hearing *your* voice the night your sister-in-law disappeared?"

Moze heard some hostility so he didn't feel much like being polite. He couldn't help it. He'd always been that way except with family and, for the most part, his students. He gave back what was given to him. "Did you record the conversation with my son?"

"No, but I did take notes. Why do you ask?"

"I'm just surprised at your lack of accuracy. I believe what he told you was that the voice he heard *sounded like* my voice. That whoever spoke to his mother had a voice *similar* to mine. And, unless Wally lied to me, he made that interpretation pretty clear to you."

Moze was certain that the smug smile that momentarily flashed across her face appeared with a purpose. "Let me ask the question again. Do you have any idea why he would remember hearing a voice that sounded like *your* voice the night your sister-in-law disappeared?"

"No. I don't. I do know that I wasn't there."

"And how do you know that? That was a long time ago."

"Because I was with somebody at a motel. I believe this was documented by the State Police in 2010."

"Yes, I read the report. But I will need you to give me the details again, if you don't mind. This is a separate investigation, so I will want to corroborate everything from 2010 that will be relevant to it."

Corroborate. Moze felt a sudden weakness pass through his being.

"According to the State Police investigation, you spent the evening with somebody named Vicky Voorhees. Is that correct?"

"Yes, ma'am."

Kendricks kept her eyes fixed on Moze for a few seconds before continuing, "I tried to contact her this morning, but I understand she is now a resident of Golden Cottages in Pine City and suffering from an advanced form of dementia. Are you aware of her situation?"

"I found out when I went to see her at her home recently."

"What was the reason for your visit?"

"I was trying to sell her *a car*?" He flashed her a look of disgust. "Sorry, ma'am. Dumb questions get dumb answers."

"I'm not in the habit of asking dumb questions, Mr. Foster. So... let's try this again. What was the reason for your visit?"

"I wanted to give her a heads-up about Chrissy's case being possibly reopened."

"Were you able to talk with her?"

"No. Her daughter Deenie told me it would be useless."

"Had you spoken with her daughter before that visit?"

"She had been a student of mine many years ago."

"And have you spoken with her *since* that visit?"

Moze hesitated. "Yes."

"Regarding what?"

Moze was beginning to feel like he was on the witness stand. "She and Wally have started a relationship so she has been to the house a few times. Both of them are divorced and have known each other since they were kids."

"Have you and Wally discussed her mother's role as your alibi with Deanna?"

Kendricks' fascination with Deenie was beginning to wear on Moze. He had committed himself to not letting Kendricks get under his skin, but now he had let her do exactly that from the moment he'd walked in.

"Ms. Kendricks, I understand that you have a job to do here, and I will be willing to answer whatever questions you have. But I am at a loss to understand your fixation on me as a suspect. I had nothing to do with Chrissy's disappearance and, as far as I know, you have nothing connecting me to it other than Wally's 45-year-old *possible* memory of someone whose voice *sounded* like mine. I was questioned in 1972 and then again in 2010 and dismissed each time as a suspect. Surely there is a record of Vicky's corroboration in 2010, so why the fascination now."

"Two reasons, really." She stopped just long enough to give Moze time to wonder about what the second one might be then folded her hands as if in prayer.

"In 1972 Chrissy Foster was only a missing person, and I have no records of any interrogation that might have taken place then. Because nobody petitioned the court to have her declared dead in absentia between her disappearance in 1972 and her discovery in 2010, she wasn't legally dead. In 2010 she was declared dead by the coroner, but the PSP investigation did not go forward because it had no suspects. There are notes from the two investigators indicating that no one could even be considered a person of interest. No sworn statements. Only notes indicating that the only other person remotely connected to her disappearance had produced an alibi involving a Mrs. Vicky Voorhees, who told the investigators that you were with her the night of the disappearance. According to the notes, she appeared very nervous about the possibility of her husband finding out about the affair she was having with you in 1972, but nevertheless was willing to corroborate your story.

"Now, fast forward seven years and it's my job to at least go through the motions of looking into the case because of your adopted son's memory of that night. I talked to the doctor who performed the procedure that caused the flashback and he confirms that it is quite likely that Wally did experience the event. Now, because of that memory, I have the name of somebody who could have been present that night. But he… you… unfortunately for the investigation, have an alibi, Mrs. Vicky Voorhees. But, unfortunately for her and you, she is battling dementia.

"Now, here's what has my interest in her piqued. When I talked to her daughter, Deenie, she, without being asked, volunteers the information that she can vouch for your whereabouts on the night in question because her mother had told her all about it after her father died. Then, oddly enough, I find out today that Deenie is now dating your son."

Kendricks stopped talking and gave Moze a long, hard stare. It seemed to Moze that she was daring him to say something.

So, he did. "You know more about this than I do, Ms. Kendricks. I was unaware that Deenie knew of my relationship with her mother. It only lasted until a few weeks after Chrissy's disappearance. I am also surprised that Vicky told her."

While he had been speaking, Kendricks' eyes had remained fixed on Moze with an accusatory look intimating that the next words out of her mouth might be *I am charging you with the murder of Chrissy Foster.* But instead, when he finished, she started speaking again as if he had never said a word.

"Reason number two." Again, she gave Moze a few moments to think about what was coming.

"After talking with Wally's doctor and looking at the paperwork from the 2010 investigation I concluded that I needed to get the public involved. You probably heard about the DA's KDKA gig." She gave Moze a moment to respond, but he ignored it.

She chuckled as she reclaimed the floor. "I didn't expect much. And the first day gave us exactly that. Nothing. Not a lousy phone call. We always get crank calls at least. But yesterday, ten-thirty-three in the morning the phone rings."

She paused to dramatize her ensuing words. "Did you ever hear of a man named – wait now, listen to this – *Moses* Hendershot?"

"No."

"Well, he's certainly heard of you. If you heard the DA's announcement on KDKA, you are aware that your name was not mentioned, only Chrissy's, and the possibility that she might have been travelling with a male."

Again, she waited for nothing. Moze tried to shake someone out of his head so he could get some sense of where Kendricks was going with her questioning, but nobody was there.

"He had quite the story to tell, complete with dates and times and names. Still doesn't ring any bells?"

"No."

"How about May 12, 1972?"

Moze did not hesitate. "The day Chrissy disappeared."

"I will correct you somewhat. That was the day she disappeared from her home, but Moses Hendershot saw her on the twelfth and then again on the thirteenth. And he swears you were with her both times."

"Impossible."

"It would seem so, except he said that when you and Chrissy checked into the motel where he was working, you showed him your driver's license and Master Charge card. Can you provide any explanation for that?"

Moze quickly scanned possible answers. He could be defiant and immediately declare the other Moses a liar. He could say he has no memory of his license ever missing.

Or he could *sort of* tell the truth. "I lost my wallet."

"So, had you applied for any replacement cards?"

"No. I figured I'd wait and see if it turned up."

"Did it?"

"No."

13

Moze v. Kendricks Part II

May 2017

Louise Kendricks had been unsure about the credibility of Moses Hendershot. But when she saw the change in Moze Foster's demeanor as she told him that her witness had seen a driver's license and credit card, she knew Hendershot was telling her the truth. Moze Foster had been surprised. He had not remembered Hendershot's name, but she'd bet that he most certainly had a recollection of showing someone his ID.

"You said my name wasn't mentioned by the DA."

"It wasn't. *Hendershot* told *me* your name.

Moze had never been very good at acting, but he took his best shot at an appearance of incredulity, quickly following it with the words, "And how does this guy remember so much detail from forty-five years ago? A name on a driver's license? Really?"

Kendricks felt all warm inside as she listened to Moses Foster become more than a *yes* or *no* participant in her interrogation. "He worked at a motel on Route 19 north of Pittsburgh."

"Yeah, but to remember a name that long ago? Seems like this guy should be looked at. And where was he when the PSP were investigating in 2010? Why now?"

"Oh, we will look at him." She paused and looked at her notes for a moment, not sure how much she wanted to tell Foster. She decided that the more he knew how believable the story was, the more he might panic and say something incriminating.

"I'd be glad to tell you how he answered the questions that most people would want to ask. Besides being a motel clerk fresh back from Vietnam, Moses Hendershot had a little marijuana business on the side. The night you and Chrissy checked in, he said he sold the two of you $100.00 worth. He took it to your room after you checked in. Said he made a pass at Chrissy while you were showering, but she had no interest in anything but the marijuana."

Moze interrupted her. "Well, that part sounds right. Chrissy enjoyed her weed. Too much so."

Kendricks once again continued her narrative as if he hadn't said anything. "He figures that she must have told you about his advances because you had a few unkind words for him the next morning when you checked out. Said you left as he was going off shift. His girlfriend always showed up about ten minutes before he left because she worked the day shift and you got him into trouble with her.

"But what really stuck the two of you in his memory besides his and your first names being the same, was getting arrested later that same day by an undercover cop who checked into the motel. He blames you for the six weeks he did. That you turned him in because he made a pass at Chrissy."

"Well, he's trying to get his revenge on the wrong guy. I wasn't there."

"Didn't sound to me like he was still carrying a grudge. He said he was calling us out of curiosity. That when he heard the DA give the date, he remembered that it matched the day he was arrested which triggered his memory of the guy he's always blamed for putting him into jail. That's when he told me your first name.

"When I asked him about 2010, he said he had been in Vegas for twenty years. Came back to Pittsburgh to be near his daughter when he turned seventy. He's got diabetes and weighs three hundred pounds. I'm going to Wexford next week to talk some more with him. Any chance you have a photo from '72 that I could show him when I tell him that you deny being there?"

"I'll see what I can find, but I have to tell you, Ms. Kendricks, I didn't hear anything that's going to change what I said earlier. Unless he has photo copies, I guess it's his word against mine, and I have an alibi. I never showed a charge card or driver's license to Moses Hendershot or anyone else the night of Chrissy's disappearance. And I would be willing to take a polygraph to prove it."

"That's good to know. I'll keep it in mind."

Kendricks stuck a few papers back into a folder and rose to her feet. "Thanks again for coming in, Mr. Foster. I'll be in touch concerning the polygraph."

Moze stood and slipped into the light jacket he had carried into the room with him. "Anytime."

"Oh, Mr. Foster, tell Wally to keep in touch. I'll especially want to hear from him should he experience any new memories from 1972." Kendricks smiled then spoke to the door ahead of her as she opened it, "Please remember the old photo. It could end up making your life a lot less complex if he can't ID you. I'll be showing him photos of several different men your age from the early seventies."

"I'll find one tonight and scan it."

Kendricks said to her secretary, "Give Mr. Foster a card with our email address, Marie."

Marie, the card already in her hand, extended it in Moze's direction.

"Just email the photo, Mr. Foster. Save yourself a trip." The tone of her voice almost suggested friendship. "I'll be in touch."

"I'm sure you will, if you're of a mind to waste your time."

"Oh, darn it. I'm so embarrassed, Mr. Foster. I just remembered a few other items that I wanted to discuss with you. May I have just a few more minutes of your time?" Kendricks watched her quarry for a reaction. It took a few moments but she got it. Moze Foster was obviously agitated.

Moze drew a quick breath. *Oh shit.*

* * * *

Back inside Kendricks' office, his coat again on the back of his chair, Moze tried to relax as he sat down. He couldn't escape the feeling that Kendricks had staged the previous ending of the interrogation, wanted him thinking that she had already emptied her gun only to now show him that she had more bullets… as if she had become the female version of the old TV detective Columbo who always had *just one more thing* he wanted to ask his suspects before he brought the hammer down.

She took her place at her desk and stared at him for what seemed to Moze like minutes. He sensed a different atmosphere in the room now… not even the pretense of civility. Finally, she said, "Did you buy a 1960 Plymouth Valiant from Pine City Motors Used Cars for three-hundred seventy-nine dollars on July 29th of 1972?"

Is there anything this attack dog doesn't know?

"I had completely forgotten about that car. I didn't have it long. It was a great little car, but once Mom and I took over the raising of the kids, I decided to get something bigger so I sold it."

"I'm confused. You'd already had one Valiant. Same year even.

He hated all the lies. There would be no good way out of this, but, at this point, he had to keep throwing stuff out there in hopes something would stop her pursuit, would actually make some kind of sense.

"I liked the first one so much and I thought the price was really reasonable."

"To whom did you sell the first one?"

"I really have no idea. Forty-five years is plenty enough time for *me* to forget a name."

"Well, I know who it was. You sold it to a William Jackson living at the time in San Diego, California. Now… how the hell did that all take place?"

Moze didn't hesitate. "I was in Pittsburgh in the parking lot outside

Three Rivers Stadium and some guy walked up to me as I was getting into my car and said he had been looking for an old Valiant and would I take a thousand bucks for it. So, I said sure. Said the woman with him was his cousin and was a Notary Public from Slippery Rock and that he'd put the sale price at a dollar and I could keep the $999. I remember that because of its location being so close to Pine City. So, we did the deal right there and I took the bus home." Moze wanted it all to stop, but he couldn't. Not now.

"What was he doing in Pittsburgh?"

"Selling drugs? How the hell would I have known?"

"What was the date of the sale?"

Moze stared at her with annoyance then said, "Really? You want a date?"

Kendricks said smugly, "July 26th 1972... does that sound about right?

"If you say so. Why the games, Ms. Kendricks? You obviously have all this information at your disposal. The only thing you are establishing is that I have a memory deficiency of at least forty-five years."

"Understandable. One thing I don't know that maybe you do is, have you ever had any contact with William Jackson since the day you sold him the Valiant?"

"No, ma'am. Of that I am sure." He paused and offered the hint of a smile then said, "I really need to be somewhere else soon, so if you don't have any more questions, I'll be on my way."

"One more question."

Of course there's one more.

"Three days later you bought the other 1960 Valiant? Why?"

"Hmmm... Let me see... Could it be that I liked the first one so much that I wanted another one? A bright red one instead of white? Oh yeah, almost forgot. I made, let's see, 620 dollars in the process and the new one had 30,000 fewer miles on it. But then I'm pretty sure you already know about the mileage and the price... probably even the color. That's on the title transfer, right?"

Without waiting for a response, Moze stood and removed his coat from the back of his chair and said, "It's been a pleasure, Ms. Kendricks."

Kendricks drilled him with an icy stare and said, "I'm sure we'll talk again soon."

"Good. It'll give me a reason to live."

14

Wally

May 2017

Wally sat in front of his computer trying to concentrate on the latest update for one of his best clients. His work, designing and maintaining websites, was something that he thoroughly loved, and being able to do it from home made him appreciate his job even more. But these days, even when he found time to work, it was sometimes more of a challenge than he could handle. He had been neglecting his job. Although he was the boss and technically could work whenever he wanted to, he was a company of one. When he wasn't coding, nobody else was either. And few websites ever remained stagnant. Companies added products, deleted products, changed descriptions, updated reviews and of course prices changed constantly. Just staying in constant catch-up mode meant working into the early-hours of the morning most nights. And now his only employee was pretty-much one handed and the other hand shook enough sometimes, that it wasn't much good either.

Any other time Wally would have been thrilled to have his sister around for an extended stay. They seldom were together more than a couple of days at a time, although since their divorces, Lisbeth had made several weekend visits each year. Wally, once his illness started progressing rapidly, liked to stay close to Moze and home. However, there were exceptions like last Christmas when he and Moze went to Philly to see Lisbeth sing one night and then, two nights later, play in the orchestra's production of The Messiah. He had been so proud of her.

From the time she had been eight or nine years old, he had been in awe of her singing and the way she would fearlessly stand in front of an audience, never forgetting a word or note. And when she had that violin stuck in the crook of her neck with a spotlight on her for her solos... she would light up the performance with her beauty and grace. To have a sister like that and a father like Moze was more than any man deserved.

What an idiot Conrad had been. To throw a treasure like Lisbeth away for some meaningless affairs. Wally had called him once after the breakup, hoping he could glean something that he could report back to Lisbeth, something that would somehow save the marriage. But Conrad had nothing but guilt and anguish to offer which did not satisfy Lisbeth. She had wanted a certain body part on a platter.

Wally and Conrad had always hit it off even though Junie, especially the last few years, would shamelessly flirt with her brother-in-law. It bothered Wally, bothered him a lot. But he hadn't blamed Conrad for that. Conrad, in that smooth way of his, always refused to play Junie's games, deflecting her double entendres and extended squeezes with wit and deference to Lisbeth's proximity, never giving Junie the slightest encouragement.

So now there was no Conrad. No Junie. But there was a Deenie whose phone calls seemed to last forever in a good way. The two newly discovered soulmates made each other feel young again. Appreciated. Each of them genuinely interested in the other.

And now, Lisbeth was here. He had hoped she would stay with Moze, but she'd had other plans. The first night following the fall, Wally had been insistent that Moze and Deenie go home. He could take care of himself. And he might have been able to if it hadn't been for the Parkinson's. His right hand and arm shook more than the left, but he could compensate one for the other. Now though, with the left elbow sprained, he was, at times, completely helpless. By the following morning he knew he had to have somebody there.

Deenie had been more than willing to move in with him, but it was too soon in their relationship for that. She had just been set free from caring for her mother. He was not about to take that freedom away from her. At least not this soon. And he was not about to have Deenie see him and his infirmities closeup. At least not yet.

Moze, too, had been ready to move in, as he had been a year ago when things started going south. Wally was not so naïve about his future that he wasn't aware that the time would likely come when he would need someone, family or stranger, to move in or he would have to find a nursing home. But neither of those choices was acceptable or needed at this point.

When Moze had suggested the call to Lisbeth, Wally had agreed only if Lisbeth would sleep at Moze's. He and Deenie would spend evenings either at her place or his, and Wally insisted he could get through the night by himself. When he would need Lisbeth most was for getting dressed. An occasional trip for groceries or errands or medical appointments would also be appreciated. Lisbeth, of course, saw it differently, and Wally gave in because he knew she was right. If he would get up in the night to empty his bladder, the trip to and from the bathroom was now even more adventurous because his left arm would be unavailable to stop a fall.

* * * *

From the living room, Wally thought he heard some noise then he heard Lisbeth. She had been gone when he woke up, leaving him a note saying she needed to get a few things from WalMart.

"Good morning, Big Brother," she called from the kitchen.

A few moments later she stuck her head into his office and said, "You're at it bright and early. Getting lots done?"

"No. Not really. It's so hard to concentrate these days."

"The headaches?

"Please don't think of yourself that way."

"Funny guy."

Wally sensed that Lisbeth was staring at him. So far, he was having a good day. Nothing had gone haywire yet today. "If you're standing there waiting for me to start the shakes, you might be wasting your time. I'm a normal guy so far today."

"Well, that's some good news."

Wally looked up at her. Something wasn't right. Lisbeth looked hesitant. He might even say a bit nervous. Not like Lisbeth at all.

"What's up?"

As soon as the words escaped him, the situation came into focus. He had expected the question the first night she arrived. Here it was two days later and she couldn't hold back any longer.

He put his hand out and said, "Wait. Don't tell me. You either want to know if Deenie and I have done the dirty yet." He paused for drama. "Or you want to know what I remembered about Moze. I'm sure he told you about the new memory, and I'm also sure he told you not to ask me. I am simply astounded that you have waited this long before an interrogation on either subject."

Lisbeth grabbed the footstool from the big leather chair by the door and slid it beside Wally. She inhaled deeply. "Do you think it's fair to Moze to keep whatever you remembered from him? Especially after his last visit with Kendricks?"

"Oh, so you don't want to hear about my sex life?"

"Of course I do. Just not right now."

Wally looked at his sister's large brown eyes. He had always been envious of them. His were a drab light blue, like robin eggs that had been left in the sun for a month or two.

"Well, I guess that since I've told Deenie, I might as well tell you. But don't tell Moze. I'll do that myself the next time I see him. He'll probably—"

"You told *Deenie?* Did you not hear what Moze said about her putting herself right in the middle of things already?"

Wally ignored his sister's theatrics. "I don't know for sure the time of the memory, but I think it's from earlier in the same day as the last one. Just after supper. You and I and Moze and Mom were in the kitchen. Mom started to cry and Moze put his arm around her waist and led her through the door. He looked back at us and said, *Mommy will be all right. She's just sad that I can't stay longer. I'll cheer her up before I leave. Be good now. She'll be back in just a few minutes.*

"I stood and watched them through the door until they got out to Moze's car, then Moze put his arms around her and Mom did the same with him. They stood there for the longest time, then Moze kissed Mom on the side of her neck. Mom's head was on the other side of Moze, so I couldn't see what she was doing. A few minutes later Moze got into his car and left." Wally looked away.

"So Moze *was* there the evening Mom disappeared."

"I'm not finished."

"Sorry."

"Mom came back into the kitchen and gathered us into her arms and said, *Moze will be back later tonight to cheer me up some more, so don't be worried if you hear me with somebody in my room.*"

"Dammit, Wally. And you told all of this to Deenie?"

"Don't worry about Deenie. She won't tell anybody. If I thought there was the slightest chance, I wouldn't have told her."

"Oh, Wally. I know how lonely you have been. And I know how much you like Deenie, but think about her taking a polygraph or on a witness stand being badgered by the DA. Being reminded repeatedly of the consequences of perjury when the DA asks her if she has heard anything from you about Moze being at the house the night Chrissy disappeared. I like Deenie, I really do, and I hope you two end up growing old together. But she's always been something of an airhead, and the thought of Moze's future depending on her testimony is unsettling at best."

"I'm not going to fight with you, Lisbeth. You know I would never do anything to get Moze into trouble. He told us that he wasn't there that day or night, so he wasn't there, no matter what's in my memory. If it comes to the point where I am put on a witness stand, although I sincerely doubt that it will come to that, I will say that I no longer remember what I experienced. Deenie will never have to testify. And I don't think they can make her take a polygraph."

Wally felt his bad arm start to tremble. He winced as elbow pain from the other arm caught him by surprise when he grabbed the one that trembled.

Lisbeth reached across her lap and tenderly helped get the arm under control. "It's all right," she said almost in a whisper.

Wally removed his hand from his arm and placed it on Lisbeth's hand. "Deenie called me this morning to say that Kendricks wants to talk with her in the office this afternoon. I think I better go with her." Immediately he felt Lisbeth's hand tighten, but only for a moment.

"No. You stay here and try to get caught up. I'll go with her. Is that all right with you?"

Still troubled by Lisbeth's airhead comment, Wally did not answer right away. But he knew his sister was right, and he knew also that Lisbeth would be less intimidated by Kendricks.

"Promise you won't bully her or make her feel like she's said the wrong thing?"

"Promise. What time is she to be there?"

"One."

"Did you tell Moze yet?"

"No. I wanted to wait and see how her visit went."

"Will you be all right here by yourself?"

"Of course." Wally pulled his hand away and reached for the phone. "I'll call and tell her that you'll be going in my place and that you'll pick her up at 12:45. I think she will be glad to have the chance to be with you by herself."

15

Deenie

May 2017

Already a nervous wreck knowing that she was going to be questioned by the DA's office, Deenie now had to do it without Wally. It wasn't that she disliked Lisbeth. It was just that she would rather be with Wally. His presence in her life had been like a much-needed drug.

Despite the support that her church had provided for her, Deenie had been in a seemingly bottomless depression. She was fifty-one years old and had been cast off by a man with whom she had not had a meaningful one-on-one conversation in years. At the same time, she had been obliged to begin caring for mother. Which had been a good thing at the time, she suspected. At least for the first six months she had been able to talk to her, share old memories, bitch with support.

And now she had Wally. Yes, she worried about how his future would impact her, whether she would become a caretaker all over again. And there was a persistent voice in her head that kept asking if her feelings for him were not being amplified by her pity, her admiration for his courage, her simple desire for companionship.

She had always felt sorry for him. For as long as she had known him, he had been the nice boy with the nice sister and nice father. But he had also been the boy whose real father had been killed and the boy whose mother had run off and left her kids without a parent.

Despite his affliction she experienced a physical attraction for him. He always had been handsome and athletic. If he ever would have asked her out in high school, she would have gladly agreed. When he told her his story about wanting to ask her out, she couldn't help laughing. Then she realized that if he would have asked her out, their lives would have been so much better. Tears followed. That story and the discovery that Wally's adopted father had once carried on an affair with her mother only made her connection with Wally more special.

But the most important aspect of their relationship was the way Wally made her feel. He cared for her, made her smile, made her feel wanted, and was *so* easy to talk to. Maybe it was just that she had so much stored up over the years that made their conversations easy. She guessed it might have been the same for Wally too. Whatever the reason, their time together brought them contentment and pleasure.

There had been sex now twice. Nothing spectacular either time. She guessed that it would be that way until she would be able to put the Parkinson's out of her mind. If it wouldn't change, she would be satisfied regardless. She knew the likelihood of ever experiencing those hormonal explosions of her youth was decreasing with every birthday. At least three women from the church who were about her age had told her stories of their menopause experiences. For Deenie, intimacy with Wally and an average climax now and then would be enough.

And now, too, there was Wally's dad, Mr. Foster... Moze. She'd had a crush on him back in the day. Must have been genetic—both she and her mother. If he had been ugly and fat -- which of course he hadn't been – but if he had, she and everyone else would still have been in awe of him. All her math teachers from middle school up had been some of the smartest people in her world, including her mother, the principal at the time that Moze had been Deenie's teacher. But besides being super smart, Mr. Foster had been so nice to everyone and especially patient with kids who had trouble with math, like herself.

Most of all, everyone respected him because of the way he had handled all of the crap that had happened to him... having hardly known his father when he was killed in Korea, his brother being murdered, his sister-in-law disappearing, and then his mother dying, forcing him to become a father to his niece and nephew.

Deenie had loved her father, had been so proud when she would sit in the congregation and watch him deliver his sermons with calm and logic and purpose in that soothing voice of his. But at the end of the day he had still been the minister. So many nights the church was his priority. It had always been easy to see, however, that Mr. Foster's kids, his *adopted* kids, had never been preempted by anything or anyone. People... adults, talked about him... in a good way. Lisbeth and Wally always seemed to be getting recognized for something.

When Deenie had told the Assistant D.A. that her mother, on the night after her husband's funeral, had confessed the affair with Mr. Foster, and then told Deenie about having been with him the night his sister-in-law disappeared, Deenie knew she was likely crossing more than one boundary.

Boundary number one— it really was none of her business. Until the day that Mr. Foster had come to the house a few weeks ago, she'd had next to no contact with any of the family since high school. But his timing had been perfect. She had just had a bad day with her mother, actually had had several bad days in a row and was starting to feel like the call from the Cottages was never going to come. And then there he was... an escape to a simpler time.

Her mother actually had already confessed to her about her affair with him, so, as she looked at him that afternoon for the first time since spotting him at her father's funeral, she was seeing him in a whole new light. Yes, he looked older, but certainly not old enough to have been the lover of the old woman in the house. When she had given him the news of her mother's dementia, the sadness that had overtaken him would not let him leave. After all the years that had passed, he evidently still had feelings for her.

But those thoughts regarding his reaction had come before Kendricks' call, before she had been aware of her mother's involvement in the situation. Mr. Foster had likely come to check her mother's memories of the 2010 investigation, only to find out that he no longer had his alibi. No wonder at his sadness. Deenie hadn't told him yet of her intervention, was not completely convinced that she had done the right thing. If Kendricks brought it up this afternoon, Lisbeth's direct nature would let Deenie know if she had done the right thing.

Boundary number two—Deenie had perjured herself. Well, not officially, but she had lied to Kendricks about her knowledge of her mother being with Mr. Foster the night that Wally's mother disappeared. She had not planned to, but there had been something in the Assistant DA's manner that had irked Deenie, a tone of voice that suggested that she was the Voice of God and you didn't want to piss off God. Besides, there was that image of Mr. Foster standing on her front porch, shrinking at the news of her mother's dementia, her new relationship with Wally, and the fact that she had always liked Mr. Foster. She just knew he could never be involved in anything that would bring harm to anyone, especially the mother of his brother's children. As much for that reason than any other, she had willingly offered the lie. She could only imagine the befuddled look her words had put on Kendrick's face.

But that had been before Wally's accident and the unsettling piece of the past that had popped into the present. Not that it changed her feelings about Mr. Foster. It had, however, affected Wally. He could say that it hadn't as often as he wanted, but he had not been the same since. And now, today, he had bailed on her.

Had he been reluctant to face Kendricks and offer lies of his own? She was very likely to ask him if he'd had any more memories resulting from his treatments. If he said no, the two of them might be sharing a cell together. No, she didn't really believe there was much chance of either one of them doing jail time for lying. Still, she guessed it was a possibility. They were both obstructing justice.

Deenie was glad she'd experienced these thoughts before facing

Kendricks, and now that she had considered Wally's possible motive for not going, she started to get comfortable with the idea of Lisbeth being there with her instead.

Lisbeth had balls, nerves of steel. At least she used to. Deenie would always remember Lisbeth stepping to the foul line after making a field goal during the state quarterfinal when Lisbeth was a sophomore. With five seconds left on the clock and Pine City losing by two, Lisbeth had done something that had been beyond Deenie's knowledge of the game at the time… Lisbeth deliberately missed her foul shot, banging the ball against the front edge of the rim. The ball directly returned to her in front of the foul line where she then retreated to a spot just beyond the three-point line, calmly set herself and sent it back up for a perfect swish through the net.

The game had been played on a supposedly neutral court, but it had been eighty miles from Pine City and much closer to the other school somewhere near Altoona if she remembered it right. Everybody for the other team had been standing, shouting, blowing horns… and then suddenly they weren't, struck dumb in a matter of a few seconds and engulfed in the sudden explosion of sound from the Pine City fans. That was the power of Lisbeth then. Deenie hoped that nothing had changed.

16

Lisbeth

May 2017

Lisbeth was pleasantly surprised at Deenie's demeanor as they chatted in the car on the way to the courthouse. The small talk at the outset mainly focused on their shared experiences with cheating husbands and the ensuing divorces. A few minutes later Deenie had the conversation focused on Wally.

"How was he when you left the house? I thought he didn't seem like himself when he called to tell me you would pick me up. No falls during the night?"

"No, he seemed fine except for the elbow. How are *you* doing? You going to be all right with Kendricks?"

Deenie laughed. "I've had beauticians I was more afraid of than her." She paused, her voice becoming more serious. "Have you met her yet?"

"No, but that doesn't mean I don't already have an impression of her. Moze has always been a pretty good judge of people, and from what he's said, I think she's somebody out to make a name for herself... facts, logic, and consequences be damned."

"I think that's pretty much my take on her, too. I would just add that she thinks a lot more of herself than maybe she should."

Several seconds passed without words between them before Deenie said, "I was remembering this morning the basketball game that you won my senior year. How poised you were under all of that pressure.

How did you ever deal with that?"

"Huh, I haven't thought about that in years," Lisbeth replied reflectively. She paused for a few moments, seemingly traveling back in time. "That was probably the best game I ever had. I had practiced that intentional miss a hundred times. And by the end of the season I had the part where I hit the front of the rim pretty-much down pat. All I had to do after that was get to the three-point line and make the shot."

"Didn't you end up going to Penn State on a scholarship for basketball?"

"Softball, but I quit playing after my freshman year. I decided to concentrate on my violin. Not much of a future in softball." Lisbeth checked the clock on the dashboard. "How do you feel about punctuality?"

"Generally, I'm for it," said Deenie, "but today I think I'm against it."

"Me, too. What do you say we make the bitch wait for fifteen minutes?"

"There's a Sheetz near the courthouse. Let's stop there for a coffee."

"Perfect."

* * * *

The clock on the wall of Kendricks' office indicated 1:20 by the time they were seated. She and Lisbeth had been ushered into the room by Kendricks' secretary who said her boss would be right in. Deenie had just finished making herself comfortable when her cell phone signaled a text message from Wally.

Lisbeth heard the cell noise and said, "I'll bet that's Wally."

"He wants to know how I'm doing."

"Tell him we're being punished for arriving late."

Just as Deenie finished tapping her response, Kendricks entered the room in whirlwind fashion. "Sorry, ladies, for keeping you waiting. I was just updating the DA on what was happening."

Before she could say anything else, in walked the DA herself.

"And as you can see, she has decided to sit in on our little get together. Let's all of us put some names to faces. I'm Louise Kendricks. Which one of you is Deanna?"

"That would be me," said Deenie who reached out and took Kendricks' hand.

Before releasing Deenie's hand, Kendricks shifted her attention towards Lisbeth and said, "And this must be Wally's sister Lisbeth Dawkins." Releasing Deenie's hand, Kendricks offered it to Lisbeth who firmly took the hand then released it with a quick, hard squeeze. Kendricks reacted with only a curious glance then immediately turned towards the DA and said, "And, ladies, this is District Attorney Barb Breckenridge."

The DA exchanged handshakes and pleasantries with each of them.

Lisbeth immediately surmised that the DA's presence was strictly a power play. Neither she nor Deenie was a principal player in the game, so no other reason made any sense. The DA was here for one reason only... to intimidate Deenie.

"I'm glad you came with Deanna, Lisbeth. Your name's been mentioned affectionately by both Moses and Wally," said Kendricks.

Lisbeth offered only the slightest smile and replied, "Well, what a coincidence. I've heard your name lately, also. Maybe not with much affection though."

A brief chuckle from Kendricks let everyone in the room know that Lisbeth had established herself as more than just another body in the room.

Kendricks' responded by immediately turning her head in Deenie's direction. "Now, first of all, let me inquire as to Wally's health. It's been a few weeks now since I last saw him. His treatments are going well?"

Deenie didn't know if it was her place to speak, so she waited to see if Lisbeth would answer. When she didn't, Deenie said, "He had a fall a few nights ago, but it had nothing to do with the Parkinson's. He just tripped on the coffee table leg."

"Oh, geez, is he all right?" asked Kendricks. Lisbeth made no attempt to hide the rolling of her eyes.

"His head hit the floor—"

"All right, Ms. Kendricks," interrupted Lisbeth. "Enough of your faux concern for my brother. Let's be honest here. Your only concern for Wally is in using him to put our father in prison."

"Not true, Mrs. Dawkins. I like your brother. He came to me, remember."

"But you're the one who has twisted his words into an accusation against our dad. Wally's only reason for coming to you was to let you know there had been someone else in the house that night, and because you have nobody else to accuse, you're using the words *sounded like* to start a witch hunt."

"Believe what you will, Mrs. Dawkins. But I am going to have to ask that we get back to business here—"

Lisbeth couldn't help herself. "And what business is that? Using the poorly chosen words of a man suffering from Parkinson's to implicate his own father for his mother's—"

This time it was Kendricks who interrupted. "Please, Mrs. Dawkins, I would like to speak with Deanna about a few things. The DA's time with us today is limited so if you won't allow us to stay on task here, I'll have to ask you to wait outside."

Lisbeth had folded her arms across her chest. When Kendricks finished talking, she raised a thumb and forefinger to the corner of her mouth and swept it across her lips, subtly and slightly extending her middle finger while making the movement. If Kendricks picked up on the intended disrespect, she chose to ignore it.

"Thank you. Now, Deanna, the reason I asked you here today was to clarify an item in the presence of DA Breckenridge. When I spoke to you over the phone, you had indicated that, prior to the onset of your mother's dementia, she had told you about her affair in 1972 with Moses Foster. Is that correct?"

Deenie answered without hesitation, "That is correct. My father had just died, and I guess Mom wanted to finally get it off her chest although I think it might have had more to do with my unhappiness with my then husband's cheating. I believe that she wanted me to understand that sometimes people do such things then realize afterwards that it was a mistake and change for the better because of it."

"And then you told me, without my asking by the way, that your mother also told you that she had been with Moses Foster on May 12, 1972, the night Chrissy Foster disappeared. Now, just to clarify, was that the entire day of the 12th, the evening of the 12th, the night of the 12th, all of the above, or some of the above?"

Lisbeth watched Deenie look at DA Breckenridge then at Lisbeth, seemingly wanting someone to tell her what to say. Because Lisbeth was hearing this information for the first time, she certainly had no idea what Deenie's answer should be. By the look on her face, Lisbeth suspected Deenie had no idea either and was just now considering the fact that there might be a right answer… or a wrong one.

Before Deenie could choose, Kendricks started talking again. "Yesterday afternoon– I believe we just missed you– DA Breckenridge and I went to the Cottages to visit with your mother. What a pleasant surprise to find that she was, according to the staff member on duty, having one of her more lucid days since her arrival there."

Deenie's mind raced back to her mother's lunch yesterday. Kendricks' was right about the state of her mother's mind. She had not fought with Deenie over her feeding, had not tried to pick any food from the tray belonging to Faith, the woman who always sat beside her. Her mother had actually asked Deenie what she had done that morning. It had been weeks since her mother had asked her a question that made sense.

"When asked about having an affair with Moses Foster in 1972, your mother said that she was ashamed to say that there had been a brief … *dalliance*, I believe was the word she used. And when we asked if she had ever told you about it, she confirmed what you had told me—that it was after your father died.

"But when we asked her if she had told you about her being Moses Foster's alibi for May 12th, she said no. Now is your mother confused on that point?" Kendricks paused. "Or are you?"

Deenie gave Lisbeth a look that said she was sorry, then started to speak, "I guess–"

"Excuse me," said Lisbeth politely. "Ms. Kendricks, DA Breckenridge, did you record your conversation with Deanna's mother?"

It was the DA who responded. "For this conversation I don't think we need to go–"

"And if you did record her, did you inform her that you were recording her?"

Kendricks jumped in before her boss could answer. "Why, Mrs. Dawkins, you are beginning to sound like a lawyer, and not a very good one at that."

"Here's the thing, Ms. Kendricks, any confusion involving the answer given by Mrs. Voorhees likely has more to do with your interpretation of her answer. Was your question to Mrs. Voorhees *Were you with Moses Foster on the* 12th? or *Did you tell your daughter that you were with him?* As you represented the conversation to us, it sounded like she could have been with him, but had never told Deanna or, more likely, considering Mrs. Voorhees current mental condition, did not remember telling her.

When the room went silent for several seconds, Lisbeth felt sure she was about to be bounced. She was ready to go anyway. To that end she decided to wait until Kendricks or Breckenridge started the eviction process before interrupting one last time.

Finally, Kendricks said, "What we asked or didn't ask Mrs.

Voorhees really has nothing–"

"Deanna," Lisbeth said, "unless one of these two ladies produces the recording of their visit with your mother, I would not try to answer any more of their questions. And since Ms. Kendricks doesn't think much of me as a lawyer, we better get you a really good one before you say anything more."

Deenie stood up immediately and said, "Great idea, Lisbeth."

She gathered her jacket from the back of her chair and added, "And having Power of Attorney for my mother, I want you to know that, should you want to speak to her again, you will need to contact me first in order to get my permission. If I should agree, you will only speak to her in the presence of my attorney."

"Oh, and one more thing," added Lisbeth as she joined Deenie at the door. "You are right, Ms. Kendricks, I am not a lawyer, but good luck trying to get that conversation with Mrs. Voorhees admissible if you go to trial. Your inquiry concerning her state of mind yesterday when speaking to the aide, would indicate to me anyway, that you were aware of her dementia prior to conducting the interview. That doesn't sound to me like something a good lawyer would do."

Deenie, without turning or stopping her progress through the outer office, put an exclamation point on Lisbeth's observation, "Ms. Kendricks had already been made aware of Mom's dementia during the initial phone call." She stopped abruptly, turned and spoke directly to DA Breckenridge, "If Ms. Kendricks had any doubts about my assessment of my mother's condition, all she would have needed to confirm that information was a call to my mother's doctor."

17

Moze

May 2017

The phone rang just as he finished doing his supper dishes.

"Moze, can you please get over here when you get some time?" Lisbeth added right away, "It's not Wally. He's fine." She was trying to keep her demeanor controlled without upsetting him, but the fact that she had called and wanted his presence strongly suggested that all was not well. She had always been that way, always wanting to appear to be poised and in control, regardless of how she really felt. Around others she was usually able to pull it off. Not so with Moze. Or Wally.

"Sure, be there in ten minutes."

"Thanks, Moze."

Moze had a pretty good idea that whatever had set Lisbeth off likely was connected in some way to that afternoon's meeting with Kendricks. Wally had texted him earlier that Lisbeth had gone with Deenie in his place. At the time Moze had felt a certain amount of relief. Lisbeth would always be a good choice when dealing with a stressful situation.

But now that he was aware that something had roiled even the always-poised Lisbeth, Moze could feel himself fast approaching a tipping point with the whole DA situation. It had become the source of too much commotion in his family. Wally's guilt, Lisbeth's irritation with Wally, Deenie's finding out about the particulars of her mother's affair, and now...well, who knew what was in play. All because of him. Maybe it was time to come clean with everybody, including the DA.

* * * *

Wally and Deenie were seated on the edge of the couch, with Lisbeth pacing through the middle of the room when Moze walked into Wally's living room.

"We've decided that we're not talking to the DA's office again without a lawyer. And we think that would be best for you also," announced Lisbeth.

"Why? What happened?" asked Moze as he sat down beside Wally.

"Kendricks went after Deenie like an unleashed pit bull." She looked at Deenie with a strange mixture of pity and irritation.

Deenie started to speak but stopped and shrank back as if the traffic-stopping hand that Lisbeth threw in her direction had pushed her backwards.

"It's not you, Deenie. There's just too much at stake here not to have a lawyer present. You can't be expected–"

The sound of Moze's cell phone ringing interrupted Lisbeth. Moze silently mouthed the word *Kendricks* then said, "Yes, Ms. Kendricks, what can I do for you?"

Moze listened.

"Yes, I can do that. Sure. Okay. Bye."

"Kendricks wants me to come in for a little chit chat tomorrow afternoon." He saw the immediate agitation in his daughter's face and said, "And no, I'll not be taking a lawyer with me."

"Did she say why?" Lisbeth asked.

"No," Moze lied. He hadn't told any of them about Moses Hendershot, so he didn't feel the need to divulge Kendricks' request to email a photo of Chrissy from 1972 to show Hendershot in addition to the one of himself that he had already given her. He had several he could scan. Nor did he see the need to tell his children that he had lied about Kendricks asking him to come in to chat. His visit was going to be with the DA and would be at his request.

"Well then, can I, at least, go with you?" pleaded Lisbeth.

"No. I can handle Kendricks. What I want is for all of you to just relax and take a deep breath. You're all getting stuck in the middle of this nonsense and I think it's about time I told you a few things that I probably should have told you earlier."

He couldn't tell them everything, but maybe he could give them enough that they would stop worrying for the time being.

"Wally, your memories are spot on. I have always known about someone else being with your mother that night, but trust me when I tell you that it wasn't me."

Before Moze could say anything else, Lisbeth said, "But can you prove it? We have never questioned your involvement. It's Kendricks I'm worried about."

"But I'm not. If the PSP have Vicky's interview, Kendricks has to disprove what's there, and there's no way she can do that.

"As for your other memory, Wally, I really *was* there. I had gone to the house to say good-bye to your mother, because I knew she was probably not going to be there in the morning. She was an emotional mess that night – depressed, sad, so afraid of the future. I tried to get her to change her mind, and she tried to convince me that she might. Had I known that I would never see her again, I think I would have done something drastic. Probably would have taken all of you to your Granny Ann's and locked Chrissy in a closet."

"But… why did she leave?" Wally's voice was full of confusion and hurt.

"She was, unfortunately, under some bad influences."

"What do you mean? People? Drugs?" The question came from Lisbeth.

"Both. I don't think telling you any more is going to make things better for either of you. I can tell you this for sure – Chrissy later regretted what she did. She had chosen to come back to you, but, well, things obviously didn't work out."

"How do you know all of this stuff?" Lisbeth had just expressed more interest in her mother in the last minute than she had in the forty-five years prior to that.

"You have to take my word for it, I guess. I *will* tell you that I did not get that information from Chrissy and I did not get it until a month or so after her disappearance."

"So, you never said anything to the police?" asked Wally.

"No. I didn't see where it could change anything. The police had investigated, conducted a search, and found nothing as I knew they would. Two weeks after Chrissy left, I got a letter from Tampa that said they were there. The next month I talked with the person she left with. That's when I found out that Chrissy had left him on June 20th of 1972 to go home."

"And who was or is that person?" asked Lisbeth.

Moze did not answer.

Lisbeth said, "Moze?"

"I can't tell you. I'd like to tell you. I really would, but I'm sorry. I can't. Please let it go at that."

Lisbeth, who had sat down in the matching chair to the sofa where Wally and Deenie were seated when Moze started to talk, rose to her feet and started pacing again before saying, "What if, God forbid, the DA would decide to file for a preliminary hearing and put you under oath. Would you reveal who told you?"

"She won't do that, Lisbeth," said Moze.

"But what if she does?"

"I guess I won't know until it happens. As far as you all getting a lawyer, I would like you to wait until I sort out a few more things. Hopefully none of you will get called back in for a while, if ever. If you do, I'll give Kendricks a choice of you being accompanied by me or a lawyer. I'm pretty sure I know what her choice will be.

"Now, unless you need me for anything else, I'm heading back home. I'll give you all a call tomorrow evening after I talk with

Kendricks. In the meantime I want all of you to forget about anything that happened today in that office. I promise you that, no matter what she said or you said, it will soon be of no consequence. Everything is going to be all right."

Lisbeth started to speak, but Moze threw up his hand, giving a good imitation of what she had done to Deenie a few minutes earlier.

"Trust me, Sweetheart. Okay?"

Reluctantly Lisbeth said, "Okay."

He looked at Wally and Deenie until he received a nod from each of them then said, "Talk to you all tomorrow then."

18

The DA

May 2017

The sound coming from the office phone told DA Barb Breckenridge that her secretary wanted to talk.

"Yes, Marie."

"The Assistant DA says that she is finished interviewing Moses Hendershot and would like to schedule some time with you at your convenience."

"She still on the line?"

"Yes."

"Tell her to give me five minutes then come over."

The DA knew that Hendershot had been scheduled for a visit an hour ago, but after yesterday's fiasco with the two women in the Foster case, the DA wasn't sure that she wanted to hear the latest news. At least Hendershot had made the trip here without anybody having to go to Wexford. She was starting to regret giving Louise the green light to investigate Chrissy Foster's disappearance.

Breckenridge had relented on her decision not to involve law enforcement's resources until there was more to go on than a memory that may or may not be real. Louise's enthusiasm had been contagious though. Her ambitious nature, bulldog focus, and fearlessness that had separated her from the other thirty-three people who had applied for the job made her hard to say no to. But the DA was starting to have serious doubts. Although this Foster case could be a big-time headline maker *if* it really was a case, it could be a big black eye if it wasn't.

Going to the nursing home had been a mistake. Breckenridge knew better. Antagonizing the two women had been a mistake. Louise knew better. It was obvious to Breckenridge that Louise had wanted that kind of atmosphere in the interview, had wanted to intimidate the two women, especially the old woman's daughter. As far as the DA was concerned, as of now, no crime had been committed.

An official inquiry was still possible. The man Louise met with today could make things more interesting for sure, but unless he has some physical evidence establishing Moses Foster's presence at the motel that night, it would just be a matter of one man's word against another's. Besides, regardless of what Louise would like the situation to be, there were the PSP notes from 2010, indicating that in an interview with Vicky Voorhees, she corroborated that she had been with Moses Foster from eight in the evening of the twelfth until midnight. That took Foster out of the timeline established for his son's memory. Somebody else had to have been with Chrissy that night.

Unless Vicky Voorhees had lied.

The one person who *had* lied was her daughter. Breckenridge had to agree yesterday with Louise that the proverbial deer in the headlights had been about to confess to it until Foster's daughter intervened.

A brief rap on the door gave way to the presence of Louise Kendricks and Breckenridge knew instantly the interview with Moses Hendershot had not gone well.

"Sit down, Louise, and give me the bad news."

The Assistant DA made a face that fit her mood. When she had herself settled into her chair, she said, "Well, I guess it could have been worse."

"How many photos did you have for him?

"Twenty-four. He narrowed them down to eight and Foster was one of them. But in the long run eight is seven too many. I needed him to put his finger on Foster the moment he laid eyes on him."

"Yeah, well, the memory of a face has a way of changing over forty-five years. How did he seem… credible?"

"Absolutely. I think he's still pissed off that he ended up in jail because of Moses Foster. But do I think a jury would find him more credible than Moses Foster, no. Not really. I would probably choose Foster myself."

"So, what's next?"

"All I can do with Hendershot is put him face to face with Foster and hope one of them convinces me that I'm right or wrong."

"I don't suppose you showed him a photo of Chrissy?"

"Yes, I thought about that yesterday evening while I was looking over my notes. I called Foster and asked him to email one."

"And? Did Hendershot recognize *her*?"

"Right away. No doubt whatsoever."

"So, we know she was at the motel and she was with someone. The someone she left her kids for."

"Somebody named Moses Foster," Kendricks shot back immediately. "The driver's license and credit card, remember?" she added when she saw the DA's eyebrows furrow.

"But Foster said he lost his wallet. And Hendershot didn't identify him. *And* he has an alibi."

"And," Kendricks sneered along with her sarcastic tone, "all that bullshit about selling his car to William Jackson at Three Rivers?"

"I don't see anything there that makes him even remotely a murder suspect. There's no logic in the sequence of the events. Everything you have referred to can be explained without a murder being involved. Not to mention that I see no motive. Why would he murder his brother's wife?"

"To get the children."

"A single, young, probably handsome bachelor in the midst of an affair with a married woman is not among the usual suspects for killing somebody to get her children.

"As far as I'm concerned, Louise, you can ask questions till the cows come home, but you cannot harass people in the process. And that's what you did yesterday. You most likely have lawyers involved now. Hell, Moze Foster might not come in again without one after yesterday. You can be sure that the women clued him in on what was said and how it was said." The DA felt her blood pressure rising, so she stopped for a moment and took a deep breath.

"Now, what's going on with that Wegener child abuse case? Anything new from the sheriff's office?"

"No, but I am planning to call over there before I leave today."

"Good. Let me know what's happening before you go."

* * * *

Half an hour later DA Breckenridge still had Moses Hendershot and Moses Foster front and center in her mind. Occasionally, Wally, Lisbeth, and Deanna were there also. But it was mostly the two men named Moses. She hadn't met Hendershot, but knew the two of them had to be nearly the same age… somewhere near seventy. What the hell was she doing, letting Kendricks think of charging Foster for something she had next to no evidence against. In fact, there was *no* evidence of a crime. The body of a person missing for forty-five years had been found seven years ago, picked clean by wild creatures and completely void of any evidence.

Moses Foster was, by all accounts and appearances, a well thought of, responsible, and loving individual. His adopted son was suffering the ravages of Parkinson's disease and had been beating himself up over getting his father involved in this mess the moment after he opened his mouth. None of this made any sense. Breckenridge had allowed herself to be unduly influenced by the ambition and the enthusiasm of her assistant. It was time to stop harassing this man and his family.

She would tell Louise the first thing in the morning. Unless something definitive fell in their laps, the case was closed.

* * * *

At a little before three that same afternoon the DA's secretary called her again.

"Yes, Marie."

"Moses Foster would like to speak to you, if you have time."

"Sure. Put him on."

"No, ma'am, he's here in the office with me right now."

"Yes or no, Marie, is he alone?"

"Yes."

"Give me two minutes then send him in."

"Okay."

I wonder what this is about? At least he hasn't brought a lawyer. She thought about calling Kendricks to sit in, but quickly dismissed the idea. Foster would likely feel more comfortable without her. Besides, this would be the DA's first experience with him other than meeting him outside Louise's office. She looked forward to it.

Rather than continuing to sit at her desk and wait for Marie to bring Foster to her, the DA went to her door, opened it, and said, "Hello, Mr. Foster. Nice to see you again. Please come in."

Moze nodded and followed the DA into her office.

When he remained standing, she said, "Please, have a seat. Now, what can I do for you today?"

"Well, Ma'am, I have a few things I wanted to pass on to you. First, I want to continue to make it clear that I had nothing to do with Chrissy's death, despite what Ms. Kendricks seems to believe. And, obviously, neither of my children did either. So, I would very much appreciate it if this office would stop treating them as if they did. They are only concerned for me.

"Secondly, these memories Wally has been having because of his treatments are mostly accurate and–"

"Wait. You said *memories*, plural. Have there been more?"

"Yes. He did not want to tell you about it because of concern for how they might affect me. He had a fall the other day that evidently triggered another one. As you know, the first one involved someone being in the house with Chrissy the night she disappeared and, according to Wally, that person sounded like me. But it wasn't. The second memory occurred earlier that same day at the house also. That one did involve me. He saw me in his memory because I was there. Chrissy had told me that she was going to leave the children that night, so I had gone to the house to talk her out of going if I could. If not, I knew that I would be saying good bye."

DA Breckenridge thought for a moment that her guest might be about to break down, but he didn't.

"Why was she leaving?"

Moze shifted his position in the chair, feeling uncomfortable because of what he would say, not because of the other person in the room. Unlike her assistant, there was an air of sincerity about her.

"Who knows why people do the things they do."

"But you know the answer to *this* question, don't you? And I'm betting that you know who she left with also."

Moze Foster's eyes went to the floor then right back into the DA's line of sight.

The brief staring contest ended when Breckenridge said, "You realize that if foul play was involved in Chrissy's death, whoever it was that left with her that night is now the prime suspect?"

"I don't know any more than you do about how Chrissy died, but I do know that the person she was with would not have allowed anything to happen to her."

"So you *do* know who it was?"

Again the staring contest. This time Moze blinked first. "Yes. I do."

The door flew open revealing Louise Kendricks with the DA's secretary close behind.

"I'm sorry, Barb. I told her you were with Mr. Foster, but she didn't stop."

"That's okay, Marie."

"I'm sorry, Boss, but I had something that I wanted to tell you and when Marie told me that you were with Mr. Foster, I thought he might be interested also."

"And what is it that's so important?"

The Assistant DA paused for dramatic effect. Instead of delivering her news to the DA though, she looked directly at Moze Foster and announced, "I think I may have located William Jackson, aka Billy Jack, the one-time owner of a 1960 Plymouth Valiant."

Moze smiled and said with an unruffled calm, "I'm afraid, Ms. Kendricks, that's just not possible."

PART II

LUKE

19

William Jackson

April 16, 1972

"Piece of shit," muttered Wires, the spindly young black man, as he threw open the door to his car and climbed out. "Someday fore I die, I'm gonna have a good set of wheels." He slammed the door shut behind him.

William "Billy Jack" Jackson, his white friend slash business associate, had already emerged from the other side. "Of course, you will, my man. A few more weeks like this one, I might just buy you one myself."

"Sorry, man. I can't git ya home now, 'n' I'm gonna be late for work."

"Hey, no problemo. Ten minutes of walkin' for me, that's all." He reached into his wallet and took out five dollars. "Here, go into the house and call yourself a cab."

"Naw, I can't. But thanks."

Billy forced the money into his friend's hand. "My treat. Now go on. See you tomorrow then?"

"You're a real pal, Billy. Thanks. Yeah, see you tomorrow."

Billy gave a short wave and started down the street.

He couldn't give a shit about Wires, especially now since his car was worthless. Billy didn't believe in owning much of anything. Possessions like a car were just one more way the cops and the government could keep track of him. He did have a driver's license, simply because there was always the odd moment or emergency when he needed ID, like for drinking. He was twenty-six but had been cursed with a baby face. It wasn't bad now that he had his regular stops, four bars with owners who looked the other way while he sold his wares in their bathrooms and parking lots. Billy Jack made sure they always received something for their cooperation. And, of course, they never asked him for ID.

All four of the bars he used were within twenty minutes of walking from each other on a route that zig-zagged south of Camp Pendleton. None of them served food and all were short on ambience, basically hangouts for lost souls to find sex, drugs and a fix for their loneliness after surviving Vietnam.

The Vietnam War, having created so much stress and idle time for its American soldiers, sent them home with new habits that needed nourished. Billy Jack had been on top of that situation since early in 1967. Although he hadn't made enough money to *live* on Easy Street, he made visits there occasionally, mostly to supply its residents with his product.

Whether he was on Easy Street to deliver highs or visit some high-class strip joint, he never felt comfortable there. He most enjoyed selling to the Marines in his four-bar jurisdiction. Not that he saw himself as anyone deserving accolades for what he did. He was just someone who provided an escape for people who needed it far more than the rich. Okay, so he was not above lifting a wallet from a drunken Marine occasionally. But it was never outright theft. More of an exchange, a silent bartering. He would remove the money in a wallet and leave in its place a suitable amount of product. But he only did that when business was slow and the opportunity looked like a no brainer.

One time, back in 1970, he had lifted a Marine's wallet… must've been a thousand bucks in it. In the bathroom stall Billy was rifling through all the photo compartments, searching for hidden cash when he found a suicide letter dated for that day. Man, what a downer. The guy had no family and had lost his best buddy in the war. In the letter the Marine confessed that he had killed a Vietnamese mother and her three kids as payback for his buddy being blown to bits by a land mine fifty yards from their hooch. In his rage he had been certain the mother had to have known where the mine was to keep her children safe. There was no name at the end of the letter, just the words "I am sorry, God."

Billy had returned the note with enough marijuana to give the guy one helluva last high. The money he kept for himself. No sense in giving it back to a dead man walking.

The guy sitting at the end of the bar tonight reminded Billy a lot of that kid from 1970. Billy had never seen him in the bar before, but he had the same lost look about him... that *been-to-Nam* look. That *these-three-beers-I've-had-aren't-doin'-it-for-me* look. The kid needed to know that other treatments were available. Besides, this was payday at Pendleton and from where Billy stood, this soldier looked like an easy mark, one way or another.

"Hey, man. You a Marine?"

The guy nodded but didn't look up.

"Mind if I sit here?"

Billy took the lack of a response as at least a yellow light.

The Marine shoved his empty glass toward the bartender who also had ID'd the Marine as a revenue source and, having watched him just empty his mug of beer, was at the ready to refill it.

Billy reached out and pulled the glass back towards the mark. Not wanting to be seen as a negative for the bar's business, Billy pushed a fiver next to the glass and slid it back at the bartender. "It's okay, Ducky. Here's a little extra on top of what he owes ya. The Marine and I need to talk for a minute."

Ducky took the glass and the fiver. He looked from the money and mug then to Billy. "But he owes me—"

"Yeah, I know. I've been watchin.'" Billy pulled a ten from his money clip. "Here. Keep the extra. Now he's even."

The Marine had remained oblivious to the resolution of his tab, his head still down, his gaze still firmly affixed to the counter.

"I've got something far better for you than a couple of lousy beers. Here." The hand that had recently held ten dollars now held a baggie with two joints. "No charge. A little somethin' to show my appreciation for your service to our country."

Only when Billy nudged him with an elbow did the Marine look at the gift. He studied it for a moment then, after a quick look around the room, accepted it. "Thanks."

"It's quality."

"So, if I wanted more, you'd be the guy?"

"I'd be the guy." After a few moments Billy said, "I could use one myself. Let's go out back and light up. What do ya say?"

The Marine finally turned to his benefactor and looked at him for the first time. "Don't I know you? You've been at a bar over on Easy Street?"

Billy was momentarily taken aback. He usually remembered a face like this one. "Yeah, I been there. Don't remember you though."

"Yeah, don't imagine you would. You were somewhat … *preoccupied*. Skinny broad. Big tits. Orange hair. A package like that is hard to forget. Know what I mean?"

"I most certainly do. Come out back and I'll tell you all about her. Might even be able to fix you up."

The Marine held out his left hand. "Ring a ding ding. Mother of my kids. I'm a shitty father and worse husband, but at least I'm faithful."

Billy stood up and put a hand on the Marine's shoulder. "Come on. I'll tell you about her anyway. You might change your mind about all that wedding ring-fidelity shit. Did I mention that she has a sister? If I can get you interested—"

The Marine stood up and waved his wedding ring in Billy's face. "Ain't gonna happen."

"Tell you what. Let me tell you about them while we have a joint or two. Then I'll give them a call and see if we can set something up. If you get interested enough, just find out what each of them has tattooed on their crotches and I'll give you a full bag of product. Twenty sticks and sisters. What a deal!"

Billy smiled and added as they walked away from the bar, "But if you don't give in to temptation, you get nothing."

"Sounds like I win either way."

20

Chrissy

June 1966

Thank God her mother had already gone out before Luke got there last night. Now, how was she going to keep her out of sight tonight? Chrissy really liked him. Nita Turnova and her often lubricated words had screwed up so many things in Chrissy's life. If she wasn't careful, it was sure to happen again with Luke.

Chrissy's father had been no prize but she had always believed that he loved her. Unfortunately, he had loved a lot of people in the Slippery Rock area, most of them married women. It was difficult for Chrissy to know whether her lush of a mother had driven her father to those other women or the other women had driven her mother to the booze. All she had known of their marriage had been arguments. Nita's voice, however, had always seemed the loudest and the least concerned with Chrissy's well-being. When the divorce had happened eight years ago, Chrissy had probably been the most relieved.

She had not known last night what to expect from her blind date with the guy from Pine City. A girl who worked with her at Giant Eagle said her boyfriend knew a guy from there who was headed into the Marines on Monday and needed a date for his last weekend at home. Said he had dropped out of IUP to enlist. Chrissy had just graduated from high school and was between boyfriends, so she figured why not? She was only a year younger than her date, but she lived seven miles away and in a different school district so their paths had never crossed.

The evening had gone so well that she would have stayed out all night and slept with him if he would have asked. But he never went south of her waistline. A real gentlemen. Maybe things would be different tonight. She hoped so anyway.

But how to keep him from meeting her wine bucket of a mother? Luke said he'd be there at six to take her out to eat before going to the movie. Her mother never left for Gothchas before seven. Chrissy thought for a moment about calling Luke and suggesting that she meet him somewhere but realized she didn't have his number. In fact, she couldn't remember hearing his last name. He had not used it. Said his name was Luke. Her eyes had been satisfied with knowing only that. She had never been out with someone that good looking. Someone that smart.

A knock on her bedroom door was immediately followed by her mother's voice and then her head leaning around the door. "Chrissy?"

"Nita!" said Chrissy indignantly.

"What?"

'You always just barge right in. What if I had been in bed with somebody? I'm eighteen now. It's possible. you know."

Having sex with Luke still on her mind, Chrissy had placed the event in her bed and Nita had crashed the party.

Her mother moved into the room and said, "Well then, I guess you would have to share."

That was just the kind of response that made Chrissy cringe at the thought of Luke meeting her mom. Nita did not know about last night's date or the one scheduled for tonight. She seldom got home until well after midnight and occasionally not at all. It was three-thirty in the afternoon now and the first time they had seen each other all day.

"Especially if it's the guy you were with last night. Where did you find him?"

"What guy?" She knew it was useless to play innocent, but she hoped somehow Nita was playing games, trying to bluff some information out of her.

"The guy slutty Shirley saw you with at Putt-Putt Land."

"Oh him. Marcy set me up on a blind date. He's off to the Marines for basic training on Monday. Nothing for you to get too excited about."

"You let him in your pants?"

"Yeah, and I'm pregnant with twins already. You going to help me take care of them?"

Nita did a momentary double take before blurting out, "Don't even joke about such things. Jesus."

She waited a few moments then asked the question Chrissy knew was coming, "Goin' out with him again tonight?"

No sense lying to her. If they couldn't avoid being seen at Putt-Putt Land, somebody would spot them eating or at the movie. Didn't matter as long Nita could be avoided. "Yes."

"When's he pickin' you up, this father of my grandchildren?"

"Don't know. He was doing something with his brother and mother first."

"His father gone like your scum-sucking old man?"

"No. He's gone like dead. Died a war hero in Korea after being shot in WWII."

"Gee, I'd like to meet this kid if he wasn't going to be leavin' so soon. Good lookin' *and* the son of a war hero. Could've been a good catch for you, maybe."

"Yeah, well, Dad could have been a good catch for you if you'd been sober enough to realize it." This really wasn't what Chrissy wanted to do – get into an argument with Nita today. But it was so easy to do. Her mother had so many faults. Her life had plastered her with *kick me, I'm stupid* signs. Chrissy mostly tried to focus on the few that said *Love me, I'm your pathetic loser mother*, but her mother's mouth made it so difficult to do.

"Let's see now, when was the last time that great catch was there for *you*? Never changed your diaper. Never took you to a doctor. Never helped you with your homework. Never—"

"Never left me alone when I was five to get soused at Gotcha's. Forgot me at soccer practice how many times? Left me alone with the creepy bartender who felt me up then jerked it in front of me when I was six. No, Nita, we've played this game too many times already. You're going to lose just like you always do."

"Okay, you win. You always do. I'm a shit mother. That doesn't mean I can't want the best for you. I can still hope you find a good-looking, war-hero kind of guy who won't leave you."

Chrissy heaved a sigh just as she always did when the game was over and said what she always said, "Yes, Mom, I know you want the best for me."

Nita took a step towards her daughter only to be immediately stopped by what was added, "And the best thing for me right now is for you to leave my room."

21

Luke

July 1966

Luke pulled his footlocker next to his cot and picked up the pencil once again. He had done this several times in the last two weeks, but each time he'd let something interfere with completing the process. It wasn't that he didn't want to write home. He missed his mother and Moze a lot. But by the time he finished his letters to Chrissy, he was ready to do something other than write another letter.

He had met Chrissy two days before leaving and had immediately made up his mind that she was the one. The next night, the night before leaving for Parris Island, they'd had protected sex.

Moze had been waiting for him that night when Luke got home. "You nailed her didn't you. At least you better have. That's the only acceptable reason that will keep me from beating the pus out of you for not spending your last night here with me instead of some little brunette from Slippery Rock. Did you at least have a rubber on?"

"Yes, Daddy," said Luke emphasizing the paternal reference as he sometimes did when his older brother needed a reminder that he was being an irritant though tonight it was meant more as a joke than an expressed irritation.

In the several hours that Luke had spent with his brother that weekend, the subject of Moze's decision to finish college only came up once. Luke had told himself that he would not say anything more about it, but the reality of them all being together that weekend and the great time he'd had with them— not to mention meeting Chrissy, Luke had become sullen and withdrawn to the point where Moze put his arm around Luke's neck and squeezed it.

"Hey, Doofus!" Moze increased the pressure then let go. "Don't think for a moment I'm happy about this… that this is what I want. But that's the way it has to be. What if I had enlisted with you as we planned, and we both ended up in Vietnam and got ourselves killed? What would happen to Mom with all three of her men dead." Moze paused. "I'll go, but I can't go until you're home safe."

After several more minutes of procrastination and eating one of the cookies his mother had recently sent him, Luke began to write,

Hey Brother,

I know. I should have written to you sooner, but I hate writing. It's always been hard for me, putting my intelligence (or lack of) on paper where the words sit and stare back at me and anybody who reads them. Spoken words go into the air and vanish. Much safer.

I have been writing to Chrissy though. She writes me two or three times a week. I don't want her to lose interest so I write back.

If I'd only met her before I enlisted. What a dumbass thing to do – enlist for three years. One real Chrissy in front of me is worth a million posters of Joey Heatherton on my walls. Oh well.

The physical stuff here is a piece of cake. I'm numero uno in all the drills. No one even close. What I have trouble with the most is the D.I. All his bullshit. He likes to get in my face and spit his wet words at me. Like I'm going to be scared of him. He's so skinny and old I could… Yeah, I know. Count to ten.

Speaking of skinny, there's Martin, this black guy

from Baltimore who I've kind of adopted. His older brother was killed in Nam and his dad was killed in Korea like ours. I think that probably has something to do with why he enlisted and maybe why we get along so well. Anyway, he shouldn't be here. He takes too much shit from everybody, even his brothers. There's this cracker from Alabama who keeps needling him. The other blacks only encourage the cracker. It's like they don't want to claim Martin as one of their own. I punched the cracker in the showers and it seems like it's helped some. It wasn't a sucker punch. You know how I feel about that. I gave him the chance to apologize to Martin for calling him a "little faggot nigger" but he just laughed at me. I warned him I was going to deck him. I even counted to three out loud for him before I swung.

The one area I need to spend more time on is my shooting. I'm better than anybody else at mid-range stuff, but three guys are better at long range. Probably not much long range needed in Vietnam though.

You wouldn't believe the heat here. If you ever do enlist, don't come here in the summer. Ninety-nine degrees today. Humidity makes it feel a lot worse. If I ever complain about the heat in Pine City again, just smack me up the side of my head and yell Oorah!

Tell Mom I'm doing okay and thanks for the care package. Hope your knee is still doing okay. Can't wait to see you both after basic. Six weeks and two days (but who's counting!)

                          Luke

P.S. Would you do me a favor? It's kind of a big one. In her last letter Chrissy said her Mom is in a coma.

Would you check and see how things are with them and if there's anything you can do. Their last name is Turnova. I don't know the mom's first name. Don't make a special trip home, but the next time you're back if you get time. I'd kinda like you to meet Chrissy anyhow. See what you think of your future sister-in-law.

22

Moze

July 1966

Leave it to Luke to wait for almost six weeks to write his first letter home and then include information that Moze knew would cause their mother to worry. Not that her son hadn't been in fights before. That had been going on since grade school. What would upset her about the incident were the racial undercurrents involved. She had been born in Pine City, never lived anywhere else. You could count the number of black family names there on one hand. All of them lived on the same end of town. Had their own church.

Ann Foster was not, nor could ever be called, a racist. She had been raised a God-fearing, Jesus-loving Presbyterian and had made sure her two boys had been brought up the same way. But she watched enough television news to know that a lot of colored folks were getting tired of the way they were being treated. The violence that had occasionally been popping up on her TV screen seemed more frequent of late. In Philadelphia now, her own state. Her husband, having witnessed incidents of discrimination in WWII and then again in Korea, had told her of the blind eye the Army had used in dealing with it. She hoped that had changed in the years since, but she doubted it. What surprised her most about what was happening in the news was that so much of the trouble was in the northern cities, places where she had thought people didn't have to *learn* how to get along together.

But as much as Moze wanted to read the letter to his mother and omit the reference to Luke punching the cracker, he knew his mother would want to hold the letter in her hands and read it herself. More than once. Especially the section about Chrissy becoming a member of the family.

So, he gave the letter to her the moment he got into the house. Luke had mailed it to the IUP address that Moze had sent him. As he had expected, the wince on his mother's face told him when she reached the part about fighting.

"I am so proud of him sticking up for his friend," she said as she set the letter down on the black wooden stand inside the front door.

"That's Luke, all right," said Moze.

"What do you think about this business with the Chrissy girl? Seems like he's made his mind up awfully fast."

Moze was surprised at her reservation. Luke had always been so particular about girls. Something was always wrong with even the prettiest or the smartest or the nicest ones. His mother had often kidded her younger son that he would end up a bachelor unless he lowered his standards some because there were no perfect girls. And then just for fun she would add, "If there is one, Moze will likely find her first."

"I take it from his letter that you have not met her yet?" she asked.

"Yes, I stopped at the A&P where Luke said she works and introduced myself. She's pretty and seems nice."

"What about her mother? Is she still in a coma?"

"She said her mother died last week."

"Oh no." Ann put her hands to the edge of her apron and twisted it. "What was wrong with her?"

"Chrissy didn't seem like she wanted to talk about it. Just said it was some kind of cancer."

"Is she still living with her dad?"

"Her dad left her and her mom a long time ago."

"Poor thing. So she's had to deal with everything by herself? No brothers or sisters? Uncles or aunts?"

"I don't really know. She didn't say and I didn't ask. I did ask her to come for dinner tomorrow. Hope you don't mind. Just seemed like the right thing to do. I think Luke would really appreciate it."

"Yes, yes, of course."

* * * *

At the dining room table on Sunday, Moze's mother peppered Chrissy with so many questions that he couldn't help feel sorry for the future other Mrs. Foster. In the answers it was revealed among many other facts that Chrissy had been an average student who didn't much care for school other than playing on the club basketball team where she had been the team's leading scorer.

When she spied the old piano in the far end of the parlor, there was momentary excitement in her voice as she asked if Luke played. When Ann said that she was the one who played, Chrissy did her best to hide her disappointment.

"Do you play, Chrissy?" Ann asked.

"Yes, but I'm not very good. Nita– Mom couldn't afford for me to take lessons, so I can't read a note, but I've got an ear for where the sound comes from. A little gift from God, I guess."

"That's really something, isn't it, Moze?"

"Yeah, I've heard that some people can do that, but you're the first person I've known that can."

"It's really not that big a deal. My dad's sister can do it better than I can."

Ann suddenly became aware that both Chrissy and Moze had finished eating. "Anybody ready for a piece of the shoo-fly pie I made this morning?"

Chrissy looked at her watch. "I feel bad about this but I got a call from my boss right before I left, asking me to work at two. I didn't want to have to cancel my visit, so I asked if it would be all right if I could wait until three. I've missed so much work this last week and a half because of my mother. I think he's trying to get me some hours back."

Ann quickly got up and said, "I'll go cut you a couple of pieces to take with you and put some extra food into a container for you to take for tomorrow's supper."

"That's real nice of you, Mrs. Foster."

Turning her head back towards Chrissy on her way into the kitchen, Ann said, "Isn't any Mrs. Foster here, only some middle-age woman named Ann."

Moze rose almost as fast as his mother and said, "Chrissy, do you mind if I ride with you? I'm thumbing back to IUP this afternoon. I've got everything already to go except a piece of Mom's pie."

"Sure. If I didn't have to work, I'd take you all the way."

"Every mile helps."

* * * *

The future in-laws were barely out of the driveway and onto Route 173 when Chrissy reached over to the radio and turned it off.

"Luke said he told you about his fight with that guy from Alabama."

When she said nothing more, Moze figured she wanted his reaction. "Luke doesn't like to see people bullied. And he's not too good at working things out peacefully."

"I can't blame him for not wanting to talk much when there are two of them after—"

"Wait. *Two* of them?

"He asked me not to tell you anything about it, but I'm worried something will happen to him."

"All I got from him was that he gave the guy a chance to apologize to his friend Martin and when the guy didn't, Luke punched him."

"Yeah, but then another guy tried to grab Luke and Luke punched him too. Broke the second guy's nose." Chrissy looked at Moze and said, "The next time you write to him..." She returned her attention to the road and continued, "tell him to please be careful. From his letters

I know how much he thinks of you, looks up to you, that you've always been like a father to him."

"Sounds like Luke being Luke. I'm afraid you'll have to get used to it." Moze laughed. "He and I had a big fight my senior year when he didn't like what some guy from the crowd said about me when I got pinned during sectionals. He went right up through the crowd that was between them and stuffed his handkerchief in the guy's mouth. The guy looked like he was about sixty. I had to watch from the floor while security escorted him from the gym. I was already embarrassed at being pinned and then to hear someone in the crowd say, *At least some one in the family knows how to take care of business*. Well, that just fractured the relationship for a while." He laughed again. "But I got over it. It was just Luke being Luke. Just Luke being loyal. Those guys he fought with at Parris Island… they'll figure it out soon enough. Unless they're dumber than dead, they'll want what Martin has. If I was in a life or death situation, there's nobody I'd rather have with me than Luke Foster, especially if I'm his friend."

Chrissy reached over and took hold of Moze's hand, gave it a quick squeeze then let it go. Moze liked her. She seemed genuine. But Moze couldn't help feeling that things had moved too fast. Luke was nothing if not spontaneous. Would Luke have been as enthusiastic about Chrissy if he hadn't been leaving town? He had never been one to think much about consequences.

23

Luke

September 1966

Every day in basic Luke had obsessed over thoughts of home and Chrissy. Thirteen weeks later here he was at last. For ten days. Ten days of not taking orders covered in spit. Ten days of no responsibilities.

The first four days had been nonstop sex with Chrissy when he could get away from his mom and Moze though they had made it quite easy for him. Moze told him their mother had made it clear that neither of them would interfere, explaining that she had been Chrissy once upon a time after their father's 1942 basic Army stint at Fort Dix.

Luke had laughed at that news from Moze, but the more he thought about it, the more uncomfortable it made him. He wasn't sure he was ready to take on any role his father had played. Soldier. Husband. Father.

The soldier part he was pretty confident he could handle. He still had his advance infantry training yet at Camp Lejeune, but he'd seen nothing yet that discouraged him from engaging in combat. The way he saw it, fighting wasn't complicated. The Viet Cong or whoever the enemy would be, was to be avoided or killed. Luke didn't remember ever being afraid of another individual – except Moze, only because he could never really hurt Moze in the way that fights often required.

On the fifth day Luke decided he'd had enough of his brother's excuses for not wanting to hang out with him. A twenty-year-old Marine should be able to spend time with his brother instead of his girl.

If their mother didn't like it, so be it. He called Chrissy and told her the new plan for the evening. He would be with Moze until ten then take him home before going to her house.

The two brothers chose Pizza Hut for supper at seven. Then maybe shoot some pool at Gotchas.

While waiting for their pizza, Moze broke the evening's first extended silence. "So, Little Brother, I understand you had more than one redneck on your tail involving your friend Martin."

Luke hesitated then smiled sheepishly. "I didn't want you guys to get worried and all, but yeah, more than one."

"Three?"

"I was doin' all right with three. If it hadn't been for the fourth one— I just didn't see him coming until it was too late."

"Did you get into trouble?"

"A little. Had to toothbrush the urinals for a week."

"What about the other guys?"

"They needed a little time to ah… *recuperate*. But they got the same. Except the last guy. He had to do the walls and floor also. We're all cool with it now."

"Will any of them be with you at Lejeune?"

"Maybe two of them? I'm not sure."

"Martin?"

"I tried to talk him out of the infantry. Even the DI said he'd do what he could to get him behind a desk, but the kid's as stubborn as you are. Wants to be with me, he says."

"Well, who could blame him. His own personal bodyguard."

Luke laughed. "You remember Dicky Waters from grade school? Moved away when I went to junior high? That's who he reminds me of. He's like everybody's uncoordinated little brother."

"I hope he's smarter than mine."

"Well, yeah, that's part of Martin's problem. He *is* smarter. Smarter than just about anybody. He dropped out of college like I did.

Like I said in my letter his big brother was killed in Vietnam in February so he's decided that he's going over there and get revenge." Luke dug his wallet out of his jeans and removed a photo. "Here, this is why he needs a bodyguard."

Moze took the photo from Luke and looked at it. "Yeah, I see what you mean. That's more of a sneer than a smile."

"I'm tellin' you, Moze, the kid's got no fear. He says what he wants to say and the consequences be damned."

Luke let Moze laugh for a moment then said, "So what do you think of Chrissy?"

Moze looked in mock bewilderment. "Who?"

"You big turd! Seriously. Is she the one for me or not?"

"What the hell kind of question is that? That's your call. I think she's a great girl. My only concern is her eyesight and common sense if she thinks you're a catch."

Luke ignored his brother's words. "What about Mom? She okay with her?"

"Mom thinks she's a slut, but figures you'll never find anyone any better."

"Come on, Moze. I'm serious, man. I want your opinions."

Luke watched as his brother's face immediately lost the smile that had been there. "I think she's a great girl, but it's not my opinion that matters. I will say this though. I'm a little concerned that you're worried about what I think." Luke looked away but his brother's eyes came after him. "Are you having second thoughts?"

"No, not at all." But Luke knew he was lying to his brother. He knew because as soon as the sex ended each time, he wanted to leave, wanted to take his duffle bag and hop on a bus headed anywhere. Or at least go and hang out with Moze... even his mother. It wasn't that he *disliked* Chrissy. But being with her was not at all what he had imagined in Basic. Now their short, forced conversations always ended in extended silence once he had answered the barrage of questions

Chrissy would throw at him, trying to keep the silence away.

He felt so bad for her. She had written him more letters than he had written to her. In the beginning, he had been able to almost match her letter for letter, writing a new letter before the previous one was answered, every second or third day. The relationship delineated in their words to one another had been genuine. He was sure of it. But by the end of basic, it was all he could do to produce one a week. Still, there had been much anticipation to be with her again.

The past few days, however, the relationship was not the one that existed in their letters. At least not for him. The two people in the letters seemed to have known each other for years, could talk about anything, saw the future as real and close as the next letter.

Chrissy had poured her heart out to him when her mother had died. Until then, he'd had no idea what her relationship with her parents had been like, assuming only that her mother had been like any other mother… like his mother.

The first few letters had been so matter of fact about her mother's death, almost giving him the sense that Chrissy had been glad her mom was dead. But then the pain began to seep into her words as she realized how alone she was, how much she missed her mother.

What surprised him most though was her assumption of guilt for the way she had treated her mother, a total contradiction of the relationship she had described in her earlier letters which had placed the blame for their problems solely on her mother and her drinking.

What if I become her with our kids? she had written. *What if they treat me the way I treated her?*

The words *our kids* had, at their first reading, forced his attention from the words that followed. *He was going to have kids with Chrissy?* No. He wasn't ready for that yet. He was a Marine now. He would soon be in Vietnam fighting in a war. Maybe dying in a war like his own father.

But, at the first touch of her body when she threw her arms around his neck and pressed herself against him, forcing him back into their corporeal lives again, *our kids* became just words in a letter from someone he used to know, all concern for the future beaten down by hormones and the sweet smells of her.

"Well, no matter how you feel about her, you better make sure you're wearing a hat on your head, Doofus."

"Yes, Daddy."

Luke tried to give his best sarcastic push to his words, but they came out flat because he was thinking that this was as good a time as any to say what he had been thinking for a few days now.

"So, brother of mine, how's *your* love life been this summer? Worked through all the blind girls at IUP yet?"

"Funny guy."

"And you can't work the sympathy angle any more now that you're done with the crutches."

"Yeah, I'm thinking about renting one of those spiffy Marine uniforms now that I see how that's working for you."

"Waste of money, Big Brother. At least from the way Chrissy talks about you all the time." Luke paused and looked at the floor for several moments. Finally he said, "Would you have been interested in her if you had met her first?"

Before Moze could answer, their waitress arrived with their pizzas. "Be careful, guys, the pans are really hot."

Luke immediately jumped at the opening, all thoughts of Chrissy suddenly vaporized.

"I'm betting dollars to doughnuts they're not as hot as you."

The girl was not especially attractive and probably didn't get many comments like that one. She blushed and lost her grip on Luke's pan, allowing it to strike the other pan that was closer to Moze. No harm was done, but she apologized with embarrassment then added "not hot *or* coordinated, as you can see."

"Don't mind him," said Moze. "He just got home from Marine basic training. He didn't used to talk to girls like that."

"And don't pay any attention to him… my *much older* brother."

Her face still flushed, the waitress quickly turned and left.

"What was that all about?" asked Moze.

"Who would you rather go out with, her or Chrissy?"

"So, we're still on *that* subject. Listen to me. I'm not playing that game. If you have a problem–"

"Do you want her? Chrissy I mean. I don't think I'm ready to be what she wants me to be. I'm just Luke Foster. I'm going to be a Marine for almost another three years, and I'm feeling a little boxed in by this relationship with her." He picked up a slice of pizza and held it in front of his mouth for a few moments. "I'm just sayin' that there's no hard feelings if you would want to take her out after I leave."

Moze still had a bite of pizza in his mouth when Luke stopped talking. He finished chewing then said in that patient and deliberate manner that Luke had learned to avoid a long time ago, "What makes you think you have ownership of Chrissy? And furthermore, what makes you think I would care whether I had your permission or not." Moze took a long breath. "She is not married to you, not even engaged. Why are we even talking about her?"

"Because I don't have the balls to break it off."

"Well, you'd better find a pair because I'm not getting involved in your love life. If you want out, get out before you go back or she'll sit around and wait for your next leave."

"But what if she is the one for me? I mean all the other stuff is great. I just don't want to spend all my time with her."

"If you don't see the wrong in what you want from her, then nothing I say will help. You're talking like somebody I don't know. Now finish your pizza then this blind date is over, stranger."

In his head the idea of handing Chrissy to his brother seemed like a good move, but Luke knew his brother was right. He would eventually have to tell her how he really felt.

Just not tonight. Maybe tomorrow.

* * * *

Tomorrow came. And then another. And when the time arrived for Moze to drive Luke to the bus that would take him to Pittsburgh, Luke had said not a word to Chrissy about his doubts. He chose instead the path of least resistance. And stepping onto the bus he knew he had done the right thing. The overwhelming sense of freedom without the drama of a breakup told him so. He couldn't get to Vietnam fast enough.

Moze had not said another word to him about Chrissy, and Luke was fine with that. The two brothers parted with a handshake and a hug, not sure when or if they would ever see each other again.

However, as the bus pulled away from the curb, Luke, his window down, caught one last glimpse of Moze pointing at him and mouthing in an exaggerated way one word repeatedly, *pussy.*

"Yeah, but I'm a free pussy!" hollered Luke then he closed his window.

24

Luke

October 1966

After basic training, the eight weeks of advanced infantry training was pretty much a walk in the park. Luke had kept Martin safe except for an incident outside the mess hall a week after arrival. That, however, had been more Luke's problem than his friend's. A white Marine about the size of Martin had bumped into him on purpose which set off Martin's mouth. By the time Luke and two other Marines interfered, Martin was looking up at him with a missing front tooth. When the white kid saw Luke and Martin walk off together, he shouted at Martin in an extreme southern drawl, "I'll see y'all later queer boy when your girlfriend's not around." Luke immediately pivoted and after several quick strides grabbed the kid by the shirt and lifted him off the ground. When the kid took a swing at Luke but missed, Luke roughly returned the kid to his feet and punched him square in the mouth.

"Better be more careful with your choice of words, Marine. And as for looking for my friend later when he's alone…" Luke looked at the two teeth on the pavement and kicked at them. "I sure won't have any problem finding you again."

Luke turned to walk away just in time to see the two silver bars on the shoulder from which he proceeded to bounce.

"Excuse me, Captain sir," said Luke straightening to attention. "My fault, sir."

"What about the rest of this nonsense… your fault, also?"

"No, sir. That is, I don't think so, sir."

The rest of the half dozen or so present had immediately set themselves at attention.

The captain slowly looked around at each Marine, focusing extended attention on the two with missing teeth, then said "You two, come with me."

"Permission to speak, sir," said Luke.

"Permission to speak first," said Martin, giving Luke a quick shake of his head.

The captain looked at Martin and said, "Private Brownlee, you have one minute to clean up this mess for me in terms of the truth."

"Yes, sir, Captain, sir. No mess here sir. Just two clumsy Marines bumping into each other, sir. Private Foster is not involved, Captain, sir."

"Is that your memory of the incident, Private Collins?"

The Marine with two missing teeth and blood dripping down his chin looked at Martin, then at the captain. "Yes sir, Captain Boyles, sir. Just two spastic Marines, Captain Boyles, sir."

"Anybody else here see things any differently because I'm pretty sure *I* saw things differently?"

A fractured chorus of *No, sir, Captain Boyles, sir,*'s replied.

Several seconds of silence followed before the captain spoke again. "Okay. have it your way." He turned his attention back to Martin and Collins. "Now, both of you dumb shits get yourselves down to the infirmary and see what they can do for you. I don't want to see either one of you again, is that clear?"

Both privates replied in unison, "Yes sir, Captain Boyles, sir."

And that had been the last of anything out of the ordinary the entire eight weeks.

* * * *

The letter to Moze with Luke's account of the incident had also included an apology to his brother for his behavior while on leave. Luke had yet to receive a reply which had him bothered. That was not like Moze. He had always been one to let go, to forgive and forget all the stupid stuff Luke had done over the years. Luke had written a second letter to him a few weeks later which had produced the same result.

Luke had also written two letters to his mother and received a reply for each. Whatever had Moze pissed, he had, at least, kept it to himself.

Chrissy's letters, though not as numerous as the ones he had received in basic, still arrived a couple of times a week. He saw no difference in her words than before. She still loved him and wanted to get married. If Moze had squealed on him, it hadn't apparently bothered her.

Luke did his best to respond to each letter. Maybe it was the guilt of misleading her, or maybe it was just easier to keep up with her pace since she wasn't writing so often. Whatever the explanation, he felt better about the relationship.

When he received his orders, he found out he was headed to Camp Pendleton in California. He would officially find out where he was going to be assigned after he got there, but everyone knew where riflemen went from Pendleton. His job for tonight was to write a letter to each of the three people in his life who cared about him and give each of them his new address. He had no idea how long he would be in Pendleton, but it seemed likely that the next letters he received might be read in Vietnam. Or possibly, never read at all. The one he wanted to read most though would be one from Moze, telling him everything was going to be okay between them.

* * * *

The flight to Pendleton was long. Three layovers long. He tried to sleep, but all four legs of the flight were in daylight. Too much on his mind to take daytime naps. One stewardess seemed to go out of her way to make sure everything was all right for him and the other twenty or so Marine and army personnel on the plane. Maybe she thought he was cute, but the more likely explanation, as he saw it, was that she knew where he was going. West bound flights to San Diego or LA or San Fran for guys in uniform were probably no brainers. Maybe she'd had a brother or relative or boyfriend who had made the same trip and returned home in the belly of a transport plane.

Being suspended thirty thousand feet in the air as he flew over the Grand Canyon, he could still comprehend the magnificence of it, but then a mass of clouds stole it almost as quickly as it had appeared.

He suddenly found himself thinking of his father. Had he flown to the coast on his way to Korea in 1950? Maybe he had seen the canyon also. For sure he hadn't seen it on the way home. Because Luke had signed on for three years, who knew how many times he'd get to see the canyon again as he moved between assignments. Unless his would also be one way.

"Please fasten your seatbelt, Marine. We're descending now," said a different stewardess than the one he had taken notice of earlier. Despite the daylight still spilling onto his lap, he had been asleep.

Because of gaining three hours in the air, it was only eight o'clock by the time his bus rolled into Pendleton. Although it had been dark for the last two hours, the base was lit up by a multitude of high pole lights, making the unloading area seem as bright as day.

The ten other Marines on the flight out had been joined by twenty more at the bus station in San Diego. Luke, being one of the first to board the bus, was directed to the rear where two other Marines already were seated. They evidently knew each other from basic training and in Luke's opinion were about as mature as junior high kids. The two-hour bus ride that followed became almost more than he could bear. But, after his close call at Lejeune, he had made up his mind that he would not get into any more trouble, so he did his best to ignore them.

Their existence, however, soon became part of what was to become a defining moment in his life, a moment that would set him on a course that, as he would look back on it later, affected his life as much as his brother's knee operation had changed his brother's life.

At the door of the bus, Luke stopped to position his duffle bag so he could descend the few steps to the parking lot when one of the two remaining Marines behind him shoved the other in one last act of immaturity before setting foot on Pendleton. The Marine closer to Luke knocked him into his bag, not yet completely shifted. The bag stuck for a moment in the exit way, causing Luke to lose his balance and fall forward with the bag His right foot momentarily caught in the gap on the door's hinged side, which sent the rest of his body twisting down the steps until his left knee slammed onto the pavement.

Lying there, writhing in pain, his only thought focused on getting to his feet and beating the idiots behind him to a pulp. He put his arms out and tried to push himself up using the leg that didn't hurt as much, but he instead collapsed in pain.

With great concern the Marine who had initially hit him bent over and said, "Jesus, man, I'm sorry!"

Luke clenched his right fist and with his left hand grabbed the kid by the shirt front. One punch, that's all he wanted to throw. Just one never-to-be-forgotten punch for the pain. But the force used to grab the Marine's shirt only brought him down on top of Luke. The kid's buddy quickly helped him up and the two of them took cover among the others. Because the bus had arrived ten minutes early, the sergeant who was supposed to meet the new Marines missed the main event, but arrived in time to sort the situation and get Luke transported to the infirmary.

25

Luke

November 1966

"I hope you're not planning on getting' a purple heart for that, you clumsy-ass fool."

Luke rolled over in his infirmary bed at the sound of Martin's voice and slowly forced himself into a sitting position on the side of the bed, letting his feet rest on the floor.

"Where the hell did you come from, you cracker's dream?"

"I got in this morning and immediately went lookin' for you. What happened?"

"Two Marines I never saw before were goofing around getting off the bus and I ended up on the pavement. The doc says my right leg just has some ligaments sprained but the x-rays show my cartilage is a mess in my left knee. It'll have to have surgery but not until the other one is strong enough to handle all my weight. The operation for the cartilage will put me on crutches for six weeks just like my brother was. Then probably another month after that before I can go back to full duty." Luke looked away from his pal. "He said it might be as much as four months' total."

"Four months! Oh man."

"I know. I'm really sorry. But you'll be all right. You don't need me. I can't even get off a bus without getting hurt."

The room was quiet for a moment until Martin said, "Maybe I can try to pull some duty here until you're ready. You're gonna need somebody to look after you while you're on crutches, right?" His mood shifted away from disappointment. "I can use your injuries as an example of how incapable you are without me."

"Sure. You can try it, but don't count on it."

"So, you got to stay here while you wait for the operation?"

"I don't know how long it'll be. That chair over there is it for now." Luke pointed to the wheelchair sitting to his immediate right.

"Nice wheels, dude. You been in it yet?" Before Luke could answer, Martin said, "Come on. Get in. I'll take you for a ride. I'm hungry. Is there a cafeteria here?"

"I don't know. They brought me breakfast this morning."

Martin took control of the wheelchair and put it in front of Luke. "Let me give you a hand."

Out in the hall Martin got directions to the cafeteria from a nurse. Five minutes later they were seated at a table, eating.

"See what I mean. You need me, man. I'm supposed to get my papers today. I'm goin' to do my best to get the orders changed to stay here. Bein' signed up for three years, maybe they'll give me a break. They have plenty of time to get this nigger's ass into Nam for a year, right?"

"Yeah, maybe, but if anybody can take a situation that might favor that, but instead put him into a jungle by nightfall, it's you."

"No, no, no. I'll be good. I'll kiss cracker ass if I have to."

Luke laughed. "I'd pay good money to see that."

The two of them sat and talked for another half an hour then even longer back in Luke's room until the doctor came in and asked Martin to leave while he examined Luke. Martin decided he'd just say goodbye, promising to be back as soon as he talked his way out of whatever orders he was getting.

But Martin did not return. Two weeks later Luke received a brief letter that had been written the same day as they had been together in the infirmary.

Hey Buddy,

How's it hanging? Yeah, I know. I was supposed to come back and tell you my news, but they wouldn't let me. Said I was supposed to have been there two hours earlier which is true. The guy wouldn't even listen to me about me wanting to get a change of orders. I was supposed to be on a cargo transport plane to Da Nang in 45 minutes, so I didn't have time to go back to the infirmary. You'll have to get along without me for a while.

I just got my final orders about an hour ago. I'm still in Da Nang but I'm headed south to someplace called Hoi An. Some infantry bunch. That was the plan all along. To kill me some of them bastards that got my brother.

I don't have much else to say, I guess. Hope you get better fast, but if you're going to be there another four months, chances are we're not going to end up together, so I won't be able to save your sorry white ass every time somebody starts shooting at you. You get better my friend and maybe we'll run into each other in some rice paddy somewhere in another six months.

I'll keep you up to date on how many of those gooks I destroy, so if you end up somewhere else let me know so I can get a letter to you. I used the infirmary for this letter. Hope you got it.

Martin

* * * *

Two weeks later, the pain from Luke's torn cartilage had lessened, flaring only when the pieces randomly shifted when bearing weight. He was very willing to deal with that situation to get out of the wheelchair and onto crutches. He just had to keep his other leg, the one with the bad ligaments, weight free until it could get its strength back. The doctor told him this morning that hopefully it would only be another couple of weeks before he could get the cartilage pieces removed.

Luke sat in his hospital room wondering once more why he'd not had a reply yet to either of the two letters sent to Moze since leaving home, and it had been a week now since he last heard from Chrissy.

A knock on his door interrupted his thoughts.

"Door's open."

The head that came around the door was on a captain's uniform.

Luke grabbed his crutches and started to get up.

"At ease, Marine."

Luke saw the name on the uniform and said, "Thank you, Captain Mowrey, sir."

"Mind if I sit down?"

"Please do, sir." Luke propped his crutches against the wall by his chair and eased himself back down.

"Doc says you're healing okay, but how do you feel?"

"I'm doing fine, sir. Just bored as all get out."

The captain chuckled. "Well, that's what I'm here to talk to you about. Sure seems like a waste of your time and the Corps' time to have you on the sideline so long. Doc says you'll be close to another three months before we can get you back into shape, so I'm thinking how best to use you, and this is what I've come up with. Let's see what you think. I don't generally offer options to a Marine when I give him his orders, but this is something a little unusual.

"Your file says you were in college when you enlisted. How was that working out for you?"

Luke had no idea where the captain's question was headed. The hesitation in his response and the look of confusion brought a smile to the captain's face.

"No right or wrong answer here, Private Foster."

"The only reason I went was to play football. I wasn't doing very well until my big brother told me he'd let me quit and enlist with him if

I got my grades up. Made dean's list second semester."

"That's says a lot about you, young man."

Luke laughed. "Yeah, I got the grades up then he flunked his physical because he tore the cartilage in one of *his* knees." He laughed again. "At least I was smart enough to let the Marine Corp pay me while I have my surgery."

"So, is he in the corps yet?"

"No. Mom talked him into staying in college. Our dad was killed in the Korean War. Said she didn't want all of us dead."

Captain Mowrey said with much gravity, "We're going to do everything we can to make sure your mother doesn't get any more flags." He paused to allow his words to hang for a moment.

"Everybody probably thinks that the only thing the Marines are doing in Vietnam is killing the North Vietnamese and the Viet Cong. Not true. We have a program that's been going on for over a year now that is trying to bring peace to the villages in the countryside. It's called the Combined Action Program." He smiled and said, "Used to be called CAC for Combined Action Company but the locals pointed out to us that the VC were making fun of the name CAC. Evidently it phonetically sounds like the Vietnamese word for cock, so we made a bit of a change.

"Most of the Marines in the program get only a few weeks of training for it when they get to Da Nang. Some basic Vietnamese language phrases, information about their culture and religion, stuff CAP Marines need to know about the people. We send a squad with a Navy corpsman into a village and they partner up with a squad of local militia called Popular Forces or PF's for short, and live in the village. Our guys train the PF's in basic rifleman skills and try to get them prepared to defend themselves and the village. The Marines help out wherever they can… fixing what needs fixed, helping with the crops or fishing, even teaching school when there's no one around to do it. In short CAP Marines do anything that will make lives easier, better, safer for the villagers. The Navy corpsman helps with the local medical problems. Most of the people in the village are women and children and old men. The young men are either in the army, with the VC, disabled, or dead.

"At night the CAP Marines spend time keeping the VC away from the villages. No more intimidating visits or confiscating their rice and other supplies. So, you *will* get shot at. The program has met with very good results." The captain removed a pamphlet from his clipboard and handed it to Luke. "Here's some info for you to check out later."

"Now, what I see here for you is a great opportunity to get way ahead of the curve, so to speak. We have a Vietnamese language school up at Monterrey that you could attend while you're recovering from your operation. We'd still have you do the CAP course in Da Nang when you finally get to Nam, but, if you study your ass off here and get good at Vietnamese, I'm going to see about getting you knocked up a grade or two because you will be a Marine of great value to us. You could teach in the village, help with interrogation of prisoners, liaise with ARVN, translate enemy communication... anything involving knowledge of the language is hard to come by over there. I was there for a year and I can't tell you how much time was wasted waiting for a translator... a *good* translator."

He waited for his words to sink in, waited so long that Luke wasn't sure if he was expected to make a response. Finally, the captain said, "After your two weeks of school in Da Nang, we'll require you to have a few months of field experience with a combat company. We can't very well put you into a village where you will be patrolling with your squad and PF's without ever having been in combat."

"I understand, sir.

"So, Private Foster, what do think of my plans for you?"

"Well, sir, what little Vietnamese I've heard sounds like it would be a really hard language to learn. But I think I'd be crazy not to give it a try. Especially if it means a higher rank and pay grade."

"Ace your class, stay out of trouble, and I think I can get you bumped up to lance corporal for sure."

"I'll be grateful for whatever you can do."

The captain extended his hand. Remaining seated, Luke offered his in return and it was immediately seized aggressively. "Great. Look forward to seeing you succeed, son. We need you. I'll stay in touch with the doctor and get back to you as to when you can start. We'll probably wait on the particulars of the language business until post op but I can get you some materials on the culture for you to start on immediately." The captain pumped Luke's hand one last time and released it.

"Thank you, sir."

"Good luck with the knees." And then he was gone.

Luke sat in the chair and thought, *What the hell just happened? Lance corporal? For just going to school?*

But now he had to learn Vietnamese. Had to sit in a classroom again. Had to study and do homework and take tests.

However, this time it would be part of his job. He would be getting paid for it... sort of. Even if he didn't get an A, he'd still likely get a promotion to private first class.

If he turned it down, he'd likely get some desk assignment until he healed and have to learn a bunch of stuff anyhow. And he'd still be a private. And he'd likely not get another chance to be in that CAP business. It did sound like something he'd like. Not get shot at as much. Do something positive.

Yeah, he guessed he'd give it a go.

* * * *

Two days later Luke was in his chair, looking through a book about Vietnamese culture that a hospital orderly had brought him an hour earlier, when the same orderly knocked at his open door again. Before Luke could get to his feet, the orderly handed him a piece of mail then quickly left.

This one was from his brother, first letter he'd received from him since returning from leave. Finally, he thought as he hurriedly tore it open.

Hey Little Brother,

So you just had to outdo me, huh. Both knees!

I hate to tell you this but Mom said she's glad for what happened. Says the longer it takes for you to get to Vietnam the better. What the hell are they going to do with you while you get things back to normal?

Okay. Enough chit chat. Now I've got to ruin your day. You left something here when you got on that bus. Don't worry. Chrissy's going to take good care of it until you get back. She should have been the one to tell you, but she wanted the news to come from me.

That's right. I wanted you to be the first to know that I'm going to be.... an UNCLE! Uncle Moze. Sounds pretty strange to me, but I'll get used to it. Better than being a FATHER, Doofus.

So now what?

I'm not going to get on your case. It's your life. It's Chrissy's life. But what you left behind is going to change everything around here. Mom is thrilled and has already told Chrissy that she is to move in with us until she is able to take care of the baby when it gets here.

Chrissy is, on the other hand, a mess. That's why this letter is coming from me instead of her. She's sure you're going to tell her to get rid of it.

Are you? I can tell her if that's what you want. We can tell Mom that something went wrong. I'm not meaning that you should tell her to get rid of it. That's not my place. If you want her to have an abortion, I'm certain she will. But she'll want to have it done soon.

The impression you gave me of your feelings toward Chrissy when you were home... has anything changed?

Whatever you decide - you must choose what will be best for everyone.

I know you will.

Moze

When the letter slipped from his hand and fell to the floor, Luke let it be, his eyes staring at the empty space where it had just been. It wasn't until some PA announcement a minute or so later that he lifted his head and let it fall against the back of his chair. His palms came together with his fingertips just touching the base of his chin, as if in prayer. But there most certainly were no deals to be made with God on this topic. The matter had already been decided somewhere in the words from his brother.

You must choose what will be best for everyone.

That was exactly what his brother *would* say! Not *best for yourself*, or *best for Chrissy*, or *best for the baby*. No, you didn't grow up with father figure Moses Foster, being told to do things the *easy* way. This was not going to be a decision that he would sit and debate for gut-wrenching hours. He had made the decision the moment the sentence was presented to him, then reinforced with the next line, *I know you will.* The contemplation that started, even before the letter hit the floor, involved only the *consequences* of his decision.

Maybe his parenthood would end somewhere in those required six weeks of combat.

26

Tomas Calgretti

June 1987

"Okay, thank you, Tom, for being so patient while our video guy fixed the problem with his camera. He assures me that we will not have to stop again. You had just started to tell us about the most memorable experience from your first serious firefight in June of 1967. You said it was in the north somewhere?"

"Yes. Quang Tri Province, not far from the DMZ. I had been shot at several times before, but this was my first all-hell-breaking-loose one. Let me give you a little background first. I can't talk about this particular day without remembering somebody. I haven't seen him or talked to him since about a week after the night in question, so if by some chance, Luke, you happen to see this someday, I sure would appreciate seeing you again, man. Okay, thanks for letting me work that in."

The interviewer, Bobby 4T (tell-them-the-truth) Wardle, an on-air personality at a popular Denver TV station, quickly added, "We're hoping a lot of people get to see these tapes with the stories of our vets from the Vietnam War. Of course, the people of Denver will be able to see all of ours during the next few weeks, and PBS is going to pick from each area some to show nationally. Who knows? Maybe you'll hear from Luke..."

"I can't remember his last name, but he'll remember Calgretti, the private that never let him out of his sight. See, a lot of guys like me, when we got to Nam and got put into a new unit, we'd look for the guy we wanted next to us when things went south. Me and this big dude from Philly met in Okinawa. He was there finishing up an R&R and I was in a holding pattern waiting for deployment to Da Nang.

"I don't remember what the deal was, but Big John was a lance corporal on his second tour and he took exception to Luke also being a lance corporal after only having been in country for two weeks. I'd already decided that Big John was going to be the guy to get me through my tour. After all, he'd survived one tour, so he was doin' something right. Anyway, he starts raggin' on Luke about how he must a been a real ass kisser to have that rank so soon. And you could see that it was starting to get under Luke's skin. Well, finally he's practically having to stand on his toes so he can get right in Big John's face and then he starts speaking Vietnamese. I mean he's running the words at him a hundred miles an hour. Now, Big John's getting angry, also, cause he don't know what Luke's sayin'. Luke, he just all of a sudden stops the Vietnamese and says, "Would you like me to translate that for you, big fella?" Big John grabs Luke by the neck with that big paw of his and starts lifting him off the ground. I mean he's got Luke nose to nose. So what does Luke do? He grabs Big John by the back of the head and starts whipping his own head side to side until Big John can't hold him anymore and drops him. Then Luke starts shakin' his head again and pretty soon he's sneezing, showering the big guy with all kinda of crap from the nose and mouth. Big John takes a step back, then Luke says, 'I told you I was going to start sneezing, then I told you I was going to put you on your ass, Lance Corporal Shaw.' And then Luke drops him with one punch, like it had come from a canon. That was it for me. The guy drops the toughest dude I know *and* can speak Vietnamese. The King is dead, long live the King. You know what I mean?"

Thomas Calgretti gave a quick nervous laugh then continued. "I expected Big John to get up and beat Luke to a pulp, but he just sat on the floor with this glaze in his eyes.

"Two weeks later our whole platoon's out on a mission because somebody else's recon is sure there's a bunch of NVA, you know, regular North Vietnamese Army, making their way from Laos towards our guys up near Con Thien. We left with nearly two hours of daylight so we could be in place without thrashing around in the dark. Our own recon had been there the day before and checked this place out. It looked like an old camp with fox holes scattered around the perimeter. A shack–"

Bobby 4T interrupted, "So this was not on a trail?"

"No, we never walked trails. Captain Kildoo kept us in the bush as much as he could. It was a pain in the ass, especially for the guys workin' the machetes, but we rotated it some. We never lost anybody under that guy. He knew how Charlie loved to booby trap the trails. Hell, we never had one go off until this particular night.

"Recon had checked all of the fox holes, but they had missed a foot-deep hole covered with branches and leaves. Goober Harris–"

"Wait. The guy's name was Goober?"

"Yeah, he never told us why. But it doesn't take a lot of imagination to come up with likely reasons, does it. As I was sayin', Goober stepped into that hole that was covered up. Right away he knows he's screwed because he feels the switch under his foot. I was about ten feet away from him and in the moonlight reflecting from his face, I will never forget the look that was there as he struggled to keep his balance with his other foot without liftin' the one on the switch. The three of us, me, Big John and Luke, we'd all heard the click."

"The click? It was a dud then?"

"No, sir. It weren't no dud. That click meant that Goober would most likely die and the other three of us end up missing a few pieces the moment he lifted his foot. That thought and what to do about it had locked my brain down for just about two seconds. That was about all of the time it took for me to see Luke start movin' backwards– like he was tryin' to put some distance between himself and Goober in case the mine exploded. I gotta admit I took a few steps back myself before I understood what Luke was doing.

"After maybe ten yards he stops his retreat, takes off his pack, drops his rifle, and hollers at Goober, 'Get rid of your gear and keep your goddamn foot on that switch, Goober. Don't you move a muscle until I move you. You understand me?' Goober started to say something… I think maybe he was going to argue, but Luke interrupted him with a loud, 'Good, now get your pack off and toss your gun.' Goober did what he was told, and then Luke says to me and Big John, and everybody else nearby, 'You guys probably want to back up some and hit the ground.' And we did.

"Luke starts running at Goober and launches himself, legs spread in a vee, taking Goober with him in the most beautiful tackle I've ever seen."

"So… anybody get hurt?"

"Just Luke. A piece of shrapnel 'bout an inch long in one of his thighs."

"Wow! That's a hell of a story. Sounds like he should have gotten some kind of medal for that."

"He did. A bronze star and a Purple Heart."

Bobby 4T chuckled, "No wonder that day sticks in your memory."

"Hey, Bobby, I'm just gettin' started. That day did not end there.

"The mine obviously exploded the moment Luke pulled Goober and his foot off the trigger switch. And then, oh man, it was like that first firecracker going off in some rich guy's Fourth of July celebration. The NVA were maybe three hundred meters away, close enough that they had a trailing squad nearby that probably heard us talking before the mine went off. Most of us near Goober hadn't even gotten off the ground before the first tracers came flyin' by. And then, well, everything else came flyin' by. We all went scramblin' for those fox holes and started returning fire. The guys with the big guns got set up and started doin' their thing. We'd have felt a lot better about things if we hadn't had those recon reports about the NVA numbers, and we'd obviously lost the advantage of an ambush.

"Captain Kildoo calls for air support. All we had to do was hold out for fifteen minutes or so. Meantime, you cannot imagine the noise of their fire coming in and ours going out. That was my first time for anything more than a few snipers.

"Then all of sudden it got real quiet. Somebody said he thought he heard a bird. Then somebody started shouting in Vietnamese not fifteen yards away from us. Immediately Luke screams at us not to shoot at the voice, and right away he starts crawling in that direction. A couple of minutes, and he's back with what looks like a twelve-year-old VC, black clothes and all. Luke had the kid's rifle. Somebody had gone for Kildoo and he was there by the time Luke was back. Luke tells him the VC kid was surrendering. The NVA had conscripted him that afternoon. This was his home area and he didn't want to go with them. He hated the NVA. They'd taken all three of his older brothers and they never came back.

"This VC kid is speaking a mile a minute telling Luke that the NVA numbered about 500 and were already leaving to avoid the air strikes they knew would come. They had not wanted to engage but had told the trailing squad to deal with us. The kid says he lit out when the chaos started.

"Captain Kildoo radios in new coordinates and not two minutes later those birds put down a carpet of bombs and napalm that brought up the stage lights. A bunch of secondaries told us the new numbers Captain called in were money and that the survivors were goin' to be minus some ammo."

Calgretti stopped talking in what appeared to be a moment of duress then added, "The platoon lost two men that night. I didn't know them much because they were in a different squad, but I've often wondered how much more sideways that night would have gone if Luke... Foster, that was his name, if Luke Foster hadn't been there."

"You got split up later, I take it?"

"Not because I wanted to, I'll tell you that. About month later he gets assigned to what was called a Combined Action Program unit. Just a squad of guys and a medic that go live by a ville and keep the VC away. I tried to get assigned with him but got turned down."

"Speaking of VC, what happened to the kid?"

"Luke kept him, like guys sometimes kept stray dogs. Luke found a home for him with one of our hooch cleaners. Then when Luke went to the CAPS, he took the kid with him to his village."

"How did that work out for you? Did you ever see Foster again? Obviously, you got through the war without him."

"No. And I've been damn grateful I didn't get to go with him. From what I've read, those CAP Marines had some of the highest mortality rates of anybody. My gut tells me he made it, though. You had to be around him to understand."

27

Wally Moses Foster

March 26, 1967

Chrissy looked at the other two people in the dining room with their heads down in prayer. If it were up to her, there would not be this ritual every mealtime. It was never done in her childhood. Her parents weren't the praying type. Not that she hadn't heard God and Jesus mentioned most days. Their names just weren't associated with prayer. She was in kindergarten before she discovered that you didn't have to be angry to speak their names, didn't have to be throwing something or getting hit or slamming a door. Even when she came to understand the absolute power most people believed to be held by God and Jesus, Christine Turnova remained outside the influence of the church and its followers.

So, while Moze and his mother finished up their expressions of gratitude and love and prayed for the safety of Luke, Chrissy was summoning her courage to deliver the latest news in today's letter from him. As of the writing of the letter nearly ten days ago, her lover, their son and brother was now officially a combat veteran.

"Amen," she added a beat behind the other two.

Her next words sneaked into the room like a distant relative not knowing how he would be received. "I got a letter from Luke today." Chrissy always took the mail from the box. She was especially diligent this past week since Moze had been home for Easter break. If there would be something in a letter that might be upsetting to Ann, Chrissy would rather not have the letter's existence known.

Right away Chrissy picked up on Ann's apprehension. "He's okay," Chrissy quickly added.

"But something's wrong," said Luke's mother asserting her words as fact.

"No, no. Nothing's wrong. It's just that he was shot at for the first time. His platoon or company or whatever it's called. They were on some mission and were ambushed. He said he's pretty sure he killed a couple Viet Cong. He said he thinks he did all right for his first time in a firefight and to tell you both not to worry and that he's going to be okay."

"Of course, he's going to be okay, Honey. That's one thing about our Luke... he knows how to take care of himself. Isn't that right, Moze?"

"Isn't anybody better. I'm surprised Ho Chi Minh hasn't surrendered yet. Probably doesn't know Luke's there."

All of them forced a laugh and started eating.

Ann was the first to speak again. "Chrissy, have you told Luke about the due date being moved up?"

The cuckoo in the clock on the wall jumped into the room and sang six times then disappeared.

Chrissy waited gratefully until the noise stopped.

"Not yet."

"You wait much longer there'll be nothing to tell... Sweetie." Ann had added the term of endearment at the last moment after hearing echoes of irritation in her own voice.

Chrissy lowered her head and said, "I just don't want the situation to be a distraction. You know, especially now that people are shooting at him."

"Of course. You're right, Honey."

"Don't either of you waste any time worrying about Lucas Foster being distracted. When he's in a fight, his mind only thinks about winning." Moze stuck the forkful of turkey that had been dangling in front of him into his mouth. "Wow, Mom, that is really tender. Sure beats the food at IUP."

"I doubt that's much of a compliment."

"Okay, let me try again. "That's the best turkey I ever had."

"That's better."

* * * *

Moze had been coming home each weekend for the last month since Chrissy had stopped working. Her car at the house allowed him to take his mother's car back and forth to IUP. The baby's arrival had been rescheduled for two weeks earlier than the original prediction so his being at home each weekend or being able to hop in the car and be at the hospital within an hour and a half from IUP made all of them more comfortable.

At home, when he wasn't in his room working on papers or studying, he and Chrissy spent most of the time together, sometimes in the presence of his mother but often by themselves. There always seemed to be something to talk about or something on TV to watch.

Moze had become Chrissy's confidant and best friend, someone to listen to her fears concerning Luke. She was sure he didn't love her and sure he was going to die. Moze had tried to make light of her fears, joking that if the latter fear came true, the first one didn't matter. But Chrissy's one character flaw that Moze wished he could change was her lack of humor. So, he decided early on that any attempt at humor should not involve Luke. After all, he realized, he had hardly ever known her when she hadn't been alone and pregnant. Mostly he felt sorry for her. Luke had invited her into his life, impregnated her, then left her with strangers.

Moze loved his brother but Luke had always come up short when it came to dealing with responsibility. Moze feared that much of that character flaw was rooted in his own willingness to fix things for his brother, accepting the role of father and brother but really only knowing how to be the brother. They were too close in age for there to be discipline other than the rare physical guidance. The great majority of the time Luke just did what his brother told him to do because he accepted the fact that Moze knew what was best.

Despite the occasional consequences of Luke's fiery temper, Moze never viewed his brother as a failure. He was in fact proud of him. Luke's heart was as big as their mother's, and although he sometimes took the circuitous path, he mostly ended up in the right place. That's what Moze was hoping for now. What bothered him the most was that he did not know where the right place was. Over the last nine months or so he had become very close to Chrissy and had no doubt what she wanted... what would make her happy. It was Luke who had him baffled.

Like the previous three Saturday nights, this one was spent in front of the TV with Chrissy and his mother. A minute or so before ten Moze got up and changed the channel to KDKA so they could watch Gunsmoke, one of everybody's favorites.

"I just read in the paper today that CBS is moving Gunsmoke to Monday night next year. I guess I won't be watching it from... here."

As he was finishing his sentence, his attention shifted to Chrissy jumping out of her seat beside his mother on the couch and hurrying back the hallway.

Ann looked at Moze for an explanation then suddenly seemed to understand. "I better get back to her."

Moze started to get up also, but his mother stopped him with her words, "No. You stay put. Just be ready."

"Be ready for what?"

"A nephew or a niece."

A minute later Moze heard his mother calling to him. "Moze!"

He jumped to his feet. "What is it?"

"Go upstairs and get Chrissy's suitcase next to her dresser."

And so began the only bookless all-nighter of Moze's college career. It ended sometime after seven the next morning with him holding a healthy baby boy, Wallace Moses Foster.

* * * *

Moze had gone home at a little after 7:30, hoping to get a few hours of sleep. But the few hours ended up being six. Surprised that his mother hadn't been home yet, he took a shower, had a bowl of cereal, then headed back to the hospital. He would sit with Chrissy awhile before heading back to college.

When he entered the hospital room, Chrissy was sitting in an easy chair holding the baby. She must have seen him do a quick search of the room with his eyes. "She just left. I tried to get her to leave all morning but she insisted that I sleep, which I didn't." She paused and lovingly looked at her child. "I think the real reason she wanted me to sleep was so she could hold Wally. The nurse tried to get her to give him up several times, but she would have none of it."

"She will be such a comfort to you in the coming weeks," Moze said as he moved to the foot of the bed and set down his mother's camera.

"Oh my god, I can't imagine doing this without her. I don't have a clue what I'm supposed to do." She looked down at her child and said, "Isn't he scary looking. Sooo tiny. Like he could break or die at any moment if I do the wrong thing."

"Hey! Finally, you are making jokes! You haven't gotten to know Ann Foster if you think she's going to let anything happen to her grandson."

Chrissy forced a smile but continued looking at her baby. "You've been as much a comfort to me as your mother. I feel so blessed to have the both of you."

Moze moved directly beside Chrissy and said, "Anything for my family, and you are family, Chrissy." He bent down with outstretched hands and Chrissy immediately offered her son to him. "You and this little guy will have me to watch out for you as long as you need me." He lifted the baby, carefully cradling his head with his right hand. "What do you think? Who's he look like? Me or Luke?"

"Neither of you. He's too pretty so it must be me."

Baby Wally spastically waved both his tiny fists then did the same with his legs. An unpleasant odor followed sounds that announced to Moze that it was time to return Wally to his mother.

Stopping the return, Chrissy put up her hands and said, "Last one to touch him. That's what my aunt always said."

Moze held Wally in front of Chrissy until he decided that she might be serious.

When he pulled him back against his chest, Chrissy smiled and said as she reached out to him, "Here, you big baby. So much for watchin' out for us."

Quickly Moze placed the baby in her hands.

Chrissy pushed her call button and smiled, "The nurse told me I had one more day of part-time motherhood since I put in six hours of labor last night."

A minute later an aide had Wally on the cart that she had brought with her and was removing the disposable diaper. Both Chrissy and Moze took mental notes as they watched her clean up the mess and put the new diaper into place. Chrissy's earlier playful rebuke had stung Moze enough that he would not shrink from that responsibility again.

When the aide had left the room, Moze took the camera from the bed and said, "Okay, it's time for some photos of Mommy and her baby. One for Granny Ann, one for Mommy, one for me, and one to send to Daddy. I put a brand-new roll of film in the camera before I left."

Moze opened the drapes to get as much light as possible into the room then snapped the photos. With her free hand Chrissy immediately reached up and latched onto the camera. "My turn, Uncle Moze." She handed Wally to Moze and tentatively stood up, the camera in one hand and the arm of the chair in the other. "Now let me figure this out a moment. Which button do I press?"

"It's a really cheap camera so there's only the one."

"This one?"

"Do you see any others?"

"Okay, smile, smart ass."

When he started to hand Wally back to her, she stopped him. "No, no. Everyone gets one of these also." Chrissy took three more photos of him holding Wally then put the camera back onto the bed.

"Keep the camera here and get four shots of Mom with Wally when she comes back. Then use the rest of the roll on Wally by himself. Mom can take it to McCann's tomorrow and tell him we need it back by Saturday. That way I can mail them to Luke before I go back to IUP next Sunday. McCann's brother will do a rush job in house if we pay an extra three bucks.

When Chrissy didn't respond to his directive, Moze added. "Okay?"

"Sure."

"Something wrong?"

"Not really." She paused. "I guess I had forgotten you're leaving today."

"It's only for five days."

"Sure. I understand. But you will be back Friday, right?" She looked up from the baby and gave Moze a very small smile.

"Of course. But Granny Ann is the one you'll want this week."

"I know. But it's not the same without you." Chrissy heard the neediness in her voice and saw how uncomfortable Moze suddenly looked. "You being a man and all. Ann and I are just a couple of helpless females." Chrissy finished her words with a smirk that ended in a full grin.

The grin helped, but Moze still wanted to leave. First, he needed to get Luke back into the conversation, remind Chrissy that Luke just a few months ago had promised to marry her.

"How about I call the Red Cross when I get back to my apartment this evening and see if they can get a message to Luke to let him know he has a son? Not that I have to do it. You are welcome to do it yourself."

"No. I would appreciate you doing it. I'd have to get to a pay phone in here someplace and get a bunch of change and – no, please, you do it."

"What were Wally's official stats again?"

"Six pounds, ten ounces, nineteen inches long, brown hair, brown eyes – at least they are now."

"Okay. I'll call Mom tomorrow and see how you're doing." Still holding the baby, he moved closer to Chrissy and, though he knew he shouldn't, the overwhelming feeling of pity for her demanded that he kiss her on her forehead. Immediately he retreated from her as he said, "Let me pull the curtains. You get back into bed and try to get some sleep. I'll keep Wally with me here in the chair for a while then give him to a nurse when I leave."

"Sleep sure sounds good," she said as she gingerly got into bed and under the covers.

Moze took his place in the chair and watched as the fidgeting creature in his arms gradually settled into sleep. He wondered if he'd ever have a child of his own. Moze was certain that fatherhood was something he could do well. Luke? Only time would tell.

"Thanks, Moze." Her back towards him, Chrissy's words were almost imperceptible. "You'll make a great dad."

"I know." It was not the first time she had seemed to hear his thoughts. Coincidence? Of course. But he should nevertheless keep the thoughts he sometimes had of her away from her presence. Just in case.

A few minutes later Chrissy was asleep also and Moze was on his feet looking for an escape from the life that he really wanted there in Chrissy's room. A life he could not let himself have.

28

CAP

August 1967

Luke sat atop a sand bag, one of thousands that surrounded the compound outside his hooch. The Seabees had finished the buildings and the tower that stood at the back edge of the camp like a pubescent erection in less than a week. The sand bags had arrived in trucks already filled, but Luke's CAP had helped place them in a triangular-shaped wall around the outside of the five buildings which served as sleeping quarters, storage area and a place to eat and have meetings. That wall was pretty much all that stood between his squad and annihilation if the NVA would ever decide his squad was important enough for the consequences of attacking it. The VC in his area were a threat, but, in the three weeks Luke had been there, the only damage done had been three incidents of sniper fire on the tower and one rocket that missed the tower by thirty feet.

The collection of photos of his son Wally that Chrissy had sent him over the last four months was spread out on the sandbag to his right. Randomly Luke would pick up a photo, look at it for a few moments then put it down and pick up another one. The stoic expression on his face remained the same regardless of which photo he held. Someone observing him would be hard pressed to distinguish father Luke from a stranger performing the same acts. Except for the photo of Moze holding Wally in the hospital on the day he was born. A quick half laugh escaped then as it always did when he looked at that one. There was always the thought that the child in his brother's arms would be better off if the man holding him were actually his father. And there was each time he looked at the photos a moment when Luke realized that he felt nothing more for Wally than he would if the photo had been of Moze and a son of his own.

Because Luke had opted for his tour of duty to begin as soon as he finished his recovery and schooling in Vietnamese, any opportunity for an annual leave ended. There were no annual leaves granted during a Marine's thirteen-month tour, a policy Luke had been aware of and willingly accepted. Especially now that he had become a father and had promised to become a husband also.

But Chrissy had other plans. When Luke had informed her that he could not get his thirty-day annual leave in July, Chrissy had researched the leave options available and had come up with a solution. With help from Moze.

After thirty days *in country* Marines were eligible for one R&R leave per tour. One of the approved locations was Hawaii, a popular choice for married men to meet their wives. Chrissy's plan was to leave Wally with Ann and fly to Honolulu, courtesy of Moze and some of the money he had made earlier in the summer while working at the Castings.

Luke gathered the photos into a pile then stuck them into his shirt pocket and tried to forget that his R&R approval could come at any moment. Unless some clerk somewhere in Da Nang had accidentally used his form for rolling a joint. It was *possible*. Hopefully.

* * * *

Because of Luke's knowledge of the Vietnamese language, he and the unit's commander Sergeant Ramirez decided Luke's best use would be teaching the village kids how to speak English and basically work as much American propaganda as he could into the lessons. That propaganda included anything he could say to the children that would help them view his CAP unit as their friends and the VC as the enemy.

A small building that had served as a school several years ago had become a storage building for the local army, but because the ARVN had pulled out of the area six months ago, the building now housed mostly rats. It did, however, have a roof and three walls. The local government was not yet sold on the Marines' presence in their village but decided that having a school for the children was a better use of the building than a home for the rats if the Marines did the work and furnished the material to get it fixed up. And that's what his squad had done while the Seabees built their compound. Except for Luke and Ben Daniels, the Navy corpsman assigned to his unit. Each CAP unit had one who served as its medic and to provide medical services to the local village. That's what he and Luke did while the school was being remodeled.

Daniels had been given a space for his office in a building two doors down from the school. Luke's day began each morning at seven with Daniels, translating for him and the locals. Luke would then leave Daniels on his own at ten o'clock and head for the school. The first hour was set aside for English, followed by a half hour of math then a half hour of geography on some days and science on others. The CAP school at Da Nang provided enough books for the ten to fifteen kids that showed up most mornings to either have a book of their own or to share with somebody else.

Luke's best student was also one of his oldest, Minh, the VC deserter he had brought with him from his combat experience near the DMZ. Minh had just turned thirteen the week he and Luke had arrived at the CAP village. An intelligent kid, Minh wanted desperately to please his teacher. Though Minh had been told why Luke had to sometimes ignore him, that didn't keep him from enthusiastically waving a hand every time Luke would ask the class a question. Luke was his hero, his savior… the only person who had shown him kindness since his parents had been killed two years ago.

Minh proved to be a great help to Luke in the classroom. Luke's

Vietnamese was excellent for an American, but there were times he would have trouble with some local expression or not understand why a certain child would be confused at Luke's pronunciation. Because most of the children were much like Minh when it came to enthusiasm for learning, Luke would know something had gone wrong when Minh's hand would be the only one in the air. Luke then could count on Minh to set him straight, if he could. Even Minh would have trouble occasionally with the local dialect. Before moving in with his oldest brother after his parents were killed, his home had been fifty miles south, which was far enough away for pronunciations, even meanings to be different.

At noon the two of them would make the ten-minute walk back to camp and have a c-ration lunch. If Luke was lucky, he would be able to fall asleep for an hour before having to join the afternoon patrols. While he slept, Minh would go outside and find a spot out of the sun or rain and read. Luke made sure Minh always had reading material of some kind.

The afternoon patrols were done by the Marines themselves. No PF's, the local militia assigned to the Marines by the local authorities. For the most part the militia consisted of soldiers who were too old, too young, or too incompetent to serve in the ARVN, the South Vietnamese Army. They were ill equipped, poorly trained, and paid half of what regular ARVN soldiers were paid. At the CAP school in Da Nang Luke had been warned not to expect too much from PFs, but he was trying to keep an open mind.

One of the stated goals of the CAP program was to turn the PF's into a force capable of eventually defending their home area without the Americans. While Luke and Doc would be busy in the morning with doctoring and teaching, the rest of the squad offered instruction on weaponry and drills to the few PF's who showed up. Of the twenty that were listed on the roster, seldom were there more than eight who regularly participated. Neither the PF's nor the CAP Marines had authority over the other. It was up to Sergeant Ramirez and his PF counterpart Trung-si Quann to work out any problems that occurred between the two forces. Quann had been shot in his left leg by the VC a month before Luke arrived in the village. He showed little interest in his men or his job. He did, however, like to drink American beer.

Besides a Navy corpsman each CAP unit had a sergeant as its leader although it was not unusual for the leader to be merely a corporal. Officers were purposely excluded. Luke had been told the reason for this was to keep the squad as cohesive as possible, something made more difficult by the inherent elitist tendencies of some officers. As Luke saw it, a sergeant was just another grunt on steroids, someone who had been where his men had been, a one-time private who had reached the top of the step stool. Respect earned not respect assigned.

In the three weeks Luke had dealt with Sergeant Ramirez, he'd found him to be worthy of such respect. Ramirez had not chosen to lead a CAP. He had been *volunteered* by the colonel in charge of his base. The colonel himself had led a reactionary force flown in to rescue the sergeant's company when it had been overrun by NVA near the northern side of the Rockpile, an area even further north from where the CAP was now located. The other two company sergeants had been killed along with the lieutenant. Ramirez and the eleven remaining men from the company had been holding off a hundred or so NVA.

Impressed by Ramirez's courage and leadership, the colonel, when asked several weeks later to recommend someone to lead the new CAP being installed southwest of Dong Ha, had immediately settled on Ramirez. After some coaxing and the promise of assigning him the best men available, Ramirez accepted. Two weeks of CAP school later he was in charge of Luke's squad.

The only other required position in the squad was a radio man. Fran Burkett, a likable kid from somewhere south of Oklahoma City, had arrived at the camp the day after Luke and quietly announced that he was that guy. Luke had decided early on in his field experience that, other than the guy walking point on a patrol, the worst job was carrying a radio on your back with a big antenna sticking up in the air announcing that *here I am, the one who can call in artillery or an air strike to blow your Asian ass to little pieces.*

Although the squad and its PF partners had been on patrol every night for the past two weeks, no enemy had been encountered. Ramirez and Quann were of the opinion that the VC were just biding their time, evaluating how seriously to take the CAP unit. The VC most certainly couldn't be too worried about numbers. CAP units ideally were to have from twelve to fifteen Marines and as many PF's. But Luke's squad was undermanned, as were most CAP squads. The original ten men assigned to the unit now numbered eight, having had two moved to a nearby CAP unit to replace two of the three men killed there in an ambush just last week. The number of PF's had yet to surpass the eight Marines.

So far, the afternoon patrols were conducted pretty much for show. The Marines would walk from their compound to town, giving the locals the chance to see them and interact with them. But the only interaction that had taken place in the first few weeks had been with the kids. It had not taken long for them to learn how to work the CAPs for candy bars. Because he was the teacher for many of them, Luke had been the first to get played. He had told his students to call him Mister Luke, but one of the kids called him *Genral* Luke one day causing Luke to laugh. Soon, all the kids were calling him *Genral* Luke.

The adults in the village were not as friendly as their children. The Viet Cong were still in charge and until the locals saw proof of the foreigners' ability to protect them from retaliation, they were not about to show any signs of cooperation with the Marines. According to Quann, most of the locals had no interest in either the VC or the Americans. They just wanted to make a living. And even if the locals hated the VC for taking their money and their crops when they saw fit, the farmers and villagers feared the VC too much to help the Americans and the PF's. From what Luke had witnessed in his short time in the area, he knew it would take time to get the locals to trust the CAP unit to protect them from the VC. Although the Marines had helped with their medical care and the education of their children, not one VC had yet been killed or wounded.

After the leisurely afternoon stroll through the town, the Marines would vary their routine but eventually visit one or more of the surrounding hamlets. Ramirez would never take them to the same one in the same order by the same route to help prevent an ambush. The hamlets were mostly a mile or so apart, all connected by a network of crude roads, but Ramirez would sometimes take the squad on circuitous routes through open fields or lightly wooded areas behind local dwellings. Luke's unit's area of responsibility encompassed six hamlets and the town next to the compound. Evening patrols, however, would extend beyond the hamlets into the jungle and the semicircle of foothills that extended the jungle in the direction of the Laotian border less than ten miles west.

For Luke his CAP life so far had been a great experience. In the mornings he used his language training from Monterrey and in the . evenings and at night he got to play soldier. The only thing that would make his life better would be more sleep. At least he had been blessed with an ability to put his head on his cot, close his eyes, and five minutes later be asleep.

29

Minh

August 1967

The sound of Minh rapping timidly on his door of bamboo awakened Luke from his afternoon nap. He looked at his watch. He still had an hour before patrol. He knew the rest of the outfit would still be working with the PF's so he guessed that it was Minh at the door.

"Come on in, Minh."

"Luke, sir," said Minh when he closed the door behind him, "Friend Huy says Mama-san Mai wants you come for Coke. Very soon. Very important."

Mai was the owner of a small café in the village and was not the least bit intimidated by the VC. She had been raised in the village then ran away as a teenager with the son of an ARVN colonel. They married and ended up in Hue where her husband used his father's connections to set up a lucrative black-market trading business when the American build up began. Two years ago her husband was knifed by a business rival and died two days later, leaving Mai with two children to raise and enough money to go back to her village and start a café. Huy and his thirteen-year-old sister Ha helped her run it. Luke and the other squad members would have lunch there occasionally and Mai would always give Luke and Minh a free Coke. It was usually warm, but it always tasted good with her cooking. Mai was a good-looking woman of thirty-one. Her daughter Ha could easily be mistaken for a younger sister. Luke was pretty sure Minh felt the same way about Ha as most of the squad felt about Mai.

"Well then, we better get going. We sure don't want to get the Mama-san mad at us, do we."

Minh smiled. "Mama-san Mai not get mad at you. She like you."

Luke liked her also, but was not sure whether he trusted her. Quann had said she had two older brothers that he suspected were VC. He had seen them go into her cafe once a few months ago, but never saw them come out. His curiosity piqued, he had asked Mai about them later. She had only laughed and said they weren't clever enough to be VC. They were just a couple of fools after a free meal.

Turning his back to Minh, Luke threw on his pants and grabbed his M-16. When he turned around Minh was holding Luke's hat out for him.

Ten minutes later Luke and Minh were met by Mai at the door of her cafe. Ha was stationed behind the counter, wiping its surface, and occasionally flashing smiles in Minh's direction. Mai motioned Luke towards the open back door that led to a partially enclosed porch used for storing trash and empty bottle cases. When Minh started to follow Luke, Mai said, "You stay, Minh. Ha, give you Coke."

On the porch, Mai closed the door. Luke did not know Mai well, but her personality usually struck him as carefree and fun-loving. He had never seen the serious side of her that was currently on display. Her dark brown eyes that often sparkled with a hint of devilishness were now focused with a sense of urgency.

"VC attack you tonight. Wait for you to go on patrol then booby trap your huts."

"How do you know this, Mama-san Mai?"

"One of them hang around Ha sometimes, always try to impress her. He in here little while ago, tell her to listen for boom boom later tonight. Then no more Marines tomorrow."

If she was acting, she was damn good at it, thought Luke. Her face was pleading before the words came out.

"Please, Genral Luke, no boom boom tonight."

"Maybe this guy was just talking big. As you said, just trying to act tough for Ha." Then another thought, "Or maybe he's testing her to see if she tells us."

"Oh. Yes, maybe it test."

"Do you think he's clever enough to do something like that?"

"Oh no. This boy, he not even little clever."

"Okay. I'll go back to the camp and talk to the sergeant. Meanwhile, you keep Huy and Ha close. Don't let them out of your sight, and if the VC kid shows up asking for Ha, make some excuse that she can't talk to him and send Minh for me."

Back at camp, Ramirez was reluctant to accept Mai's story. He was still of the opinion that she was a VC sympathizer.

"It's just possible that the VC will be waiting for us if we would come back early."

"But we're coming back here sometime tonight. Why make up a story to get us to come early?" argued Luke.

"Maybe they have something going on out in the bush that they want to make sure we don't stumble on. Maybe an NVA unit on the march? I don't know."

"Well, I believe her, Sarge. If we come back after they've been here, there's always the chance we'll miss something they've done. All it takes is one trip wire missed and someone's dead. But it's your call."

Ramirez said nothing for a while, then stood up. "Get Burkett in here with the radio. I'm letting the CO make the decision."

Luke found Burkett in his hooch cleaning his recently acquired M14, an act that every soldier who possessed one did religiously before every patrol. Luke had refused the new weapon because he had heard all the rumors of the problems that Marines were experiencing with the guns jamming. On patrol before joining his CAP unit, his squad and a group of VC had surprised each other. The Marine in front of him had pulled his weapon up to fire and it jammed. Luke's M16 had not. Luke survived. The other Marine took a bullet in the throat and died.

"I'm with you," said Burkett after Luke filled him in on their way to the hooch that served as Ramirez's office. "What would you do? Go out on patrol and sneak back or hide out here and wait for them?"

"Not my call. I'm just glad Ramirez is getting the CO involved."

A minute later Ramirez was on the radio with Colonel Barnes at Dong Ha explaining the situation with Luke and Burkett listening. When Ramirez finished, the colonel said, "Got your map in front of you. Sergeant?"

"Yes, sir."

"Good. Now use it to find a way to get back to camp before the VC then kill every goddam one of them. Got that?"

"Yes, sir."

"That's all, Sergeant."

"Yes, sir."

Ramirez handed the radio back to Burkett. "Okay, guys, I'll get back to you in about an hour when I figure out what we're goin' to do. All I can say is that the mama-san better not be setting us up."

* * * *

Luke thought it was a good plan, especially now that Ramirez had decided to enhance the CO's orders. The patrol that left the camp would have the usual eight men but two of them would not be Marines. Tonight two of Quann's most trusted and largest men would replace Private Carl Murdock and PFC Elijah Jones, the only black member of the unit. Quann's two men were smaller than any of the Marines but bigger than any other PF's, making the exchange of uniforms a better fit. Jones and Murdock would stay in the camp with the assignment of firing off two illumination flares should the VC get to the camp before the squad could get back.

With sunset in the middle of August coming at a little after six, Ramirez had the squad on the road at five thirty. His route was to take them in the direction of the Laos border and head into the jungle-covered foothills as they sometimes did, but then, in the cover of the trees and darkness, they would swing southwest and then back towards the village and find the road that mostly paralleled the route out of the town. Eventually they would meet that road a mile south of town and work their way back to the camp in the fields and brush where they would set up a perimeter nearby and wait. If the VC were aware of their usual patrol times, and Luke was sure that they were, they would not expect the squad back until after midnight, and would not show up until the villagers had retreated into their homes for the night.

Luke had sent Minh to Mai's for the night and ordered him not to return to camp, assuring him that he would see him in school the next morning. Knowing how Minh felt towards Ha, Luke knew Minh would have no trouble doing what he was told.

No illumination flares had lit up the night and nothing unexpected had happened by the time the patrol made their way back to their positions outside the camp... except for PFC Denton's encounter with a monster spider. He was walking point through the edge of the jungle just before the turn back towards the village was made. When he felt a web against his face and then the presence of something moving on his shoulder, he instinctively reached for whatever it was to get it off him. Finding that it filled his whole hand, he shook his hand hard and the creature went to the ground. The PF behind him tried to slam the butt of his rifle against it, but only crushed one leg before it disappeared into the darkness of the jungle floor. Listening to Denton describe the size of the spider, Luke had been thankful that he hadn't been the one on point. He hated spiders. Moze had always told him to be nice to spiders. Luke was pretty sure Moze might feel differently about one the size of his hand.

An hour after the patrol had set up its positions around the camp, the first movement was spotted by Luke, who was positioned closest to the back of the camp. He, Ramirez and Doc Daniels were within ten yards of each other and all of them soon had an unobstructed view of several moving figures nearing the five-foot-high wall of sandbags that surrounded the camp. Ramirez had chosen their positions so the initial fire would be away from the camp structures and those of the nearby village, some of them as close as five-hundred yards. Ramirez waited until as many VC as possible were exposed but not yet on the sandbags then fired an illumination flare as the signal to start firing. It was also the signal to the two Marines in the camp that they should be looking for targets coming over the sandbags.

When the light from the illumination round exploded into the darkness, the other five Marines farthest away from Luke immediately opened fire, dropping two VC immediately. From inside the sandbags Murdoch and Jones quickly dispatched two more VC coming over the top.

On the outside of the wall, Luke, Ramirez and Daniels had done the same to two others. In the fading light from the flare Luke counted five more that had already turned and were running away from the camp. Another one had earlier broken rank and seemed to be headed more for the backyards of the town.

Luke turned his head back toward Ramirez and said as if he were the one in charge, "I'm going after the loner. I think I know where he's headed." Although he knew it was a race he could not win because of the VC's head start, he could only hope that somehow, he could get there in time to prevent the worst from happening. Half way there he heard the shots.

The VC had entered Mai's from the rear door. He found her in the café with Minh listening to loud music on the radio. Their backs turned, they were oblivious to his presence. A quick burst of gunfire from the VC's AK-47 passed between them and exploded the radio.

"Where Yankee whore Ha?"

Mai jumped from her stool and stuck her chin out. "You get out my house."

"VC dead because of her."

"No. VC dead because of you, blubber mouth."

The VC started for the living area that opened beside the café. When Mai tried to grab him, the VC shoved her hard into a stack of chairs. Minh launched himself in the direction of the VC and took him to the floor, in the process separating him from his rifle. With an advantage of several inches and many pounds, the VC quickly reversed his position. His hands grasping Minh's wrists and the rest of his body perched on Minh's stomach, the VC quickly scanned the floor in search of his rifle, only to see Mai reaching for it. A quick hop forward on his knees placed them on Minh's arms freeing his hands to remove the knife sheathed at his waist. A second later it was slicing Minh's neck. The VC sprung to his feet and turned towards Mai who now had the gun in her hands and was screaming at the sight of the blood squirting from Minh's neck, and was, for a few split seconds, oblivious to anything else.

When the VC lunged at her with his knife, her body recoiled, causing a quick spasm of gunfire. One of the bullets ripped into the hand holding the knife.

"Mai! Mai! Set the gun down!" Luke had just entered the back door and had his gun pointed at the VC. He could not see Minh on the floor on the other end of the lunch counter.

Mai went to her knees and slid the gun in Luke's direction then scurried towards Minh while yanking her blouse off. "Minh need help," she cried in desperation as she tried to stop the blood.

"Minh?" Luke had already started moving towards the gun when he saw Mai slide out of sight. Confused by her words and actions he took the few extra steps to see what she was doing. Seeing Minh's blood oozing through Mai's blouse, a quiet moan escaped him. "Oh, Minh." When he saw the massive amount of blood collected against the bottom of the base of the counter with spatter on the boards lining the front of the counter, his attention returned to the VC. Then he remembered Ha.

"Where's Ha?"

"Hiding under bed probly," Mai answered without taking her eyes off Minh. She had wrapped her blouse around his neck and was tying the ends together as tightly as she could.

"Ha?" Luke forcefully hollered toward the living quarters, still glaring hard at the VC. "Come here. Hurry!"

"You," he growled at the VC. "You did this?"

The VC said nothing as he stood holding his mangled hand against his ribcage.

"Yes, Genral Luke," said Ha, her voice wavering as she appeared in the doorway.

"You need to run to the camp and get Doc Daniels. Tell him Minh needs him immediately." He paused not sure how much to say then, as he saw Ha focusing on Minh cradled in her mother's arms, he calmly added "Please, Ha, hurry."

As soon as Ha was out the back door, Luke kicked the AK-47 in the direction of the front door then set the butt of his gun on the floor, resting the muzzle against the end of the counter wall, never once taking his eyes off the VC who was cowering away from Luke with his bleeding hand now covered by his black shirt. He had stretched enough of it away from his stomach so it could cover the torn flesh.

Luke looked at Minh, his blood now barely soaking through Mai's blouse then grabbed the knife lying on the floor three feet from the VC. Again he stared at the VC. *Why was this piece of shit still breathing?* Besides being Luke's best student, his best friend, an invaluable resource on all things Vietnamese, Minh had become family. So much so that Luke had started investigating how to take Minh home with him. But having enlisted for three years was going to be the problem. Unless he would do the whole three years in Nam, he would have to leave him there while he finished his enlistment somewhere else.

Luke took one more look at Minh and heard Mai start to sob.

Why was this piece of shit still breathing?

And then he wasn't.

* * * *

Five minutes later Ben Daniels with Ha close behind burst into the room. Mai was standing over the sink behind the counter, her blouse and her hands in soapy water.

"Where is he?"

"Other side of counter with Luke."

Ben took his medical kit off his shoulders and hurried around the counter to where Luke sat with one leg extended, the other tucked under himself, cradling Minh's head in his lap."

"He's gone, Doc."

Daniels let his bag cascade to the floor. Pointing at the VC on the floor beside Luke, he said, "That the guy who did it?"

Mai called over her shoulder from the sink, "Piece-shit fall and break neck."

Without any hesitation Daniels said, "That sounds about right from what I can see. Come on, pal, let's get Minh back to camp."

"You go on without me. I need to help Mai clean up first then I'll take him."

"Yes, Mai need to take trash out somewhere other VC's find it."

Daniels looked at Luke and sighed. "Okay. I understand. I'll let the rest know what happened. We all thought a lot of Minh."

* * * *

Luke's physical exhaustion didn't knock him down until the middle of the next afternoon. He had carried the dead VC to an open area on a trail Mai knew to be a favorite of the local VC. She was adamant that none of them should get any impression that she feared reprisal. Word was sure to have spread through the VC that this particular one had gone after Ha to take revenge. In spite of Luke's arguing, Mai wanted the rest of the VC to see what happened to someone who tried to harm her family.

When Luke and Mai had returned, they finished cleaning the cafe then Luke carried Minh's body to an area just outside the sand bags on the front right side of camp. He then retrieved a shovel from the storage shed and finished burying his best friend just as the first light of dawn broke through the bank of clouds crawling across the horizon. Standing in front of the mounded earth with the sunlight slightly warming his back, he let his mind wander back the short trail of memories he had shared with Minh. He had experienced familial love from his mother and brother, but not the kind of love Minh had given him. That love had had no bounds, no demands. Never a cross word had either of them given the other. Minh had been a puppy who always knew where his master's slippers were, knew when his master didn't want any slippers.

All his students, including Ha and her brother Huy, were in their seats when Luke arrived at his usual time. As he looked around the room. each face offered him a look of worried concern. Minh's empty chair was pushed against one of the three tables that stretched across the width of the room. Luke was pretty sure that the white flowers piled on the table in front of Minh's chair had been sent by the mothers and fathers of the children. That was the moment when the emotional exhaustion hit him. Breathing suddenly became impossible. He turned and wrote on the blackboard in Vietnamese *Please remain in your seats* and then slipped out the back of the room.

A minute later Luke found himself sitting on the floor of Mai's empty café. He had entered from the rear. The sign on the front door said Closed. Mai, having gone to bed in the hope of getting a little sleep before opening for the day, heard his noise. When she found him on the floor, tears streaming out of the sobs, she sat down beside him, gently slid an arm around his neck and let him mourn the loss of the boy she had secretly hoped would become a part of her own family.

30

Honolulu

September 1967

The sound of someone knocking on the door yanked at the knot in Luke's stomach. When not sleeping, he had been sitting in the hotel room off and on for the last forty-eight hours, riding a nearly constant marijuana high. Chrissy had called the day before yesterday with the news that she had been bumped from her standby status at the last minute, then called again yesterday saying she had been bumped again. The good news was that there were seats available for today's flight from Seattle.

A chopper had arrived at the CAP camp an hour after the call telling him his seven-day leave would begin in an hour. Following a brief layover in Da Nang he flew to Okinawa then took a commercial flight to Honolulu, leaving him with five days there then a day of flights back to his unit. He had called Chrissy the minute after his notification, waking her in the middle of the night and putting the onus on her to make flight arrangements.

And now she was just outside his door.

Having had two full days to think about what he would say to her had not made any difference. The pot had made his situation seem so much less complicated. But he was sober now and would somehow have to find a way to convince her that he still wanted to marry her. Still wanted to be a father. As soon as he could convince himself.

Another knock. This one sounded different. Angry?

"Luke! You there?"

Luke jumped to his feet, knowing that the voice he had just heard belonged not to Chrissy but to his brother Moze.

A few moments later without even looking for Chrissy, he had his arms wrapped around his brother. Only after Moze pulled back did Luke force himself to look for the mother of his child.

"Chrissy?" he asked when he could not find her.

"She's in my room. I'm supposed to let her know when she should come. She's terrified, Luke."

"Scared of me?

Moze pushed his brother back into the room and shut the door. "Since the day you left. More so now that she has Wally.

"She thinks I would hurt her?"

"No. Not physically."

Moze knew he had to choose his words carefully. He would not offer Luke any choices like he had in his letter announcing Chrissy's pregnancy. Moze was too attached to Chrissy and Wally now to want anything but what would be best for them, too aware of how much damage Luke's abandonment would cause everyone because of the relationships formed. Chrissy and Wally had become part of the family.

"Does she want to get married? Right now? If that's what she wants, we'll just do it." Luke heard the words after he said them and wondered where they had come from. Not once had he considered that option during the past few days. He had only wanted to get through the visit without any drama, have enough sex with her to show her that he still cared, listen to her talk about their son.

Then get back to Vietnam.

"You will have to ask Chrissy those questions." Moze paused then said with the hint of a smile. "I can tell you that she made a call to Hawaii to find out what was needed for a marriage here while we were waiting for your R&R to get approved. She came prepared... just in case.

"Which brings us to the main reason I am here." Moze stopped, knowing that his brother would, sooner or later, figure out what had been left unsaid.

After several moments of silence passed, Luke said with noticeable frustration, "And the answer is?"

Instead of answering his brother's question, Moze went to the window and cranked it open. "Well, one reason I'm here is to get this strange smell out of the room. Since when did you start smoking?"

"Shortly after the slanty-eyed little bastards started trying to kill me."

With his back still to Luke, Moze did not see his brother close his eyes and sigh in disgust. Moze did though hear him say, "I can't believe I just said that."

"Said what?"

"Did Chrissy tell you anything about me wanting to adopt a thirteen-year-old Vietnamese kid?"

Moze turned and said, "Yes. She said she would do her best with it if it was what you wanted. I'm telling you, Brother, you've got a great girl there."

"Well, there won't be any adoption now. Minh had his throat cut trying to protect his girlfriend from a VC. If I'd been there a minute earlier…"

Luke sat down on the end of the bed and put his head in his hands. "He was such a great kid, like a little brother, Moze. I made him stay off the base that night because we expected an attack, and he still gets killed."

Moze walked to the bed and sat down beside his brother. He had wanted to get Chrissy into the room as soon as possible so that she and Luke could reconnect and make their way closer to marriage. But seeing Luke hurting could not be ignored.

"Should I say anything to Chrissy about what happened to the kid when I go back to the room to get her?"

Luke dropped his hands to the bed and said, "No, I'll tell her about it later." Regaining his composure, he gave Moze a shove against his shoulder. "So why *are* you here? What about classes?"

Moze returned the shove as he said, "I can't go to class with the flu now, can I? Besides, you're going to need a best man if you decide to get married, Doofus. I rented a movie camera at home and took some movies of Wally to show you later if I can find someplace here to rent a projector. If you and Chrissy decide to get married, maybe we can find some leatherneck to go to the wedding and take some movies to show Mom when I get back. Although she said she'd rather stay with Wally, I know how much it must be bothering her to not be here."

When Moze finished, Luke looked away and waited as long as he could before saying, "So what do you think? Should I go through with it? Maybe I should just wait until my tour is over and do the wedding business on my annual leave. You know, so Mom can be there."

Once again Moze was in a position he didn't want to be in. If he could only be sure that Chrissy would speak her mind to Luke, he could keep his mouth shut. But he couldn't be sure, and Luke needed to be aware of what was going on in her head. "Here's the thing, Little Brother. At this point in Chrissy's life, she needs you to marry her for several reasons, but what's driving her to do it now is Wally. She does not want him being looked upon as a bastard. It may be hard for you to understand, being that you have not experienced him yet, but from what I've observed, there is nothing more important to her than her son. Not even you. In her mind every day that there is no marriage is another day closer to the possibility that there won't ever be one."

For a moment Moze thought he was finished talking. But something else suddenly needed to be said, something rooted in all the moments he had spent with Chrissy and Wally.

"I will not tell you to marry Chrissy, and I will not tell you not to marry her. And I will not talk to you about your responsibilities. But you hear me, Luke, when I tell you this— if you don't marry Chrissy, marry her soon, I will."

Unless his little brother had been changed by the dynamics of war or what had happened with Minh, Moze was dead certain that Luke was incapable of deserting Chrissy and Wally.

Luke's first words, however surprised him. "Do you love her?"

"I do. I've spent hundreds of hours with her in the past year and I'd do anything for her, including marriage. But my love for her is rooted in proximity and pity. She deserves better than that. She wants better than that."

Luke looked hard at his brother and said, "I don't love her. I can't help it. I just don't. I know how messed up this sounds but I loved Minh more than either Chrissy or the kid. I—"

"I can understand that. You are in a different world over there. Your very existence is being threatened every day. But—"

"Let me finish, Moze. Minh is the first person I've ever lost who meant anything to me except for Dad, but I don't really remember him much at all. Minh's death gives me a better sense for the importance of the people I love. You and Mom specifically. And I absolutely will not put Chrissy and the baby on you two. Just won't. I only asked you if you loved her to find out if I could give you a gift of them if you really wanted them."

"And what a gift it would be, but the better gift would be serving as your best man. I'm betting you'll get through this Vietnam horror, return to Pine City and find out what a great wife and mother Chrissy will be. And once again acknowledge that your older brother knows what's best for you."

Although Moze finished with a smile, Luke knew his brother was not joking.

* * * *

Luke had hoped that the moment Chrissy entered the hotel room he somehow would be so taken by her, so enchanted by her sexuality, that he would suddenly shake off his doubts about marriage and fatherhood. But, no matter how much he fought it, what he experienced instead was the feeling that he was in the presence of an enemy, a threat to the existence he had become accustomed to. His freedom. Freedom from the future he had just offered to his brother.

That was not to say that he didn't enjoy the sex that followed. Unintentionally or not, he had remained faithful since his returning from leave last August, so the anticipation for the sex had helped mitigate the negative stuff.

When they lay spent after the act, he pulled a couple of joints from his uniform on the chair beside the bed and offered one to Chrissy. As the air clouded, he broke the initial silence with the announcement concerning Minh's death.

"Oh, Luke, I'm so sorry."

"I just want you to know how great you were in going along with me wanting to bring him home. You were way better than I would have been if you had done that to me. But he was really special."

"Do you want to talk about it?"

"No. Not really." He paused and looked at the ceiling. "Except to let you know what kind of man you will be marrying. I was going to cut the throat of the VC that killed him but instead I chose to break his neck. I had to put my hands on him, to hold him up against me as I whispered into his ear in my best Vietnamese, 'Rot in hell you little piece of shit.' Then I grabbed the far side of his head with my right hand and snapped it down and back towards me."

As he spoke, his voice quivered with excitement as if he were committing the act again. He wanted to look at Chrissy to see her reaction to his words, but then decided that he just didn't care. The VC had been an enemy who only a few minutes earlier had been trying to kill him in battle. Luke had not slit his throat and left him to bleed out as the VC had done to Minh. So why should Luke need to explain himself. At least he had told her what he had done.

"Did Minh suffer?"

"No, I don't think so. He was unconscious by the time I got there. The mother of the girl that Minh was protecting held him in her arms while she tried to stop the bleeding."

Chrissy reached out and placed a hand on Luke. "Hopefully he had some kind of awareness that he was being held, that someone was caring for him."

"He was gone by the time I got to hold him."

As that first joint was followed by several more, Luke told her how the families of his students had sent flowers with their children to the school the next day and the ceremony his squad had held for Minh later.

Chrissy had hoped they would be able to talk about getting married but when Luke kept the focus on Minh, she was reluctant to intrude. She saw his need to talk about his loss as an opportunity for her to be included however indirectly in the relationship. By the time his stories of Minh came to an end, both Luke and Chrissy were ready to sleep.

* * * *

It was Moze who finally brought up the subject of marriage. At ten that night he decided to call their room. After an interminable amount of ringing, Luke picked up the phone.

"Is the wedding still on?" Moze asked.

"We haven't talked about it yet."

"How many days of leave do you have left?"

"Ah, two? Let me think. Yeah, two. Three nights counting tonight. Why? Isn't that enough time to make it happen?"

Moze heard the hope in his voice.

"Barely, if you want to have a day to yourselves afterward. You need to find what's called a marriage agent tomorrow, fill out an application and get him to issue the license the same day, then find someone to marry you. And, if we want a movie of it for Mom, we need to find somebody who will be available both tomorrow and the next day in case you can't get the prep done tomorrow. You want me to go out tonight and see if I can find somebody willing to do the filming?"

"I can go."

"Why don't you two just stay there and get to know each other again. I'm ready to go. I'll get up early tomorrow and try to find an agent. If I run into any problems, I'll let you know. Okay?"

"Yeah. sure. Thanks."

"I'll give you a call tomorrow when I know something."

"Okay. See you tomorrow then."

Moze put his finger on the phone cradle button then lifted it and called the front desk to ask the receptionist if she knew of a bar or night club nearby that served as a hangout for Marines. She didn't, but she told him to hang on while she asked the bartender at the hotel's bar if he knew of one. Two minutes later she was back with his answer which was no, but a bunch of Marines were in the hotel bar at that moment shooting darts and another one was at a table with a woman. Moze thanked her and hung up.

Downstairs in the bar Moze quickly discovered the group playing darts. No uniforms, but a few t-shirts with USMC or Leatherneck Brigade supporting the bartender's claim. Moze also spotted a young guy with a girl in the most secluded corner of the room. One other couple was at the bar but because of the man's slovenly appearance and lard ass, Moze was pretty certain that he wasn't a Marine. Moze chose the couple in the corner.

"Excuse me. Could I have a moment of your time, please?"

The couple exchanged looks before the one with dog tags around his neck said, "Sure. As long as you're not here to take me back to Da Nang."

Moze offered a quick laugh as he looked for wedding rings. Each had one. "Not likely. My brother Luke is the Marine. I'm here with his fiancé. If everything goes according to plan, she and my brother will get married tomorrow before he has to go back to Vietnam two days later."

The female looked maybe thirty and her husband a few years older. The wife immediately said, "Oh, that's great. Are you–"

Her husband interrupted, "She means, of course, that it's great they're getting married, not that your brother's gotta go back to Nam in two days." He waited for Moze and his wife to respond to his joke then said, "What part of that hellhole is he in?"

"He's with a CAP unit up north pretty far. That's about all I know. I know he's mentioned Dong Ha. He went to school in California to learn Vietnamese."

The Marine stood up and said, "I'm stationed on a hill outside of Da Nang, probably not very far from your brother." He extended his hand and said, "I'm Will Montgomery. This is my wife Julie. We're celebrating our tenth anniversary."

Moze shook hands with Will and said, "Moses Foster, but please call me Moze," then nodded in Julie's direction. "Nice to meet you both."

"Won't you sit down with us, Moze?" asked Will as he returned to his seat.

"Well, I guess that kind of depends on whether I can talk you into coming to my brother's wedding tomorrow." He paused then added sheepishly, "Or the next day if we can't get the legal stuff worked out. There's no waiting period or blood test or anything really. But Chrissy and I just got here today after waiting two days in Seattle for connections and she hasn't had a chance to fill out the application yet."

"So, you need witnesses?" asked Julie.

"No, you don't even need a witness here other than the person performing the marriage. What we need is someone to film the wedding. I rented a camera back home. My mother had to stay there and take care of Chrissy and Luke's little baby, so we really would like to be able to show her the wedding when we get back. I wish I could give you a specific time on a specific day, but we won't know until we find an agent."

Neither Will nor Julie said anything right away so Moze said, "That's all right. I certainly understand, especially when you're celebrating an anniversary. I'm glad I had the chance to—"

"Tomorrow's good. We'll make it no matter what the time. I've got a court martial the day after tomorrow that I have to be back for."

"You're being court-martialed?"

Will laughed. "No, I'm a lawyer, Marine defense counsel. One of over two-hundred fifty lawyers in Vietnam."

"Wow. That's... How come you're in Vietnam?"

"Couldn't say no to an old boss."

"I can stay an extra day if you need me," offered Julie.

"Oh, that's super," said Moze. "That makes everything simpler. Hopefully, it'll all happen tomorrow. Are you staying at this hotel?"

"Yes." Will took out a pen and wrote their room number on Moze's hand. As soon as you find out anything, call the desk and leave us a message. We'll check with them every hour or so when we're out."

"Oh man, you guys are great. I've been trying to leave them alone since they haven't seen each other in more than a year, but they're going to want to hear the news." Moze reached out his hand again to Will. "Thanks so much, Will. And you, too, Julie. Hope to see you tomorrow." Moze started to leave then turned back and said, "Almost forgot, Happy Anniversary."

Both said thanks together then Julie added, "Tell your brother and Chrissy we can't wait to meet them."

"I will."

31

Luke

September 1967

His plane was flying west, yet Luke, eyes staring at the blue Pacific below, felt like he was headed home. He was married. He was a father. But he was alone and didn't feel like either condition was real. Yet something was different now.

Watching the movies Moze had brought with them had been so much fun. The quality of the film was not the best at times. Out of focus, too much light, not enough light, but Luke at least now had some idea what little living Wally looked like.

Wally. Luke would never have chosen that for a name. Under cross examination Chrissy had finally confessed that she had chosen the name because she'd always had a crush on Wally Cleaver, from watching reruns of *Leave it to Beaver*. Luke did his best to hide his irritation with the choice. He still had two years left in the Marines and didn't see how he'd be doing much parenting before then, so what the hell. It was Chrissy's call. He had, though, approved of Moses for a middle name.

Luke was surprised at how much film there had been of Moze playing with Wally. In one segment, although there was no sound, it was obvious that Wally was doing some serious screaming until Moze lifted him out of his crib and rocked him in his arms until eventually Wally calmed down. A few moments later he was staring intently at Moze, eventually smiling then laughing. As the three of them watched the film in the hotel room before heading to the airport, Moze had been quick to point out that, had there been sound, Wally's sudden mood change would have been easily understood. *A fart of epic proportions* was the phrase he had used.

But the part of the film he had most enjoyed was the footage of his mother. For his son there had been no real emotion, only curiosity. Seeing his mother, however, had been such a treat. The joy of her being a grandmother was so obvious. In fact, Luke saw a radiance about her he had never noticed before, as if she were aging in reverse. Until seeing her in the film, he had felt guilty about dumping Chrissy and the baby into his mother's life. But now, at least on film, his selfish act had given her life new meaning.

The wedding, much to his surprise and relief, had been a positive experience. Randall Kikikoa Manaloa, their marriage agent, had been recommended by the hotel concierge. By eleven thirty that morning Luke and Chrissy had completed their paperwork and after a few rejections by people recommended by their agent, a Navy chaplain friend of Captain Will Montgomery agreed to marry them at 3:00 beside the USS Independence anchored in the harbor.

After the wedding Captain Montgomery insisted on buying dinner for everyone at an open-air restaurant right on the waterfront where he and Luke bonded immediately in their common knowledge of the area west of Dong Ha. Before everyone went their separate ways after eating, Luke and the captain exchanged addresses and promised to meet up in the future.

Yesterday, Luke and Chrissy had slept till noon then had their honeymoon… a bus tour of Honolulu before ending up at the beach for some swimming and a dinner cruise headlined by some well-known Hawaiian entertainer. The only negative of the day for Luke was not having much alone time with Moze. During the three days that the brothers were in Hawaii, the only time they were alone together was the little bit of time in Luke's room before Chrissy came down the first day.

But Luke was surprised that the regret that he had for lost time with

Moze was more for his brother's loss than his own. He felt like he had deserted Moze for Chrissy.

Luke's time with Chrissy had surprised him. He had actually enjoyed her company. The relief he had experienced at being able to talk about Minh and the guilt at not being able to protect his friend, not being able to make good on the promises he had made to him involving his future... Chrissy had just listened, just let him unburden himself.

He was aware that part of the closeness he had felt with her had come from the pot. They had smoked a lot of it. Chrissy had liked it. A lot. So much that she wanted to have some to take home with her. Luke had given her the rest of his stash although he still worried that she and Moze might get caught with it on the way home. At least there would be no customs to deal with.

Then there had been the sex, even better than he had remembered. She had devoured him. He had sensed none of the fear that Moze had spoken of when he first arrived. If anything, Chrissy seemed more confident in the way she carried herself. The clingy neediness that had been there before was no longer apparent.

Was it possible that he might really have enough feelings for her now that he could make marriage work? He guessed there were no choices that had to be made now. The rings were on their fingers. Thanks to his mother. She had given hers to Chrissy and her husband's to Luke.

* * * *

A few hundred miles east of Honolulu Chrissy stared at the wedding ring on her finger as she half listened to Moze talk about how good the trip had been. Then suddenly she was aware that he had said something that required a response from her.

"Sorry. Huh?"

"I said, *what do you think?*"

"About what?"

"That guy you married a couple of days ago, you know, Luke?"

"What about him?"

"He seemed different, didn't he? More serious. More... responsible, maybe? Probably has something to do with all the death around him."

"Yeah. Maybe." The tone of her voice indicated continued distraction if not disinterest.

"You all right?"

"Why wouldn't I be? I finally have a wedding ring on my finger. And tomorrow, I'll be back home with my baby boy."

"I wonder how Mom is making out. I thought about calling her this morning, but the calls are so expensive and you know she would never tell me anything other than what she thinks I want to hear. I'll call her when we know if the flights are going to work out."

Chrissy's attention was already wandering again before Moze finished talking. She wasn't thinking of Luke and she wasn't thinking about Wally. Her attention had drifted to the plastic bag inside her suitcase stored in the bottom of the plane. She was wondering when and where she would find an opportunity to enjoy its contents. Ann, now her official mother-in-law, almost never left the house, meaning that if Chrissy was going to get high, she would have to leave the house to use the weed. That would mean having to drive home under the influence to some degree unless she stayed away long enough to return to a responsible state. That might make for a long trip.

But having Wally with her when she got high was out of the question, so she would have to be alone in the house long enough to get up and then back down again before Ann and Wally would get home. The only way to get enough time was going to require Moze's involvement somehow.

"Did Luke talk about his Vietnamese friend much?"

Oh shit. Moze is talking to me again. Vietnamese friend? Must be Minh.

"Minh?"

"Yes."

"He told you about him?" Chrissy was trying to find out what Moze wanted to know?

"Yes. He sounded like he was feeling pretty guilty," said Moze.

"For what... killing the VC that killed Minh? If breaking the bastard's neck was what he felt like doing, it shouldn't matter. It's a war and one of the enemy is dead. Big deal."

"He didn't tell me about breaking his neck. Did he seem upset about it?" Moze had always had that fear for his little brother and his temper... that he would someday seriously hurt someone, possibly kill him. They had talked about it often after the incident at football practice. Even in war, being enraged to the point of being out of control was probably not the way to kill an enemy. What would happen to awareness in that situation?

Chrissy had managed to keep her focus and answered immediately, "I have the impression that he had thought about it and had decided that he had made the choice that was best for the VC and for him. But the fact that he felt like he needed to tell me because I might be upset about it probably means that *he* was upset about it. So, I don't know. I think it's probably all tied together with the guilt thing over not being able to protect Minh. Luke didn't mention it again after the first day. In fact, he even said he felt better after talking to me about it." She paused and put her hand on his thigh and squeezed. "Don't worry about him, Big Brother. He'll be all right."

"Yeah. I know. I'm just not used to this new version of him. The one that doesn't seem to need me as much."

She smiled at his confession and squeezed his leg again. "Well, I still need you."

32

Mai

A Day Later

No reason had been given when the sergeant at Danang intercepted him twenty yards from the chopper that was waiting to take him back to his CAP unit. Luke's first thought was that he had misunderstood which aircraft he was to board. Another chopper a hundred yards away sat empty and quiet.

"Corporal Foster!" shouted an unfamiliar voice.

Luke turned around. "Yes, Sarge!" he shouted back.

"Please come with me!"

An uncomfortable sensation sprang into his consciousness. Something unexpected had turned him away from his unit. He could see nothing good coming from this. Across the tarmac he saw a Jeep racing toward him. A few seconds later the passenger's image came into focus and Luke saw his CAP leader Sergeant Ramirez headed his way.

When the Jeep pulled up beside him, Ramirez said, "Get in Foster." And then the Jeep was rolling again. A minute later it stopped in front of a Quonset hut where Ramirez got out and said, "Come with me."

Inside the dimly lit building, Luke suddenly heard a hard rain start pounding on the metal overhead. The area in front of him was divided into several walled cubicles that opened into a common ceiling that was the roof of the Quonset hut.

"Have a seat," said Ramirez when they had entered one of the cubicles."

At this point Luke was pretty sure he was about to be informed that his wife and brother had crashed somewhere on their way home. He braced himself for the official news.

"First off, let me set your mind at ease. Nothing has happened to your family. But I do have some bad news."

"I didn't figure this was some kind of special welcome." He was so relieved at hearing that his family was okay that he had to say something no matter how lame.

"Two nights after you left, a squad of VC kidnapped Mai and Ha. They took them out into the jungle and raped Mai repeatedly then made Mai watch them rape then kill Ha. Both of them were found in the street in front of Mai's place at daybreak. We had been on patrol that night and got back about two. I don't think the VC would have done anything until after we went back to the camp for the night. Doc wanted to fly Mai here for treatment but she refused. Didn't want to leave Huy there by himself and wanted to be there for Ha's burial.

"That brings me to why we're here, Luke. The VC have really fucked themselves by doing this. The people in town are beyond being scared. They're incensed. They've been after us to do something since the morning after it happened. But whatever we do has to be done by the book. I've already had it made quite clear to me that all patrols must be organized and approved by Company. We have limited personnel and resources so number one priority is we don't get anyone killed just because the townspeople are upset. We'll hunt these guys down and we'll kill every one of those involved. But we'll do it with our heads on a swivel, not charging blindly after vengeance. Hear what I'm saying?"

Luke only continued to stare at the concrete floor.

"I know you have a special relationship with that family and I think we both know why Mai was targeted. If I am you, I want to do what I just said we're not doing... at least not the way I know you want to.

"So, here's what this meeting is all about. I'm giving you a choice, and I've already discussed this with the CO. Either you return to camp with me now, understanding the way we are going to go about our business, or you will be sent to another CAP unit. Barnes already has one picked out for you outside of Hue. You can be there in an hour.

From his sergeant's first words concerning Mai and Ha, Luke's emotions had been all over the place. Horror, guilt, misery, sympathy, anger… eventually they all became one tangled mess leaving him unable to think straight. Fortunately, the decision Ramirez offered him involved no thinking at all. Under no circumstances could he abandon Mai. He needed to see her. Needed to make her understand that what had happened to Ha was not her fault. He should've stopped her from flaunting the death of the VC. Had he not been blinded by the loss of Minh he would never have let her do it. But there had been satisfaction in it for him, too.

And how could he give up his teaching. He loved his kids. He didn't want to go anywhere else. There was no way he could ever have a better class, a better CAP outfit.

But most of all, he had unfinished business. He would not disobey the terms Ramirez had laid out for him to remain with the unit. He understood the need to be smart about what had to be done. He understood there could be no blind fury involved. But the guilty were going to suffer and then they were going to die for what they had done to Mai and Ha. He would agree to anything to get to that moment in time. After that, he really didn't give a shit what happened.

"Are we on patrol tonight?" Luke finally asked.

"Yes, we are."

"Then we better get headed back to camp. I want to see Mai before supper.

* * * *

The main door to Mai's shop was open as the sign on the screen door advertised. Inside though, ten-year-old Huy was the only one in sight. When Luke asked him in Vietnamese where his mother was, Huy pointed in the direction of the living quarters. The door that led there was propped open by a chunk of cinder block.

Luke gave a thumbs-up to Huy as he headed for the door. Stopping in the doorway, he called, "Mai? Mai? It's Luke. Can I come in?"

After a few seconds of silence, Luke looked back across his shoulder to Huy and said, "You sure she's here?"

Huy nodded. "She sad for Ha."

Luke turned back to the living quarters and said, "Mai, I'm coming in, okay?"

Still no answer. The light fading from the eastern-facing window on his left was all that lit the room in front of him. It appeared to be the living room with a couple of wooden chairs and a beat-up blue sofa against the wall. A small bamboo table with a few books scattered on top separated the chairs. A wall with a door on each end and one in the middle separated the living room from the rest of the house. Only one of the doors was ajar so Luke went in that direction. Though he only knocked lightly, the bamboo door moved until it hit the inside wall.

"Mai?" He stepped into the room and immediately saw her tiny body curled up on the bed. The left side of her face and shoulder, both covered in varying shades of purple, confirmed the information Ramirez had given him. Even from eight feet away in the fading light he could see there was still some swelling under one eye.

Without raising her head, Mai said quietly, "I did not listen to you. Now Ha is dead. All my fault."

With soft deliberate steps Luke moved to the side of her bed and got down on his knees. He took one of her hands with his left hand and placed his right hand on her forehead and stroked her hair on that side.

Speaking in Vietnamese Luke said, "Oh Mai, I am so sorry for what's happened. Please forgive me."

Mai raised her head and opened her eyes in confusion. "It's not your fault. Mai's fault."

"No, I should have stopped us from putting that kid's body on display for the VC. I let my anger and grief for Minh cloud my judgement."

Mai put her head back down. "Poor Minh. Maybe the two of them are together now."

For the first time since he had taken her hand, she looked at it and noticed his wedding ring. "You got married?"

Luke heard both the surprise and disappointment.

"I did." Quickly he tried to think of some way to make the situation less impactful. "I kinda had to. I have a baby boy."

"Minh would have had a brother then?" she asked.

"Yes."

Mai studied the ring for several moments then removed her hand from Luke's grip. Holding the hand up to him she said, "My husband got my ring from man who owed him money. He said man killed somebody to get it."

"You still wear it even though your husband is dead. Why? Do you still love him?"

"No. I wear it because it is pretty. That's all."

She put her head back down and closed her eyes. "I wanted Ha to have it."

And then she was sobbing.

Luke stood up and pulled Mai out of the bed and onto her feet without any resistance. A moment later he wrapped his arms around her. Almost immediately she started to calm down. When her sobbing stopped and her breathing became normal again, he said, "My squad will find the ones who did this to you and Ha and they will die. I promise you."

She opened her eyes and looked at him. Her words desperately raced from her mouth as if to stop Luke from doing the killing right then. "No, Luke. They will kill Huy next. No more. Not for me. I beg you, please?"

"You don't want them punished for what they did to you and Ha?"

"Oh yes. I want to kill them myself. But I cannot risk my little boy's life. I don't want anyone else dead." She put her head against his chest and closed her eyes. "I think Huy and I should leave as soon as I can sell my shop. I have cousin near Hue. I will help her run her café. That would be the best thing." After a brief pause, "There is nothing for me here now. Only bad memories. Everybody wants to kill VC for me, but I will be the one blamed."

"Will you stay if I promise not to find them and kill them?"

"Your new wife... is she beautiful?"

Luke felt Mai's body tense even more than when she was expressing her fear of retaliation.

"She is not beautiful like a movie star, but she is pretty."

Gently he took her arms into his hands and pushed her back from his body. "I don't want you to leave, Mai. Not now, especially after all that has happened to us. I am married, but I want you here where I can be with you and talk to you. You are the only one who can understand how much I felt for Minh. I watched you hold him while he died. I know how much he meant to you also. I watched your ferocious spirit stand up to that kid with the knife. I think you are beaucoup tough and if I weren't married to my wife, I would want to be married to you. But I met her first and I have a child with her, so I have to stay married to her.

"Truth is, I feel more connected to you. You and I, we share loss together, though yours, of course, is much greater. Ha was not my child but I saw enough of her to understand how special she was. She and Minh, two innocent children, destroyed for no reason. I get so angry when I think about them. I really want those VC dead. But at the same time, I really don't want to lose you. I need you, Mai. I will keep you and Huy safe. Please stay."

Mai put her head against his chest and Luke wrapped his arms around her again. Neither said anything. Finally, Mai, without pulling away from him, said, "I can't stay. I have lost my daughter and now you are married. You will leave me when it is time for you to go home and I will be alone with Huy, so I must leave you first."

The sound of voices from the shop were almost immediately followed by Huy's voice, "Má?"

Mai pulled away from Luke. "I must go."

33

Da Nang

May 1968

"At ease, Corporal Foster," said the thirty-something Marine nonchalantly. "I know you requested Captain Montgomery, but he's in Saigon for a few days. My name's Captain Roberts. I've been assigned as your counsel." The chunky lawyer extended his hand.

So much for that idea. Luke took a breath and shook his hand.

"How do you know Will?"

"He and his wife were in Hawaii when my girl and I got married last September. He was kind enough to take a movie of the wedding for us."

Roberts said, "Sit down," and pointed at the empty chair on the other side of a small desk. They were in one of several Quonset huts on the side of Hill 327 just southwest of Da Nang. Half a dozen other desks were nearby, but only three of them were being used by other lawyers and their clients. "He's a good guy all right. He's been showing me the ropes around here for six months now. Been a huge help to me. I'm sure he would have taken your case if he hadn't been re-assigned to Hue for all of this Tet shit."

"I assume you've been told that you'll be staying here on the hill until your case has been adjudicated. You'll be free to move about. Just sign in and out when needed."

Roberts picked up a folder and removed a paper that was loose inside. "Since your problem occurred just yesterday, there's not much here but some basic information… time, arresting officer, offense. Why don't you give me the details as you remember them."

"There's not much to tell, sir. I went to Bangkok for a week's R&R instead of my annual leave. Bought some marijuana. Smoked it and brought some back with me. I know I screwed up. So, I'm willing to take my punishment. All I'm asking is that I can return to my unit when all is said and done."

"Wait a minute. I'm having some trouble understanding something. You just said that you got married last September. But you didn't take your thirty-day annual leave? Did your wife meet you in Bangkok?"

"No, sir."

"And you're still married?' he asked with a chuckle.

Luke let the captain's attempt at humor suffer a slow death then said, "I just didn't feel like going home. My sergeant and two of my squad were killed in Hue. I was in Hue for a month then went back to my CAP where I was put in charge. It's been a tough couple of months. I just needed to get away from everybody, but now I really need to get back to my CAP. I couldn't leave them for thirty days. Things have kind of gone to shit for us too since Tet."

"Okay." Roberts set the piece of paper on the desk and reopened the folder. After some study he said, "I see here that you have one bronze star and have been recommended for another one because of your conduct in Hue. That's pretty impressive, corporal. I also see that you received a field promotion there as well, from lance corporal to corporal. And a second and third purple heart. *Very* impressive." He turned another page in the group of papers that was clipped together. "Says here you went to the language school in Monterrey for Vietnamese."

"Yes, sir. I used to teach English to the kids in the village but the school was destroyed while we were in Hue. I'm hoping my men will have finished rebuilding it when I get back to the unit."

"You know what you did is a general court-martial offense, right? Just a piece of a joint in your pocket is enough to get you kicked out for good."

Luke straightened in his chair. "Seriously?"

"Yeah, somebody somewhere along the line told you that. Probably more than one somebody."

"I guess it's possible I wasn't listening." After a moment he added, "If I heard it, I probably thought it would never apply to me, I guess."

Captain Roberts grunted in agreement. "From what I've seen, I don't think many Marines had any problems with that rule until the last six to nine months or so. The number of cases here has been like a car peeling out from 0 to 60. And I don't think 60 is anywhere near the top speed we're going to hit.

"That's the bad news. The good news is that a general court martial is *not* what's in your immediate future." He stopped for a moment and put his elbows on the table and created a church and a steeple with his fingers. "The Corps cannot follow that policy any more. If it did, there wouldn't be anybody left to fight this goddam war. In fact, if it weren't for us getting a new SLO– Staff Legal Officer– two days ago, I would've bet, with your record and Vietnamese skills, you'd get nothing but a shit job for a week cleaning toilets or some such thing. But I really don't know what to expect from–"

Luke interrupted him. "Tell him that I'll give him my word that it won't happen again, and, if he'll let me go back to my unit, I'll sign on for another tour."

Captain Roberts kept his hands together, moving his elbows from the desk to the arms of his chair. As he leaned back, his eyes remained locked on his client. Finally he said, "Ooookay. But that's a bit drastic." He stared hard at Luke and asked, "Are you sure? Because I think we can get the same result if you let me question you about your experience in Hue in front of him. From what I've heard, smoking a few joints for what you guys went through there would likely be forgiven."

"Yes, I'm sure. I haven't signed anything yet, but I already told my CO that I was going to re-up as soon as I got back from leave."

"Well, damn good for the Marines then." The lawyer put his hands on his chair and pulled himself closer to his desk. After putting the piece of paper regarding Luke's arrest back in his folder, he set it aside and picked up his legal pad and pen. "Okay. Tell me about Hue. That will be our trump card. We'll play it even though it probably won't be necessary."

Luke leaned forward and put his hands together just as a rocket struck the ground nearby. The metal building vibrated and some dust drifted down from the ceiling.

"I don't think the VC want me talk about it," he said leaning back.

Roberts smiled. "Don't take it personally. It happens several times a week. I don't think they aim at anything. They get lucky once in a while knocking the power out, but not much else since Tet. They pretty much exhausted their fireworks at that party."

Luke leaned forward again in his chair. "Where do you want me to begin?"

"How did you get there?"

"Wait, I need to say something first. Everybody likes to refer to Tet as a big surprise. That's a bunch of bullshit. On at least three different occasions in the middle of January our squad leader Sergeant Ramirez informed the CO of an unusual amount of activity in our area. Hell, I interrogated a wounded VC and the last thing he said before he died was that he would see me after Tet." What Luke chose not to tell his lawyer was that the prisoner's wounds had been inflicted after his capture. And that the interrogation had concerned Ha's rape and murder.

"The leader of the other CAP unit near us had experienced the same indifference when he had reported his concerns. Our reports were disregarded because our CAP squads don't have officers. In other words, truth can only come from officers."

Whether Captain Roberts' response was due to his rank, or Luke's remarks did not have any value in the case before him, or the captain genuinely had no other way of reacting to Luke's statement, all he said was "Hmm."

"Hmm? Okay. I guess I *am* talking to an officer."

"Son, you're not telling me anything I haven't heard already. Westmoreland still refuses to believe that he was wrong about Khe Sanh. That Tet was going to be all about its fall. He had Johnson convinced that Ho wanted it to be our Dien Bien Phu, the battle that sent the French back home in '54. Had the whole armed forces in Vietnam redeployed just to keep that from happening, which left a whole lot of units undermanned. And then there was the idiot at Phu Bai who sent three hundred Marines to Hue to fight ten thousand NVA, but I'm sure you're aware of that part of the story." Roberts paused. "Now, tell me what really happened."

Luke stared at the folder on Roberts' desk. Finally, still staring at it, he said, "Long version or short?"

Roberts cocked his head to one side then said, "The one most likely to prevent you from serving time in the Marine prison here in Da Nang and get you back to your CAP unit by tomorrow night."

34

Hue City

February 1-20, 1968

"I had been asleep for three hours after returning from a night patrol with my CAP unit up in Quang Tri province when a call came from our CO at Dong Ha telling us to get our gear ready. Some Marines were in trouble in Hue. An hour later a chopper picked us up and took us to Da Nang to get us attached to a regular Marine company. As you said there'd just been a major shuffling of personal so Westmoreland could get more troops to Khe Sanh. Two hours later and we're on a transport truck with three other CAP units headed north to Phu Bai.

"We weren't more than half an hour out of Da Nang when we were ambushed. Fire coming from both sides of the road with us in the open back of the truck. That was where we lost Doc Daniels, our corpsman. I was sitting next to him. A bullet to the head. That's an image I'll take with me to the grave. Shot in the back of the head with the exit through the face. Probably the first round fired at us. Another CAP unit in our truck lost its radioman.

"By the time we got to Phu Bai, the company we were to be attached to had already gone to Hue, so we were told we'd have to wait until the next day when another company would likely be sent. And it was. Hotel Company. But once again we didn't go. We started to get the feeling that nobody wanted us, that CAP Marines weren't good enough.

"The next day, Saturday the 3rd, we became temporary members of

Alpha Company First Marines, the company that had been the first into Hue on the 31st and been ambushed before reaching the city. We were filling a lot of dead and wounded Marine boots. Guys were referring to us as the Fucking New Guys, but we'd probably had as much contact with the enemy as a lot of them since arriving in Vietnam. Another company, Bravo, was going with us. So once again we piled into transport trucks and, along with some big guns and tanks, we headed the ten miles north to Hue. It wasn't long before we were taking fire once more, but we made it to the MACV compound then on to the university where we spent the night.

"Nobody slept much that night. We had been told we were to be ready before daylight. We were going to work up the left side of LeLoi Street and meet three other companies at the building where much of the NVA was headquartered on our side of the river. From what we'd heard, a lot of Marines had died the past three days with only a few buildings gained, and now we were expected to somehow take several blocks.

"The first building we took was a chapel, a beautiful Catholic church that had a bunch of the enemy inside. One of our tanks brought down the steeple and by the time the big guns and rockets and grenades finished with it, it didn't look much like a church. The enemy inside were dead or had run out the back.

"Our next target was a school that had a couple of two-story, L-shaped wings with an open courtyard in the middle. We took the east wing pretty easily, but the west wing was like a fortress. The NVA had machine guns on each end of the building, which put anybody who tried to cross the courtyard into a crossfire. Hours later we were still there. Well, some of us were. By the end of the day we had lost over half of the 147 we started with and by the end of the next day our company had 7 left—123 wounded, 17 killed. I was one of the 123 wounded.

"I had been firing from the second floor when a mortar blew a hole through the wall to the right of my window. A chunk of concrete exploded into my side, and another one left me with this little reminder." He pointed to the ragged scar from the side of his jaw to the edge of his sideburn. "Another hit me on the side of my helmet and knocked me unconscious. I didn't come to until I was in the air on my way back to Phu Bai. X-rays showed that the bottom two ribs on my right side were broken. The next day I was told I'd be going back to my CAP unit after two weeks of recuperation. Meantime I was to help out with any interrogations of captured enemies."

"But I doubt you got a bronze star for that," Roberts interrupted.

"No, sir, I didn't. The first few days my face hurt, my head hurt a lot and every breath I took was painful. But after that, things started getting more tolerable and I had a lot of time to sit and think about all the death and injuries I'd seen in Hue and, of course, Doc Daniels. He and I had spent a lot of time together and had come to be pretty good friends. I'd given him as much time as I could, helping him with the language so he could understand his patients.

"I guess I'd be lying if I said those FNG comments didn't bite me some. We weren't new guys. We were there to help our fellow Marines. And then there were a few *gook-lover* remarks about CAPs. But those guys are just ignorant, so I can deal with that. But there were a few officers in those four days that made us CAPS feel like we were not up for combat. Almost like we were just doing the CAP work to get out of the real Marine Corps. Not that there wasn't some truth in that, just not their version.

"So, after a week I went back to Hue. Breathing and moving still hurt like a mother, but the headaches were much better. My trip back was on one of the big Sea Knights that had brought me to Phu Bai the week before. One of the crew said the south side of the city, where I had been, was pretty much secure now, but inside the walls of the old city, what's called the Citadel, all hell was breaking loose.

"For some reason I eventually got attached to Alpha 1/5 inside the Citadel instead of Alpha 1/1 on the south side where I had been. My first day there, my new company was nearly wiped out. For the next week to ten days I spent most of my time in Hell. My CO finally convinced the head honchos in Phu Bai that we needed their big guns to start firing into the Citadel or we'd be part of an even bigger blood bath. That was the only way we could win the battle. In other words, to take the city, we had to destroy it.

"At the height of the shelling, I'm not sure what day it was... they all kind of run together, my squad was clearing our way through a neighborhood late in the afternoon... might have been the 19th, when another guy and I ran into this swanky house, one of the few houses left pretty much intact, to escape some really intense mortar and machine gun fire coming at us from several directions.

"Going in we were so intent on not running into a bunch of the enemy that we each let loose a volley of fire at nothing in particular. When nothing came back at us, I turned to see who all was still behind us and found nobody there. The misty rain that was falling, coupled with all the smoke and dust from the shelling going on, made it almost impossible to see anything. And, as I said, it was late in the day. I hollered out the only name I knew of the three others who had been with us. The other two were real FNGs who had arrived in Vietnam two days before. The only response I got was a burst of gunfire from some distance away.

"The other Marine with me was a private named Alton Tobias from Mississippi, a couple of years older than me. He had been at Parris Island only three months ago. Most of our conversations since his arrival had been filtered through the sounds of guns and screaming and dealt with our survival. The two nights we'd had together in the homes our squad occupied had involved the usual getting-to-know-you stuff which was just enough to let me figure out he was a bona fide cracker. He didn't know what a CAP Marine was and didn't seem to have any interest in finding out.

"Because I didn't trust him with my back yet, I decided we would clear each room in the house together. He seemed fine with the idea. After a thorough search, we decided to spend the night downstairs, which had a bedroom in the back of the house with a large glass door that opened onto a patio. We sat in the dark at a table with the drape pulled across the door. With only a little bit of light from a nearby burning building leaking around the drapes, we ate our C-rations and talked about the events of the day. We decided that we would take turns showering then we'd each take a shift of guard duty while the other one slept in one of the three real beds in the house. I hadn't showered since leaving Phu Bai nearly ten days ago and was aware how bad I smelled. Neither had I been able to get more than four hours sleep in any night during that period, so it sounded like a great plan to me.

"I took my shower first then dressed and went downstairs to the living room where Alton was sitting in the dark, smoking a cigarette.

"I sat down on the bottom step as he passed me on his way upstairs. A few seconds after he reached the top of the steps, I heard the bathroom light switch click.

"'Turn it off,' I shouted in half a voice. Alton hollered back that he was sorry, but it didn't matter how sorry he was when half a minute later an RPG exploded through the bathroom wall. Ten seconds later another one came through the back-bedroom glass door where we'd had our supper and destroyed the dining room beside it.

"Upstairs I found Alton unconscious on the floor with his arm ripped off just above the elbow, muscle and bone dangling in a steady flow of blood. He also had a large gash across his forehead. I grabbed the towel I had just used a few minutes ago and tied it around the remaining eight inches of his arm.

"I don't think of myself as a quick thinker, but I did know I had to get Alton to someone who knew more about helping him survive than I did. My best guess was that he had about thirty pounds on me, so I wasn't going to carry him down the stairs, not with my broken ribs. With my hands under his arms I dragged him down the steps backwards and then to the front door. The small fires still burning from the Phu Bai shelling from the south and the naval gunship shells from the east would be little help in lighting a path through the maze of destruction in the streets. The tank we had followed into the neighborhood after the shelling was long gone.

"Alton moaned but still seemed unconscious. I stood my rifle on its butt against the door frame and maneuvered him up across my back and shoulders, got to my feet, grabbed my gun and let gravity take us down the three steps and into the street without going to the ground. I thought for sure I'd be shot immediately.

"I hadn't gone more than fifty yards or so when I tripped over a body. Both Alton and I went down. It was so small it had to have been a child. In my struggle to get us back up, I saw that what I had tripped on was not a child but a part of a torso in an NVA uniform. A couple hundred yards later I was beginning to think I was lost. The darkness and the fear were messing with my sense of direction. And then two things happened.

"Not more than five yards to my right, I heard the weak voice of a Marine calling out for a medic. I stumbled in his direction and got down on my knees and lowered my head, letting Alton slide into my arms and then onto the rubble-covered street. The missing weight felt awfully good.

"I recognized the man on the ground as one of the FNGs in my squad. His shirt was soaked in blood. He had chunks of broken bricks across one leg and several broken cinder blocks behind him that kept him from falling backwards. His chin was on his chest. He mumbled that he was cold and couldn't feel his legs. I told him I would come back for him as soon as I got Tobias to the ARVN base we had been using as headquarters."

"You said you saw *two* things." Roberts said.

"The other was the Dong Ba tower that Delta Company had taken a few days earlier. An illumination round had lit up the sky to the west and there was the tower, or what was left of it, two hundred yards away from me. So now at least I had a reference point to make sure I was going in the right direction.

"I got Alton to the ARVN compound then I went back for the FNG. Fifteen minutes later I was shot in the arm by somebody firing in automatic bursts. After the third burst I was able to locate a muzzle flash. Given how far away it seemed, I think it was just some VC who had taken a pair of night vision binoculars off a dead Marine. Twice I tried to start back on my journey to cross the street, but each time he gave another quick burst. Finally I moved behind the remnants of a building to my left and continued to crawl in the direction of the wounded Marine. The shooter lost me.

"The FNG was dead when I finally found him. While I was loading him onto my back, I heard what sounded like somebody crying. The sounds were muffled, like they were coming from below the ground and then they stopped. I set the dead Marine down and began looking for the source. Five yards away I heard the noise again. I called to him and identified myself just as the ground gave way beneath my feet. I slid for a few feet then went down on my butt. When I put my hand down to support myself in an attempt to stand up, it was against a human shoulder. I pivoted immediately and put my other hand down and it went into a gooey substance that I soon discovered to be an open human torso. In horror I shifted my weight to my legs and jumped upright.

"There was distress in his voice, but the crying had stopped. His head and shoulders were above the rubble. The rest of him was in a mass of broken concrete and bricks that had both of his arms pinned against his sides. The next day I would find out that the Marine I removed and the one whose mangled body I had slid into had been taking cover in a crater created by an RPG when another one landed right beside them, shredding one body and burying the other.

"I spent the next few minutes uncovering the live Marine whose blood-saturated uniform was held together by small groups of threads.

The light being almost non-existent made treatment of his many cuts impossible. When he said it had been three in the afternoon when they were hit, I figured any arterial bleeding would have killed him by the time I found him, so I loaded him on my back and headed back.

"Both men I brought back survived. I had every intention of going back for the dead Marine, but I had to get my arm treated first. It had still been bleeding. A retrieval unit found him the next day and brought him back along with three other bodies. My CO gave me hell the next day for not getting help when I went back out, but then said he was proud to have me in his unit and would see what he could do for me."

35

Da Nang

Next Day

Just as his lawyer had promised, the judge had delivered Luke from any jail time. His last words to Luke had been, "I sentence you to a long life without any more of Hue's horrors."

At the advice of his counsel, Luke had pretty much repeated everything that he had offered the day before, a narrative that he had tried to keep as emotionless as possible. Now, as he passed over Hue nearly three months and a couple of thousand feet away from the event that would define so many of his conscious and subconscious thoughts, he could still smell the death. It was in his head. He had never seen any official numbers for the civilian dead, and now that he thought about a number, he didn't see how coming up with that number would be possible. Day in and day out bodies had littered the streets like trash after an outdoor concert. He witnessed a few family members, or whoever they were, risk their lives trying to drag bodies out of the mayhem, but he also saw some of those same people killed trying to do so.

Inside the walls of the Citadel, he had seen two different piles of bodies that had remained in the open for days at a time until the ARVN sent a squad to incinerate them with a flamethrower. Another time he witnessed a dozer scoop out a trench in the middle of a street and push a pile of rotting bodies into it then push nearby rubble on top. The NVA and VC had sporadically executed families who were known

supporters of the South Vietnamese government or the U.S. No trial.
No presentation of evidence. Just herded them together and shot them.
Then left.

Luke had also omitted from his narrative how he had wretched at
the feel and the smell of the dead Marine he had found with the one still
alive. How his hand had been covered in the contents of the open
intestines and how he frantically wiped it against the dead man's clothes
then his own. But the smell had remained. Still remained when he
thought about it.

Then, of course, there had been the matter of his ribs, the pain
worse than anything he had ever encountered. Repeatedly he had
dropped to the ground as he carried each man to safety. Even now,
months later, deep breathing was avoided, and sleep was never available
on his right side.

Maybe what bothered him more than the pain in his ribs was the
experience he'd had during the first few days in the Citadel. He had
been on a patrol with his platoon, one squad on each side of a street.
Suddenly a local jumped out of a doorway with his hands in the air. His
sergeant had grabbed the man who, with the lines on his face and his
rotted teeth, looked like he was an old sixty. The sergeant then threw
him to the ground and kicked him a couple of times.

"I don't like to be surprised," Sarge said, "especially by an old gook
like you."

A boy, maybe thirteen, then came out the same door calling, "Ông
nôi! Ông nôi!" and rushed to the old man.

Sarge smacked him hard on the side of his head with his rifle and
the kid went down on the bricks.

"Now that one looks like he could be a VC."

The kid knew the term VC and scrambled back away from the
Sarge. "No VC! No VC!"

"The old man's his grandfather, Sarge," said Luke.

The sergeant turned his attention back to the old man. "Is your gook grandson a VC?"

The old man looked confused and frightened and didn't answer right away, so the sergeant brought the butt of his M-14 down on the old man's shoulder.

Luke stepped forward, making sure he was between the sergeant and the boy. "Let me talk to him, Sarge. I don't think he knows any English."

After a short conversation with the old man, Luke said, "They were thrown out of their house by the NVA. They've been on the street for a week just trying to stay alive."

"And how do you know he's not lying? That he won't lob a grenade at us the moment we turn our backs. Oh, wait, I know how to make sure. You just put a bullet in each of them. Problem solved."

The sergeant turned around and said to one of the FNGs. "Put a bullet in the kid, Mulroney. I'm not wastin' one of mine." He turned back towards the old man and said, "This old shit bird certainly isn't worth it." He raised his M-14 and slammed the butt into the old man's head. The sound of the skull crunching was like a bunch of eggs falling to the floor at the same time.

For a moment Luke was immobilized by his shock. When the sergeant turned away from the old man's body in front of him and called Mulroney's name again, Luke stepped backwards bumping up against the boy.

A split second later a zipping sound with a sniper's bullet exploded the sergeant's left eyeball.

Luke whirled around and pushed the kid away from the group and told him to get back inside the building. Although a few of the squad reacted with a burst of fire in several directions, nobody knew for sure the spot where the bullet had originated.

Luke felt no guilt at his lack of remorse for the sergeant's death. In fact, he had been glad the guy was dead. What he did feel bad about was his reluctance to take a stand. The old man would not have died if

Luke had acted as he should have. And it was the sniper who had saved the boy, not Luke. He wasn't sure what his next move would have been. He was aware of how the chain of command worked, and he had been in Hue long enough to know how many Marines were paranoid about whose side anybody was on. He had already heard several stories about innocent-looking locals of all ages with concealed weapons or explosive devices. Nobody up that chain of command would've likely understood his reason for choosing a Vietnamese life over that of a US Marine sergeant if it had come to that.

Since returning to his CAP unit after Hue, he had been on patrols that had encountered the VC, but the encounters since Tet had been fewer and less intense than before. So many VC had been pulled from the outlying areas to bolster the attacks made on the cities and so many of those attacks had resulted in horrific losses for the enemy. There just weren't as many VC as there had been.

Eventually he was certain that he would see death again in Quang Tri Province. But he doubted he would ever see death and the destruction of the human body on the same scale he witnessed in Hue. He couldn't get back to his CAP unit fast enough.

36

Luke

Saturday, April 15, 1972

Luke had been to this bar once before. It was close to Pendleton, an easy twenty-minute walk. He had been with some other Marines then and one of them had bought a bunch of reefers there. Tonight, he'd felt like being alone. He was still trying to figure out what he was going to do next after his second three-year enlistment ended in June.

With no one on either side of him, he sat on his barstool nursing his third beer, wondering how he was going to finally handle being a husband and a father. He hadn't seen any of his family since his wedding day. A letter from Chrissy a few months later telling him that she was pregnant again certainly hadn't helped. The best he had been able to do after that was write a few letters each year, usually in response to the guilt that Moze would lay on him each time Luke would choose not to go home for his leave.

Unlike Wally's birth notification by way of the Red Cross, Luke didn't receive the news of his second child's birth until getting a letter from Chrissy almost a month after the fact. The sentence she had used started with *In case you're interested...* That had been in June almost four years ago. She had been justified in questioning his interest.

Letters from Chrissy still came, but much more infrequently now. Pine City no longer seemed like a real place. His reality had been his life in the villages. It had demanded so much attention that he'd had little time for thoughts of his past life. When he had made time to think about his family, it was Moze he thought about the most. He certainly missed his old relationship with his brother, but he couldn't allow himself to dwell on it. The Moze of Luke's youth, had become a muscle, atrophying from lack of use. And the more photos Chrissy and his mother would send of the kids, the more Luke distanced himself from the old Moze. After what Luke had done to his brother by dumping his responsibilities onto him, their relationship could never be the same. In freeing himself Luke had inserted his brother into his place. And he had done this because he knew Moze would never let anything go wrong.

This past Christmas Luke had not received anything from Chrissy. No photos of the kids and the family, no letter, not even a card. It had upset him, yet there had been a sense of relief to think that maybe she had finally tired of his lame excuses for not coming home and had given up on him.

A few days after Christmas he had received a card from his mother with a letter inside telling him about the kids. She had never faulted him for his behavior. She and Chrissy always left that to Moze, probably because he was so good at it. Just not good enough to make Luke come home.

Luke had not heard anything from Moze since last June's decision to not go home for his annual leave. He had written him one of his annual letters asking for Moze's understanding for not going, but this time nothing had come back. Not until two weeks after Christmas. Luke turned his body sideways on the barstool and fished a folded paper from his pocket and placed it beside his glass on the bar. In the dim light he read the letter one last time.

Luke,

I promised myself I was done lecturing you on your responsibilities, but here I go again.

God, you are one dumb son of a bitch. A sweetheart of a wife, two great little kids, and a brother and mother who love you no matter how much you ignore us.

I don't know how else to say this, but you have turned your wife into a pothead. She's been using the stuff ever since you were married. Mom and I have tried to talk to her about it, but she insists that she can take it or leave it. Every year it's gotten to be more of a problem. She barely makes it from one paycheck to the next now, including the money you send her. And that's with getting free room and board and daycare.

It's taking its toll on Mom. I help as much as I can, but I can't be here and be teaching at the same time. I worry for the kids. Too many times lately they have been put to bed without being bathed and teeth brushed. Chrissy seems only to care about getting to the couch and her joints at the end of the day.

You either need to step up, Little Brother, or step away.

Moze

Luke put the letter back into his pocket and finished his beer. For several minutes he just sat there with his head down until some stranger sat down beside him and started talking. Ten minutes later they were outside the rear of the bar, smoking the guy's dope like they were long-lost buddies.

He should have known better. But after four tours in Vietnam, four years of looking over his shoulder and fostering a sense of alertness, he hadn't felt the need once he had returned to the good old U.S. of A. In truth, he had done five tours. He had agreed to the fifth one at the last moment when he was promised he would be a full-time resident instructor at the CAP school in Da Nang. That was when he had started to get careless. He'd had his evenings to himself and had smoked more than his share of marijuana. It wasn't that he was addicted to it the way Chrissy evidently was. He'd just been bored.

He would have stayed with his CAP unit, but when the unit's personnel frequently changed for the worse and was relocated twice, first to a village west of Hue and then later south of Da Nang, he was ready to leave. But he had never regretted his decision to stay in Vietnam with the CAP program. After his second Bronze Star he had been promoted to a full corporal, and when he had returned to Quang Tri Province, he was given command of his CAP unit. Ramirez had been one of the hordes of severely wounded in Hue and spent the rest of his tour rehabilitating.

While at his CAP village near Hue Luke had spent a few days of his R&R trying to find Mai and her son Huy. As far as he knew, she had never been informed that justice had been delivered to those responsible for her rape and the killing of Ha. He would sometimes fantasize about telling her, occasionally even allowing himself to be unfaithful.

The fantasies ended, however, when he finally found Mai's sister-in-law. She told Luke that when the Tet offensive had started, she and Mai had closed their café located about a half mile beyond the northwestern edge of the walled city. Mai and Huy had continued to live in a room attached to the café when it took a direct hit by errant shelling from Phu Bai. From Mai's sister-in-law's account, the hit had happened about the same time Luke had been in the Citadel, being grateful that the big guns there had finally gotten involved.

But now, here he was in an alley behind a bar, smoking dope with some punk who was obviously trying to get him high so he could separate him from his wallet. All the talk of setting him up with the orange-haired broad with a tattoo next to her crotch and betting him that he wouldn't be able to resist her charms was just part of the game. As they started walking alongside a dumpster, Luke, feeling that old familiar unease that he'd experienced on night patrols as a CAP, heard the click of what might've been a switchblade knife pop out of its housing. The punk kept it hidden but Luke was pretty sure it was there.

"You know, Marine, if you're so sure you're not going to be interested in my lady friend and her sister, then I guess that it's not really a bet I want to make. Let me offer you something else. I'll give you all the dope I have on me for all the money you have in your wallet. Deal?"

The punk brought both of his arms to his chest and folded them in such manner as to let the knife be visible.

"Look, man, I don't want any trouble with you, all right? But you're not getting my wallet, and I don't give a rat's ass about your dope. From what I've had to live with the last five years, that little chunk of metal in your hand... it doesn't impress me much. If you're willing to die for the money in my wallet, so be it."

William Jackson, alias Billy Jack, had never done anything with his switchblade but flash it as a point of emphasis. He had never even been in a fist fight. And there was something about this Marine that demanded that he be careful. The absence of fear maybe?

Yet William Jackson was too used to being in charge... getting what he figured belonged to him. He had the knife, and the Marine had the money that Billy Jack had already decided was his.

Luke leaned back against the dumpster and took one last drag on his joint then flicked it at the punk. "Nice talkin' to you," he said and started walking away.

Billy Jack hurried to a point in front of Luke and brandished his switchblade. "Hold on, motherfucker. I ain't done with you yet."

Luke pulled up. Any open knife demanded some respect, no matter who the idiot holding it was. "Hey, look, man, my life sucks too much as it is without having to spend time with you. Go on back into the bar and sell your drugs." Luke felt a rush of irritation that the punk was still in front of him, but he kept his cool and started away at an angle to avoid contact.

Billy Jack was getting irritated also. Why was this guy not afraid of him and his knife? His frustration at not being able to gain control of the situation was mixed with just a touch of fear. Some of these military guys had training to deal with knives. He'd never encountered one, but then he'd never pulled a knife on a Marine before.

Again he circled in front of Luke, tightening his grip on the knife. Again he took a stand a few feet ahead, his mind suddenly made up to take action.

Luke had already started his knee forward to deliver a message to his attacker's midsection when he saw the streetlight flash off the four-inch blade coming at him. Instinctively he reached for his attacker's wrist to protect himself. His leg off the ground and the force of their collision caused both him and the punk to lose their balance. Luke's hand held tight to the wrist as they hit the ground. As Luke's body fell atop Billy Jack, the knife disappeared into his chest.

Luke pulled his hand away immediately and looked for witnesses. He saw no one. His first thought was to do something to save the punk's life. But no matter what direction his mind went flying, it always came back to the fact that the guy had tried to kill him. If Luke got help and the guy lived, he was likely to say that he was the one attacked. If he died, there would be a much bigger mess to deal with... just because the idiot wouldn't take no for an answer.

How to explain it then. Death by suicide? There was dead body with its own hand holding the knife. But who killed himself like that? In an alley? Holding the knife at that angle?

Quickly Luke dragged the body out of the streetlight and into the shadows on the other side of the dumpster, leaving a trail of blood like a red arrow pointing to its final resting spot. He checked for a pulse but found none. At least that decision had been made for him. No further assistance required.

Luke's back against the dumpster he searched for his next move.

Did there have to be a next move? Why couldn't he just leave? Just take the guy's product and his wallet like he was going to do to Luke. He reached inside the unzipped jacket where the bag of joints had come from, then rolled the body enough to get the wallet out of the pants.

"William Harold Jackson," said Luke reading the driver's license. "You dumb bastard."

Thirty seconds later Luke was still holding the license, his mind racing once again. And then, finally it stopped. Debate over. He was about to perform a miracle.

William Harold Jackson was coming back to life and Lucas Mark Foster's military survivor's benefits were about to stabilize the financial situation for his wife and children. But most importantly, he was going to finally be free to do what he wanted.

Luke checked all the other pockets in the clothing of William Jackson but only found one key. He took it and then placed his own wallet minus its cash in the pants pocket that had held the dead man's wallet. Finally, he removed his dog tags and placed them around the dead man's neck. One last check of his own pockets found his letter from Moze. He held it for a moment then decided it belonged in William Jackson's pants.

Hoisting himself up over the long side of the dumpster, he looked around for some large trash bags but saw nothing big enough or empty enough for the body. Reluctantly he lowered himself into the large, rectangular, steel pit whose bottom was only about three-fourths covered and searched some more but again without finding anything suitable. Finally, he took the three largest bags he could find and emptied their contents. Returning with them to the body, he removed the knife from William Jackson's chest and hand. After closing the blade, he put it into his own pants. From the dead man's pants, he removed the belt.

Lifting the head and shoulders from the ground, Luke slid the top edges of all three bags underneath the body then maneuvered the bags further down the torso until he had the entire body inside. He lifted and tipped the bags up so that the body settled into the bottom. He felt the bags for the spot where the ankles were and made sure the head was below them. He then threaded the strap end of the belt through the buckle as many times as it took until he could angle the pin through the closest hole in the strap, locking the body into the bags. Once he had the body up the side of the dumpster and over the edge, he let it fall inside. Exhausted, he sat on the ground for a few moments then climbed into the dumpster once again where he maneuvered the body into the densest area of trash and made a place for it at the bottom, But, in doing so, the the tops of the bags got pushed back far enough that the punk's Air Jordans became visible. Quickly he emptied another bag and forced it over the tops of the other bags until they were completely covered then cinched its strap and tied it off.

He knew the plan was an imperfect one. If the body would be discovered before any compacting occurred, the identification of Lucas Foster would go sideways. Jackson's blood type was likely different. Dental records might be checked. A photograph sent to the base or home would cause all kinds of problems.

Home.

The thought of Chrissy being on her own he could handle. She was young and would find somebody else. Hell, they hardly knew each other. But knowing how upset his mother and Moze would be stopped Luke's plan dead its tracks for a moment. If it hadn't been for his six years away from Moze, the plan could not possibly have reached the point that it had. As much as Luke knew that he had strained the relationship with his brother, he was certain that news of his death would still devastate both Moze and his mother. It was a lousy thing to do to them. If there was only some way to let them know his pending death had been staged without compromising his escape. He was after all committing several crimes… theft, desertion, failure to report a dead body and probably a bunch of others he didn't even know about. And there was the death itself. He certainly didn't want to have to defend himself against a possible murder charge.

But at that moment he really didn't care about the legal

consequences of what he had done. He just wanted to disappear. Start a new life and forget all the death and blood of Vietnam. Forget about being a husband and a father. Forget about being Luke Foster.

PART III

LUKE and CHRISSY

37

Chrissy

Wednesday April 19, 1972

The house was small and falling apart, but the rent fit her budget and the location kept her within half a mile of Ann and Moze. It had been tough shedding the security of living with Luke's family. But the time had come when she felt that she had to make the break. She could never have done it when the kids were smaller. Except those times when the kids would be sick, Ann was only needed now to keep Wally for an hour after school and to babysit Lisbeth afternoons after morning kindergarten. As long as Chrissy had her job and Luke kept sending money each month, she could afford the rent for this dump of a house.

It hadn't been just the privacy that Chrissy had needed for smoking a joint. When Luke had chosen not to come home for the first of his annual leaves, she had begun to doubt that he ever would. After he had re-enlisted, she had steeled herself against his indifference with the love from his family that surrounded her. But this past fall when he had been deployed to San Diego and had chosen once again to not come home on his annual leave, she finally accepted the fact that it was time to move on. And to move on, she first needed to move out.

There had also been the matter of Moze. She had already embarrassed herself with him at least twice. Probably more. Remembering specifics could be difficult in the fog of a good high. Sometimes, while in that state, she could convince herself that Moze might have serious feelings for her. Not only did he treat her children like his own, he made sure that she never wanted for anything short of an orgasm. Although he would not be directly involved, images of him in her fantasies often were part of the experience, more so in the last three years than images of her husband. She used to feel guilty afterwards. Not any more, especially since Luke had gone AWOL from the marriage. She had not seen him since the days surrounding their wedding. If it weren't for having watched the wedding film fifty times, she might doubt that it had ever happened.

Lately fantasies of Moze had been more difficult to come by. Literally. He had been dating someone he worked with at the high school. Now that Chrissy didn't see him every day, say good night to him every night, experience the touch of him during the occasional hug, he had become the inanimate face of a movie star in a supermarket tabloid.

The lack of proximity also had forced her to see *herself* differently, helped her to see the reality of their true relationship. She was just someone he felt sorry for. Someone who needed a father for her kids. All of which brought her to the realization that if something had not already happened between Moze and her, it was even less likely to happen now that he was dating someone. Better to just let Moze have whatever life he wanted. Too late now for her. She had simply chosen the wrong brother.

So many times over the past few years she had wished she had cut Luke loose... had wondered what Moze would have done if he had not felt the need to honor his brother. Would he have come after her? She had certainly provided him with enough opportunities. Especially the years after the wedding after Luke had re-enlisted. Many were the nights that she was so stoned when Moze came to check on her and the kids that he could have taken her and she would have been oblivious. Not that she would have required that state to have surrendered herself. But, if it were ever to happen, she would want to be able to remember it.

Although she didn't like to think about it, she had left for another reason involving her kids and Moze and marijuana. She had started to have doubts about her fitness as a mom. Moze had tried so hard to be careful not to hurt her feelings, but she had deserved hurt feelings. Getting high had started getting in the way of taking care of her kids, placing undeserved demands on the two wonderful people who had taken her into their home, had helped her through two pregnancies and births, had helped her through the difficult and scary times of early motherhood, fed her, loved her. The embarrassment for Chrissy's missteps had become too much for her. More time on her own would give her more time to schedule her highs without interfering with motherhood.

But she had been on her own for two months now and little had changed except that she was not getting exposed as often for the bad mother she had become. That was the thought in her head when the phone rang.

It was Ann.

"Hey, Sweetie, I just received a call from Pendleton Navy Base in California. Someone wants to talk to you about Luke. I gave him your number and new address, so he should be calling soon. I just thought I'd give you a heads-up. You going to be... you know... do you need me for anything?"

In other words, am I too high to talk, thought Chrissy. More focused on what the phone call might be about than the fact that Ann felt the need to check on her condition, Chrissy said, "I'm fine, Ann. We just finished with baths, thanks. You okay?"

"Yes." She hesitated then said, "You'll let me know what this is about when you're finished talking with him?"

"Sure."

"Thanks. Talk to you then. Bye."

"Bye."

Five minutes later the phone rang again.

'Hello."

"Is Christine Foster there, please."

"Speaking."

"Mrs. Foster, this is Captain Mix, US Marine Corp calling from the US Naval Base at Camp Pendleton, California. I'm calling concerning your husband, Corporal Lucas Foster. It appears that he is missing. He was last seen on the base on 16 April with a possible sighting later that evening at a local bar. Have you seen him during that time or been in contact with him?"

"No. No, I haven't. The truth be told I have not seen my husband since two days after our wedding in September of 1967."

"Not even on his annual leave?"

"No."

"Well, that just makes this whole situation even more bizarre."

"Why is that?"

"Your husband– I mean he is still your husband, right?"

"Yes."

"All of his clothes, his uniforms, his medals, his books, his toiletries… everything is still in his room here at the base. Everything except him. We don't know what to make of it."

"You said something about a bar?"

"Yeah, the bartender said he thought he recognized him from a photo the MP's showed him, but he wasn't one-hundred per cent on it. We've got the highway patrol looking for him now. I just thought I'd check with you. You have any idea where he could be or anyone else who might know anything?"

"Luke and his brother used to be close. He lives at the same number you called earlier if you want to speak with him."

* * * *

The sound of Moze steadied Chrissy just as it always did when things seemed ready to fall apart. The reason she had never abandoned

Luke for his brother was simple. She loved Luke. Had loved him since the day she met him. Not that she wouldn't jump at the chance to take up with Moze. Moze was a definite close second. Problem was, neither wanted her.

"Moze, Luke's missing," she said as soon as Moze picked up.

"Chrissy? He's missing from where?"

"Pendleton. I just had a call from some captain. Said Luke hasn't been there for three days. I don't suppose you've heard from him?"

"No."

"I'm worried, Moze. The Marine Corps seems to be all he wants now. He wouldn't just disappear. The captain said all his stuff is still in his room including his medals. Did he ever write to you about any medals?"

"No, but then he didn't write to me much about anything."

"I guess the Marines have the Highway Patrol looking for him." She was quiet for a moment then said softly, "Something's happened to him, Moze. Something bad. There's no other explanation."

"Chrissy, now think about this for a moment. Luke did five tours of combat in Vietnam and survived. That's what he does. He survives. Whatever his problem is now, it's more likely about his temper than his health."

"But he wouldn't just desert, just disappear unless he was forced to because he was hurt. A car accident, or a fight against one too many guys?"

Moze was just as worried as Chrissy. Luke had to be in some serious trouble to have gone AWOL. Moze sure hoped Luke's disappearance had nothing to do with his last letter telling him *to step up or step away.*

"Don't worry, Chrissy. He'll be calling us one of these days with some wild story, asking us for a bus ticket to Canada. Probably want all of us to go with him."

Chrissy was quiet for a few moments. "Would you?"

"No. Mom would never go, and I couldn't leave without her."

"Would she go to visit him?"

"Oh, sure. Especially if her grandkids were there."

Again Chrissy was quiet, this time longer than before. "What a nice thought." She allowed herself a few moments with the image of the four of them together then said with a touch of bitterness, "But he'd leave us. There would be no love."

38

Chrissy

Friday, April 21, 1972

Wally pushed against the door just as his mother turned the deadbolt, causing the door to fly open. He and Lisbeth made a beeline for the TV while Chrissy headed for the kitchen at a much more deliberate pace. It was nearly five-thirty and she'd had no ideas for supper yet. She'd hoped Ann would send something home with them as she sometimes did, but nothing was offered today. Chrissy had just reached for the cupboard door to check for a can of SpaghettiOs when the doorbell rang.

She opened the door to a sight she had imagined over the course of the past five years every time the doorbell rang at Ann's house. In front of her were two Marines standing stoically in their dress uniforms.

The older of the two men said, "I am Staff Sergeant Richard Hardy and this is Captain Louis Meade. We are looking for Christine Foster, wife of Corporal Lucas Foster."

"I'm Chrissy Foster." Chrissy's confusion became audible. "But I don't understand. Luke has been back from Vietnam for over a month now. You can't be here for that reason."

"May we come inside, Mrs. Foster?"

"Sure."

Inside the house the captain said, "I think it would be better if we all sat down."

Fifteen feet behind Chrissy at the far side of the living room, her two children had watched their mother lead the two uniformed strangers into the room. Both children quickly assessed the situation and decided that their show would be more interesting and returned their attention to the TV.

Chrissy looked at her children and decided to take the Marines to the kitchen table. "This all right?"

Both men nodded then waited for Chrissy to sit before taking their seats. Sergeant Hardy then said, "We regret to tell you that the Commandant of the Marine Corps has entrusted us to express his deep regret that the body of your husband Lucas was discovered outside the city of San Diego yesterday afternoon, the possible result of foul play. An investigation has begun and will be ongoing until there is a determination of the cause. The Commandant extends his deepest sympathy to you and your family in your loss."

"But–"

"An assistance officer will be contacting you in the next day or two with more information as it becomes available and will assist you with anything that you need concerning the return of your husband, his interment, dealing with expenses, recovering his possessions, and claiming any benefits to which you are entitled." He paused for a moment then continued. "Is there anyone you would like us to call who could provide you with support?" When Chrissy did not answer, the question was repeated.

"I'm sorry. I'm so confused. So Luke was murdered here in the U.S. after–"

"The investigation is ongoing ma'am. Now is there anyone you would like me to call?"

"Uh, no. I'll be fine. Thank you."

A minute later they were gone, and Chrissy was on the floor with her back against the closed door staring into her future, a future now officially without Luke. Maybe that was why there were no tears. She had been looking at that same future for so long that there was nothing new to see or cry about.

She wanted to call Moze but she wanted to smoke a joint more. Moze would take the news much harder than she had. And then he would have to tell Ann. No, she would rather get high. Let Moze and Ann have another day with the living version of Luke.

.

39

Luke

Saturday, April 22, 1972

Moze had never been much of a believer in the occult, ESP, or the Bible's version of God, for that matter. But when the phone rang at 12:15 on Saturday, the earth stopped spinning for a moment. A sense of foreboding washed over him. When the phone rang a second time, it seemed to be daring him to pick it up. His mother had gone to the A&P for groceries, so he could let it ring until the caller surrendered to boredom and hung up. On the seventh ring, however, his curiosity overcame the reluctance to pick up. Who stays on the line for seven rings? Then he remembered Chrissy telling him that he might be getting a call from the guy who called her from Pendleton.

"Hello?"

The other end of the line remained silent.

Moze repeated, "Hello?"

A few more moments of silence and then a familiar voice, "Moze?"

"Luke! Where the hell are you?"

"I don't know. Oklahoma? Texas? Wherever my last ride dropped me."

"Are you coming home?"

"I can't."

"Why not?" Moze, expecting to hear his brother say that he couldn't because he was AWOL, instead got an extended silence.

"Luke?"

"I killed a man, Moze."

"How?" A second later he added, "Why? Was it your temper?"

"No. It was self-defense. But then I really screwed up. It just seemed like the only thing to do. I stole his identity and gave him mine. He was a drug dealer, Moze. He was trying to roll me but ended up stabbing himself with a little help from me. I put him in some trash bags and threw him into a dumpster."

"Well then, you've really done nothing much wrong, just turn yourself in and—"

"I'm AWOL, didn't report a death involving my actions, stole someone's identity, stole money, put my wallet and dog tags on him… I think I'm pretty fucked, Brother."

Neither of them spoke for several moments.

Moze broke the silence, saying, "A Captain Mix called Chrissy Wednesday looking for you."

"I don't know that name, probably somebody with the MP's.

"So… what do you want me to do?"

"First of all, I just wanted you to know I'm not dead. If they find the body, and I'm hoping they do, Chrissy will get notified. You and Mom might get notified also as secondary kin. You can tell Mom I'm okay, but she absolutely can't tell another living soul. Otherwise they will hunt me down and throw me in prison. She has to know that."

"What about Chrissy?"

"I guess I'd rather you didn't tell Chrissy. I can't take the chance that she might rat me out to get even for the way I've treated her since the wedding. This way she'll get my insurance money. Besides, I doubt she will be too busted up about me dying."

"You're wrong there, Luke. She's still crazy about you. She'd take you back into her life in a heartbeat. You know she moved out of here a month or so ago?"

"Yeah, Mom mentioned it in a letter."

"What's this I hear about my little brother getting medals?"

"Hard to believe, I know, but I'd rather not talk about it now. Maybe the next time we see each other I'll tell you all about them."

"Any idea when that might be?"

"No. I can't come near Pine City until they find the body. By the way, the guy's name, my name now, is William Jackson. I'm him for the time being. I don't think anybody in San Diego is going to miss him. And, Moze, I really did give him chances to back off. He had a knife. I was defending myself when it went into his chest."

Moze let his brother's words hang in the air for a few moments. He couldn't care less whether Luke had been in a rage when William Jackson died. "I believe you. Case closed. Now, how am I going to get in touch with you if I hear you're dead!"

"I guess I'll have to keep checking in with you. Maybe call you every week or two?"

"Okay. This is a good time if it works for you. Mom is usually getting groceries Saturday morning. I know she will want to talk to you, but long distance from a phone booth can be expensive and a pain having to use quarters. Hey, I know. Just call collect. Anytime. If Chrissy would happen to be here, we'll just refuse to accept the charges. That'll make it real simple. Speaking of money, how's your supply?"

"I'm good for now. William Jackson was doing all right in his craft. But Chrissy's probably not going to be getting her next check from me. She'll be good to go once Luke Foster is found. And that's another thing I wanted to tell you. If the body is found, it will likely have been crushed by a compactor and seriously decomposed, maybe even picked over by the birds and rats at the dump, so tell Chrissy to just have me cremated. My dog tags and wallet should be enough ID for the Corps. As far as my belongings are concerned, don't let Chrissy throw them out. Tell her that you want anything that she doesn't."

The line went silent again.

"And, Moze? I want to say I'm sorry for not being the kind of brother I should have been. I have no excuses for not coming home other than I became somebody else. I found something over there in myself that I didn't want to lose, and I saw what was back in PA as a threat to keeping that new part of me intact. I don't mean that as an excuse for what I did to Chrissy and the kids. Having sex with her was selfish. Not dealing with the consequences, cowardly. I *want* to be a father to the kids and a husband to Chrissy but that new me sees that trying to do those things would be sure to end in failure.

"See, Moze, what I can't get past is the image of you taking my place. Those kids would be so much better off with you as their dad. You were *my* dad, so I know what I'm talking about. And I could see it so clearly in every photo I got from Chrissy that had you with them.

"I felt like a dad for a while in Nam. Minh was my friend and I felt sorry for him, but I loved that kid like he was my own. When he needed me most, though, I failed him. The pain of holding his dead body in my arms is still gut-wrenching. I don't ever want that pain again. So, no more kids for me. I could not survive another failure.

"I know the old Luke Foster failed you and Mom and Chrissy and the kids, but the new guy succeeded in some other ways. My work with the CAPs was so rewarding. I was a teacher, Moze. Can you believe it? The kids loved me. They called me *Genral* Luke and we had such a blast. Most of them loved learning. They were so proud of themselves when they got an answer right. I think I helped make life better for a lot of people in my villages. And I saved a few lives in the hell that was Hue during Tet.

"Even though I didn't write home much and never came home on any of my leaves, I never stopped thinking about all of you, especially you, Moze. Hearing your voice today just reminds me how much I've missed you. If somehow I can get this mess behind me, I hope we can figure out a way to stay in each other's life."

"I am so relieved to hear that Vietnam turned into something good for you. Something–"

"Not so much though for Chrissy," Luke interrupted.

"She'll find someone. She has too much going for her. Maybe she'll end up with enough money to get an associate degree in something or some musical training. She has such—"

"Please deposit twenty-five cents to continue."

Moze could hear the quarter click into Luke's phone.

"Man, you must have put in a lot of quarters to start," said Moze.

"Yeah, but I kept one so we'd be able to say good-bye."

"Don't forget to check in next week."

"No. I won't." A pause then, "Love you, Moze. You've always been the greatest brother I ever could have had. For all the problems I have caused you, I will find a way to pay you back."

Before Moze could reply, Luke hung up.

* * * *

Chrissy did not call Moze and Ann on Saturday as she had promised herself. The promises started again on Sunday and continued through two joints until a little after four when she loaded the children into the car and drove the half mile to the home she had been such a big part of for six years.

When she entered the house, Ann immediately went to her side and hugged her while Moze lied and said that they too had been visited Saturday evening. He asked Chrissy to tell them what the Marines had told her to see if they had been told everything that she had, so she told them the little information that she had been given.

When she finished, she asked, "Did you get a call yet today from the assistance officer?"

"Assistance officer?" Moze did not try to hide his confusion.

"I guess not then," said Chrissy. "They probably only call the primary survivors. But Moze, you'll probably be getting a call anyhow. I hope you don't mind, but I told them that I wanted you to handle all the financial and body disposal stuff. I just can't do any of that now. He said it would be all right since you are immediate family."

Moze, knowing that Luke was not dead, was only half listening and let several moments of dead air hang after her words before realizing that she wanted him to agree. "Of course."

"Thanks." She smiled gratefully then continued, "So, if he hasn't called, I guess you don't know all the details. Are you sure you want to hear this, Ann?"

Not sure whether Moze had told her everything, Ann hesitated then looked at her son for guidance but received none. "Yes, I want to learn as much as I can."

"They think Luke was murdered. The coroner's report showed that his heart had been penetrated by a sharp object, most likely a knife causing a quick death. They think it's likely that his body was hidden in a dumpster and then compacted with the rest of the stuff in it. Workers at the San Diego landfill found the remains when they were spreading the truckloads of compacted trash across the landfill using bull dozers. The assistance officer said that Luke's head was crushed making any dental identification impossible.

Ann turned her head away, truly upset by what she was hearing.

"I'm sorry, Ann. I know that was hard to listen to. That was about all the information he had other than the identification was based on Luke's dog tags and his wallet. There was a letter in his pocket that was apparently from you, Moze."

Moze recoiled at the thought of the words he had written, sure that Luke's possession of the letter on the day he went AWOL was not a coincidence.

"I told the assistance officer to have Luke's remains cremated if that's okay with you guys. He sounded like he would likely meet with you in person before anything gets done." She stopped for a moment and looked at her kids playing back the hallway in the room where they always hung out when they were with Granny Ann. "How would you feel about splitting up the ashes three ways?"

"No, I think you should have them," Moze said, wishing he could tell her that the ashes were the remains of a drug dealer who attempted to kill her husband. But he couldn't, at least not yet.

40

Moze

Tuesday, May 9, 1972

Luke did not call Moze the following Saturday, nor did he call on the Saturday after that Saturday. Each day that the call did not come, Moze's pessimism increased. Had Luke been caught by the MP's and put in the brig somewhere, or worse yet, had he been arrested by civilian authorities and charged with murder?

The following Tuesday night Moze was seated at the kitchen table, correcting test papers from that afternoon when the phone rang in the living room where his mother was watching her favorite show Ironside. Moze knew right away by the warmth in his mother's voice that the caller was Chrissy. A few moments later Ann was extending the lengthy coiled phone cord to the kitchen where she gave the handset to Moze then returned quickly to the TV.

"Hey, Chrissy, what's new?"

"Luke's alive, that's what new! You knew that and didn't tell me?" She was confused and angry, yet Moze heard something else also. Excitement?

"He asked me not to tell you for fear that you would turn him in because of the way he had treated you. I really didn't think that was a possibility, but I had to honor his wishes."

"So, whose ashes have I been talking to for a week now?"

"The guy who tried to kill him."

The phone went dead quiet for so long that Moze wondered if they hadn't been disconnected. "You still there?"

"Oh, Moze. I don't know what to do," said Chrissy, her voice full of distress.

"About what?"

"Your brother. He wants me to run away to Florida with him. Just the two of us."

"When did all of this happen?"

"Just now. I just got off the phone with him."

"Did he say where he is?"

"No. Only that he will be here Friday night to get me and my things."

"But not the kids?"

"Right." Silence. Then, "He wants you to have them."

"Absolutely not!" Moze fired back immediately. "They need you, Chrissy. They need their mother."

"I know," she said quietly. "I didn't give him an answer. I know I should have said no, but I didn't. If I'd said no, I don't think I would ever see him again. It's been almost five years, Moze. I have to see him and find out what's there. If I can't find anything of me in his heart, I'll stay and file for divorce."

"And if you do find something?"

"Then I'll try to talk him into—"

"I know what he's going to say, Chrissy. He made it clear to me that he does not want kids, will not accept fatherhood. You will not win that battle. I am sure of it. Beside the fact that he doesn't want them, consider this: How can they have a dead man for a father? His name now is William Jackson. Lucas Foster is deceased. What is the name on your marriage license? The name on your children's birth certificates?"

"He said we would remarry with his new name. He could adopt them."

"Stop it, Chrissy. Now, think about the last five years. Has he ever sent them a birthday present, a Christmas present? So much as a card?

And now he's going to risk getting caught filing government forms for marriage and adoption, using the name of someone who will likely be sought as a murder suspect? Maybe he will come up with a way of acquiring a new identity, but it won't be used for adopting the children he has been running from since their conception."

Moze stopped and waited for an argument, but she didn't respond. He knew that she knew that he was right.

"That is not to say that he doesn't think that he loves you. But can you leave your children for the kind of love he's shown you since your wedding day?"

"I'm not a good mother, Moze. You know that. It'll just get worse if I don't go with him. I'm weak and lonely and bored and always looking for an excuse to get high. I love my kids but—"

"But what? If you love them—"

"Love them as kids, Moze, but not as a mother should love her kids. I'm a shit mother. My mother's daughter. My worst fear. She wanted her booze and a man to drink it with. I need my weed."

Moze heard the TV go to commercial and hoped his mother would not come to the kitchen. She didn't need to hear any of this drama.

Quietly he said, "Sounds to me like you've already decided to go with him."

"No. No, I haven't. But if I do, will you and Ann take care of the kids? I dream about them being with you."

Moze realized that a *yes* would for sure facilitate her desertion. What made his decision so difficult was his need to do what was right for the children. Much as he hated to admit it, his earlier response to the same question had been an answer that best suited him, not the children as he had said then. He wasn't ready for parenthood. He was dating someone that he found very interesting but unfortunately was married and had a child a year younger than Wally. He certainly didn't see himself as a homewrecker, but he wasn't ready to eliminate that possibility should the relationship eventually demand that consequence.

First, his brother and now Chrissy. If he could be sure that his consent to take the children would result in a happy marriage, he would do what they wanted him to do. But on some level, he knew Luke and Chrissy would never be able to make the marriage work.

For a week he had believed that the change in his brother, the one that had resulted in the new Luke, might be able to overcome the old demons, but when he reverted back to the brother who couldn't make a promised phone call and nearly three weeks later still hadn't made the call, Moze suspected the new Luke really wasn't a lot different than the old one.

And now this phone call to Chrissy? What had changed his brother's antipathy for marriage, for Chrissy? Had it come from the loneliness of being on his own? A life without a base to return to each night, without structure, without a paycheck, without the original Luke Foster. He couldn't come back to Pine City to live because people knew him, and those people had already read the glowing obituary that Moze had written, including the information provided by the Marine Corps concerning the two Bronze Stars. The more Moze thought about this the more certain he became that his brother needed Chrissy to help deal with this new world he found himself adrift in. Eventually though, he would realize that she couldn't be what he needed her to be.

How could Moze send little Lisbeth and Wally into that world?

"Yes, I will take the children, but only if you promise me that you will come back for them when he leaves you. Or you leave him. And I want you to really think about what it will be like for them when they wake up Saturday morning and find their mother has left them."

"What will you tell them?" asked Chrissy timidly.

"Nothing. What *can* I tell them? Nobody can know that you are with your husband because he's dead. There will be an investigation with police asking questions to everybody, including the children. There will be the tears of the children and lots of tears from Ann. Everybody will assume that you have had a breakdown because of the murder of your husband. I suppose there will be a few who might suspect foul play... that maybe whoever killed Luke came after you too for some inexplicable reason. Or that you've committed suicide in some secret location. Face the facts, Chrissy. When you leave, you'll be leaving a real mess behind for the rest of us to clean up." His irritation was audible.

Moze could hear Chrissy swallowing her tears and then the sound of short quick breaths. "I will try to stay, Moze. I really will."

41

Chrissy and Luke

Friday May 12- June 20, 1972

When Chrissy finished reading the story that Wally had picked, she had tears in her eyes. Lisbeth was almost asleep and didn't see them, but Wally did. "Mommy, why are you sad? I think that story is funny."

"It *is* a funny story. I was just thinking about something sad."

Lisbeth came to life when she heard her brother's voice. "Can we have another story?"

"No, Sweetie, it's nine-thirty. *Way* past regular bedtime. Now, scooch over to your own bed. I'll be right there."

Chrissy pulled Wally next to her and held him. "You're going to be such a good boy. I just know it. Mommy loves you so much." She tucked the covers up under his chin then leaned in and kissed his forehead. "Good night, my darling boy."

"Night, Mommy."

Lisbeth was always more of a challenge to get settled for the night. There were either questions about the story or questions about life in general, anything to stall her mother's departure. But tonight Lisbeth was in bed when Chrissy got across the room, her covers already pulled up and her eyes half closed.

"Mommy, I'm really tired tonight."

"Good. You'll have a good sleep then. Now give Mommy a kiss."

With new found energy Lisbeth pulled back her covers and threw her arms up and around Chrissy's neck.

Chrissy squeezed her daughter and said, "That's my girl, my beautiful little girl." Finally, Chrissy let her go and said, "Now, back under the covers and straight into happy dreams you go." With the covers under her daughter's chin, Chrissy quickly tapped Lisbeth's nose and said, "Mommy loves you."

"Night, Mommy," said Lisbeth.

Neither child was still awake five minutes later when Chrissy returned from some last-minute packing in her room and closed the door completely.

* * * *

By the time Chrissy reached the kitchen, her heart was racing and her breaths were so shallow that it was as if she had forgotten how to breathe correctly. At the front door, she surveyed the driveway. Nothing but her own piece of junk that had been her mother's. She had no idea how Luke would arrive. He hadn't mentioned having a car. If he didn't have a car and she would leave with him tonight, they would need her car. She was searching for her title when she heard the door open.

"Luke?" She said his name in disbelief.

"Come on, Chrissy, I don't look that much different. It's only been *four and a half years!*"

She closed the drawer that she had been searching and said to herself *Seems longer when you're raising two babies by yourself.* To Luke she said, "I was worried you would change your mind."

She wanted to run to him but she feared she might scare him away. Still standing inside the door, he had yet to make a move in her direction. He looked different, but didn't everybody after that much time. Mostly, she decided, he looked tired. And older.

"No chance of that," said Luke. Finally, he took the steps needed to start them both across the bridge that was four and a half years long.

The passionless embrace that ended their journey was one of

caution, as if one of them might break the other one. It was an embrace that searched for the familiar, for memories of past embraces. Chrissy's head settled on his shoulder and remained turned away. In his arms and his hands was a tenderness she could not remember, an absence of the sexual energy that would always bubble into their clinches.

"You *have* changed, Luke."

"Yes. I have."

Neither of them spoke again for the better part of a minute until Chrissy said, "Come look at the two perfect children that you and I made together."

Luke pulled back but Chrissy held onto him. "Please, Luke. Just look at them. You don't have to touch them. Once they're asleep, nothing can wake them."

She sensed an easing in his resistance and added, "Just one look."

At the bedroom door she turned off the hallway light, carefully opened the door and listened. When she was convinced that it was safe, she flipped on the light and led Luke to each of their beds for an extended look. A few minutes later she and Luke were back in the kitchen.

"See what I mean?" She didn't wait for an answer. "And all you saw were their physical beings. Wait till you hear them say *I love you, Daddy*, or *Daddy, my tummy hurts*, or–"

"Chrissy, I'm not going to change my mind on this. Did you talk to Moze?"

"He came by earlier tonight to say good-bye and try to talk me into staying one last time. He seems pretty sure you and I won't be able to make this work. And, you know, Moze is usually right."

"But did he agree to take the kids?"

"Yes, but he was not pleased."

"He will be, trust me. He will be a great dad."

Chrissy turned away from Luke and said reluctantly, "Yeah… he will. He promised to be here first thing in the morning to be with the kids when they get up and find I've gone."

Sensing that her imagination was already at work on visualizing Moze finding the kids tomorrow, Luke changed the subject, "I'm starved. Do you have anything to eat?"

"I bought a pizza for you. We each had a slice for supper, but there's lots left. I'll put it in the oven. Take about ten minutes to get it warm enough. There's some Coke in the fridge."

"Sounds perfect."

* * * *

When Luke finished eating, he went to his duffle bag inside the front door and pulled out a large matchbox. "A little present for you."

Chrissy's earlier disappointment at his refusal to take the children with them had abated. Instead of retreating into a bunker as he used to do when there would be arguments, Luke had remained affable, offering conversation in the form of questions about Moze and his mother and answering Chrissy's questions concerning his trek across the country.

By the time they had finished sharing their second joint, they had somehow managed to make their way into a serious conversation.

"What do think about Florida?" asked Luke. "I hear a guy like William Jackson can get lost down there real easily. We can leave as soon as you're ready."

"I'm ready right now. I packed everything last night after the kids went to sleep." She paused. "But let's make love here once before we go."

"We can stop at a motel after we get on the road," countered Luke.

"Please. One time here before we go. One time with all of us in the same house together. Like a real family."

"What if we wake the kids? You know how loud you can be."

"I'll lock their door then unlock it after we're finished. I'll want to look in on them anyway before we go."

* * * *

It was Luke's idea for her to be the full-time driver. The car was in her name and it just seemed silly to risk getting pulled over with him behind the wheel. Besides, he hadn't driven a car since he had finished boot camp in 1966. She could see that he was even more relieved when she had handed him Moze's driver's license and credit card. Now each of them had ID that used a common last name, something usually quite helpful for two people claiming to be married. And, of course, Luke was more than a little grateful to be done with William Jackson. At least for the time being.

The trip to Florida proved to be long and uneventful except for the first night when Luke almost lost his temper with the clerk at Mom's Motel for making a pass at Chrissy. But at her insistence Luke had pulled it together and let it go. Although she'd had a lousy night of sleep because of being so depressed over her children, the weed they'd bought from the clerk earlier helped keep her from going over the edge.

After that first morning she'd hoped that she'd get used to the idea that the kids were now with Moze and Ann, but she found herself every bit as depressed as she had been the first night. She was aware of how much of a downer she was being to Luke. He did his best to be patient with her and kept telling her that, although it would take time, she would eventually get used to the idea of the kids being out of her life. There were times that Luke's certainty about the kids being better off with Moze did make her feel better, but it didn't last.

A rental trailer outside of Tampa, recently vacated by some snow birds from the north, became their new home. Luke found a job with a local construction company while Chrissy resumed her checkout career at a grocery store within walking distance of their trailer.

For the first couple of weeks she had managed to keep her depression under control with the help of a couple of joints each night. Mostly Luke had remained patient with her, but one evening, after a particularly bad day at work where his temper had backed him into a corner with his boss to the point that he had to back down or lose his job, he came home and found Chrissy high and sitting on the couch staring at a photo of Moze.

"I sure do miss Pine City. Ann and the kids and… Moze," her voice oozed with nostalgia.

"How long have you been high, Chrissy?"

"Awhile."

"And how long have been making eyes at Moze?"

"About that long. Just wondering how my babies are."

"Do you know it's after seven? Any idea what we're having for supper?

"I'm not hungry."

"Well, dammit, Chrissy, I am. I haven't had anything to eat since lunch. Could you please put down my brother's photo and make me something. Doesn't have to be anything special. Just make a few eggs and I'll heat up some frozen veggies." After a quick look in the refrigerator and freezer he found no eggs or frozen veggies.

"Jesus, Chrissy. You work in a goddam grocery store and you can't keep the fridge full. All you want to do is smoke dope."

"Here." She extended her joint in his direction. "Have some. You'll feel better. Promise."

Luke slammed the refrigerator door shut then walked in her direction, until he was standing over her. She still had the photo of Moze in one hand and the joint in the other. Luke reached down and ripped the joint from her fingers and threw it to the floor then did the same with the photo.

"Hey! Whadja do that for? That's my favorite picture of Moze."

And then the words came flying out. Although he had thought about it for years, he had always kept his suspicions to himself.

"Tell me the truth, Chrissy. Is Moze the father of the kids? It's not them that you miss. It's not them that have you in this haze all the time. It's Moze, isn't it. Moze has been slippin' it to you since I went into the service. That's what you miss. I want the goddam truth. Are they mine? You and Moze been doin' it behind my back all these years?"

Her head cocked to one side in confusion Chrissy looked up at Luke like a dog not understanding why it had been struck. "No." She decided it was best that she didn't tell him about all the times she wished Moze had.

"No? I don't believe you. All of the time he spent with you. I don't believe it."

"He spent all that time with me because of you. You didn't want me and he felt sorry for me. And somebody had to help me with the kids because you sure as hell were never there."

Luke turned and swatted her words away in defeat, and several tired steps later he was out the door. Half an hour later he was back with Big Macs and fries from McDonalds for each of them and nothing more was said about Moze or her marijuana.

* * * *

It was not uncommon for her to dream of Wally and Lisbeth, but one morning, after a particularly vivid dream involving the kids, Chrissy awoke to Luke's usual multiple attempts to rouse her from sleep. In the dream she and Moze and Ann and Wally were all singing *Happy Birthday* to a laughing Lisbeth, her eyes twinkling, the pink bow in her hair. Awake, Chrissy hurried out of bed to the little calendar sitting on her dresser where she found that June 23, Lisbeth's birthday, was just a few days away. That moment of realization following the euphoria of the night's dream set something loose inside her mind that she could not control. The fixation on being with Luke had been like a thick fog that had been suddenly dissolved by the dream and its joyous rapture, revealing with great clarity what mattered most in her life. It was not Luke that she needed for her happiness. She had been unhappier in the month she'd been with him than any month she'd had with her kids. And, except for the blowup the other evening, Luke had been the best version of himself that she'd known since their first weekend together. The reality of Luke had become no match for the absence of her life in Pine City. She was astonished at the simplicity of the path to her happiness. It had been there all along. The option that Moze had allowed for, that chance for a redo was still there.

She heard Luke come out of the bathroom next door. His next stop would be in the kitchen to get a cup of coffee and the car keys before heading to work. She didn't want to get into fight before she left, but she couldn't leave without saying good-bye.

She caught up with him in the kitchen as he was pouring his coffee. He finished, leaned towards her and kissed her on the forehead. "You're around early this morning."

"I'm going to need the car today."

"What's up?"

A few moments passed before she said, "I've decided to go home." She saw the confusion her words caused and quickly put her arms around him. Not looking at him she said, "I'm sorry, Honey, I just can't do this anymore. I'm miserable. I'm making you miserable... I miss my kids too much."

She felt his arms envelop her, but he said nothing. Finally, "Are you sure?"

"I'm so sorry." She was bewildered by her lack of tears. Evidently, she had room for only one emotion at a time and right now it was the joy of going home.

Without words he held her while birdsong filtered into the kitchen through the sink window screen as it usually did in the mornings.

She stepped completely out of the embrace and looked at him. "My leaving has nothing to do with you. You've done everything to help me that you could.

"Now, I have to ask one more time, will you please come with me? I've seen so much of Moze in you since you've come back. You'd be a great dad, Luke. I know we can make it work."

In the silence that followed, Chrissy thought maybe she had finally won him over. Her heartbeat went crazy waiting for his reply.

"Chrissy... how can I? We couldn't stay in Pine City. We'd have to pull the kids away from Moze and Mom after they've just spent over a month with them. And who knows what would happen then. I still don't think I could do it without screwing things up. Remember, they won't know who I am other than a stranger named *Dad* who's been dead for a couple of months. Maybe someday we'll be able to figure out a way but today I can't go."

A sudden serenity overtook her. Then confusion as she realized she had been relieved at his answer. "Okay." She swallowed the moisture that had collected in the back of her throat. "When you're ready, I'll take you to work then come back and pack my stuff."

"No. You stay here and get yourself ready. I'll take the bus."

She hugged him again. "I'll be sending photos of your children so you can see what you're missing. Maybe... well... you know."

After a lengthy kiss she said, "Please keep in touch, Sweetheart. I need to know that you're okay. And you know that I'll always love you."

"Yeah, I know. Be happy, Chrissy." Luke kept his attention on her as he shuffled his way to the door. "You never know. I might just show up and surprise you someday." He opened the door and called back, "Be safe, Chrissy."

"I will." She smiled as he turned and the door closed behind him, her mind already filling with thoughts of home.

42

Chrissy

Tuesday - Thursday June 22 - 24, 1972

In her haste to get on the road Tuesday afternoon Chrissy had forgotten to take the last three sticks of weed with her. She couldn't care less. She was done with that part of her life. All she cared about now was getting home to her kids.

Considering that the car radio in Florida had talked of nothing but the impending hurricane as she headed north, the weather so far had been nothing but showers. Things changed though once she crossed the Georgia state line. After that, it seemed that she spent more time sitting along the side of the road, waiting for the rain to let up, than she spent driving. When she stopped at a motel a little before midnight, the night clerk told her the eleven o'clock news had said the hurricane, Agnes, had made landfall and had been downgraded to a tropical storm. By the time Chrissy was back on the road the next morning, her car radio was announcing that Agnes was reorganizing off the coast and was likely to become a hurricane again that would be dumping huge amounts of rain inland as it made its way north. Hurricane or not, Chrissy had decided that nothing was going to keep her from getting home in time to celebrate Lisbeth's birthday.

The second day the rain was steady but without the heavy downpours she had experienced the day before. The tread on her tires had not passed her last state inspection, but there had been no money for four new ones. As she occasionally felt the car's light rear end start to hydroplane on the excess water accumulating on the roads, she had a newfound understanding of the need for good tires. She promised herself to take care of it as soon as she got home. There would be money from the Marines soon. If not, she'd borrow the money from Moze if she had to.

By evening the forecasts were becoming even more ominous. The word *record-breaking* seemed to be a part of every new report. When darkness came, the constant stress of keeping the car centered on the road against the wind and the rain pulled hard on her eyelids. At ten o'clock she stopped fighting sleep and found a motel just outside of Richmond.

On Thursday morning she awoke with a new sense of optimism. She decided that she would not stop for another night in a motel. The next bed she slept in would be her own bed, in her own house with her children in the next room. Her positive outlook only got better as she made her way from the motel to her car through a light misty shower.

An hour later it was pouring and continued to pour as she drove north towards Washington. The weather reports on the radio were starting to sound biblical in their warnings. By noon she had made two unwanted exits because of being in the wrong lanes and had several misadventures trying to get back to the interstate.

A few hours later she found herself again in the wrong lane and, instead of heading northwest towards Fredericksburg and on towards the Pennsylvania turnpike at Breezewood, she found herself headed north to Harrisburg. She pulled off the road and with the sound of the rain rattling on her roof and the wipers slamming back and forth across the windshield, she studied her map again as she had done too many times already that day. If she stayed on I-83 it would intersect with the PA Turnpike in about an hour, then it was a straight shot to Pittsburgh and I-79 North, and from there an hour until she was home.

At eight o'clock she got off the interstate to get something to eat and fill her gas tank. She had been aware that her cash supply was dwindling, but tonight there would be no need for motel money. Still, it would take at least twenty dollars of gas to get all the way home and she would need something to eat again. A quick check showed she had only twenty dollars and change left in her purse.

Then she remembered something else she had in her purse. Tucked away in one of its pockets was a gas card she had received after coming back from Hawaii. The pre-approved card needed only to be used to activate it. She had assumed that she'd received it because of her marriage to a Marine but she'd never used it. When it came time to pay for her gas, though, the card was declined. She guessed it had something to do with the nearly five years that she'd had it without ever using it. Now that she thought about it, she vaguely remembered getting something in the mail a while back about her account, but she couldn't be sure. Didn't matter. She would make do with a sandwich and a Coke.

The rain and low clouds had conspired to make an early nightfall. When Chrissy pulled out of the McDonald's, she turned right instead of left on the road leading back to the interstate. Three miles later, with someone's headlights blinding her eyes through her furiously flapping wipers she made another wrong turn and soon became completely disoriented. She opened her map once again and thought she had her location figured out. After fifty yards or so in the pitch-black countryside, she became aware that her car was now plowing through water on the roadway. Opening her door to investigate the possibility of turning around, she discovered in the little bit of light escaping from the car that she seemed to be in a small pond of water that was concealing any definition of the roadside. She closed her door and decided to put the car in reverse to see if she could back out of the water without getting off the pavement. A few moments of backing up though resulted in a sudden drop that told her that her rear wheels were no longer on the road. She put the car back into forward and pressed the gas pedal gently and found herself back where she thought she had been.

She had no choice now but to keep going forward. Hopefully, her headlights would help her find her way through the water. She had been lucky she hadn't ended up stuck in the mud when she was going backwards.

What she really wanted to see now was a house, someplace where she could get her car off the road and call Moze. He would come for her if she asked. He would be so glad to see her... help her make everything all right.

And then she suddenly forgot Moze. The car was *floating!* Then it wasn't. She needed to get out of the car. But then it was floating again. She pulled up on the door handle and, although there was resistance, it did start to open. Her handbag. She grabbed it from the seat and started pushing against the door again, but this time it wouldn't open. The car had stopped bouncing on the pavement and was floating faster now. She had to get out.

She reached for the window crank and frantically rolled the window down, half expecting water to come sliding into the car, but it didn't. Only a sheet of blowing rain. She pulled the strap of her bag over her head, grabbed the steering wheel with one hand, and got onto a knee. After some awkward moves she had one leg on the windowsill and had both hands on the steering wheel to support herself while she extended her other leg onto the sill. It was then that the car lights went out.

She could hear water starting to slosh on the floor of the car. When the front end of the car started to tip downward, she knew she should let go of the wheel, especially when water began its rush around her and over the top of the door, but she still held on. She didn't want to be alone in the water. The car was supposed to take her home to her kids. To Ann. To Moze. Letting go was giving up. But not letting go probably meant drowning.

The moment she let go, Chrissy knew she had made the right choice. There was freedom in her movement into the water. She was soon being swept with the water much faster than the car. She turned her head back to find the car, just in time to see the roof slip below the surface. She would have to figure out another way to get home. It might take a little longer than she had planned, but she still felt hopeful.

Ahead and to the left, she thought she could see some lights. If she could find a way to get to them, she was certain Moze would come for her. Take her home to little Wally and Lisbeth. Moze.

43

Luke

July 24, 1972

The long bus ride had given Luke plenty of time to think everything through. Again. Nothing had changed though. It had been as if both he and his wife had drunk the same potion. The one that crystallized life's most complicated situations into a moment of clarity. Chrissy, choosing not to abandon their children. Luke, choosing Chrissy and whatever it took to be with her.

He suspected she had not left the photos of her and the children on her dresser because of forgetfulness. The month that he had spent with her in Florida had been as good as he could ever have imagined. Just finding her beside him every morning, cooking for him, talking with him, listening to him, making him feel like he was king of the world.

Not once had she nagged him about their children. Maybe she knew that seed was already growing. The one that she had planted the night she had taken him into their room. The seed that had brought him to this point of surrender.

When he had come home that first night after she had left him, he had brushed her abandonment off like the last snowflakes of winter, something that was annoying, inevitable but of no consequence. Being alone was being in familiar territory. He'd been there much of his adult life.

But this time it had been different. That month with her had put him on the bus in Florida and now had him in a motel in Slippery Rock, waiting to pick up his phone and talk to her, make sure that he was still wanted.

When he finally mustered up the courage to dial, it was not Chrissy's voice that he heard. It belonged instead to a stranger who said, *the number you are trying to reach is no longer in service* then repeated when he called a second time to make sure he had dialed correctly.

Although Chrissy hadn't mentioned it to him, he guessed it was possible that she might have had Moze sell the house sometime during the month she had been in Florida. Luke's next call would be to Moze.

After several rings a child's voice said, "The Fosters."

My son's voice!

"Is your Uncle Moze home?"

Luke heard Wally calling out "Moze! Phone!" into the far corners of the house. After an extended wait, he heard the rustling of the phone being passed from his son to his brother.

"Hello?"

"Hey, Brother."

"Luke? Hey, it's about time. How's everything in the Sunshine State?"

"Ah, I don't really know, but it's not bad in Slippery Rock."

"What the hell?"

Luke laughed. "Yeah, I know. Crazy, isn't it?"

Moze took a few steps towards the room where the kids were and listened, before asking his question, "Is Chrissy with you?"

Luke's confusion lasted only until he understood that Moze was messing with him. "Yeah, she drove down yesterday and brought me back this morning, you wise ass."

"No, no, Luke, I'm serious. Please tell me she's in Florida at least?"

The other end of the line went silent.

"Luke?"

"Didn't she come home a month ago?" His tone said he didn't really want to know the answer.

"Oh God, you haven't seen her in a *month*?"

"She left sometime during the afternoon on Tuesday the... ah... nineteenth. She had decided to go home."

Moze tried to picture last month's calendar. "The nineteenth? Oh, shit! She drove up the coast the week of Agnes. If she had decided to leave you for the kids, a hurricane is about the only thing that could have stopped her. The cops–" Moze's words started jumping with his thoughts, "She could still be alive. If she was dead... the cops were already looking. I mean we told so many lies that week, but after a few days they *were* looking. They still think you're dead, so– A body... but we would have been told." Moze realized he was rambling. "Aw shit, Luke, we thought she was with you. She was coming *home*?"

"And I thought she was with you, still mad at me for not coming with her."

"Why are you here now?"

"Everything you've been telling me all these years... I guess I figured out that I was finally ready. I mean I'd already figured out I was ready to be a husband before she left. But these last few weeks... I missed her so much, I had to let her have a father for the kids. At least try to."

"You were going to live *here*?

"No, not possible."

"Where then?"

"Had no clue. I just knew that wherever we were going to be, Chrissy and I and the kids, we'd all be together."

"Just a minute. I think I hear one of them coming." He stepped over to the wide arched doorway that separated the dining room from the living room. Lisbeth was only a few steps away.

"What do you need, Sweetheart?"

"I'm getting hungry."

"Granny Ann is outside hanging wash. She'll be in soon. Can you wait a few minutes more? I'm on the phone with somebody."

Lisbeth brightened. "Is it Miss Vicky? Can I talk to her?"

"No. It's not Miss Vicky."

"Oh." She walked on by him. "I'm going outside and see Granny Ann then."

"Okay."

When Moze saw his niece disappear out the back door, he put the phone back to his ear and said, "Okay."

"Who's Miss Vicky?"

"A teacher I went out with for a few months."

"Is it serious?"

"No. We broke it off a week or so ago. Much to Lisbeth's disapproval."

Moze thought for a moment then said, "Mom and Lisbeth will be coming back inside any minute. Where are you staying?"

"The Cavendish Motel. Room 11. It's right at the I-79 Slippery Rock exit on 108. I got the bus driver to drop me off."

"Do you want me to find somebody to watch the kids so Mom can come with me?"

"Not today. But for sure before I leave."

"Okay. So, you don't have a car, I take it."

"No. Not since Chrissy left." After a moment he added, "What do think's happened to her, Moze?"

"We'll talk about it later. I have some things to take care of first, but I'll try to get to the motel by supper time. I'll bring a sandwich for you."

"Great."

"Okay, gotta go. See you then."

* * * *

The brothers sat in the Cavendish Motel and ate their sandwiches without much conversation, their focus more on speculation than the facts concerning Chrissy's whereabouts. Moze tried to support Luke's need to have Chrissy alive someplace with some remarkable explanation for not making it to Pine City to be with the children that she had been so desperate to see, but he found it difficult. She was dead. There could be no other explanation.

He told Luke how neither the state police nor the local police had wanted to take her disappearance seriously for the first few days. In fact, he didn't think they ever thought it was anything but a woman on the run. At worst, a possible suicide. Either of which was fine with Moze and Ann. They had, of course, known there would be no body, dead or alive, to find because of the letter Chrissy had sent them from Florida. They had been quick to point out Chrissy's problem with marijuana which offered even more support for the theory of a troubled, young, newly-widowed mother, choosing to run away from all the inherent problems. How could he go to the police now with a completely different desired outcome? What new information could he offer?

Not that he really wanted a body. He just wanted Chrissy back home.

As they sat and talked, Moze wanted to tell his brother how difficult the last month had been for all of them, especially his mother. But he also wanted to tell him how much he had enjoyed having Wally and Lisbeth back in the house, how much he enjoyed his new role as a de facto parent, even if it sometimes meant getting up in the middle of the night to reassure them after bad dreams or wanting to know where Mommy was.

He wanted to tell him these things but he couldn't. He did not want to exert any influence on how Luke would answer the question Moze had been wanting to ask since the moment he realized Chrissy would never be coming back.

"Luke, will you be taking the kids with you?"

"Hell, no!" When he saw Moze cringe, he was quick to add, "My opinion on that hasn't changed. You'll be the better dad, hands down. They have no idea who I am. I can't stay here or I'll end up in prison, if not for murder then for a bunch of other things. And I can't take them with me. They would be traumatized, having their lives suddenly separated from family and placed in the care of me, somebody they've never seen. All of that said, now I'm going to *ask* you again to *please* keep them. I know the sacrifice I'm asking of you and Mom. But I am truly not asking you for selfish reasons. I'm asking because it will be the best thing for them.

"I really had started getting used to the idea of being their father. That's part of the reason why I decided to come back to Chrissy. She took me into their room the night I came to get her, showed me the two of them sleeping in their beds. I gotta tell you, they looked pretty awesome, especially knowing that I'd had something to do with making them. But being enchanted by sleeping children and knowing that their mother would be doing all the heavy lifting would never in a million years match the commitment needed for me to raise them by myself.

"What they need now is their Uncle Moze and Granny Ann. So, what do you say? Please?"

"On one condition. Just one."

"Anything. And I do mean anything,"

Moze got up and started walking to the door then turned towards Luke and tossed him the car keys. "I need a ride home."

"I don't understand."

"I drove yours down. Well, it's not yours yet, I guess. Not until we stop at this used car place just this side of Slippery Rock. I called the owner this afternoon and asked if there was a notary on site. He said his wife was the one who did their books and that she had her license. She'll be there until eight. The Valiant is yours for a dollar. It's got a full tank of gas—"

"But what are you going to drive?"

"I've got my eye on something a little better. I just hope the old girl won't break down on you. It's been good to me, but it *is* twelve years old. Until I buy something, I'll use Mom's. I've got the rest of the summer to find something."

Luke took the only step needed to reach his brother. He wrapped his arms around Moze and Moze held on even as Luke spoke. "You just keep on taking care of me, don't you."

Moze had lifted his arms to make room for Luke's and to return his brother's hug. The two of them held onto each other, neither one wanting to be the first to let go. Finally, Moze moved his hands to Luke's shoulders and held him so he and Luke were face to face.

"And I'll do the same with Wally and Lisbeth. I promise you."

Dropping his hands, he changed the subject, "You still have your William Jackson ID?"

Luke turned his back and privately wiped his eyes then cleared the emotion from his throat. "Yeah. I do."

"Listen, Moze. When that military money-business gets settled, make sure you use some of it for your car. Promise?"

"Sure," said Moze, knowing he would never do that. First, he doubted the money would ever come as long as Chrissy remained missing. And, if and when the money would come, he would make sure it was set aside and kept in a special account for the kids to use when they were old enough to understand that the money had come from their biological father. It would be one of the many lies he would have to tell them over the years concerning their parents.

On the way back to Pine City Moze started thinking about tomorrow's schedule and remembered something he had planned to take care of before leaving for the motel. "Dammit."

"What's wrong?"

"I forgot to call Vicky this afternoon. I wanted to ask her if she would sit with the kids tomorrow while I take Mom to the motel to see you."

"Can't call her tonight?"

"It's complicated."

"Uh oh. Complicated sounds like she might be married?"

"Yes. That's part of the reason we decided to end it."

"Do I know her?"

"No. She moved here about a year ago. Her husband's the minister at the Lutheran Church."

"Oh, Brother, you're going to Hell for sure."

"I know. But she's the one that's having the sleepless nights over it. Then on top of that, she had to tell the cops that she was with me the night Chrissy took off. I don't think they said anything to her husband though. At least as far as we know.

"I'll try to get somebody else if she can't. Or I can just wait until Mom gets back. Either way we'll see each other tomorrow. It's better we see you at the motel. I know you'll get stuck with paying for another night, but I'm concerned that if we try to get together any place else, we open up the possibility of somebody recognizing us. Man, you are famous around here now after that obituary I gave the newspaper. They called and wanted to do an article on your murder, but we talked them out of it because of the kids. We did allow them to print a photo of you in uniform."

Moze reached over and turned the radio on then asked his brother, "Where do you think you'll go when you leave?"

"I'm thinking I'll go back to Tampa, try to get my job back."

"I don't even know what you were doing there."

"Just a laborer in construction. I looked into getting a teaching job, but that would mean going back to college. Starting over really. The credits I already have were earned by some dead guy. "I hear there's a growing number of Vietnamese in Tampa. Maybe I can get some kind of translator's job, but I'll have trouble with that, too, because I can't use my Language School or CAP training as references."

"Hey, maybe you *can* get a teaching job there. Something unofficial. Maybe set up as a private tutor for Vietnamese kids who want to learn English."

"Yeah, that's sounds good. I could do that. As long as I don't need government certification."

"Don't know why you would. You wouldn't be working for anybody but yourself."

Moze looked at his brother and said with an intentional air of sarcasm, "Don't suppose you could stay in touch this time? It would be nice to know that you're okay occasionally. You don't have to call, just a postcard now and then. Maybe we could even get together for a visit once in a while?"

"Yeah. North Carolina would be about halfway. You can bring photos and movies of the kids. Tell me all about them. Just curious, did Chrissy ever show them the movie of our wedding?"

Moze knew right away why Luke wanted to know. "We've all seen them a dozen times." He paused. "But if we don't show them anymore, unless of course, they ask us to, they won't recognize you. Especially Lisbeth. So, yeah, in a few years we could all meet you, whoever you wanted to be."

Luke recognized Chrissy's rental as they neared the edge of town and saw several children playing outside. "Were you able to sell the house without any trouble?"

"No. It was a rental."

"Oh sure. That makes sense."

"Hey, ah, I'm sorry, Little Brother, I wasn't thinking too well. There's too much daylight left for us to be seen in town. Take a right here in SEATECH's parking lot. Nobody's here now. Just go around back and I'll take the wheel. You can get on the floor in the backseat. I left Mom's car out so when we get to the house, I'll pull into the garage. You just get up on the backseat and relax for fifteen minutes or so. It'll be dark enough by then that anybody who sees the car go back out onto the road will just assume it's me."

* * * *

When Ann returned to the house the next morning, it was almost

10:30. Moze was surprised she was back so early. She had only been gone an hour, meaning she'd had, at best, fifteen minutes with Luke. The air of sadness about her he attributed to having to say goodbye to her seldom-seen son so soon after just the one visit.

"Mom, you all right?"

"Where are the children?"

"They just left for Teddy's house. His mom called first thing and asked if they wanted to come over."

"That's nice." She made her way to the kitchen table and slumped into the closest chair. "He's gone, Moze. I knocked on his door even though your car wasn't there. Then I went to the office and asked if he had left any message about when he might get back. The girl said he'd checked out about eight this morning and there was no message."

"Goddam him!" snapped Moze.

"It's all right, Son. I'm sure he doesn't mean to hurt our feelings. He's been through so much."

"I really thought he had changed." His anger became disappointment. "I don't understand how he can blow us off like that. Especially you. Not getting to see him since basic, almost six years ago. He really sounded last night like he was so happy that he would get to see you."

"I know. I'd be lying if I said it doesn't hurt. But he's always been such an emotional boy. Maybe all the Marine stuff and the war stuff forced all of that inside." Ann put her head into her hands, shook them as one. After a few moments she pulled her hands away then clasped them together in front of her face as if praying. "He lost that boy in Vietnam. You said he told you the boy had his throat cut. I'm sure there was a lot of stuff like that, maybe worse, that he saw. Then having to kill a man who was trying to kill him. And now losing Chrissy just when he thought he had it all figured out." She paused for a few moments then looked up at her son. "I choose to forgive him, Moze. I just want him to find peace."

Moze stood over his mother and cupped his hands around her head, "Me too, Mom. But you're a better person than I am because I'm still pissed at him for not saying good bye to you, at least."

* * * *

A week later when Moze checked the mailbox, he found two letters in Luke's handwriting, one addressed to himself and one to his mother. Neither had a return address. They were each postmarked, however, with the same city of origin, Philadelphia. He took the letters inside and called to his mother so that each of them might finally have a letter from Luke. He waited for her to join him in the kitchen then handed her the envelope with her name on it and waited for her to open it. Her hand shook as she took control and tore the seal open.

On the single sheet of paper that she unfolded with her trembling fingers were two words, *I'm sorry*. Moze knew, without opening his, that his letter would say the same thing. It did.

Ann sobbed without the knowledge that those two written words would be the last she would ever get from her younger son.

Moze crushed his and threw it into the trash can.

"Hey kids," he called back the hallway, "get your swimming suits on. We're going to the pool and have a fun day."

PART IV

MOZE

44

Now, where were we…

May 2017

Moze sat in the DA's office and watched a smug smile spread across Kendricks' face as she had dramatically announced to him and DA Breckenridge that she had located William Jackson. If Moze would ever hit a woman, his choice would have to be Kendricks.

Even though he felt he was safely beyond her obsessive pursuit of him, that there was no way she could have found William Jackson because the real William Jackson had been dead since 1972, Moze was curious as to what she was up to. She evidently thought it was the proverbial smoking gun, although in today's world of law enforcement, the smoking gun is a DNA match.

The DA had looked more than a little annoyed with her assistant when she had first burst into the room, but Kendricks' information combined with what Moses Foster had just told her changed her disposition dramatically. "Well, Louise, I'm not sure that *anything* you could tell me now could top what Mr. Foster was about to tell me."

"Oh? And what was that?"

Moze looked at Breckenridge with a sigh, twisting his mouth in a way that let her know that he was not pleased. He had felt much more comfortable talking with her than with Kendricks.

"He knows who left with his sister-in-law the night that she disappeared, and he was just about to tell me before we were interrupted. But since you're the one whose pants are on fire here, let's hear what else *you* have to say."

Kendricks wanted to hear what Moze was about to say, but she relished her opportunity to take center stage more. "William Jackson sold the 1960 Valiant that he had purchased in 1972 from you, and in 1976 he purchased a used 1971 Renault. In 1980 he traded the Renault in for a used 1976 Plymouth Volare. His address for each transaction was listed as 1302 Terrance Road, Philadelphia. Ten years later he sells that car to a Thomas Baxter in Seattle, Washington." At that point she stopped her narrative.

After a lengthy pause Breckenridge said with frustration, "And? That's it?"

"It's the last time his name comes up. He just vanished. Or died. But I'll see what I can find on him when he was in Philly."

DA Breckenridge turned to Moze. "I hope you have more for me than she did." She paused as if she thought he would be eager to take up the challenge, but he didn't.

"Mr. Foster, you were going to provide me with the name of the person for whom Chrissy Foster left her children on 12 May 1972?"

Moze looked at Kendricks, momentarily closed his eyes, and shook his head. "That was one helluva an entrance. You're not old enough to know the song, but way back when, somebody named Peggy Lee had a hit called *Is That All There Is?* Those are exactly the words I'm thinking right now. But I'll let you and your boss work that out. I *can* save you a lot of time though… William Jackson is *not* in Philadelphia and, to the best of my knowledge, never was."

Moze paused, staring hard at Kendricks all the while, waiting for a verbal reaction. Finally he turned toward her boss. "Now, Ms. Breckenridge, I will tell you who was there with Chrissy, but you have to understand that this person knows no more about Chrissy's death than I do. Or the two of you. Or the Pope. Chrissy left her husband in Tampa, Florida on Tuesday, June 20th, travelled north directly into the path of Hurricane Agnes, and none of us ever saw her again. The location of Chrissy's remains supports the fact that Agnes did her in. My guess would be that if the river had been dragged a few days later upstream from that cave, her car would have been found. Hell, it could still be there. She came north for one reason... to leave her husband and come back home for her kids. A little over a month later her husband decided to follow her. On July 24th he called me from his motel room outside of Slippery Rock and that same day I sold him my car. And that day was the last day I would ever again see my brother, Lucas Foster."

"The same Lucas Foster that died in April of that same year?" said Kendricks in disbelief.

"Yes." Moze couldn't help himself. "And, by the way, Ms. Kendricks, on behalf of the taxpayers of Mercer County I thank you for providing me with my brother's car buying history. Valuable information. But I am *not* pleased to hear that he traded my precious Valiant for a lousy *Renault*.

* * * *

For the next hour, Moze provided the two women every detail he thought pertinent to the inquiry, including his brother's shortcomings as a husband and a father. Moze did not reveal the bitter disappointment he harbored for his brother regarding their own relationship. Instead, he focused on Luke's eventual willingness to take on the challenges of marriage and fatherhood, his broken heart at Chrissy's disappearance, and how much the attack by William Jackson had cost him.

"Are you sure you have never heard from him since?" Kendricks wanted to know.

"Not even a post card." The one sentence letters to him and his mother were none of their business.

"How disappointing that must have been for you." After a brief pause she added, "How close the two of you were and all."

Kendricks was trying to reconcile all this new information with the conclusions that she had already reached and was reluctant to let go. "You see, Mr. Foster, what I am having trouble with here, is the fact that the United States Marine Corps had declared your brother dead. Notifications were made. The State of California, County of San Diego, the California Highway Patrol, and you, being that you accepted his death benefits, all have affirmed his death. I've done my due diligence in studying this case. After all these government agencies have said Lucas Foster died in 1972, what proof do you have for me that he *didn't* die in 1972?

"My word."

"You'll have to forgive me, Mr. Foster, but given the circumstances, your word seems a bit suspect, doesn't it? You lied to the local and state police in 1972, then again in 2010, and now to us. Not to mention your lies to the Marine Corps in perpetuating the fraudulent collection of your brother's benefits over the years."

"Every penny of which was used in raising and educating–"

"Doesn't matter. If you're telling the truth about his death, none of the money you received should have been accepted. You knew he was still alive. As I said, I believe the term used in that situation is fraud." She waited for a response, but Moze said nothing.

"Be that as it may, let me return to my previous question. What proof, other than your word, is there that your brother did not die in 1972?"

"None, I guess. But here's the thing, Ms. Kendricks, I don't *need* any proof. I saw him. I sold him my car. He was alive the last time I saw him on July 24th of 1972. I'm not a lawyer, but if you're thinking of charging me with fraud, good luck with that because it's been probably thirty years since I've received any money from anybody for the children. Can't say I'm one-hundred percent on this, but I'm pretty sure the statutes of limitation have long since expired on fraud."

The two women exchanged looks, but neither said anything until Kendricks shrugged her shoulders and said, "I, of course, can't speak for

D.A. Breckenridge, but you've told us that your brother assumed the name of William Jackson, a person that the San Diego County D.A. wanted to question regarding the death of a U.S. Marine in 1972, and not long after that, you, the brother of that Marine, sold your car to a William Jackson from San Diego, California. I think this office should at least make that information available to people out there who might find it interesting enough to reopen that case.

"As for the disappearance of Christine Foster, although I find your version of what happened that night in May of 1972 and the following month interesting, I'm not ready to let that go until I know that Lucas Foster did not die in San Diego." She was looking at her boss for support when she finished speaking. Instead she got a lengthy silence.

Because of the length of the silence, it appeared to Moze that the DA was not saying anything because she could not make up her mind how she should reply. Finally, he decided that she needed some help. "Ms. Breckenridge, I leave this thought with you. Your assistant, although a hard worker and competent, does the county a great disservice by wasting its time and resources in pursuing a seventy-one-year-old man who made a choice forty-five years ago to raise his brother's children rather than see them turned over to youth services and eventually fostered by strangers. My choice ended one possibility of marriage and possibly precluded others. My choice was also made the more difficult because of my mother's death a few years later, at which time I truly became a single working parent. For Ms. Kendricks' to believe that I would kill Chrissy for the purpose of stealing the children would have required a complete perversion of my character. If she puts that out there in the public in the form of a murder charge, she will not only make a laughingstock of herself, but you, also. And I promise you that there will be legal repercussions. I came here today to stop you from harassing my kids by telling you information that not even they know." Moze stood up and put on his jacket. As he passed Kendricks he handed her a card. "My kids and I are done talking with you regarding this matter. Any further contact with us will be handled by this firm.

"Oh, and one *more* thing." He turned and walked back until he was standing face to face with her. "I brought a photo of my brother that the Marine Corps gave me to use in his obituary. Show that to your Moses Hendershot the next time you see him." He handed it to her and added, "But you've already seen this, haven't you. As thorough as you are in your *due diligence,* I'm sure you have read Luke's obituary more than once. Did you show it to Hendershot?" Moze did not wait for an answer before responding, "I didn't think so."

Moze was already out the door when Louise Kendricks handed the card to her boss and headed for the same trail Moze had used for *his* escape until her boss stopped her. "Is that true? You had the photo and didn't show it to Hendershot?"

"Why would I? We all thought Foster was dead."

"I think we need to talk," said Breckenridge.

45

Moze

June 2012

This time last year he had been ready to move. Except for his four years at college, he had never lived anywhere else. The house had been old when his parents took possession. His father had not lived long enough to make many improvements and the four short years he had been there after his return from World War II had involved a lot of overtime doing the hard labor that went with foundry work during the post-war boom at Pine Castings. After many mostly ten-hour days, he hadn't had the energy or interest in home improvements.

Moze, being a teacher with his summers free, had over the years made a few major changes and several minor ones, especially once the kids had set out on their own. His biggest project and by far his messiest one had been completed ten years ago to help his children sell the house after he was gone. Moze knew nobody would want a house with ancient plumbing and wiring and no insulation, so he had replaced the old wiring and plumbing then filled the outside wall cavities with foam. The inside walls were then sheathed with plywood before being topped with three-quarter-inch, tongue-and- groove butternut boards.

This past year, however, he had done something just for himself, involving the room that used to belong to his mother, then later became Lisbeth's room, and now was his study. He replaced the thirty-inch wide window there with one that spanned fifty-four inches, giving him a much more interesting view of his backyard. Despite all the expansion that had occurred in the Pine City area over the years, the yard still adjoined a wooded area full of hemlocks and white pines.

Years ago he had erected a pole that supported four birdfeeders, providing him with much entertainment. One of the feeders had a battery-operated electric motor that would start spinning the perch if the weight on it approximated the weight of a large bird or a squirrel. Moze couldn't help laugh out loud, especially at the squirrels that would refuse to let go until they became so disoriented that they'd end up on the ground and fall over trying to get back on their feet.

Today as he watched a cardinal light on one of the feeders, his mind was thinking about the faculty meeting earlier that afternoon, the last one that he would ever attend. The school year was officially over. His teaching career finished. No statute prevented him from continuing to teach after turning sixty-five, but in the past few years he had sensed a growing disconnect with the kids. Whether it was real or imagined, the gap seemed even more pronounced when he would look around faculty meetings like the one today and see the ever-increasing number of young faces with their innate optimism and energy. The kids didn't want to relate to some wrinkled old guy with a head of white hair. Besides, he had a nice pension to look forward to and an unending summer vacation. The freedom to look at birds and flying squirrels… or to take care of Wally.

From the front of the house he heard the doorbell ring. He wasn't expecting anyone. A quick glance out the kitchen window on his way to the front door told him he was getting something from UPS.

He opened the door and was greeted by one of his former students, a bright kid from a dull background.

"Hey, Jerry. How are things in the delivery business?"

"Busy, Mr. Foster. How *you* doin'? I hear you're retirin'."

"Yeah. Today was my last day at the old mill."

"That's great for you, but I was hopin' you'd stick around long enough to teach my kids."

"How much longer would I have to stay?"

"Uh, ten years, maybe?"

"Let me get back to you in about… oh, say, twelve years, Jerry."

Jerry laughed and said as he handed Moze his electronic pad, "Hey, I need you to sign this for me. Somethin' for you all the way from Vietnam. Must be you left something there? You in the war back then?"

Moze signed the pad as he answered Jerry's questions. "No. That was my little brother. He earned two bronze stars and three purple hearts. And listen to this, he did *five* tours there."

"Oh, wow. That's really somethin'."

Jerry bent over and hoisted a large heavy-duty cardboard box off the floor of the front porch then held it for Moze to take control. "It's heavy, Mr. Foster. Got it?"

"Yeah," said Moze expecting more weight than he received. At least he didn't offer to take it into the house for him like some guy did early in the spring. Moze would rather get old on his own. Without witnesses.

"You take care, Mr. Foster. See you 'round. Oh, and enjoy your retirement!"

"Thanks, Jerry."

Inside the house Moze set the box on the dining room table staring at the shipping label, his attention focused primarily on the sender's name… Mrs. Luke Foster. Chrissy? Couldn't be. Chrissy was dead. Her DNA had left no doubt about that. So, his brother had remarried. Without telling him. Just one more nail in the coffin that contained the little that was left of their relationship. Forty-years of emptiness, no phone calls, no letters. Nothing. And that didn't take into account the six years of pretty much being ignored during the war.

Moze had been willing to overlook Luke's choice to have no contact the first few years, chalking it up to the chaos that had taken the life of his wife and the control of his life, his identity, his freedom to openly be part of the family. But when their mother had died without any word from him, Moze, even though he knew Luke would likely have been unaware of her passing, decided that the bond had been irretrievably broken. He had already grown tired of hearing his mother's excuses for Luke's behavior... they were the same excuses Moze had been making for him for years. Besides, it was difficult to feel anything for ghosts. If it hadn't been for the guilt Moze had harbored for sending his brother to war by himself, the bond wouldn't have lasted nearly as long as it did.

He never spoke ill of him in front of Wally and Lisbeth, but that didn't involve much of an effort. They'd never expressed much interest in him. Other than the investigation in 2010 after Chrissy's bones had been discovered, Luke's name had little reason to be mentioned. His was a name with mostly historical value, devoid of any emotional connotations, like a foreign name on a family tree. The effort that Moze had made in the early years to keep Luke's role in their lives relevant had waned with each year that passed. In the last five years, Moze had finally conceded the futility of hoping for any kind of reconciliation. In the beginning of the estrangement he had wished for contact. Then for many years, as his bond with the kids deepened, he feared Luke's return. But once the kids had set out on their own, he just did not care. He had no brother.

Whatever was in that package held no interest for Moze. A million-dollars in guilt money, letters petitioning Moze for forgiveness... nothing in there could be worth the energy needed to open the box simply because it came from Luke or from a new wife. He picked it up and started towards the back door to put it into the trash but immediately set it back on the table. Wally and Lisbeth had a right to see it. He would let them make the final decision as to its fate. For now, the box would go into the closet with the rest of the junk that would need sorted after his death.

46

Moze

May 2017

Moze called his children as soon as he got into the house and asked them to come over at 7:00. He told them only that he had spent the afternoon with Breckenridge and Kendricks.

When they had all seated themselves around the table, Lisbeth took control as she always did. "Okay, you obviously have some news for us. How did it go?"

Moze smiled as he looked at each of them. "Let's just say I don't think we'll be seeing much of our dear friend Louise Kendricks anymore."

"Details please, Dad," Lisbeth demanded as if she were the parent and Moze had just missed curfew by half an hour.

"There are lots of those."

This time Wally spoke. "We have lots of time."

Moze took a deep breath and began a recap of his earlier narrative, but every time he tried to skim, one of them would interrupt and press him for more details.

"So you knew all along about Chrissy leaving with Luke?" asked Lisbeth. "You lied to the police. You lied to us all of this time?"

"How could I tell you anything? You were so young. I couldn't let anybody know Luke was still alive. He might have been accused of murder and certainly would have been charged with desertion and several other crimes, including fraud for faking his death and for giving us his benefits. That money helped pay for a lot of your expenses. If there were no statutes of limitations on some of that stuff, I'd probably be headed for jail time myself for accepting the money. At least if it were up to Kendricks.

"After Chrissy left with Luke in May, I never heard from her again except for a short letter a couple of weeks later. I didn't find out about her trip back until six weeks after that."

"It's comforting to know that she wanted us again," said Wally.

Moze was about to start back into his story when Wally added, "And it helps explain my memory of the voice the night that she left. Being brothers, your voices probably sounded similar. I heard *him*, not you. I guess that was likely the only time I ever heard *his* voice."

"Actually, you heard it one other time. You answered the phone when he called from the Slippery Rock motel the month after Chrissy died. I'll never forget that call. The information that we each knew was harmless by itself but when put into words to each other, we discovered Chrissy was dead."

He wanted to tell them about Luke's last look at them the night he stole their mother from them, but he was reluctant to allow his brother anything positive. There had been nothing good about what Luke had done that night.

"Well, it's nice to know that he had decided to follow Chrissy back to PA," said Lisbeth. She reached across the corner of the table and took hold of her father's arm. "But I'm *so* glad he didn't stay."

"Me, too, sweetheart." Moze took her hand and squeezed it.

"Now where was I…" Moze was ready to go on with his story but Lisbeth was too quick for him. "Poor Granny Ann. Luke really dumped on her. She never got to see him again after he went back from leave. How could he do that to her?"

"I have no explanation. All I ever got for an answer to that was his guilt and shame. I think it just snowballed. He was in another world when it started and then it became too big for him to stop. And finally, it became part of who he was. But I really don't know. My brother, as they say, was something of an enigma."

Lisbeth had let go of his arm but reached for it again. The hair on it was white but she always marveled at how much definition there still was in the muscles of his forearm. "He dumped a lot on you, too. Didn't you ever just want to punch him? I think I would have for sure."

"I don't think I ever wanted to hit him. Maybe shake him a little."

Wally said, "But, Sis, think about it. Luke, in the big picture of things, made the decision that was best for everybody. Of course, we can never know for sure, but he had no reason to believe he could do anything but screw up fatherhood. And having to be William Jackson would only have increased the chances."

Moze laughed.

"What? What'd I say?" asked Wally

"Luke did exactly what I told him to do in the letter I wrote to him in the fall of 1966 when I let him know that Chrissy was pregnant with you. She was sure he would want her to abort you. You have to remember that I was sometimes more of a father to him than a brother, so he used to listen to me more back then. He said he'd wanted my letter to say that he should do whatever was best for him or best for Chrissy, but instead I'd told him to do what was best for *everybody*. Which he did. Thank God. It just took a while for it to all work out. For everybody, that is, but Chrissy."

"You haven't told us how Kendricks took all of this," said Lisbeth.

"She thinks I'm a liar. Which I have to agree that I've given her a lot of support in that area as you pointed out earlier. She likely figures I made up the story about Luke stealing William Jackson's ID."

"Then why do you feel you're in the clear?" asked Wally.

"Her investigation into the night that Chrissy disappeared will end up proving me innocent instead of guilty. Unless her witness decides to lie or *Kendricks* does."

"What witness?" asked Lisbeth.

"Because Luke used my driver's license to register at a motel that night, a clerk named Moses Hendershot thinks I was with Chrissy. Kendricks only ever showed him my photo and Chrissy's because she had been working under the assumption that Luke had been killed. I gave her a photo of Luke today to show to the other Moses. If he identifies Luke's photo, it proves that I wasn't there and it proves that Luke wasn't dead."

"Do you trust her?" asked Lisbeth.

"No. But it would really come down to the motel clerk's credibility. He would have to either lie under oath just for the hell of it or lie for some reason that would benefit him, and who would have any reason to offer him money to do that? I can't believe Kendricks would want to get herself mixed up in some kind of payoff scheme just to *possibly* win a shaky case... But I guess stranger things have happened."

The room was quiet as each person gave consideration to Moze's last words, including Moze.

Then the phone rang.

"Call from Breckenridge Barbara." The phone's caller ID repeated the name another two times before Moze picked up.

"Hello, DA Breckenridge."

Moze's hearing had fallen off during the last few years to the point that he had begun to rely on the speakerphone button for hearing his callers better. With others present he would often choose not to use it for privacy. Tonight though, he thought his children should hear whatever the DA had to say.

"Mr. Foster, I was hoping to have a few more minutes of your time."

"Sure. What can I do for you?"

"Well, first I want to apologize for all that we have put you and your family through during these past few weeks. Louise still wants to show your brother's photo to Mr. Hendershot just to cross her t's, but from what I've heard from you in our visits, I have no doubt as to what the man will say. I have been so impressed with how you have handled this whole situation and even more so with how you've handled the challenges your brother gave you."

Moze heard some commotion behind him and turned to see his kids silently clapping.

"I was just talking with my mother on the phone. She has been fully engaged with what has been happening with your story ever since she saw my appeal on KDKA when this whole fiasco started. She said she had vivid memories of the first reports of Chrissy's disappearance back in '72. She was two years behind Chrissy in high school and recognized her name and photo when they were first looking for her. She had still thought about her from time to time even before the news broke in 2010 that her remains had been found. As you, I'm sure, are aware, there was some talk about you back then and your involvement in the disappearance. She thought at the time how ridiculous it was for the police to even consider that you could be involved. She reminded me recently that she felt like she knew you from friends of hers who knew teachers in Pine City High School."

Moze was dumbfounded about where the DA was going with this story. He started to wonder whether the time had come to turn off the speakerphone.

"In case you haven't figured this out yet, Mr. Foster, my mother has been widowed since 2005. She would be mortified if she knew I was doing this, but I think she would love to have the chance to sit down with you over coffee and get to know you a little bit."

Again Moses heard commotion behind him. This time he did not turn around.

"Given our recent history, DA Breckenridge, I'm a little surprised that you would trust me with your–"

"Don't confuse me with my assistant, Mr. Foster. I've been a fan of yours since we first met. I gave her only the latitude that her position entitled her. If I weren't married, I'd be after you myself."

"Well, now I *know* I'm knee deep in it."

"I think I have your email address on my laptop. I'll find a photo of Mom and send it to you just so you won't have any concerns about her appearance. You'll see that she cleans up well."

"Really, I am flattered, but I'm getting a little old for that scene. If she doesn't know what you're up to, then I won't be offending anybody by saying no. Although you are the District Attorney and I suppose you could–" He interrupted himself, "Oh no, that's the other one that would do something like that."

"I'll send you the photo. Just in case you might be susceptible to hot-looking sixty-somethings. I'll send her phone number with it."

Moze laughed. "A DA with a sense of humor. What'll they think of next."

"Good night, Mr. Foster."

"Goodnight."

Before he could hang up, the sound of a bell from his laptop on the kitchen countertop announced an email.

"Wow," said Lisbeth, "she fired that off in a hurry." Lisbeth jumped out of her chair and had the screen flipped up before Moze could get there. She opened the screen and opened the email. "I think you better dial this number immediately, Moze. Her daughter was not kidding you."

Moze looked over his daughter's shoulder and said, "Not bad. Not bad. But I think I'll pass."

"Why?" asked Wally. "She has a really nice smile."

"Don't know a thing about her. She could be some needy nut case for all I know."

"Do I hear a chicken in the house? I do. I do hear a chicken in the house," teased Lisbeth.

Wally quickly added, "And the expiration date on all of those excuses you used to use involving the raising of your children… they all expired a long time ago. It's time to have some fun, Dad."

"Yeah, she definitely must have the hots for you," said Lisbeth.

Moze felt himself redden. "Knock it off you two. If I started having wild sex at my age, I'd likely blow a gasket and die on top of her. Is that the last image you want for that old woman? Or for yourselves for that matter. It's making me want to throw up just talking about it."

"Puleeze, Moze. Stop! You win," groaned Lisbeth.

"Thank you."

And then, for some reason… maybe it was the security of the love in the room. Maybe it was the relief at the DA's acknowledgement of his innocence and that the pall of the unknown had been lifted. Maybe it was hearing that people like the DA's mother admired him. Maybe it was just simply the right time. Whatever the reason, he said to Lisbeth, "In the back closet in the room I used to have when you were kids, there's a box on the floor all the way in the back. Would you bring it out here?"

Lisbeth looked at her brother then at her father. A faint smile flashed then was gone.

"You mean the box from your brother?"

47

Luke

May 2017

The box sat on the table like something returned from another planet. A box of mysteries. A box with something waiting to be unleashed… diseases, pestilence, radioactivity. Or a box of answers to questions not yet asked.

None of them expected it to be a box of chocolates.

"So you knew it was there?" asked Moze.

"I found it a year ago while I was looking for my old yearbooks. When I saw the date on the postmark and realized it had been sitting there for four years and was still unopened, I figured you didn't want it opened. Both Wally and I have talked about how your feelings for Luke have changed over the years. We understand, Dad. After all you did for him, you couldn't be anything but frustrated and saddened by his silence. If Wally had treated me like that, I would be crushed, bitter, and lots of angry."

"He gave me the two greatest gifts I could ever receive as compensation."

Moze smiled at them then looked away. "Yet, I still have trouble all these years later forgiving him. I thought for a while I had it figured out… how to handle him. Just become numb. But this DA stuff has brought it all back to the surface. I just… miss him."

Wally jumped in, "That's all on me, Dad. None of this stuff would have come back on you if I'd kept my mouth shut instead of going to the DA."

"Are you kidding me? I've been looking for a way out of all my lies to the two of you over the years but could never find the cojones to tell you. I'm so relieved that you finally know the details."

"Are you sure you want to do this, Moze? Open the box?" Lisbeth asked. "Wally and I aren't likely to find a problem with what's in there as much as you will."

"Whatever is in there, I'll deal with it. I choose not to ignore my brother any longer." With a paring knife Moze opened the box and the years between him and his brother and their two children merged.

Resting atop a cushion of crushed newspapers was an unsealed envelope with the word *Moze* on the front.

Moze opened it and read it aloud.

Dear Moze,

My name is Tam. I am the wife of your brother. I am sorry to tell you that he is very sick and the doctor says he will die soon. Several weeks ago when his condition worsened, he had me put these things in this box so that you could have them. I think he is very sad that he did not talk to you for so long. I know he misses you because I sometimes find him crying when he looks at pictures of you and your family.

Moze handed the letter to Lisbeth. "I can't read this. You do the rest of it. I'll be bawling like a baby if there's much more of this."

"Sure, Dad." She kissed him on his forehead as she took the letter from him and found the last words he had spoken.

With these things in the box he sends to you and your children each a letter. He hopes all of you can forgive him for his behavior.

He asked me to tell you about his life here. In 1990 he saw a film about some CAP Marines returning to their villages in Vietnam to see what had become of them and the people who had lived there. He decided that he would like to come back for a visit by himself. He bought a fake passport in Philadelphia with the name William Jackson then later bought papers here that gave him back his real name. Easy to do in Ho Chi Minh City.

He also wanted me to tell you about him and me. Luke was my teacher from 1967 when I was 10 years old until he had to move in 1970. He was my best teacher ever and made me want to go to more school to study English. After the war was over, I graduated from university and taught English in a Da Nang school. When he returned to my village late in 1990, my parents called and I came home to see him. I wanted so much to thank him for what he did for me. Well, I thanked him so much we fell in love. We have two adopted children, a boy Minh and a daughter Ha. I knew both Minh and Ha before the VC killed them, so it was like we replaced them. Minh is now twenty-five and is an English teacher in my hometown, and Ha is twenty-four and a nurse in the hospital in Dong Ha, a fifteen-minute drive from here. Luke and I moved back here when the children finished their university.

Ha has been helping me take care of Luke. He was diagnosed with pancreatic cancer last year but too late to have hope.

Luke has been wonderful husband to me and father to Minh and Ha and he knows you have been a great father to Lisbeth and Wally. If they read this, he wants them to know that he couldn't have been a good father to them at that time. He has never doubted that he did the right thing for them because of how you treated him. I think they will see in their letters that he loved them in his own way. I know that he did. You will see.

What I am writing now is something that he did not tell me to write and would not want me to write. I know that you probably have circumstances that will not allow it, but if you could somehow find it possible to visit us <u>very soon</u>, it would mean so much to him. Please don't think me a bad person for this, but I have told him that you called me after receiving the box to thank me and say you are coming. Forgive me for doing this, but I know he will stay alive longer if he believes you are coming.

Much love to you,
Tam Foster

Lisbeth set the letter on the table and said, "Oh wow, Daddy." She spoke the words without looking at him. "That means—" She had already started to speak before she saw that he was in distress and had his hands over his eyes.

She reached for her father's arm once more and said, "How could you have known. He probably would've died before you could've gotten there. The shipping time alone for the box... maybe two weeks or more." She let go of his arm and slid her chair close enough to him that she could put an arm around his shoulders. "Don't you dare start beating yourself up over this. Not after the way he hung us out to dry all these years. Anything that might have happened to us all this time, he would never have found out in time to get here. If he would have even tried."

Moze had taken hold of her hand that was resting on his shoulder while she was attempting to console him. By the time she had finished speaking, he had his act together again.

"That only says I was no better than he was. I should have opened the damn box, should have known something had happened."

"But there is a sort of irony in it," said Wally. "Luke waiting to hear from you, experiencing a little of what it had been like for you and Granny."

"Are you sure you want to do any more of this now, Dad?" asked Lisbeth.

"I think we owe him that much, don't you?   Not to wait any longer?"

Wally pulled the box towards him and picked out the wads of crushed newspaper, setting them in a pile on the table until he found the envelopes, then distributed them.

Moze rubbed his palms against his eyes and took a quick breath. "I'll read mine last. You want to go first, Wally?"

"Sure."

Wally opened his envelope, his hands, steady as he started, were visibly shaking by the time he had it open and ready to read. He quickly dropped their positions so that his forearms rested against the edge of the table.

Dear Wally,

Let me say first, in case you didn't see the letter from Tam, I am not sorry for giving you to Moze. I do apologize for not doing more to help support him in providing for you. He helped raise me so I knew what you'd be getting.

Because you were first, I felt like I had some connection to you. Your mother often bragged about you in her letters. She wanted so much for me to love you the way she did, but I was too much a part of another world to be able to do that. My failures at that had absolutely nothing to do with you.

I don't know if your dad told you this or not, but I told him that when I came to your house that night to get Chrissy, she took me to the room where you and Lisbeth were sleeping, trying to get me to change my mind and stay, but of course, I couldn't or wouldn't. That was the first time I actually felt something like a father. The two of you in your beds looked so much like little angels that I was sure

I would only make a mess of things if I hung around.

If you believe any one thing that I say to you in this letter, believe this... your mother did not want to leave you. She would never have left you if she hadn't believed that Moze would make a better father than me. A better father and mother than both of us. But she adored you.

What has been the hardest thing for me to deal with during this look back at my past is knowing that your mother would still be alive if I had gone back with her or if I hadn't made her leave Pine City with me. I don't know exactly how she died. All I know is she'd still be alive if it weren't for me.

I did abandon you but I never stopped thinking about you and the family. I lived in Philadelphia for many years. And every year I was there I subscribed to the Pine City Reporter. The issues would often take more than a week to get to me, but I eventually got them. Most days there wasn't anything of interest, but every once-in-a-while I would get a nugget of info on you that would just light up my life with a burst of pride.

The first time I saw you was when you made the All-Star team in Little League and advanced to the regionals in Franklin. You were twelve. You went one for three and made a nice catch in centerfield. That pitcher for the Erie team sure looked a lot older than twelve, didn't he.

Then in 1984 when you took second place in the state finals of the senior math contest in Harrisburg, I was also there, just barely. I got the issue that said you were in the finals on the same day as the finals. I jumped in my car and took off for Harrisburg. I wore my usual disguise that I used when I would have to risk being seen by Moze or anybody that might recognize me. I had a pair of big, thick, black-frame glasses and a full beard that I would glue to my skin with this special adhesive. Made me feel like a spy. I guess I was.

Three months later I was at your graduation. Seeing Moze give you your diploma... what a great night that was for the two of you and for me. Even though I was way in the back, I could still see how you both beamed. I remember when I graduated and saw teachers handing diplomas to their kids. I thought that would be so cool.

I had returned to Vietnam by the time you married but I did see the photo of you and your bride. I hope you have been happy and have a family of your own by now. Any articles that I found over the years I have saved and are in the album that should be in the bottom of the box.

May you live a long and prosperous life, Wally.

Love you like a son,
Uncle Luke

Wally sat and stared at the letter still in his hands, eventually letting it slip and settle onto the table. "I don't know what to say. It sounds like he was really there." He looked at Moze. "You didn't see him?"

"No. I had no idea."

In a hurry to speak Lisbeth clipped the air at the end of her father's response, "I did. I saw him. Not at your events, but I saw him at several of my concerts in Harrisburg after Conrad and I were married. He sat in the front row. I remember feeling a little creeped out. He was always smiling at me. I even said something about him to Conrad. He wanted to confront him the next time he showed up, but I talked him out of it. For all I knew he was a rich eccentric donor to the symphony. Those front row seats weren't cheap. Besides, I never saw him anyplace but there. He probably didn't feel like he had to worry about being recognized in Harrisburg." She paused. "Maybe he'll mention his visits in my letter."

She smiled then chuckled.

"What's that about?" asked Wally.

"Just thinking about what my Marine, war-hero uncle might have done to that prick of an ex-husband."

"My guess… Luke would have politely vanished," said Moze. "He would not have wanted to upset you."

"I'm sure you're right, but I can dream, can't I."

"Okay," said Moze. "Your turn."

Lisbeth unfolded her letter and scanned it for a few moments. "Yes, it *was* Luke at my concerts." A few moments later she added, "His first paragraph is the same as yours, Wally, so I'll skip it."

Dear Lisbeth,

To the darling girl that looks so much like her mother. Yes, you do. I'm sure people have told you that all your life, especially your father. I think both of them had a crush on each other. Wouldn't that have been something… if you'd have had both of them for parents? If your dad hadn't been such a great brother, he'd have taken her away from me in a heartbeat. I did offer.

Lisbeth lowered the letter. "Really, Dad? Did you and Chrissy have a thing for each other?"

"I loved Chrissy like a sister. There were moments…" He stopped as he searched for the right words. "Sometimes love and pity can get mixed up a little. And I really did feel sorry for her.

"But—"

"Yes, Luke did offer, but I didn't… couldn't. She was family."

"Do you think she would have wanted…"

Moze sighed. "Yes. I think so. But… you know… life went on."

Lisbeth sat motionless, her eyes unfocused as if she were rewriting history to accommodate this new piece of information. Finally, she lifted her letter and continued.

As I told your brother I've had a mail subscription to the Pine City Reporter since 1973. The first thing I saved was in April of that year, a photo of Moze and you on the front page. The two of you were at the Summit Avenue playground on a warm spring day during Easter vacation. The paper evidently employed a roving photographer to record special moments for the front page, and that day he captured Moze with you sitting on his shoulders, preparing to dunk the ball into the eight-foot high junior hoop. It was not a great photo. Grainy black and white. The camera positioned under the basket did not capture much of your faces. But it was my first look at you since I saw you asleep a year earlier. I've always loved that photo.

I was in the Altoona gym the night you made that shot that put Pine City into the state semifinals when you were a sophomore. God, you were a ballsy player. I think I remember Chrissy telling me that she played basketball in high school. I know you sure didn't get your shooting eye from me.

Your freshmen year at Penn State I went to your softball game at Temple. You played a great game at shortstop and went three for four at the plate. I have the box score from the Philly paper in the family album that Tam put in the box. I want you guys to have all of the stuff I collected over the years. It will be of no value to anybody here.

Did your husband ever tell you how he threatened to

punch me out? For some reason he didn't like me watching you in the Harrisburg Symphony. I used to go whenever I could until he stopped me one night on the way out of the auditorium. I guess my disguise was a little over the top. He told me that if I ever told you that he said anything to me, I would regret it from my wheelchair for the rest of my life. Said he knew people! I'm sure he has told you about it by now and the two of you have had many laughs about it. Anyway, your violin was always the highlight of the evening. You are so talented. I'm sure Moze has told you that your mother could sit at a piano and play without any printed music.

Chrissy would have loved to watch you live your life. Me too.

Love you like a daughter,
Uncle Luke

Lisbeth threw the letter to the table. "Dammit!" she shouted. "Not fair. He got to throw words at us from half a world away while he's dying. That doesn't make it all right." She tipped her head back and closed her eyes for a few seconds. "What if you hadn't been there for us? Wally and I could've been split up."

She stood up and eased herself into her father's lap the way she used to do as a child. With her head under his chin and her cheek against his chest, she forced her arms around him and said quietly, "Oh, Moze. Your brother only showed up for our successes. You were there for our failures. You created the moments he got to see. Thanks, Daddy."

From a few feet away Wally, as he often had as a child, felt left out. He was a man with Parkinson's now who, disease or no disease, was unable to physically be part of what was happening between Moze and Lisbeth. But that was okay with him.

"Amen to that, Dad," he said as he reached a hand in his father's direction. Moze leaned towards him enough that their hands could join.

Wally would choose his moment for an embrace with his father when it wouldn't be an intrusion on his sister's moment with him. She would be back in Philadelphia before long and his life with Moze would resume its normal course. A shudder passed over him as he considered what his life would have been like with Luke as a caretaker. Although, from what his wife's letter indicated, their roles would likely have been reversed eventually.

A few moments later Lisbeth's continued dead weight prompted Moze to shift his legs which prompted Lisbeth to stand up and return to her chair.

"Your turn, Moze. Let's hear what Luke has to say to you," she said as she sat in her chair.

"I think I'll wait until later. He pulled the box toward him and said, "Let's see what else is in here." He removed five dark blue boxes. "These will be his medals. The Marines returned them to me with the ashes of William Jackson. The only information I ever learned about them was from the Marine Corps. But when I gave them to Luke with my car and the rest of his belongings, he seemed really pleased to get them back. I know that the Bronze Stars each involved saving lives by risking his own. Once near the Laotian border not far from the DMZ and the other time in Hue during Tet. As for the Purple Hearts, the first one was for a piece of shrapnel in his leg, the second one from an exploding wall that knocked him unconscious, put a scar on his face and broke ribs. The last one was for being shot in the arm. I know that scar was still there four years later.

"As proud of his medals as he may have been, I think, in his mind anyhow, his biggest accomplishment, the thing he was most proud of, was his time teaching in the CAP schools."

The three of them passed the medals to each other, taking turns studying them.

Moze then pulled out three notebooks and gave one to each of them.

It was Lisbeth who offered a guess as to what they were. "Looks like a list of names, a lot of them look Vietnamese. My book, anyhow, has a year at the top of each list and an address. The years listed are the years he was in Philadelphia. I see some familiar street names."

"I'll bet those names were the kids he taught English. I would say my notebook is from his CAP days," said Moze thumbing through the pages. "The years stop in the spring of 1971. Each name has several notes under it. Evidently what the child liked to eat and what his favorite subject was." Moze thumbed back to the beginning and stopped. "This boy named Minh must have been the one he lost. Under his name he wrote 'my best student' and under his likes it says 'Crazy about hot dogs, baked beans and Ha.'"

"This one then has to be a list from the days after he returned to Vietnam according to the years," said Wally. "A lot of names here."

They spent a few minutes looking through their respective notebooks then exchanged them until everybody was finished.

The scrapbook that Luke had mentioned in Wally's and Lisbeth's letters was the next item lifted from the box. The three of them drew their chairs together with Moze in the middle and looked at it together. Several additional newspaper items not referenced in the letters were included. Moze also had a kept a folder that included the items that were in the album, but it was nice to see everything as organized as Luke's material was. In the back was Granny Ann's obituary and a photo of her headstone bearing witness to a visit Luke had evidently made to the cemetery during one of his trips to see his children perform.

In another section just before his mother's obituary, Luke had grouped several articles and photos that had appeared in 2010 following the discovery of Chrissy's remains.

In the very back was a small clear plastic baggie stapled to the inside back of the album, the contents visible … two clear bags with little swatches of hair clipped from Lisbeth and Wally labeled with each name and the dates they had been clipped.

"What happened to my beautiful blond hair!" exclaimed Lisbeth.

The last item removed from the box was a folding black plastic DVD case with a sticker on the outside that said *My Second Family*.

"Oh, good, this should be interesting," said Lisbeth. She immediately jumped up and retrieved Moze's laptop from the other end of the table. A few moments later the homemade title *Our Family* stretched above a still photo of Luke, Tam, Minh, and Ha, labeled 2016 and another photo of all four of them taken in 1993.

"Look at them, Dad. They all look so happy. Luke looks like he's a lot thinner in the second photo than the first."

"Cancer can do that to you, I guess. But he looks happy. I know I can't remember the last time I saw him with that kind of smile on his face. That photo from 1993 is the first recorded image of him I've seen since his wedding video. The Marine photo for his obit doesn't count. I've never seen anyone smile for those. When we're finished with this, I'll get out the transfer DVD I had made of the old wedding film."

"Did you ever see that, Wally?" asked Lisbeth.

Before Wally could answer, Moze said, "You don't remember me asking you if you wanted to see it back in 2010? That's when I had it done. I didn't want you to think about your mother as a pile of bones, but you said it had no interest for you."

He looked at Wally, "I know *you've* seen it."

"Several times, but not in the last five years or so."

Moze hit the play button and Luke's DVD started playing.

As the movie progressed it was obvious to Moze that he wasn't going to see much of his brother who was evidently the designated cameraman. After the children became teenagers, they occasionally replaced him. Those few times before then, when he did become visible, Moze was surprised at the size of his brother's paunch. By the time he was in his sixties, the girth had begun to reach the point of obesity. But he did look content with his life.

Tam's appearance never seemed to change. She was very attractive in her younger years and was obviously in love with Luke when they shared the camera's spotlight. She seemed to enjoy having the camera on her, at least that was what her perpetual smile said.

At one point there was footage of headstones for the original Minh and Ha. And then towards the end another marker for someone named Thanh Foster. Because of the birth and death dates, it seemed obvious to Moze that the child was Luke's grandson from Minh and his wife, and that he had died in infancy. Moze was saddened at the realization that he and Luke then would finish their lives without having the chance to spoil grandchildren.

"They seem to be such a happy family," said Lisbeth when the DVD finished. "I think I would like to meet them someday. What do you think, guys?"

Moze was dumbstruck, this from the child who never had any interest in her birth parents. "Maybe. I'm not sure how welcome I would be after never responding to Tam's letter."

Lisbeth turned her attention to Wally. "What do you think, Brother? Want to take a little trip? Meet some Fosters?"

For a few moments Wally said nothing. He seemed to be looking at everything in the room but his father and sister. Finally, in a quiet voice he said, "Of course I would like to, but, at this point with the disease, I think staying home would be the smart thing to do. You and Dad should go, though. Take lots of video to show me when you get back. Deenie and I will be fine here."

Moze smiled. "*If* I choose to go, it'll only be on the condition that all three of us go together. We'll talk about it after we get a chance to think about it some. Right now I'd like to watch the wedding DVD. I really want Lisbeth to see her mother and father."

"You were the best man, right?" asked Lisbeth.

"Yes, I was."

"Well, roll that ancient footage," said Lisbeth. "I want to see what my real dad looked like on his brother's wedding day."

"I hope the camera zooms in on Chrissy's midsection, because if it does, we might see where one of my favorite people just took up residence. If she wasn't there then, she'd be there by the end of the next day."

"Wow, that's really weird, isn't it?" mused Lisbeth.

"Who knew," said Moze as the video without any title page began.

"Hey," said Lisbeth, "this really is *old*. No sound? Luke's at least had sound. I want my money back."

"Luke's was almost thirty years newer. Quiet or I'll have my usher show you to the door."

"Yes, Daddy."

But she wasn't quiet. The film began with the camera panning around the room and stopping on a female Lisbeth did not recognize. "Who's that? Hope that's not Chrissy if I'm supposed to look like her. Besides, she sure seems to be flirting a lot with the cameraman."

Moze laughed. "It's his wife. They were celebrating their tenth anniversary. I found them in the hotel bar. He was a lawyer stationed in Vietnam somewhere near Luke. They couldn't have been nicer. They even took us all out to eat afterwards."

The footage brightened suddenly then Luke and Chrissy were walking into the room and taking their places beside the person officiating. Transfixed by the sight of her mother, Lisbeth said almost reverently, "Oh, Moze. She really was pretty. No wonder Luke came back for her. But how could he have ever not wanted to be with her." It was an observation rooted in amazement, not confusion. She didn't want an answer.

"Look at the difference between this Luke and the one we just watched in Vietnam," said Wally.

"That's what forty or fifty years can do to you, Son."

"Wonder what Chrissy would have looked like today?" said Lisbeth, her eyes still glued to the laptop.

"I don't know about now, but I'll bet you'll see her at fifty the next time you look at a mirror." Moze looked away from the screen then added, "If she'd been able to get rid of the marijuana crap."

Five minutes later the wedding was over. After a brief blackout several more minutes of film from the after-wedding dinner followed. Then there were a few more minutes that Moze had shot of Wally and Granny Ann when he and Chrissy had returned home.

"Nothing of baby Lisbeth?" asked his daughter with disappointment.

"The camera was rented. That's what I should have done with that first check from the government for Luke... buy one. How many times I've regretted not doing that."

"No worries, Dad," said Lisbeth. "We've got more than enough photos.

"I'm so glad we have this film of Granny Ann though. We have a bunch of photos of her, but seeing her alive, moving... this is much better. I really don't remember her other than the photos."

When Moze had removed the DVD and placed it in its case, he said, "Would either of you want me to make a copy for you?"

"Yes, for sure," said Lisbeth.

"Me too," added Wally.

Moze reached for the box. "Did we see everything that was in there?" After a moment of investigation he answered his own question. "Yep, I guess that's it then."

"Except your letter," said Lisbeth.

"Yeah, I know. But I think I'll read it later. If there's anything you should know, I'll show it to you." He gathered up the wadded papers and returned them to the box.

As Wally and Lisbeth got up from their chairs, Lisbeth said, "I am serious about seeing Luke's family, Wally. I agree with Dad. I think it would be so great for all of us to take a trip like that together. I can miss another week of work if I have to. That's all it should take. Do you have any treatments scheduled in the next week?"

"Yes, but I can postpone it if you're sure I won't slow everybody down."

"What about your business?" asked Lisbeth.

"My office is where my laptop is."

"Super!" She turned to her father. "Moze?"

"Unless I find something in Luke's letter that would make it a bad idea, let's do it. You two can make the plans when you get home tonight and let me know what you come up with. It's all my treat."

48

Moze

May 2017

The pileated woodpecker with his massive body glided smoothly onto the crossbar that held the suet feeder. He looked to his right, then to his left half a dozen times, each time with his head cocked slightly upward as if he were worried about being attacked from the sky. Wariness seemed to be his mantra, though Moze could never understand why, having never seen anything foolish enough to challenge the huge bird with its long, streamlined bill, a jackhammer that could startle a forest with one quick series of explosive hits on a dead oak tree. He came every evening just before dusk for his daily dose of fat. Moze watched him longer than usual tonight, though it probably had more to do with postponing the reading of Luke's letter than any interest in the woodpecker.

That he had missed the chance to see his brother one last time only made him feel even more reluctant to see what was there. As if Luke somehow had known that Moze wouldn't come and included some vitriolic rebuke for deserting him in his final hours.

But it wouldn't matter what Luke would have to say to him now. Whether it was unequivocal kindness or a deathbed plea for forgiveness would not matter. The self-deprecation Moze held for himself at refusing to open the box, for denying himself and his brother the opportunity for any reconciliation would color everything in the letter with his own guilt.

Still, he had to read it… his brother's last words to him.

May 18, 2012

Dear Moze… brother, father, friend,

How can one person be all those things to someone? Shouldn't someone like that be treated like a god? Certainly better than I treated you. I have no doubts that the thought has lingered in your mind often over the years. So once again, I apologize.

Yeah, I know. Big Whoop. Same old Luke. Been there. Read that. Heard that. I know I have some serious explaining to do.

I've had a lot of time to think about this, especially since the cancer showed up. CANCER. Do you believe it? Me? The guy who survived five tours of duty in Vietnam. Still can't believe it sometimes. Either fact.

Anyway, I guess it's true, so it's time to get on with it. What I'm about to tell you is probably going to sound like the biggest bunch of horseshit you've ever heard, but believe me when I tell you… I really thought it was true. Which will probably only lower your image of me even further.

But, of course, it wasn't true.

Drumroll….

I believed you were the father of Wally and Lisbeth. As recently as last year.

After getting the news that I likely would be dead in another year and a half to two years, I started sorting through all my personal stuff from my first life. That was when I came up with the idea to send you whatever I had that you and the kids might be interested in. It's probably no surprise that I put the actual sending of it off as long as I could.

Hopefully you found the hair that Chrissy saved from the kids. She had left the little envelopes on her dresser with the kids' photos and casts of their foot and hand prints, trying to get me interested in joining her. The casts broke when I dropped the box that they were in many years ago in Philly. Sorry.

Not all of the original hair is there. I found a place in Japan that tested my hair and theirs for DNA and what do you know...a perfect match.

So why did I think they were yours?

Probably because I wanted them to be. But that didn't keep me from being crushed that you would actually do that to me. I know, I know. I tried to talk you into taking Chrissy. I guess I couldn't believe that you wouldn't. How could you not want her? You kept telling me how great she was. How stupid I was for not treating her better. It wasn't much of a stretch for me to assume that you would eventually take me up on the offer.

But I could never let you know that was how I felt. Because deep down I couldn't convince myself that it could be true.

How could it, you were Moze.

As long as I played it the other way— that you were that guy who could do such a thing— I could justify the way I acted. So I went back and forth, believing, not believing, and a lot of the time... just not caring.

When Wally was born, there were the photos, proof in living color. You and Wally, you and Chrissy and Wally. All the time you spent with Chrissy... hell, you lived together in the same house. You had to want her eventually.

Then along came Minh. A real kid, not a photograph, someone who needed me every day. Did not ask a thing from me yet transformed me into someone who wanted to give him everything. I failed him though, couldn't even keep him safe. I think that's when I really started to believe my own lies about you. I somehow had to make you worse than I was.

Chrissy's letters, praising your kindness to her and the children, didn't help. <u>Can't you see that he's just trying to get into your pants?</u> I would write in invisible ink. No matter that she only got pregnant after being with me. In my twisted mind that was all part of the plan to cover your dirty deeds.

But, of course, when you showed up in Hawaii and I was in your presence, you were the real Moze and all those sick and crazy thoughts vanished.

After the wedding, though, something changed in Chrissy's letters and the insanity returned. It was like she didn't care as much. Like she had someone else. And who else would it be if not you?

I understand now it was only the marijuana.

Florida got you off the hook, at least for a little while. It started the night Chrissy and I left Pine City. When she was so fired up about wanting to take the children with us, I just knew she couldn't do that to you if they were yours, not after you and Mom had given them so much.

Florida was supposed to be about just the two of us but it wasn't. She was so depressed. All she wanted to do was get high. She said that she missed the kids too much, but I knew the truth. It wasn't the kids she missed, it was you. We had a huge blow up over it. That's what I keep thinking of. How likely it was that it was those insane accusations that finally pushed her away from me and sent her home to die. When I apologized the next day, she said she understood. That she forgave me, but it was less than a week later that she left. If only I had... ah well, regrets are like left-over foreign coins. You stick them into a drawer then stumble upon them once in a while. But they're basically useless.

I stewed about her dumping me for a few weeks before I realized how much I missed her. The time with her had changed me every bit as much as Minh had changed me. I needed to be with her, to do as much for her as you had, even more. If the kids were mine, so be it. I was going to be the one with them, not you. If they were yours, that would be my revenge. To take them from you.

Then suddenly the kids didn't matter to me anymore. Chrissy was dead. And the reality of you, and the kids being without their mother... I was not about to force my way into that mess, no matter whose kids they were.

So here I am, at least for a little while longer, acknowledging my idiocy and confessing my crimes against you. Lisbeth and Wally were my kids and I blew it.

But not really. I saw enough of them from Philly to say that I gave you the greatest gift a brother can give. Yes, it ruined our brotherhood to some degree. And Chrissy died. I screwed up her life in lots of ways but at this point in mine, I'm ready to blame Hurricane Agnes for her death.

On the plus side, you and I both raised other people's children and I think we did a great job. Although I'd be a fool not to give Tam most of the credit for mine. She has been my salvation.

You, however, you're the one who allowed me the chance for that salvation... the opportunity to escape and to find her and Minh and Ha.

Because you're Moze.

And because you're Moze, I know you'll forgive me for thinking that you were ever anybody else.

Love you Brother,
Luke

49

Vietnam

June 2017

Fifty years can mess with your memories. That's how long it had been since Moze had traveled to Hawaii with Chrissy. That's how long he'd had to forget how tedious and irritating long flights could be. The five hours from Pittsburgh to Seattle had been almost a pleasure. But the ten hours from Seattle to Tokyo? *What the hell had he been thinking! He was way too old for this.* One thing was certain, the seats were definitely smaller, and the leg space more cramped than in 1967.

The three-and-a-half-hour layover in Tokyo had seemed like eight. Then another hour and a half in the air from Saigon – he still couldn't think of it as Ho Chi Minh City – to Hue on a plane that shook his bladder like a cocktail mixer. And now the hour and a half they had been in the car with their private driver Phuong who knew how to find every pothole on Highway 1 and had promised them they would be at Tam's house half an hour ago.

Moze had tried to get in touch with Tam the day after opening the box, but the address, except for the name of the town, was buried under international hand stampings and barcodes and torn when the box had been opened. After an unsuccessful internet investigation and trying to call the local police and school, he had decided to roll the dice with his six-thousand dollars on the table. Surely someone in the town would know a woman named Tam Foster with an American husband and school-teacher son.

The driver of the car suddenly announced that they had finally arrived in the town listed on Luke's box. The first stop was at the local police station to find information on the location of the school. Ten minutes later they not only had found the school but also Minh, who had a room full of teenagers discussing Moby Dick in English. Not wanting to be a distraction, Moze waited in the hallway while the driver told Minh that he needed his mother's address because he had a package for her that required a signature. Not suspecting anything Minh quickly wrote the address on a piece of paper and handed it to the driver.

The house belonging to the address was near the western edge of town with a large golden field behind it that held three, medium-sized wind turbines a quarter of a mile beyond the backyard. The house was a stucco-covered story and a half with a porch extending forward from the house but covered with the same red metal roof that protected the rest of the house. The porch was reached by four concrete steps.

As he got out of the car, Moze took a deep breath, trying to calm himself. When that didn't work, he waited for Lisbeth to come around from the other side and take his arm.

He leaned inside and said to the driver, "I don't know how long we'll be here."

"Phuong wait as long as needed. You have car and me for 'nother twenty-four hours. I wait till you ready to go back. Many hours left."

Wally shuffled his way until he was beside Lisbeth and said, "You ready, Dad?"

"Yeah, except I forgot my bullet proof vest."

"I'm sure those old photos of Luke you brought for her will work just as well," said Lisbeth.

The front door was open with only a screen door separating them from the Asian music playing somewhere in the back of the house. Moze tried to knock on the door but it gave way to the pressure without making much noise.

"Hello?" he called.

"One moment, please," came a tiny voice back at him, barely climbing above the music.

From a side hallway not far from the door the tiny voice sounded again as its owner appeared. "Hello... what—" She stopped midsentence as her eyes took in the sight of the three of them. Suddenly she was screaming in Vietnamese then immediately switched to English.

"Oh my god! Oh my god! Oh my god!" She put her hands to her face and sobbed."

Timidly Moze opened the door, half expecting her to start pounding her fists on him. When he sensed there was no danger, he reached out to comfort her by placing one hand partway around her back and the other on her near shoulder while she continued to sob. When the emotion subsided, she withdrew her hands from her face and looked up at Moze, she started to speak only to lose control again. This time Moze fully enclosed her in his arms and patiently waited for her distress to end. Meanwhile, Lisbeth and Wally slowly worked their way around the screen door.

It only took Tam a few moments this time to recover. She gently pushed herself away from Moze and looked at all three of them.

"You all came. Thank you. Thank you very much. I am so happy to meet you at last." Her words moved with her gaze. "Lisbeth. Wally. And, of course, you are Moze."

"I'm so sorry we did not come when you sent the box," said Moze. "If I had opened the box when I received it, we would have come then. I didn't know he was dying. I'm so sorry, Tam."

Tam's eyes suddenly brightened and her words flew from her with great urgency. "Oh, no! No, no, no, no, no! Luke is not dead! You will see!" And she punctuated her words by leaning into Moze and squeezing him, then pulled back and smiled at him with a joyful radiance.

"But the cancer? Nobody survives pancreatic cancer. Not even Luke."

"Stupid Vietnamese doctor. Luke had something else that looks like that cancer… pancreatic lymphoma. It can sometimes be cured with chemo and drugs. Much better chance than the other cancer. He is still sick but the doctors are optimistic. Maybe only a few more weeks of chemo. He is walking now on the trail out back. Come. All of you sit down while we wait for him to return."

"Can you show me how to get onto the trail, Tam?"

"Yes, of course. I will take you now. Yes. Yes. You should see each other alone. Yes. That would be much better."

* * * *

There was a moment when Moze first saw his brother that he feared he had fallen. Luke was on the ground in the high grass with one leg outstretched, the other bent almost underneath his rear end, his weight steadied by an outstretched hand against the ground. His eyes were gazing into the direction of his straightened leg, his head tilted up and moving ever so slightly, reminding Moze of the pileated woodpecker, but after a few moments of watching him Moze decided his brother was just looking at the clouds.

Moze was too far away from him to be recognized as anybody but an old man with white hair. He moved a few steps to the side, so he could be mostly hidden by a large bush while he continued to watch his brother. For a moment he was clueless as to what he would say to him. All the mean-spirited remarks he had cast at Luke over the years were certainly inappropriate now. Life had become way too short for such irrelevancies.

What Moze wanted to do was to take Luke and his family back to Pine City. Surely the care he would get there, especially with all the specialists available in Pittsburgh would be better than here. But his family's roots were here now. Luke obviously felt more connected to Vietnam than Pennsylvania. Still, he would make the offer. Except Luke's return to the U.S. would now be something of a risk, assuming

Kendricks would make good on her threat to inform California and the Marine Corps of her discovery. Sometime before Moze left for home Luke would have to be told the possible consequences of ever visiting the U.S. again for any reason.

* * * *

The trail wound to the right behind a small copse that prevented Luke from seeing Moze approach until he was but five yards away from him. Luke must have heard him before seeing him because he had his head turned right at Moze but then tilted it back in that sudden moment of surprise and recognition.

There was surprise in Moze also, although he tried to hide the shock of seeing the dramatic difference between the Luke he had seen in the home movie and the emaciated one in front of him now, the weight loss even more drastic than the 2016 image on the DVD.

"It only took you fifty years, but you finally made it to Nam, Big Brother," Luke said as he struggled to get to his feet.

"Yeah, thank God for Jack Baird putting me on the dorm floor and then the operating table."

On his feet Luke staggered for a moment in steadying himself then disappeared into Moze's arms. The two brothers stood in the still bright light of the late afternoon sun at the edge of the golden field. With the rhythmic sound of the nearest wind turbine whooshing behind them, the two seventy-somethings lost their battle to control their emotions.

When the storms finally passed from their old bodies, Moze gently pushed his brother's shoulders back and was the first to speak, "Come on, Doofus. Let's go back to the house. We have a lot of catching up to do." Grabbing Luke's neck he playfully put him into a headlock as he often had when they were kids, then quickly released him. For several seconds he stood and smiled at his brother in disbelief that they were together. As emotion started to well up again, he once more threw an arm up and around Luke's neck, this time stopping it to rest on his far shoulder.

"But first, I want you to finally meet our two children."

Luke blinked away the last of the puddles left by the storm and leaned into the offered comfort. "I would like that very much."

Acknowledgements:

These books were invaluable resources:

Hue 1968:
A TurningPoint of the American War in Vietnam
by Mark Bowden
Atlantic Monthly Press: June 6, 2017

Marines and Military Law in Vietnam:
Trial by Fire
By Lieutenant Colonel Gary D. Solis
U.S. Marine Corps
Published by History and Museums Division Headquarters,
U.S. Marine Corps, Washington, D.C., 1989

About the author

James Christie graduated from Indiana University of Pennsylvania with a B.A. in English and received his M.S. from Elmira College. He has also written *Blink Once to Spread Snow* and *From I-80 to Galway Bay: Searching for an Exit*, both available in paperback and digital formats from Amazon.com. More information available at GracehillPress.com

The author can be reached at
JAC@GracehillPress.com
Mailbox@JamesAChristie.com
JamesAChristie@icloud.com